The Soul Collector

(PREVIOUSLY PUBLISHED AS
A POCKETFUL OF PARADISE)

KATHLEEN KANE

St. Martin's Paperbacks

The Soul Collector was previously published under the title *A Pocketful of Paradise*.

THE SOUL COLLECTOR

Copyright © 1997 by Kathleen Kane.

All rights reserved. No part of this book may be used or reproduced in any manner whatsoever without written permission except in the case of brief quotations embodied in critical articles or reviews. For information address St. Martin's Press, 175 Fifth Avenue, New York, NY 10010.

ISBN: 0-312-97332-2

Printed in the United States of America

St. Martin's Paperbacks edition/January 1997
St. Martin's Paperbacks movie tie-in edition/September 1999

St. Martin's Paperbacks are published by St. Martin's Press, 175 Fifth Avenue, New York, NY 10010.

10 9 8 7 6 5 4 3 2 1

To my husband Mark, for twenty-five years of love, laughter and unfailing support. Here's to the next twenty-five!

Prologue

"It's a miracle!"

The young mother pushed her way past the dumbfounded doctor, still standing over her infant son's crib. The baby, deadly silent a moment before, wailed again and his mother laughed her delight. Bending down, she scooped him up into her arms and held him close. He continued to scream and she treasured each shriek, blessed each hiccoughing breath he drew. She grinned when he kicked his plump little legs furiously against her rib cage.

Turning to face her husband and the doctor, she said it again, more firmly this time. "It's a miracle, I tell you."

"Doc?" Her husband moved hesitantly across the floor to gingerly cup the back of his son's head in the palm of his large, calloused palm. "What happened?"

The doctor winced as his patient screeched again, then the old man's face split into a wondering smile. "If I had to hazard a guess," he said, "I believe I'd have to side with your wife. It's a miracle."

"I don't understand," the young father whispered and looked into his wife's teary, triumphant eyes.

"Me neither, boy," the doctor said and began to pack up his medical bag. "That baby was as near death as any I've seen. In fact, I would have bet money I don't even have that the child had actually stopped breathing." He shook his head and shrugged. "According to everything I've learned over the last sixty or so years, that boy ought to be dead."

The mother hugged her son even tighter as if afraid that the man's words would bring about a change in the tiny, warm body wriggling against her.

"Then how . . ."

The doctor interrupted the young father's anxious question with a simple statement. "I've lived long enough to know not to question some things." He removed his glasses and looked at the couple in front of him. "And you two shouldn't either. You've suffered enough."

She paled slightly at the mention of the two children they'd already lost, now lying beneath tiny white crosses in the town cemetery.

The tired doctor noticed her reaction, reached out and patted her hand. "Enjoy this gift you've been granted. Don't ask questions we none of us can answer."

She nodded and leaned into her husband's broad chest, their son cradled between them. The man wrapped his brawny arms around the two most important people in his life and promised himself to never ask the Lord for another thing.

"I could explain it for them." Another voice spoke up, but none of the mortals in the room could hear him.

"Blast it!" Zacariah jumped, startled, and spun around to glare at the newcomer.

A tall figure stepped from the shadows in a corner of the room. Clothed in soft, shimmering gray, the same color the sky took on just before dawn, the being frowned at his friend and asked, "You did it it again, didn't you, Zacariah?"

"God's Blood, Mordecai. Must you sneak up on me like that?"

"I didn't sneak. You weren't paying attention. Just as you neglected to pay attention to your collection."

Zacariah scowled at him and shoved one hand through

his thick, black hair. *"I don't need a sermon. As for paying attention . . . I'm here, aren't I?"*

"Late."

"Only a few moments."

"You were already warned about this. When you're sent to collect someone, you're supposed *to collect them."*

"I was detained," he protested. *"By the Path, am I allowed no recreation?"*

"Recreation?" his friend echoed solemnly. *"Exactly where were you?"*

"Hmmm . . ." Zacariah shifted his gaze away, only to find himself staring at the happy little family. He frowned slightly and shuddered.

"You were in England again, weren't you? I simply don't understand the fascination you have for Parliament."

"For your information, I was not attending a session of Parliament," Zacariah said. *"In fact, I was here. In this Path-forsaken town at my appointed time."*

Mordecai took a step closer. *"If that's true, why weren't you here to collect the child?"*

"There was a minor delay." He frowned again and straightened the fall of his robe.

"And did your horse win?"

Zacariah flinched and glanced at his oldest friend. Rubbing his jaw with one hand, he replied stiffly, *"What makes you assume that I was attending a horse race?"*

Mordecai sighed. *"Because there are no gladiator challenges to watch in this century."*

Zacariah ignored the jab. *"Why exactly are you here, anyway? The child was my collection."* His gaze narrowed thoughtfully. *"Have the Minions assigned you to check up on me?"*

"No." Mordecai drifted further into the room. He reached up to lift his cowled hood off. Shaking his blond hair back from his face, he replied quietly, *"The child was your collection. The child's mother was mine."*

"Oh."

"Yes." He shook his head again. *"With the child's death, the mother would have died almost immediately. She's already lost two other children, poor soul. The third would have killed her."*

Zacariah's head snapped up and he looked into the other Collector's fathomless blue eyes. *"Are you still taking her?"*

"I can't." Mordecai frowned and shrugged. *"By not taking the child at his appointed time, you've ruined the whole family's schedule. Now the Minions will have to determine new times of Collection for each of them. And who knows how long that will take? It will probably be years, now."*

"Does it really matter?" Zacariah asked indifferently. *"In the grand scheme of Collections and eternity, what do a few extra years mean? After all, they're only human."*

Mordecai scowled at him. *"You don't understand, Zacariah. You never have. For every collection missed, years of human life are altered. Not always for the better."*

Zacariah glanced at the people in the room. They didn't seem the least bit concerned that he'd missed his collection. So why should the Minions care? It wasn't as if he always missed his appointments. Why it had only happened . . . as he realized the number of times he'd arrived too late over the centuries, he decided to abandon that particular train of thought.

"Still," Mordecai muttered. *"They do look happy, don't they?"*

Zacariah grumbled as he allowed his gaze to swing around the simple, poor cabin. Dirt floor, blanket-covered windows, one room for the family to live in. His upper lip curled and one dark eyebrow lifted into a ridiculously high arch. Oh my yes. Who wouldn't be happy in such surroundings?

He couldn't understand humans, no matter how he tried. Though he was honest enough to admit that he didn't bother to try as often as his friend did. For all the good it did him.

Mordecai moved closer to the three adults and stared fondly at the tiny boy, tucked into his mother's protective embrace.

"Do you ever wonder, Zacariah? Do you ever wish you could know what that kind of joy feels like?"

"No." He glanced at the family and shook his head. In point of fact, except for actual collection times, Zacariah tried very hard not to think about humans at all. Beyond, of course, the various forms of amusement they provided.

He smiled to himself over memories of other times, other places.

A rumble of distant sound reached them and Mordecai turned in response. Glancing back over his shoulder at the friend who was getting himself in deeper trouble by the decade, he said, "We may as well go. There's nothing to be done here now and the Minions are waiting for you."

In a blur of mist and movement, Mordecai faded away. The Minions.

No doubt, he would have to do some quick thinking and even quicker talking to soothe his superiors.

Zacariah glanced at the family one last time. Shaking his head he told himself that it was a shame these people couldn't know what he'd done for them, however inadvertently. By the Path someone should know and appreciate him.

Because he had a feeling that the Minions were going to make him pay dearly for this latest mistake.

Chapter ❀ One

"Blast and damnation!"

The new fence post toppled over and as it went, Rebecca Hale felt a sliver the size of an oak tree pierce her palm. Grabbing her left hand, she stared down at the jagged splinter of wood jutting up from her flesh.

If she'd worn gloves, this wouldn't have happened. But then, if her husband Daniel hadn't died four long years ago and left her to run the ranch practically single-handedly she wouldn't have been fixing the fence posts at all. Her lips quirked. And, if she had wheels, she thought, she'd be a carriage. Rebecca grinned, then glanced down at her worn, split skirt and battered boots. No. Not a carriage.

A farm wagon, maybe.

"You cussed, Ma," a young voice interrupted her thoughts and Rebecca winced a bit at having been caught.

"So I did," she said, since it was pointless in arguing the obvious.

"What do ya think your punishment ought to be?" Danny asked, unable to hide the laughter in his voice.

She swiveled her head and looked at the boy. As always, it took only one look at Danny's impish expression to bring a smile to her own face. And like males of any age, he'd learned how to use that expression to his own advantage. Rebecca shook her head, unable to resist the sparkle in his eyes or the gap-toothed grin he flashed at her. Sometimes, her six-year-old son seemed too smart for his own good. But then, she could hardly blame him for enjoying himself at her expense. Especially since he'd spent most of the week before listening to lectures about not mimicking the cursing he heard from Buck and Scotty.

"Well I don't know, Danny," she said finally. "What do you think?"

He curled his arms tighter around the top slat in the gate, gave himself a push with the toe of his shoe and tilted his head back to stare at the sky while the gate swung lazily. "I think you better make a double batch of cookies today. The extra work'll help you think about your mistake."

"And give you more to eat."

He flashed her another grin. "That, too."

She snorted a laugh, lifted her palm to her mouth and pulled the sliver out with her teeth. No point in trying it any other way. It had been years since she'd had fingernails long enough to get a grip on a splinter.

"Storm comin'."

Rebecca looked at her son again, then turned in the direction he was pointing. Warily, her gaze swept over the sky, noting the black and gray clouds racing across the wide expanse. An unusually fast-moving storm by the look of it. From a distance, a low rumble of thunder echoed through the mountains nearly encircling her ranch.

"Should I go set out the pans?" Danny asked, already jumping down from his perch.

"Guess so," she said and sighed ruefully.

A spring storm *should* have meant a cozy hour or two by the fire. Reading stories to Danny while he ate his way through a double batch of cookies. Instead, it meant running around the ranch house settling pots and pans under the leaks in the roof. She sighed. At least, though, she had Danny to help.

"Know what the silver lining is?" the boy asked.

"What?" She grinned at her son as she realized that he was beginning to sound a lot like her.

"Even if the roof leaks, we got enough pans to go around!" He shoved his honey-brown hair out of his eyes and gave her a crooked smile that displayed his missing front tooth.

Rebecca laughed and lunged for him as another clap of thunder rattled down around them. He jumped back but he just wasn't fast enough. She wrapped her arms around him, lifted him high off the ground and planted several quick, noisy kisses on his dirty neck.

"Ah, Ma . . ."

She set him back on his feet, ruffled his hair, then gave his backside a quick swat. "Ah Ma, yourself. Now you get on inside and set the pans out. I'll be right along."

Danny stalked off toward the house, rubbing at his neck and muttering something about "dumb girls."

Bending down, she snatched up her hammer and the crumpled paper sack containing the last of her tenpenny nails. Then she stared at the cloud mass again. From what she could tell, there looked to be a lot of rain coming. Enough to make the house downright soggy.

No matter what else needs doing, she decided suddenly, the minute this storm passed, she would get Buck and Scotty to fix the roof. No doubt her foreman and the young cowboy would complain heartily about having to do work that didn't require sitting atop a horse . . . but there was no other way.

Frowning, she acknowledged silently that a patchwork job would work on the roof fine. For now. In the spring and summer, all they would have to worry about was rain. But come winter, they would be in real trouble. The heavy snows they usually got during winter would crash through that aged roof like an avalanche and folks would have to wait until the following spring just to dig her and Danny out of the mess.

There was no help for it. They needed a new roof. But then, they needed a lot of things. Somehow, they had to get to the bottom of the rustling going on at the ranch. They had to stop the thieves while Rebecca still had enough horses left to sell for cash money to last them through winter. Her fingers tightened around the hammer until the wood dug into her palm.

Dammit, she wasn't about to lose the ranch she'd worked so hard to hang onto.

A sharp, wild wind blew up out of nowhere, whipping her split skirt around her knees and slipping up under the hem long enough to leave a chill that crawled into her bones. Her hair was plucked from its loose, haphazard knot, and as she faced into the wind, the long strands lifted into a straight, chestnut brown curtain streaming out behind her.

She lifted her chin and closed her eyes, relishing the feel of the fierce, frigid air rushing around her. Thunder smacked against the clouds in an ear-bursting crash of sound and Rebecca's eyes flew open.

The clouds had rolled down the mountainside to settle in closer to the ranch. As she watched, the gray, rain-heavy mist touched down low to the ground like some great crouching beast taking up residence in her south pasture. She shivered and tightened her grip on the tools still clasped in her hands.

Wisps of vapor streaked from the cloud mass as if searching for something to hold onto. The mist itself seemed to be moving, as if gathering itself together. Light and dark shifted, separated, then intermingled again, blending the sun and shadow into a shimmering, dazzling shade of gray.

Rebecca stared, spellbound by the ever-changing mist. Her breath caught in her throat and her heart began to pound wildly. She'd never seen anything like it before. Unconsciously, she took a step toward the mist and narrowed her gaze, straining to see through the vaporous curtain to what lay beyond.

There was something in there.

Something alive.

She could feel it.

"Isn't there *something* you can do?" Zacariah gave a quick look at his surroundings and only barely managed to suppress a shudder.

"No. The decision has been made."

Decision. This was no decision. The very word implied thought, consideration.

This was . . . well, he wasn't sure what this was. Humiliating leaped to mind. Barbaric.

"Do I at least get a horse?"

"No." The response came quickly and echoed through his brain. "It's not far. Just walk."

Walk? Zacariah glared at the swirling patterns of light and shadow surrounding him, then glanced at Mordecai before turning to face Gabriel, the Minions' representative.

Gabriel's gray robe caught the shifting patterns of the mist and became one with it. He frowned and his steely blue eyes fastened on the Collector who had finally made one mistake too many.

"One month," Gabriel intoned and his thoughts invaded Zacariah's mind. *"Remember that. You have one month to study and learn about mortals. Then you must make your collection and return to the Path."*

"What exactly am I supposed to learn from these creatures?" His temper boiled despite the fact that he knew anger was not the way to deal with Gabriel.

"Respect would be a good start."

Zacariah bit back the oath hovering on his lips.

"You have shown repeatedly your disdain for the beings in your charge, Zacariah. Now, you have been called

to account.'' Gabriel paused. ''You might also learn compassion.''

"Compassion?" He threw his hands up wide and let them fall back to his sides. "*This* sort of compassion, you mean? Make a mistake and be banished?"

"Hardly a banishment, Zacariah. It's only one month.''

"I really don't think I'll need an entire month, Gabriel."

"This isn't up to you, Zacariah. And may I remind you that it is precisely because of your own thinking that you are in this situation?''

There was no need to be nasty about this, Zacariah told himself. Silently. He glanced down at himself and experimentally flexed his knees. He frowned. Hard to believe that a few simple mistakes had brought him to such a pass. He would have thought that his superiors would have shown a bit more understanding. Or some of that *compassion* they were so interested in. After all, he'd been a Soul Collector for eons. What were a dozen or so missed appointments in that length of time?

For centuries, he'd wandered the earth, collecting souls and guiding them to the Eternal Path. And for centuries, he'd watched as the humans in his charge fought and railed against his coming. Even those who should have been most eager for his arrival ... the sick, the injured, struggled against his presence until the last.

Is it any wonder that he had so little affection for them? They all mouthed platitudes from their various religions. All of them professed to believe in an afterlife, be it Heaven or Nirvana or whatever ... yet none of them were willing to take the one step that would usher them into eternal life and peace.

How was an intelligent being supposed to overlook such nonsense? And what was the harm of showing up a little late occassionally? True, at times being late meant that a collection wasn't made at all and the being went on to live for many years. But most of the time, a delay was simply that. A delay. An hour. Two. All right, a *day* at most.

Most of his fellow Collectors followed the rules strictly. They were always precisely where they were supposed to be at precisely the given time. Their supreme devotion to duty was probably what had brought about Zacariah's punishment. After all, next to those paragons of perfection, his simple errors in judgement looked far worse than they actually were.

Of course, to give them their due, the Minions *had* been patient. Until the fiasco with that last infant. Apparently, that had been enough to push the Minions beyond the barriers of their supposedly limitless forbearance.

He had thought about appealing this banishment by going over the Minions' heads, so to speak. After all, though they were Zacariah's superiors, the Minions themselves were answerable to the Angel of Death and, finally, God. Minions. Their very name insisted that they, too, were servants. But their combined dignity and authority served to mask that truth.

Zacariah recalled standing before the Minions trying to explain exactly what had happened. He also clearly remembered that his superiors hadn't been interested in explanations. He closed his eyes and let the memory come.

"As you know," Ezekial had begun, *"millennia ago, we, too, walked the earth with the mortals. We lived as they do, only showing ourselves as what we are to those whose time it was to join us."*

Zacariah nodded and offered up hearty thanks that he had not been a Collector during those dreadful years. He shuddered at the thought of actually having to live—permanently—among mortals.

"But as time passed," Ezekial went on, *"we came to see that we couldn't serve humanity by pretending to be like them. Rather, it was our duty to remain apart. To become one with the Eternal Path and to stand ready to usher our charges forward on their journeys."*

Zacariah knew all that. He'd learned it all long ago. And it made perfect sense. What could a Collector possibly have in common with beings who lit candles against death?

"My brothers and I"—Ezekial's voice had grown louder, as if he'd sensed that Zacariah's attention was wandering—*"have decided that your own sad disregard for collection schedules and the humans in your charge must be addressed. To that end, you will live as a human, among them, for a period of one month. You will spend your time in a place where, at the end of that month, a collection is to be made."*

Zacariah had been almost too stunned to react. Live as a human? Him?

"However," Ezekial's voice boomed and even Mordecai took a single step back, *"when your punishment is complete, there must be no more nonsense from you, Zacariah. You will make your collection in a timely manner and you will return to the Path."*

"Who is it I will be collecting?" he asked. The very least they could do for him was tell him this much.

Ezekial fixed him with a stony stare. "You will not know the identity of your collection until the time is upon you. We will brook no more mistakes from you, Zacariah. Is that understood?"

He nodded, but told himself silently that a month among mortals just might be enough to cause more mistakes than it would prevent.

Zacariah opened his eyes again, pushing his memories aside for the time being. No point in thinking about his return to the Path already. He had one long month stretching out in front of him. He would be better served to concentrate on the matters at hand.

"Are you ready?" Gabriel asked suddenly.

"No." He lifted both hands, palms up. "What am I supposed to do for this month?"

"I suggest," Gabriel told him with a sly smile, *"that you find a job."*

"A job?"

"Yes. You'll need to earn money in order to feed and clothe yourself, after all."

Food? Clothes? *Money?* By the Path, this punishment was getting worse by the moment.

"I'll ask you again, Zacariah." Gabriel's eyes narrowed slightly. *"Are you ready?"*

He nodded to his superior. It was pointless to argue further. There was no way out of this and the sooner it started, the sooner it would be over.

"Very well." Gabriel inclined his head briefly, then stepped back into the surrounding mist, becoming a part of the light and shadow. *"One month,"* he repeated unnecessarily. *"We shall await your return. With your collection."*

When the elder was gone, Zacariah looked at his friend. "I'm *freezing!"*

Mordecai shook his head. "You'll need a coat, too."

"By the Path! You'd think *someone* might have thought of that."

Mordecai rolled his eyes.

Suddenly, all sorts of questions were occurring to Zacariah. "How will I explain being on foot? What happens when they ask who I am? What will I say? What sort of job should I get?"

Mordecai tugged at the fall of his robe and shook his head solemnly. "You should have thought of these things before."

"I know," he said and glanced through the curtain of clouds at the Hale ranch. "I suppose I didn't really believe that the Minions would go this far to teach me a 'lesson.' "

"I can't believe they did."

He scowled at him. "Listen to my teeth chatter, if you still need evidence." Disgusted, he snapped, "What am I supposed to tell these humans?"

"Don't even consider telling anyone the truth, Zacariah. For one thing, no one would believe you. And for another, you can't afford to anger the Minions further."

Zacariah couldn't think of another thing that the Minions might do to him that would be worse than this. But, he allowed silently, he wasn't ready to test that theory.

"Of course I won't tell them the truth, but I have to say *something* to explain my presence. Even a *human* will have some questions."

"Tell them your horse threw you and that you hit your head. You can't remember a thing. Not even how you came to be here."

"No one will believe that." Zacariah frowned and realized that he was actually feeling . . . nervous.

"Say it with sincerity," Mordecai advised.

Clearly, Mordecai was determined to be no help whatsoever. Zacariah frowned and slapped his palm against his flat stomach. The unexpected churning inside him was unsettling.

"It's not too late to change things," he said.

"Yes it is." Zacariah pulled a deep, unsteady breath into his lungs and coughed. It felt as though a cold, wet knife had sliced down his throat. Although, he admitted to himself, it did seem to help that strange, fluttery feeling in his stomach.

"If you went to the Minions and begged forgiveness, they might change their minds. Grant you mercy."

Beg?

Plead for mercy?

He stiffened and ignored the whistle of wind humming around him. "No. I don't beg."

"Not even for this?"

Not even to dig himself out of this humiliating punishment would he humble himself like that. "No."

"I don't understand you at all."

He smiled wryly. "I know."

Mordecai glanced over his shoulder into the swirling

mist behind him, then turned his sharp blue gaze back to Zacariah. "You realize that the Minions are furious," he whispered. "I've been a Collector for six hundred years, and I've never seen them mad before. In fact, I didn't think you could get that angry while on the Eternal Path."

Neither had Zacariah.

"I have to go." Mordecai stiffened and cocked his head, listening to a call only he could hear. "I've a collection to make." He paused, then frowned.

"What is it?"

"I have to take Fenwick along with me," Mordecai muttered.

Zacariah laughed out loud and startled himself with the hearty sound of his own laughter. Mordecai's frown deepened.

"I'm gratified that your first real laugh was at my expense," he said. "This isn't right, you know. You being sentenced to Earthly life while I am forced to initiate Fenwick into the role of a Collector."

Fenwick, a good-hearted, recently collected soul, had been chosen to become a Collector himself. And though Fenwick was eager to please, it seemed that not even being on the Eternal Path was enough to rid him of his Earthly clumsiness. Apparently though, his pure heart had shone greatly enough to overshadow his inadequacies. Of course, the Minions made the decisions. It was up to the Collectors to train initiates.

Mordecai glanced over his shoulder into the mist again and nodded. "I must go. Fenwick is waiting and the collection is imminent."

Zacariah nodded. "For your own sake," he said with disgust, "I advise you not to be late."

"Coming," the Collector assured someone waiting just behind the curtain of mist. Turning back to his friend again, he said finally, "A month isn't so long, Zacariah. I'll come to see you, when I can. Of course," he added

as he stepped back into the surrounding clouds, "Fenwick will probably have to accompany me."

Mordecai's voice drifted away along with the last of the clouds.

Alone.

Momentarily, he paused.

A splash of sunshine fell on the meadow grass at Zacariah's feet. A harsh breeze rushed past him and lifted his too-long black hair off his collar. He turned his face into the wind, and gasped at the sharp, cold sting of air against his flesh.

Below him, in the heart of the valley ringed by mountains, lay the ranch where he would live as an ordinary man for one, long, *interminable* month.

The warmth of the sun pulsed through him and he took one hesitant step forward. His booted foot came down on a stone and he staggered slightly before recovering his balance.

Walking.

Already, he didn't like it.

Chapter ❁ *Two*

Rebecca shook her head and laughed at her own wild fancies. Clouds? Alive?

She pushed her hair back from her eyes and watched as the low-hanging mist slowly lifted and swirled with the wind. A small smile curved her lips. She really had to get some sleep. Too much work and worry and not enough rest had her seeing shapes and shadows that didn't even exist. Soon, she'd be joining her son Danny at bedtime, in checking under the beds for monsters.

Rebecca shook her head, glanced at the fallen fence post, then up at the blackening sky. She'd never finish the repair work before the coming storm broke. Even as that thought raced through her mind, the wind picked up, twisting her hair into long, tangled threads flying about her face.

Lowering her gaze, she looked back to the spot where the low-lying clouds had been a moment before.

It was then she spotted him.

He seemed to have come from the heart of the mist—though he was much closer to her now than the clouds had been. A man. Alone. Walking.

A small curl of worry began to thread its way through her. She tossed a quick glance at the house, a hundred yards away, then looked back at the man steadily approaching. Briefly, she wished that she'd allowed Danny to ride out with Buck and Scotty that morning. She'd feel a lot easier if she only had herself to look out for.

Immediately, she told herself she was borrowing trouble. Most people were decent. The chances of someone arriving out of the blue . . . and on foot, to do her harm, were pretty slim.

Her fingers tightened around the hammer. Still, she couldn't help wishing she had her rifle with her.

Rebecca studied the stranger coming steadily closer. Wind rushed past her and the clouds overhead seemed to dip and sway under the heavy burden of rain they carried. A single drop of water plopped into the dirt at her feet.

She silently took the stranger's measure, despite the distance still separating them. A tall man, with long, jean-clad legs, he walked stiffly, as if carefully planning each step. His movements seemed almost clumsy, like a man not used to walking.

She smiled to herself. A cowboy. Rebecca'd never met a cowhand who would walk when he could ride. Most of the men she knew looked a little out of place when they were out of a saddle. Besides, the high-heeled boots cowboys wore were designed to keep their feet in stirrups. Not for walking.

But where was his horse?

He came still closer and Rebecca could see his eyes. Even at a distance, she was stunned by their color. A clear, startling blue, they shone like sunshine on a mountain lake. His night-black hair was too long in back and shaggy on the sides. It fell across his forehead and ruffled in the wind. As he pushed one hand through his hair, she noticed for the first time that he wasn't wearing a hat.

Everybody wore hats.

Protection from the sun and the rain, a hat was as much a part of a westerner's outfit as gloves or a horse.

Another solitary raindrop splashed against Rebecca's shoulder. Thunder rattled across the sky and lightning lit the clouds from behind, giving them an eerie glow. The first crash of thunder was followed quickly by another.

"Ma!"

Rebecca tore her gaze from the approaching stranger, and spun around to look at her son. Standing in the open doorway, Danny shouted, "I can't reach the big pans."

As if the sky had waited for the news that not all of her leaks were looked after yet, the clouds tore apart and a hard, heavy rain fell onto the ranch.

Drenched in seconds, Rebecca strained to see past the wall of water to the man headed toward her. Instinctively, she raised her arm and waved him on, silently telling him to hurry. Then she turned and ran for the house.

She stopped on the porch, under the overhang, just long enough to kick off her muddy boots.

"Who's that?" Danny asked as she tossed the hammer and nails into a corner of the porch.

"I don't know yet," Rebecca told him and gently pushed him back inside. "Stay there till I find out."

"Maaa. . . ."

"And hand me the rifle." Rebecca ignored her son's whine and stood on the threshold, ready to bar the way into her house with her body if she had to. Without another word, Danny slapped the rifle stock into her outstretched hand. Rebecca's fingers curled around the worn wood and she held the weapon barrel down, but ready. Lord knew, she didn't mind helping a stranger in need, but she wasn't about to take chances with her son's safety, either.

A moment later, the stranger leaped up onto the narrow porch and shook himself like a dog after a swim. He wiped one hand across his face, then stared at his wet palm as if he'd never seen it before.

"It's raining," he said and his voice sounded scratchy and rough.

She frowned thoughtfully. What if the man wasn't quite

right in the head? What if he'd escaped whoever was supposed to be caring for him?

"Yes," Rebecca agreed, keeping a wary eye on him.

"I'm soaked through." He shook his head and stared down at his own clothing, now hugging his tall, lean frame.

He sounded almost surprised that his clothes were drenched. Hmmm. A man who didn't know rain was wet, obviously shouldn't be out on his own. Maybe she should just slip inside the house, bar the door and wait for Scotty and Buck to return.

The man shivered. "Cold, too," he remarked.

"'Course ya are," Danny piped up. "You're all wet."

"Danny," she said softly.

Then the stranger sneezed and he looked so surprised she almost laughed aloud. She stared hard into his eyes, looking for what, she wasn't sure. But there was no sign of madness in his clear blue gaze. Instead, she saw just what she would have expected to find in a man in his condition.

Disgust.

He turned his head to look out at the deluge and Rebecca studied his profile. Pitch black, sodden hair clung to his high forehead and lay just above slightly arched black brows. His straight nose had never been broken in a fight and his lips, still twisted in a grimace, were well-shaped. She even noticed what was probably a dimple in his right cheek.

Ignoring her completely, the stranger suddenly stretched out one hand, palm up, from under the porch overhang. When he'd caught a handful of rainwater, he dumped it onto the ground and grumbled something unintelligible.

Rain. Raindrops. Hundreds of them. Thousands of them.

Zacariah inhaled deeply and tried not to shiver. He was cold right down to his bones. Bones! By the Path, he actually had *bones*. Something tickled in his nose and he wrinkled it in reaction. It didn't help. That same, helpless feeling he'd experienced a moment ago swept over him. He inhaled sharply, his head jerked and he shot the air out of his lungs in a powerful sneeze.

Blast it anyway. Why he was forced to endure such privations for a few paltry mistakes was beyond him. Wouldn't it have been kinder to sentence him to the dark road for Eternity? A half smile lifted one side of his mouth. At least then he would have been warm.

He felt the cold caress of water droplets rolling down his back beneath his sodden shirt and twitched his shoulders uncomfortably. Wind brushed past him, knifing through his flesh, pushing the cold even deeper.

Everything was so . . . *awful*. By the Path, why would a human fight against a Collector's presence? To escape such misery, he would leap across the chasm separating life and death! He drew another deep breath and inhaled the mingled scents of pine trees and muddy earth. He listened to the drumming patter of the rain against the dirt. He shivered again as the wind taunted him.

"Where you from, mister?"

Zacariah straightened, glanced at the woman and ignored the suspicion in her eyes. How difficult could it be to sway this one human female to sympathy?

"I'm not sure, really," he said and knew the instant the words left his mouth that it had been the wrong answer.

"Is he crazy?" the boy asked in a whisper loud enough to be heard by everyone.

Zacariah frowned briefly at the child.

"I don't know," his mother assured him. "What do you mean, you're not sure?" she asked, cocking her head to look at him harder. "And while you're at it, where's your horse?"

Horse. Hadn't he told Gabriel that he would need a horse? Disgusted, Zacariah realized he would have to use

Mordecai's suggestion. All he needed now was the proper note of sincerity to make it all believable.

"My horse threw me," he said, glancing at the boy to avoid, however briefly, looking into the woman's suspicious gaze. "I must have hit my head when I fell, because I can't seem to remember anything."

He hoped it sounded like a plausible explanation for his sudden appearance. Although, he thought, sending a silent message to whoever might be listening, none of this would have been necessary if his superiors had outfitted him for his punishment properly.

He took a step closer and smacked his forehead on the low-hanging curve of the warped wooden overhang. Yelping, he jumped back and rubbed the painful spot. By the Path! Why had no one warned him about this? Had it *really* been necessary to force him to feel *pain* on top of everything else? Under the relative shelter of the porch roof, the sound of the rain was loud, insistent.

It drummed on his nerves and pounded against his now throbbing head.

Dropping his hand to his side, Zacariah noticed for the first time the rifle in the woman's right hand. Shooting him wouldn't do her the slightest bit of good—although he was almost tempted to let her try it. Maybe he could be collected. No, it wasn't his 'time' yet. And it certainly wouldn't set the right tone for his visit, either.

"Well," the woman said with a cautious smile, "that's an interesting tale." She looked him up and down carefully, then added, "I suppose you're harmless. I've never yet turned away somebody needing our help . . ."

He sneezed again. Violently.

The woman handed her rifle to the boy butt first, then reached out and grabbed Zacariah's forearm. Tugging at him, she drew him nearer the light-filled doorway.

"We can finish talking inside," she told him. "After you dry off and before you catch your death."

Zacariah smiled at that.

She, of course, misinterpreted that smile and warned, "Now don't you make me sorry I invited you in, mister. You mind your manners or you'll find yourself back out in the rain, with a bruise or two to keep you company."

He looked down into her green eyes and believed her. *Anything* was preferrable to standing in that deluge, so he told himself to be charming.

"Thank you," he said softly.

The woman paused, smiled, then gave his arm a friendly pat. "You're welcome."

She drew him inside and said, "Warm yourself by the fire. I've a few leaks to look after, or soon, the inside of the house will look just like the outside."

Zacariah stepped across the threshold and stopped. Warm, fragrant air met him and wrapped itself around him like a blanket. His body shuddered again, then he drew a deep breath, inhaling a delectable scent hanging in the room. His mouth watered and his stomach grumbled in anticipation.

His eyebrows lifed. Apparently, he was actually *hungry*.

Ignoring his new body's complaint, he looked around at the ranch house. In direct contrast to the gloomy weather outside, the house was bright with color. The main room was bigger than it appeared from the outside. Log walls surrounded him. Shining white chinking separated the dark, ancient-looking timbers, making sharp, deliberate stripes around the room. There were several portraits in handmade frames hanging on the walls and blue-and-white gingham curtains hung in starched precision across the windowpanes.

A stone fireplace with a hearth tall enough for a man to stand in it upright, took up most of the far wall and the flames dancing across the firewood seemed to call to Zacariah, whispering of warmth. He moved forward on still shaky legs, surveying the rest of the room as he went. A cluster of chairs, each of them covered in a different, boldly colorful fabric, were arranged in a half circle in front of the hearth. In the center of the room stood a long, pine table. The benches drawn up on either side of it had been padded and covered with a flower-sprigged material. In the middle of the gleaming tabletop, a handful of wildflowers stood proudly in a cut-glass vase.

Everywhere he looked, there was evidence of a well-loved house carefully maintained. At least, he told himself, it appeared to be in better shape than some homes. Except, of course, for the roof. The woman hurried around the room, a tin washbasin in each hand. She set one of them down directly under a leak and immediately, a drop of water plinked into it. She muttered something he didn't quite hear and moved off to the far corner of the house.

Behind him, the front door slammed shut and Zacariah turned around.

The woman's son grinned at him in welcome and he nodded cautiously. He'd never had much patience with children. But then, whenever he'd popped in and out of people's lives, it always seemed that children were shrieking or shouting or breaking something. And the children he'd collected were never in his company long enough for him to change his opinion that as a breed, young humans were noisy, dirty and altogether fairly unpleasant.

Apparently though, his feelings weren't obvious.

"Ya cold, mister?" the boy asked as he walked up, grabbed Zacariah's hand and began to drag him closer to the fireplace.

He frowned at the boy's attentions, then glanced down at their joined hands, amazed to actually *feel* warm, healthy flesh against his own. Odd, these new sensations. From freezing to warm in a matter of seconds. Now, the touch of a human hand.

It was a bit disconcerting, though not entirely unpleasant.

"Bet ya are," the child went on without waiting for a

response. "I been caught in the rain sometimes, too. Especially back when I was younger."

The boy was a smaller version of his mother. He had her soft, green eyes, the finely arched brows and the same stubborn tilt to his chin. The only thing missing was the flash of wariness shining in the woman's eyes.

Strange, Zacariah thought. It was uncomfortably strange, noticing things that usually escaped him. He wasn't entirely sure he liked it, either. This business of actually being welcomed into a home rather than having candles lit and prayers chanted to keep him out was unsettling, too.

"How come you was out there just wanderin' around?" the child asked. "Ma says only drunkards and fools don't know enough to come in outta the rain."

Wonderful.

"Danny!" The woman interrupted her son sharply, but the boy wasn't nearly finished.

"You a drunkard, mister?" He leaned in close, wrinkled his nose and sniffed. "I don't smell nothin' funny like the last time Buck went to town on Saturday night."

Good God.

"Danny Hale, hush this minute."

The boy ducked his head and looked at his mother out of the corners of his eyes. A slow grin crept up his features.

"Oh no you don't, you little devil." She hurried to her son, spun him around and gave him a gentle shove. "You go set up the pans in the other room."

"But Ma, I'm talkin' to this fella about man stuff."

"So I heard. Now git."

Danny kicked at the braided rug beneath his feet, hunched his shoulders and stuffed his hands into his pockets. "I'm goin'," he said, and flashed the two adults a quick look. "But I'll be back."

Zacariah watched the boy go. He had enough to think

about at the moment without having to listen to a child's ramblings.

"I'm sorry," she said softly and looked up into Zacariah's eyes.

"About what?" he heard himself ask.

"Danny." She shrugged helplessly. "He's a good boy, but we don't get many visitors and I suppose his mouth runs away with him. I'm sorry if he said anything to bother you."

Zacariah shook his head. After what he'd experienced so far that day, the boy was the least of his problems.

"Well, good then," she said and shifted her gaze to the fire. Snatching up a poker, she stabbed at the burning logs until fresh flames erupted from the center of the blaze, then she set it back down and turned to him again.

In the background, Zacariah heard the rain on the roof, the gentle "plink" of drops falling into metal pans, and the sound of Danny's voice as he talked to himself. But when she began to speak, he ignored it all and concentrated.

"I noticed you didn't have any gear with you."

He wasn't sure what "gear" was, but he knew he didn't have any. He nodded.

"Then I'll go and get you some of my late husband's things. You can wear them while your own clothes dry by the fire."

He turned to watch her as she walked across the room to an intricately carved wooden chest sitting beneath one of the front windows. Zacariah frowned before turning back to stare into the fire. He'd never felt more . . . alone. And blast it, he didn't like it one damned bit. Tentatively, he held out one hand toward the flames and relished the heat rising toward him.

So many times over the centuries, he'd watched people draw close to a fire and stare into its depths as if seeking answers to a puzzle. He'd observed that even when a fire wasn't necessary for warmth, humans would gather around the flames. Now, he realized that there was comfort in a fire. Not just for the body, but comfort for the soul, as well. Maybe it was the sounds of the fire itself— snapping and hissing as if whispering long-forgotten promises. Maybe it was the light flickering against the darkness.

And maybe, he told himself, he should just stop thinking. He didn't have to understand these people—despite what the Minions said. All he had to do was survive the month.

Danny hurried back into the room and began talking again, completely unconcerned with whether anyone was listening to him or not.

Zacariah wasn't. Instead, he was watching the child's mother. He noted her quick, sure hands as she set a stack of clothes down on one of the nearby chairs. Then, she quickly dragged a stool across the floor and climbed atop it. Lifting both arms, she reached for a piece of canvas tacked to the beams overhead.

While she worked, Zacariah found himself noticing the lines of her figure. From her narrow waist and long legs to the gentle swell of her breasts beneath her soaking wet shirt. Startled, he looked away again quickly. What difference did it make what the woman looked like?

None.

He'd never really taken much notice of humans' appearances before this. But now that he was, he was forced to admit that comparatively speaking, this particular woman was fairly . . . *attractive,* he supposed was the right word.

God's Blood! He was actually assessing her as if he really *was* a human male. Now *that* was a hideous thought.

A strange, somehow unsettling feeling began to stir deep within him and Zacariah scowled to himself.

"Mister?"

Her voice broke into his wayward thoughts and he gave

himself a shake before answering. "It's Zacariah."

She spared him a quick glance, nodded, then said, "Fine. Zacariah. I'm Rebecca. This is the worst leak in the roof and this canvas may just keep us from floating away in the night. Could you help me with it, Zack?"

Zack? One dark brow lifted. Good God.

Still, he'd do well to ingratiate himself. If he had to find a job, it would certainly be easier to do it here. He couldn't imagine anything worse than having to wander around a hostile countryside trying to find employment.

It would entail entirely too much walking, for one thing.

He crossed the room in a few long strides and stopped beside her.

"I'm just not tall enough to fasten this tight," she said and let her arms fall to her sides. She looked down at him, their eyes met and for a heartbeat, neither of them spoke. Then she looked away from him deliberately before asking, "Can you do it?"

Hard to say, since he hadn't the slightest idea what it was she was trying to do. But then again, how difficult could it be? If humans could manage it, he certainly could.

"I think so," he said and knew it was the right answer when she nodded.

Rebecca set one hand on his shoulder and hopped down off the stool. A lancing arc of heat sliced through him and once again, that strange sensation unfurled in the pit of his stomach.

"Go ahead then," she said, her eyes challenging him.

He ignored the odd feelings swimming inside him, climbed up on the stool and immediately wobbled unsteadily.

"Here now," she said quickly and wrapped both arms around his knees. "You really *did* hit your head, didn't you? You feeling dizzy?"

In a lightning-like flash, awareness of the woman pressed against him shot through Zacariah. And he didn't like it. He stared down into her upturned face and reminded himself that she was human.

It didn't help.

"Zack?"

He inhaled sharply, then deliberately looked away from her to the ceiling. "I'm fine."

"I'll just hang onto you to make sure," she told him.

He nodded absently and studied the piece of canvas while trying to ignore the woman's hold on his legs. The coarse material was damp, but seemed to be keeping most of the rainwater from passing through to drop onto the floor.

What exactly was it she wanted him to do?

"Do you need a hammer, or something to pry up one of those tacks?" she asked.

A hammer? He wasn't sure what a hammer was, let alone how to use one.

He frowned at the ceiling. Tacks, she'd said. So there was more than one of them, whatever they were. He looked at the canvas again and noticed the four small brass heads positioned at each corner of the material. Ah. Quickly, to cover up his earlier hesitation, he reached for one of the brass tacks and worked it free with his thumbnail. The edge of the canvas fell and several drops of rainwater splashed onto his face.

Perfect. He hadn't been nearly wet enough.

"Oh, good," Rebecca said. "Now just tighten up the canvas and put the tack back in."

That certainly seemed easy enough.

Zacariah smoothed the fabric flat, then holding it in place with one hand, pushed the tack home with the other.

"Finished?"

"Yes." And he hadn't even needed a hammer. That should prove his worth. He hoped the Minions were watching.

She let go of him and moved back. "Well then, come on down and Danny'll show you where you can dry off."

Her steadying hold gone, Zacariah shifted. The stool teetered and his eyes widened as his balance dissolved and he fell to the hardwood floor. The back of his head smacked the polished planks and stars spun before his eyes.

Pain rocketed around inside his head. Waves of it rolled over him only to crowd together on one side of his skull before rushing back to the other side again. He reached up and cradled his head with both hands, hoping to stem the tide of agony.

By the Path, this was a much stronger pain than he'd felt before! Immediately, he wondered just how much *more* pain there might be in store for him.

"Zack?"

Her voice added to the tumult behind his eyes and he winced before blinking the stars away. Once his vision cleared, he noticed both Rebecca and Danny staring down at him.

"You all right, Zack?" Danny asked and bent over, hands on his knees.

The boy's high-pitched voice drove a spike through his head. At last though, the pain subsided into a dull, throbbing ache and Zacariah carefully pushed himself to his feet.

"You sure you're all right? Now you've had two knocks on the head instead of the one you told us about." Rebecca eyed him warily. "You seem to be fairly accident-prone."

Only since being encumbered with this clumsy body, he wanted to say, but didn't. She should have seen him at his best. Drifting through clouds, becoming one with silent shadows. Appearing and disappearing in the blink of an eye. Existing in the space of a single heartbeat.

Rather than making him feel better, his thoughts only served to disgust him. To be brought so low as to trip over his own feet!

"I'm fine," he muttered and heard his stomach grumble loudly as if demanding to be heard.

Rebecca nodded slowly, an understanding smile drifting across her face. "Now I get it." Planting her hands at her hips, she cocked her head at him and asked, "Just how long's it been since you've had a decent meal?"

He didn't suppose she'd believe 'never,' so he simply said, "It feels like centuries."

"Well, no wonder you're so weak!" She looked to her son, tweaked his nose and said, "Zack can get dried off in your room, all right?" She snatched up the stack of clothes and handed them to the boy before looking at Zacariah again. "We'll get some beef stew into you and then you can start explaining how you came to be on my land."

He nodded. He would agree to anything at the moment, just for the promise of being warm again. Surely, he'd be able to come up with *something* to tell her.

Chapter ❋ Three

Danny Hale's bedroom was just like the boy himself. Small and busy.

The log walls were decorated with half-finished drawings and pen-and-ink etchings torn from newspapers and catalogs. A desk and chair stood along one wall with a kerosene lamp and a child-sized saddle stacked on the obviously unused desktop. Hanging from pegs on the far wall were shirts, pants and a flat-brimmed black hat with a long black ribbon trailing from its brim. Zacariah's gaze shifted to a low line of hastily built shelves where a row of intricately carved wooden toys marched in surprising precision. Sculpted lions roared alongside friendly dogs, and patient horses stood, locked in wooden traces, forever chained to miniature wagons.

Intrigued despite himself, by the clever workmanship, Zacariah took a step closer and hesitantly touched the tip of one finger to a running cougar.

"Buck made those for me back when I was a youngster," Danny said.

"They're very good," Zacariah said and glanced briefly at the boy behind him.

"I got more," Danny offered, "if ya want to see 'em."

"I'd like that," Zacariah said and was surprised to realize that he meant it. He looked back at the rows of toys and smiled to himself. Every detail was perfect. From the tusks on the trumpeting elephant to the rings on the coiled rattlesnake's rattle. Imagine being able to coax such wonders from a block of wood.

And a *human* had done it.

"So how come you was afoot?" the boy asked and Zacariah winced.

Was even the child going to interrogate him? "I told your mother," he said. "My horse threw me. It must have run away after that."

The boy shook his head. By the Path, his story didn't even convince a child. Grimacing, he turned away and began to yank at his cold, wet shirt. The buttons seemed far too large for their matching holes and they fought his every effort to move them.

Disgusted with the entire situation, he told himself that his superiors should have been able to come up with a better explanation for him to give these people. Surely the Minions of Eternity could have dredged up a *bit* of imagination.

"Zack?"

He hated that name.

Glancing at the boy, who lay with the upper half of his body hanging upside down over the foot rail of his bed, Zacariah sighed. Naturally they would shorten his perfectly good name. There didn't seem to be a spark of formality about the place.

He yanked at his shirt again and the buttons popped free of the fabric to skitter around the room.

Danny's shock of straight, dark brown hair swayed on end as he shook his head. "I didn't know men could get thrown off, too. Buck says it's only whippersnappers like me who get tossed off 'cause we ain't learned enough yet to hang on proper."

Perfect. Now people would see him not only as a man who couldn't remember a blessed thing, but as a fool too inexperienced to sit a horse.

Oh yes, this month was going to be a charming one.

As he peeled his soaking wet jeans off his long legs, Zacariah told himself that it didn't really matter what the people here thought of him. He wasn't here to make friends. He was only there to observe. To learn his 'lesson,' whatever that might be.

Then he could go back to where he belonged.

Just the thought of returning to the Path made him smile.

"You sure got lots of hair," Danny commented, dragging Zacariah's attention back to the moment at hand.

"I suppose so," he agreed and glanced down briefly at his nearly nude body. His broad chest was covered by a thick mat of curly black hair that tapered down across his abdomen to a narrow line of curls which disappeared beneath the waistband of his long underwear. Absently, he lifted one hand and brushed it over his chest. He looked like a bear.

"You best get out of those drawers, too," Danny told him.

"Why don't you go tell your mother I'll be right out," he said. He'd prefer to undress the rest of the way without an audience. Lord only knew what he'd find when he was finally free of the wet clothing.

Danny paused a moment or two before nodding. Abruptly, he swung his legs high and back, then did a quick flip over the foot rail. He staggered before catching his balance, then said, "All right," and pushed his hair out of his eyes. "But hurry up, 'cause supper's waiting."

Zacariah nodded.

He waited until the bedroom door was closed again, then stripped off his underwear. Standing with his back to the door, he quickly reached for the dry clothes Rebecca had provided.

Rebecca.

Instantly, an image of her wide, green, *suspicious* eyes rose up in his mind. She didn't seem nearly as pleased to

see him as her son was. But somehow, he had to allay
her worries about him. He was stuck there for a month
and he'd already discovered that he didn't much care for
walking.

If Rebecca asked him to leave, that's exactly what he'd
have to do. And Lord knew how far it was to the next
batch of people. He might be forced to walk for days. In
the cold. In the rain. Without food.

He shook his head firmly. No. Whatever else he had to
do, he would find a way to convince Rebecca to allow
him to stay on her ranch. He remembered her smile and
the warmth in her eyes when she looked at her son and
knew that underneath her suspicions lay a tender heart.
All he had to do was reach it.

At thoughts of Rebecca, something stirred into life in
the pit of his stomach and he swallowed heavily in response. He ignored the curl of sensation as best he could
and bent to pull on the dry underwear.

Before he could get dressed again though, he gave himself a thorough, yet quick, assessing glance. His eyebrows
lifted slightly.

He looked more like a bear than he'd thought. It wasn't
just his chest. The same dark hair covered his lower body,
surrounding a groin that seemed to be entirely too active
at the moment.

Zacariah rubbed his bewhiskered jawline, frowned, then
continued dressing. Whatever was the matter with him
would probably end as soon as he became used to these
wayward feelings. As he pulled his borrowed jeans on,
then shoved his arms through the sleeves of his new shirt,
Zacariah focused on the world around him, hoping to distract his body.

The rich aroma of food cooking in the other room
drifted to him and he inhaled deeply as if he could taste
it already. He concentrated on the sound of the rain
pounding against the roof, then listened to the steady
"plunk" of raindrops leaking through the ceiling to

bounce out of a pan set in the corner. As he pulled the edges of his shirt together, and fumbled with the impossibly small buttons, he admitted that the dry shirt felt soft, warm.

He stuffed the tail of the shirt into his jeans and buttoned them, too. When he snatched up a pair of socks and bent over to tug them on, Zacariah noticed that the hems of his pants ended two or three inches above his ankles.

He frowned slightly. That wasn't right. Was it? He shook it off, telling himself that short pants were hardly important when the rest of his world lay in tatters around him. He pulled on the socks, stomped into his still wet boots and decided that no one would notice, anyway.

Straightening up, he caught a glimpse of himself in the mirror across the room and scowled at his reflection. This was going to be an eternally long month.

"You say your horse threw you?"

Zacariah swallowed another mouthful of stew, reached for his glass of milk and nodded before taking a long drink.

"And you hit your head?"

He winced. "That's right."

"What spooked him?" Rebecca asked and idly moved her spoon through her untouched beef stew.

"I'm not sure," he answered, then mentally kicked himself. He should have said *something*. Now that it was too late, any number of possibilities occurred to him. Rattlesnakes. Bears. Wolves. Mordecai. A brief, rueful smile darted across his features. Unfortunately, eternal life hadn't taught him a thing about how to lie successfully.

"What about your hat?" Danny's legs kicked against the table leg as he finished his supper.

Zacariah's mind went blank. This was all the Minions' fault. Hadn't he *told* them he would need a hat? Hurriedly, his brain raced for an answer to the boy's question and came up with nothing. He glanced at the two people staring at him and told himself to keep chewing. Stall for time. *Think!*

"It must have blown away in the wind," he said finally.

Rebecca and the boy exchanged a look that clearly told Zacariah he should have kept his mouth shut.

Slowly, she shifted her gaze to him again. She set her elbows on the table and propped her chin in her hands. "Before or after your horse ran off with the rest of your outfit?"

"Uh, before." The more he said, the worse it sounded.

For several long moments, all he heard was the fire's insistent snapping, the rain beating heavily on the shingles overhead and Danny's feet bouncing off the chair rails. Zacariah deliberately ducked his head and began eating again.

He hadn't expected food to taste so good.

In a miserable day, this dinner was quickly becoming the only bright spot. He reached for the stew pot, set on a folded cloth in the center of the table.

"That's hot."

He ignored her warning, gripped the iron handle, then let it go again, quickly. "Ow!" He sucked in a gulp of air through gritted teeth and glanced down at his palm. Zacariah watched as a flaming red line appeared on his hand. Pain pulsed through him in time with his heartbeat.

"I told you it was hot." Rebecca reached for his hand. "Let me see it."

Still wincing, he turned slightly and held his palm out for her inspection. The tips of her fingers smoothed over the bright red burn line.

"It's hardly touched," she said and released him.

"But that red line," he argued.

"Is already fading."

So it was. His eyebrows lifted as he studied his hand. A dull, throbbing ache reminded him of the burn even as evidence of it disappeared.

Standing up, Rebecca said, "Hand me your bowl and I'll get you some more stew."

He flexed his fingers carefully while she ladled another helping of beef, potatoes and gravy into his dish. All in all, he felt he was getting better at dealing with pain. Although he'd had no idea that pain actually *hurt* as much as it did. She set his food down in front of him and the tantalizing aroma rose up to tease him. Zacariah glanced from his still smarting, injured hand to the chunks of potatos and meat swimming in a rich, brown gravy.

Abruptly, he decided to ignore the burn and its pain, in favor of enjoying more of Rebecca's delicious meal. Reaching for a nearby plate, he snatched up a second slice of fresh bread and focused on his supper.

Rebecca studied the stranger. No gear, no horse, no clothes and, as far as she knew, just one name. A man who didn't know that rain was wet and who seemed surprised to burn himself on a hot pan. She slanted a look at her son and watched him grin at the man opposite him. It didn't seem to matter to him that the man didn't return the smile.

Obviously, despite Zack's strange story and even stranger behavior, Danny approved of him.

That was one point for Zacariah. Most children, she'd noticed, were excellent judges of character. For whatever reason, they seemed able to look inside a person and see them for what they really were. Fancy clothes or smiling faces didn't fool children. Maybe it was because they were young enough to see past a lie to the truth beyond.

Because Zack's story was most definitely *full* of lies. Rebecca ducked her head slightly to hide what she was thinking. She hadn't heard such a tall tale since the last time Buck went fishing and came home empty-handed, complaining about the one that got away.

Oh, men were thrown from their horses every day. And it wasn't so surprising that the animal would run off, taking its rider's things with it. But it seemed mighty damn easy for him to claim forgetting everything because he hit his head on a rock.

One thing she was willing to give the good-looking stranger—if he told such god-awful lies, he wasn't used to lying. Another point in his favor.

Hell, any number of things might have happened to Zacariah to put him afoot. He could have been robbed and was too ashamed to admit it. He might have lost everything in a card game—not many men wanted to own up to something like that.

Or, a small voice in the back of her mind suggested, he might have escaped from a jail somewhere and was just trying to steal a new outfit and get out of the territory.

If that was true, though, he would have made a move for her gun earlier.

Her eyes narrowed as she studied him.

He helped himself to another slice of bread and she shook her head. Zacariah ate like he hadn't had a meal in years, but his frame was lean and muscular. The piercing blue of his eyes looked even more startling against sun-browned skin that told of years spent outdoors. His too-long black hair lay over his collar and brushed the tops of his shoulders.

"You all right, Ma?"

She straightened up at the sound of Danny's voice and told herself that she should be asking a few more questions.

"Yes," she said, then added, "I was just wondering where Zack was headed when he stumbled onto our place."

He paused in his eating long enough to look up at her. "I don't remember that, either."

"That's too bad."

"Yes."

"Be a shame if there's someone waiting on you somewhere."

"Oh, I don't think there is," he said quickly.

"Really?" Rebecca cupped her chin in her hands and watched him. "Now why would you say that? Thought you didn't remember anything."

"I don't," he countered. "But if there were someone waiting, I doubt I'd forget it."

"Hmmm . . ."

He smiled at her and she had to admit it was a handsome smile, for all that she doubted its sincerity.

He finished his meal and laid his fork down in the empty bowl. "Thank you. It was very good."

She nodded, still wary. Even Jesse James probably had good table manners.

"If ya don't remember where you were goin'," Danny spoke up into the silence, "what're you gonna do now?"

Zacariah shot her a quick glance before leveling his gaze on her son. "I guess I'll have to find a job somewhere for awhile."

Danny glanced at her quickly and she shook her head slightly. She didn't want him speaking up and offering a job to a man who'd strolled in off the range without so much as a decent explanation of what he was doing there in the first place.

"Actually," Zacariah said, as if reading her mind, "I was wondering if you might need some extra help."

Off-guard and ill-prepared, she stammered, "I don't think—"

"Only until my memory returns, you understand," he interrupted smoothly.

"That could take years."

He smiled again and Rebecca had the distinct impression that he was aware of the power of his smile every bit as much as Danny was of his. The hint of a dimple she'd seen earlier now deepened into a slash in his right cheek.

Something fluttered to life inside her and she deliberately swatted it back down. She was a little too old to be persuaded by a handsome face.

"I'm sure I'll be back to normal in a few weeks," Zacariah told her.

Maybe, she thought. But what exactly *was* normal for him?

"Come on, Ma," Danny piped up again and she wished her son would keep out of this. "There's lots to do around here and Buck and Scotty can't do it all."

She flushed.

Rebecca felt heat rush into her cheeks and there wasn't a thing she could do about it. It was embarrassing to have to admit that she only had two hands working for her. A ranch this size would normally support twenty or more.

But with some thief making off with her stock, she hadn't been able to afford more cowboys. She hadn't had a yearling or even a gelding to sell at market in over a year. Cash money was scarce and getting scarcer all the time.

"Danny . . ."

"I would do a good job," Zacariah put in.

She sighed, feeling control of the situation slipping from her grasp. "Do you know anything about ranching?"

"I don't—"

"Remember," she finished for him. "Look, Zack, you wouldn't want to work for me, anyway. I couldn't afford to pay more than"—she paused, then swallowed and spit out the truth—"ten dollars a month."

That should do it, she told herself. Any cowboy worth his salt would be insulted over the offer and tell her so just before riding away.

He looked at her for a long minute, then asked, "Is that a lot?"

She laughed. A choked, short laugh that scratched at her throat and stung her eyes. "No, it's not."

"Oh. Well, it seems plenty."

"See there Ma?" Danny asked. "It's fine with him."

She sighed, torn between the fact that she could use

some cheap help for awhile and the very real fact that she knew nothing about the man.

And why would he be willing to work for so little money? Before she could stop herself, she asked him point-blank.

Zack shrugged. "I don't have a horse or any *gear*. It would be easier to stay and work for you than to walk into the nearest town to look for work."

Well, that was certainly true. A man without so much as a saddle to call his own didn't have a whore's chance in church of finding work in ranch country.

"Besides," Zacariah added, "if I stay here, in the area where I lost my horse, maybe my memory will come back sooner."

She couldn't tell if he actually believed that or if it was just a clever ploy. Still, she could keep a watchful eye on him. And Lord knew, she could use the extra help, if only for awhile. Though she thought she might come to regret it later, ten dollars for a month full of work was too good a deal to pass up.

"All right," Rebecca said finally. "You can stay."

Danny grinned.

Zacariah sagged against the chair back as if relieved.

"Ten dollars a month and room and board."

"Does that mean food, too?" he asked.

"Yes," she said wryly and told herself that the money she saved on his salary would no doubt be eaten.

"Good." His eyebrows arched and he gave her a slow smile that sent sparks dancing through her bloodstream.

She was forced to admit that Zacariah was a fine-looking man. Even in Daniel's ill-fitting clothes. Those high-water jeans didn't look nearly as funny on him as they should have.

That was a point against the stranger.

Rebecca frowned slightly and shifted uncomfortably in her seat. Handsome men had no place in her life. Nor for that matter, did ugly ones. But a handsome man was definitely trouble.

She wasn't looking to be sparked and courted.

Courted? She straightened up at the thought and glanced wildly at Zacariah, hoping he couldn't really read her mind. When his expression didn't change, she laughed silently at her own wild imagination. One look at an attractive man and her thoughts took off at a dead gallop. Besides, Zacariah was clearly far more interested in food than he was in her person.

Ordering her brain to keep quiet, Rebecca forced herself to listen to the conversation that had leaped into life around her.

"She sets some store by schoolin' and such," her son was saying, "but I told her I ain't never goin' to need no schoolin'."

"I'm never going to need schooling," Rebecca corrected gently.

"Me neither." Danny turned, a small, teasing smile on his face.

"That smile of yours won't get you out of this one. You'll go to school, Danny Hale." She grinned right back at him, glad to be on safe, neutral ground again. They had this conversation at least twice a week. Already dreading the start of school in the fall, Danny was busy trying to find a way out of it. "And you'll do well, too. You're a smart boy."

"I know." He nodded once, sending dark brown hair falling into his eyes, then he squinted up at Zacariah. "I already know how to read and write some. Ma teached me at night."

"Taught," she corrected again, and watched her son fondly. It seemed that every day, he looked more and more like his father. From the impatient way he brushed his hair out of his face to the crooked smile he used to charm her, he was every inch Daniel's son. How proud his father would have been of him. She smiled softly,

remembering Daniel and the good times they'd had together. How she missed talking to him and laughing with
him in the evening.

"You all right, Ma?"

"I'm fine, Danny," she said and reached for the coffeepot just as Zacariah did the same. His fingers brushed
against hers and sent a skittering sense of awareness
shooting up her arm to tremble through her chest. She
jerked her hand back and pulled in a shaky breath. Looking up at him, Rebecca felt his clear blue gaze as powerfully as she had his touch.

Who *was* he?

"More coffee?" he asked and didn't wait for her nod
to begin filling her cup before his own.

She curled her fingers around the hot china cup and
lifted it to her mouth. Glancing at him over the rim, she
asked, "You said your name's Zacariah?"

He smiled and nodded.

"Zacariah what?"

"Sorry?"

Confusion showed in his eyes and even before she
asked her next question, Rebecca knew she wasn't going
to get an answer.

"Well, since you're going to be working for me, I figured I should know your last name."

"I don't remember."

Strangely enough, this time, she felt that he was telling
the truth.

The front door blew open and slanting rain carried by
a sharp, cold wind rushed into the room. Two men hurried
inside and slammed the door closed behind them. Their
voices sounded unusually loud as they cursed the weather
and each other while taking off their rain slickers and
hanging them on a hook by the door.

"I looked all over the mesa for you and you was nowhere to be found," the older man accused.

"Hell, Buck, I was there!" the younger man countered

and ran one hand through his blond, wavy hair. "Where else would I be?"

"That's what I want to know."

"Damn, man, in this rain, no wonder you couldn't find me. My horse nearly got lost heading back to the ranch."

"I could see fine, boy. And I *didn't* see you."

The blond laughed too loudly, and clapped the older man on the back.

"Buck. Scotty. Glad to see you made it back all right," Rebecca said, successfully interrupting them. "Come on in and eat."

Both men turned to look at her. Buck pushed wisps of gray hair back from his face, tossed one last look at the younger man beside him, then said, "Sorry we're late, Becky. I couldn't find this young fool anywhere on the mesa."

The younger man shook his head, pushed past him and walked quickly to the table. Rebecca groaned inwardly as she realized that Scotty was headed for a seat close to her. He stepped across the bench, straddling it, then jerked his head toward Zacariah. Staring directly into Rebecca's eyes, he asked, "Who's he?"

She poured more coffee for each of the men, kissed Danny good night and promised, "I'll be along in a few minutes." Then she took her place at the end of the table again. Deliberately seating herself a few more inches away from Scotty, she wasn't even surprised when he simply moved closer. Rebecca glanced at him, nodded at his ingratiating smile and looked away again.

Zacariah helped himself to a third slice of apple pie, apparently oblivious to the frown Buck directed at him. Mentally, Rebecca made a note to buy extra flour and sugar in town later that week. If Zacariah were going to be staying, she'd need to stock up.

The warm, soft glow of lamplight bathed the faces of

the three men at her table. Slowly, her gaze shifted from one man to the next.

Buck's bushy gray eyebrows were drawn down low on his wrinkled forehead as he studied the situation. He hadn't gotten any better answers out of Zacariah than she'd been able to. And she knew he wasn't pleased at all, by the way he kept tugging at the whiskers on his chin.

Since Daniel's death, Buck had taken over more and more of the responsibilities around the place. He'd worked at the Hale ranch since before Daniel had been born and probably figured he had as much right to call the place home as she did. He was right.

Without turning her head, she glanced at Scotty, the one other hand she'd been able to afford to keep. Young, he had a ready laugh, pale gray eyes and blond hair that had every young woman in town nearly swooning whenever he passed by. He was also the best man with a horse that she'd ever seen. For that reason alone, she'd kept him on when her common sense told her to get rid of him. Too often lately, that laughter of his had seemed forced and he spent far too much time watching her with a shine in his eyes that told her she didn't want to know what he was thinking. And the looks he was shooting Zack now had nothing to do with friendly curiosity. He was almost acting the part of a jealous beau.

Before she knew what she was doing, Rebecca spoke up.

"Zack's going to be staying on here for awhile."

"What?" Scotty swiveled his head and stared at her like she'd just grown another eye dead center in her forehead.

"Now, Becky," Buck started, "maybe you ought to think—"

"It's already decided," she told them both firmly.

"If he don't remember a damn thing, what good will he be?" Scotty asked, throwing his hands in the air.

"Hell, you don't know a thing about him, Rebecca."

She wasn't sure if it was Scotty saying her name in such a deep, familiar voice or if it was having both men question her judgement that strengthened her decision. Maybe it was a little of both. She always had been too stubborn for her own good.

"While you two are out on the range, rounding up what's left of the herd, I can use some help around here." She turned to Buck, deliberately avoiding Scotty's gaze. "Will you take him out to the bunkhouse? Get him settled?"

"If you're sure . . ." Buck paused, waiting.

"I'm sure." She knew she sounded more confident than she felt, but for now, that was enough. She stood up and looked down at Zacariah. "Tomorrow morning, come to the house and I'll show you what I want you to do." Before any of them could say anything more, she turned and headed for her son's bedroom.

Scotty glared at Zacariah, then pushed himself to his feet, stomped across the room and grabbed up his slicker. When he stepped outside, he left the door wide open to bang against the wall in the rainy wind.

"Damn fool," Buck muttered and hurried over to close the door again. Turning to look at Zacariah, he said thoughtfully, "Hit your head when your horse threw ya, huh?"

"Yes."

The older man slowly nodded and lifted his rain slicker off the hook. "You don't remember nothing, huh?"

Zacariah stood up. "No."

As he slipped the rain gear on over his clothes, Buck said softly, "Well, I reckon I'll believe ya. I been kicked in the head a time or two, forgot whole parts of my life." He glanced at the other man and winked. "That ain't necessarily a bad thing, you understand."

No, he didn't. Not really, Zacariah thought. But why

argue the point? He winked back and paid no attention to Buck's startled expression.

As for Scotty's reaction to his presence, Zacariah could only laugh silently. Whatever notions the angry young man had about Rebecca, he was welcome to them. In one month, Zacariah would be back on the Eternal Path, happily putting this time behind him.

"So," Buck said, as he reached for a spare slicker and tossed it to Zacariah. "You don't remember anything about ranching, huh?"

He shook his head.

The older man scratched his cheek thoughtfully. "Well, suppose it don't matter much, anyway. Me and Scotty'll be doing the range work. You reckon you can find your way around a hammer and nails?"

"I'm sure I can," Zacariah said confidently. First thing in the morning, he would ask Danny which tool was a hammer.

"Uh-huh," Buck nodded, then opened the door. "Well, I guess we'll just have to wait and see, won't we?"

"I'll do the work," Zacariah said, his deep voice carrying an echo of the power only recently stripped from him.

"Damn right, you will." Buck motioned him to start walking. As they stepped out onto the porch, the older man added, "And you'll not start up any notions about Becky, either. Scotty's bad enough. I got to keep an eagle eye on that young fool. Feel like a damned mother hen guardin' her last chick. I ain't got eyes enough to keep watch on both of ya."

Zacariah dipped his head and pulled the slicker on over his clothes. Flashing the other man a long, steady look, he said, "Don't worry about me. I won't be here long enough to be a bother."

Buck looked into vivid blue eyes that seemed to hold the secrets of the ages. Instinctively, he took one step back and admitted silently to relief when the other man looked away. "Head on over to the bunkhouse. I'll be right along."

He stood under the overhang and watched the tall, dark man run clumsily across the muddy yard. He watched as a slash of lamplight streaked through the rain, then disappeared again as the bunkhouse door was opened then quickly closed. He waited silently until his heart had stopped racing and his breath could fight its way past the knot in his throat.

There was something . . . *familiar* about the new man. Almost as if he'd known this Zacariah before. Though he knew that if he'd ever stared into those eyes before tonight, he would have remembered it plainly. Because along with the familiarity, there was something unnerving about the man, too.

For one thing, this Zack was a bald-faced liar. He'd said he could handle a hammer and nails. But when Buck had tossed him the slicker, he'd gotten a good look at Zacariah's hands. Those palms of his had never known hard, physical work.

There wasn't a callous or a scar on them.

So, if he wasn't a rancher, and he wasn't a working man, just what the hell was he?

And what did he want at the Hale ranch?

He shivered as a cold, solitary drop of water sneaked under his collar and rolled down along his spine. Now he had two men to watch. Between Scotty acting like a bull in a field full of seasonal cows and this new fella springing up out of nowhere, peace of mind was going to be in short supply around here.

Buck reached up, pulled his hat brim down low over his eyes and squinted at the bunkhouse through the driving rain. One widow, one randy cowhand with a burr under his saddle and one stranger with familiar, knowing eyes.

Hell, Buck thought as he stepped off the porch into the rain. He was getting way too old for this nonsense.

Chapter ❀ Four

Eternity wasn't as long as the night he'd just passed.

Zacariah's eyes felt like two rocks in a sack of sand.

Why had no one bothered to tell him how difficult it was to sleep? Never mind the terrifying experience of having his body slide slowly toward unconsciousness—whether he wanted it to or not. How did humans sleep through the hideous noises crashing around them?

Rain had slammed against the roof with the determination of thousands of hoofbeats. But it wasn't the rain that had made sleep impossible.

He slanted a disgusted glare at the two men responsible for his aching eyes and miserable temper.

If he hadn't suffered through it himself, he doubted that he would have believed that such sounds could erupt from human bodies. Snoring. He'd heard about it of course. But he'd never been subjected to a night filled with the long chorus of snorts, mutterings and growls before. The hellish night had given Zacariah a whole new appreciation for the quiet serenity of the Path.

"You ready to get started?" Buck asked as he buttoned his shirt.

Good God. The man kept him awake all night and now he expected him to leap up and rush into only God knows what kind of menial labor? Huh. Gabriel wanted him to learn *compassion* from these people? He rubbed one hand over his face and frowned at the rough stubble dotting his cheeks.

"I said, you ready?"

"Yes," he answered because he was in no position to argue. If he didn't work, they'd fire him and he'd only have to *walk* somewhere else and hope to find a job. Besides, maybe if he kept moving, he would wake up.

"We really going to ride out and leave him here. Alone. With Becky?" Scotty's fingers expertly strapped a holstered pistol to his hip.

Zacariah scowled at him. The woman was perfectly safe. Even if his spirit were willing to seduce her—supposing he knew how—his body was far too tired.

"Rebecca can take care of herself," Buck reminded him. "Besides, it ain't up to you."

"I don't like it," Scotty said flatly.

"Nobody asked you."

First snoring, now fighting. Couldn't they be silent for awhile? In that effort, he spoke up.

"As I explained to . . ." Zacariah waved one hand at the gray-haired man.

"Buck," he provided.

"Of course. Buck." He must remember that. Turning to face the blond man, he went on. "As I explained to Buck last night, I won't be here long. There really is no point at all in your being so upset."

"Upset?" Scotty laughed shortly. "This ain't upset, mister. But you stay the hell away from Becky or I'll *show* you upset."

By the Path, he'd tried to be cooperative. Polite. But after the night he'd spent, he was in no mood to deal with tantrums.

"I'll do whatever it is that Rebecca tells me to do. She hired me." His voice, roughened by the lack of sleep, seemed to reverberate in the small bunkhouse. "Now, if you'll excuse me," he turned his back on the man. "I have to get dressed."

Silence stretched out for a moment or two and Zacariah luxuriated in it. Though he knew that Scotty wouldn't be quiet for long. He wondered what the man's reaction might be. With humans, there was no way to be sure. Hopefully the man would see reason. Starting off his quest for compassion with a fistfight probably wouldn't be a wise idea.

"Fine," Scotty finally said. "But just don't you get comfortable around here."

Zacariah glanced at him. "I won't." He hardly thought that possible, anyway. Between the snoring and the misery of what they called a bed, comfort was not something he was counting on.

"Scotty," Buck said, giving the younger man's arm a tug. "If you've got so much spit and fire twisting your guts this morning, get yourself out to Pine Creek and start them horses to the south pasture."

A long moment passed and Zacariah thought Scotty would argue the orders. It was in his eyes. But finally, he nodded briefly to Buck, then looked again at him.

"I'm goin'," the blonde said softly. "But you mind what I said, drifter."

"Oh," Zacariah nodded, a grim smile on his lips. "I will." There. Should Gabriel or the Minions be watching, surely they'd be pleased at how well he'd contained his own temper in the face of such overwhelming temptation.

"Get goin'." Buck gave the other man a shove. "I'll be along directly. And make sure you're at Pine Creek when I get there."

Scotty nodded stiffly, glared at Zacariah, then left, slamming the bunkhouse door behind him.

Buck kneaded the muscles at the back of his neck and grumbled, "Don't pay him any mind. Hell, if I didn't need his damned help, I'd fire him right now." He looked up then and added, "Around here, you take your orders from Rebecca. And me."

Zacariah nodded and told himself it would be wise to keep as far from the irritating younger man as possible in the coming month.

Month.

How would he ever survive an entire month among these people? He bit back a groan and finished buttoning his borrowed shirt.

Forcing himself to face Buck, he asked, "What do you want me to do today?"

The man rubbed his smooth jaw with one hand and shook his head. "I reckon Becky'll be tellin' you that. No doubt she's got somethin' planned out for ya."

Remembering the suspicious gleam in her eyes the night before, he shuddered to think what that plan might be.

"Ain't you gonna shave, boy?"

"Hmmm?"

"Shave." Buck nodded his head at him. "Don't you want to shave before we get started?"

"Uh . . ." Zacariah turned and glanced into the jagged slice of mirror hanging on the wall behind him. His reflection looked as bad as he felt. Dark circles stained the flesh beneath his eyes and heavy, dark stubble shadowed his jaws.

Whiskers.

Blast it.

He lifted one hand to his cheek and thoughtfully scratched at the rough stubble. There were two choices here. He could attempt to shave and slice his face to ribbons. Or, he could ignore the whiskers and grow a beard.

One corner of his mouth lifted slightly.

A beard it was.

"No," he told Buck as inspiration struck. "I don't have any of my things with me, remember? That horse of mine ran off with all of my *gear*."

"Don't worry about that boy," Buck said. "You can use mine. Just give it a strop or two."

"Thank you, but it's not—"

"No trouble, no trouble," Buck assured him. "Just get on with it. Got to get to work and I ain't leavin' the ranch till you're settled in at a chore."

Grumbling under his breath, Zacariah walked to the pitcher and bowl resting on a table just below the mirror. Apparently, he was going to shave.

The only consolation was, he couldn't recall a single instance where a soul had stepped onto the Path while shaving. With any luck at all, he wouldn't be the first.

"Something wrong?" Buck asked and stepped up behind him.

Zacariah jumped. "No," he said quickly. "Nothing."

"Well then, get a move on, boy."

Zacariah sighed and tried to remember exactly how Buck and Scotty had accomplished this seemingly easy feat. He'd tried to watch them carefully, so they wouldn't notice him staring. But they'd performed this daily chore so quickly and efficiently that they'd finished almost as quickly as they'd begun. Teaching him nothing.

Buck took a seat on the bunk directly behind the new man and settled down to wait.

His bushy gray eyebrows lifted high on his forehead as he watched the other man carefully lift one end of the razor strop. Holding onto the straight razor gingerly, as if he expected it to bite him, Zack stroked it down the leather strip to the very end and came within a hair of slicing off one of his own fingertips.

Narrowing his gaze thoughtfully, Buck leaned against the wall, propped a pillow behind his back and made himself comfortable.

Next, Zacariah whipped up a paltry lather in the shaving mug and dabbed it on his face with the care of an old maid using freckle remover. Buck frowned. The fella looked as though he'd never done this before. When the thin soap shot up his nose, Zacariah sneezed violently and Buck offered, "God bless."

"I hope so," Zack whispered and picked up the razor again.

Buck tensed and wondered briefly if he had any clean rags he could use for bandages when the bloodletting started. A man that ignorant about shaving was bound to cut off an ear or something. Jesus. Just how much could a man forget about living? Zack tilted his head back and struggled to watch himself in the mirror. Buck took a deep breath and held it when the man settled the razor's edge against his throat.

Christ . . . the way his hand was shaking, he'd be lucky to survive the first slice.

Instantly, Zack hissed and jerked the razor away from his skin. Even from five feet away, Buck saw blood well up from a sizable nick and he winced in sympathy. He then hid a small smile when Zack looked down at the razor's blade as if he expected to find drooling fangs rather than a gleaming edge.

Still, the younger man couldn't be faulted for being a quitter. While the lather on his neck slowly turned a darker shade of pink, Zacariah shifted position and lifted the razor to his cheek, then licked his lips.

Buck muffled a chuckle while Zack spit soap into the washbasin.

"That tasted awful!"

"It ain't candy."

Leaning forward slightly, he watched, fascinated, as Zack aligned the razor's edge and carefully tried again.

"Damnation!" the man shouted, dropped the offending blade into the washbasin and clapped one hand to his bleeding ear.

Shoving himself to his feet, Buck decided to interfere before the whole damn bunkhouse was awash with blood.

"How does a body forget how to shave?" he wondered aloud and stepped up beside the wounded man.

"A better question would be, why do we have whiskers in the first place?"

Buck snorted a laugh. "Well now, that is one I've asked myself a time or two."

"Seems pointless, doesn't it?" Zacariah gingerly moved his hand from his cheek and scowled at the fresh spurt of blood. "If we needed them, why the devil would we shave them off every damned morning?"

"You're preachin' to the choir here, boy."

"I just won't shave," he said to the bleeding man in the mirror.

"S'pose you could grow a beard," Buck allowed. "But for me, the itchin' liked to drove me around the bend the last time I tried it."

"Itching?"

"Lordy yes. Easier to shave than it is to scratch all the time."

Zacariah sighed heavily. Bleed to death or spend an entire month scratching? Shaking his head, he solemnly regretted every mistake that had brought him to this place.

It had been quite a morning so far. He'd already experienced anger, pain and humiliation and he hadn't even left the bunkhouse yet. Centuries of knowledge at his command and he couldn't manage to accomplish a simple chore that most human males performed daily.

"Hell," Buck said disgustedly, bringing Zacariah's mind back to the problem at hand. "I reckon I best show ya how to do it proper. If not, you're like to bleed to death and then I'd have to go to the trouble of diggin' a grave and such."

A reluctant smile touched his face briefly. "I'd hate to put you to the bother of grave digging."

"That's real kind of ya," Buck allowed. "Now, pick up that razor again and pay attention to what I'm goin' to say."

As Buck took him through the morning ritual step by step, Zacariah's confidence grew. Though it wasn't easy by any means, he thought that by the end of the month, he would be fairly proficient at ridding himself of whiskers. Just in time to not require the skill at all.

When they were finished, he admired the results in the broken mirror. Running one hand along his now-smooth jawline, he understood why it was that humans took the time to scrape away the coarse stubble. His face certainly looked better—except for the bloody spots.

"You sure you never been around these parts before?" Buck said suddenly and Zacariah's gaze shifted to meet his.

"I don't know," he said. "I told you, I don't remember."

"Uh-huh, so you did." Buck scratched his head and his brow furrowed into deep lines as he studied the other man. "But I could swear I seen you somewheres before. Can't put my finger on it . . . but it'll come to me. It always does."

Zacariah frowned uncomfortably.

"Till then though, we got work to do," Buck turned away abruptly and crossed the room. As he snatched up his coat and hat, he glanced at Zacariah over his shoulder. "You come on. We'll go see Becky and get you started on whatever it is she wants done. Me and Scotty'll be back a bit before suppertime. We got supplies with us, so we'll cook up somethin' at dinner and eat on the range."

Food. Suddenly there was a saving light shining through the misery of his morning.

"You watch your manners with Rebecca, Zack. Keep in mind that I taught her how to shoot a long while back and she ain't afraid to use a gun."

By the Path! Did these people think of nothing else?

"I am not interested in your employer."

Buck ignored that statement and went on with his warning. "I got my eye on you and Scotty both. Don't you give her cause for grief. You'll regret it. When she's through with you, I'll come down on you like a rock slide.'' He rubbed one work-worn hand over his wispy hair and continued. ''Don't let this gray up here, fool ya. You give Rebecca any trouble at all and I will personally show you the road to Hell.''

Since he already knew more about the dark and shadowy Path to Hell than Buck could possibly guess, that particular threat was an empty one.

''I don't know what else to say to convince you that you have nothing to fear from me.''

Curling and uncurling his hat brim, the older man went on. ''I'm trustin' you, or I wouldn't be leavin' the ranch at all while you're here. But you got to know something, son. Becky's had it rough these last few years.'' He squinted at Zacariah as if mentally debating just how much to tell him. Then he sighed, his decision made. ''Since her man died, she's been losing horses.''

''Losing horses?'' That hardly seemed possible. Surely not even humans could actually *lose* an animal the size of a horse.

Buck scowled at him as if reading his mind. ''She ain't misplaced 'em. Somebody's stealing them. Haven't managed to catch the bastards yet, but I will. And when I do . . .'' He shook his head. ''Anyhow, with the ranch losin' money like that, she had to let the other hands go. Couldn't afford to pay 'em. So it's just me, Becky and Scotty takin' care of this place. And now you. I'm here to see she don't lose anything else. Anything a'tall. You understand me, mister?''

Not completely, he thought. Still, he recognized loyalty when he saw it. All right, he was willing to admit that perhaps there were a *few* human characteristics that were worthwhile.

''I'll only be here a few weeks,'' he said. ''And I assure you that I have no designs on Rebecca *or* her horses.''

The older man nodded abruptly. ''Fine. But I warn ya now. Rebecca better be all right when you decide to leave.''

"All right?" Why wouldn't she be? Unless, he thought suddenly, it was Rebecca's soul he was expected to collect when his month ended.

"I'm old, boy. Not blind. I saw how you was lookin' at Rebecca last night."

Startled, Zacariah quickly thought back to the night before. How *had* he looked at Rebecca? Silently, he admitted that he would have had to be blind not to admire her beauty. But there was nothing more to it than that. By the Path, the woman was a mortal! And he, as a Soul Collector, had absolutely no interest whatsoever in the mating rituals of humans.

Although, Zacariah amended as memories filled him, he distinctly remembered that slow curl of pleasure that had unfurled deep inside him. Vivid recollections of his body's response to the woman rose up to taunt him. The unexpected tightening in his groin. The racing beat of his heart.

But wouldn't *any* woman have caused such a reaction in a male body?

He sighed and tried to focus his attention on what Buck was saying.

"I ain't gonna stand still for you and Scotty to be fightin' over that woman like two mangy dogs over a stray bone. She deserves better than either one of ya."

Zacariah frowned and straightened up. Wasn't it enough to be chastised and demeaned by his own kind? Must he listen to sermons from humans as well?

If Buck only knew how ridiculous their concerns were!

It didn't matter if he reacted to Rebecca or not. In one short month, these very human responses would end and he would be gone.

"Rebecca is safe from me," he said tightly. "But I'm afraid you'll just have to take my word for it."

"I'll do that. For now." Buck's eyes narrowed as he looked at Zacariah long and hard for a full minute before jerking him a nod. "I still say there's something almighty familiar about you, son."

Zacariah followed the man outside and stepped down off the porch onto the muddy ground.

Why would he seem familiar to a human? Had he been here before? With centuries of collections behind him it was always difficult to keep track of where one had been. But even if he *had* been here before, even if the older man *had* been close enough to death to see him . . . Buck couldn't recognize him. It was impossible. No one who had seen a Collector and lived ever remembered. At least, he'd never heard of such a thing happening.

The older man slipped in the mud, then caught himself. Continuing on toward the house, he muttered a string of curses that had Zacariah smiling in admiration for his creativity.

Ridiculous.

Buck couldn't remember him.

Slogging through the mud-choked yard toward the house, Zacariah told himself that as soon as he had a chance, he would try to sift through his memories. Try to find a recollection of Buck. Not that he was bothered by this newest turn of events.

But still, if there were the slightest chance that he and Buck had met before, Zacariah had better know about it.

"What did you say these are called?"

"Flapjacks," Rebecca said, and refilled both of their coffee cups.

"They're very good."

"I guess so." She'd never seen a man eat sixteen flapjacks in one sitting before. Watching him as he finished off the last of his breakfast, Rebecca told herself that if he worked half as well as he ate, she'd be getting much more than her ten dollars worth out of him.

He took a gulp of coffee, set the cup down again and

turned to her. "What do you want me to do first?" he asked.

"Well," she said. "The roof needs fixing, but since you fell off a two-foot stool, I'd rather not put you to work so high up."

His eyebrows lifted.

"So why don't you start with both feet on the ground."

"Doing what?"

"Think you can fix a fence?"

Hesitation flickered in his cool blue eyes momentarily, then he pushed away from the table. "I think so."

"Good. Danny's in the barn feeding the horses. He'll show you where the tools are."

"Tools." He nodded and walked to the front door. "Thank you for the meal."

She shrugged. "Just holding up my end of the deal we made. Now it's your turn."

"Blast and damnation," he shouted and dropped the hammer to grab onto his throbbing thumb. With every beat of his heart, pain pulsed through his hand.

Glaring at the fence post, Zacariah gave it a good kick and muttered viciously. He'd only been actually working a half an hour or so and already he'd nearly broken his thumb and two fingers.

Tipping his head back to stare at the sky, he grumbled, "I hope you're all happy!"

"Who ya talkin' to?"

He straightened up and spun around to look into Danny Hale's wide, curious stare.

"Nobody," he said and bent down to snatch up the damned hammer again.

"Ma talks to nobody a lot, too." The boy scrambled up onto the lower rung of the fence, draped his arms over the upper rail and watched him. "Especially when she's mad. She says that there's somebody up there laughin' over the trouble that happens down here."

"She's right," Zacariah told him with a small smile. At least, she was right about the laughter directed at him. He had a feeling that the Eternal powers didn't spend much time laughing at humans.

"Your thumb hurt much?" the boy asked, squinting at him.

"Not much." The pain had, in fact, lessened until now it was merely a blinding ache.

"Ma's not too good with a hammer either. But my pa was."

"Is that right?"

Zacariah lifted a fence rail, held it into position braced on his knee, then reached for the sack of nails. If what the boy said was true, he heartily wished that the child's father was here to take over this chore.

"Oh yeah." Danny nodded and smiled, displaying a wide gap in his teeth. "Ma says that my pa could do anything."

Wonderful. Just what he needed. To be compared unfavorably to a perfect human.

" 'Cept he's dead, now."

"Yes, I heard that." Zacariah glanced at him. "I'm sorry," he said, and surprisingly enough, meant it. Faced with a boy obviously hungry for a man's company, even he could see that it was a shame the child's father had died.

"Oh, that's all right. I really don't remember him much."

Zacariah nodded as the boy went on talking. Obviously, his input wasn't required. The child could probably talk for hours with no more than an occasional nod in response. Instead, he concentrated on the fence post.

Holding the nail gingerly between his thumb and forefinger, he swung the hammer back and made a tentative strike. Metal smacked against metal. Pleased, he did it again. And again. When the nail had been driven flush with the wood, he admired his handiwork. True, the nail-head was bent to one side, but it was holding.

Hmmm. He smiled to himself as a flush of success rushed through him. Being human wasn't so difficult. In fact, it was rather . . . *pleasant,* this feeling of satisfaction at a job well done.

Confident now, he reached for the sack, eager to try it again.

Well, whatever else he might turn out to be, Rebecca thought, Zack was no quitter.

She glanced up at the cloudless, blue sky and squinted against the sun. Then she shifted her gaze back to the man struggling with the last of the fence posts. He'd been at it for hours already and despite the noonday heat, he showed no signs of stopping. Even though having Danny perched alongside him, chattering like a busy squirrel, had to be bothersome.

Setting her palms at the small of her back, Rebecca slowly stretched, wincing slightly as her muscles pulled. Maybe she should have set Zacariah to work digging the garden and taken over the fence-post chore herself. She grinned at the realization that she would indeed rather wrestle cumbersome fence posts than spend another moment hunched over muddy, stubborn dirt and even more stubborn weeds.

But, if she wanted fresh vegetables next winter, she'd have to spend at least a good part of the coming summer planting, weeding, harvesting and canning. Just the thought of it was enough to make her tired.

But the silver lining was, she wouldn't need as much hard-won cash money for supplies during the winter.

She yawned and stretched, enjoying the deep warmth of the sunlight. After a morning of hard work, she longed for a nap. Scandalous, to even think of sleeping in the middle of the day—but lying awake half the night had made her tired enough to consider it.

Rebecca told herself that it was only natural that she

had spent a good portion of the night before thinking about Zacariah. After all, he was a stranger. She knew nothing about him, save that he knew nothing about himself. Most folks would think her crazy for letting him stay on.

She leaned back against the side of the house. The wide, shingled overhang shadowed her face from the sun as splinters from the rough log walls poked through her blue cotton shirt to scratch against her back. Finally, she lifted one foot, braced it on the wall behind her and looked across the yard at the man occupying too much of her thoughts.

Forgetting who the hell you are was odd enough. What she wanted to know was how a man could get to be grown and not know how to swing a hammer without hurting himself.

She remembered the look of astonishment on his face the first time he'd smashed his thumb. It was almost as if he hadn't know there would be pain.

Now, as she watched him, Zack tossed the hammer into the mud and took a step back from the last fence post. He held both hands out toward it, as if expecting the darn thing to topple over. But it didn't. Even if it *had* taken him most of the day, he'd finished the job.

Despite himself.

He turned toward Danny and she heard the boy's laughter ripple out into the sunshine.

Though she couldn't hear what Danny was saying, she smiled. Undoubtedly, her son had come up with a few dozen more questions for Zack. One more point for the man, he was endlessly patient with a boy who had for some reason decided to attach himself to him.

Zack bent, picked up the hammer and turned toward the barn, Danny just a step or two behind him.

Even the way Zack moved was unique. He took each step as if measuring its cost. A careful man, apparently. And a secretive one, too. Why was he lying about how he'd come to be there? More importantly, why had she let him stay?

There was just something about him, she decided absently. Yes, a voice inside her whispered. Vivid blue eyes that when turned on her made her feel things she had no business feeling. Things she'd never thought to feel.

Oh my, we *are* being fanciful today, her brain whispered. Apparently, she'd stayed out too long in the sun. Grinning at her own stampeding imagination, Rebecca straightened up from the wall.

"Hey, Ma!" Danny called. "Zack 'n me are hungry."

Now there was a surprise.

She swung around to answer him and her gaze collided with Zack's.

He smiled at her.

Her insides turned upside down.

And a small voice in the back of her mind shouted, "Stampede!"

Chapter ❈ Five

The town consisted of a single, wide street, with a couple of dozen buildings crouched behind wooden boardwalks that rose and fell like waves at sea. Both sides of the street were crowded with wagons and carriages, their owners shouting to each other like long-lost relatives. Saddle horses, tied to hitching rails, dozed in the afternoon sun. In the distance, a blacksmith's hammer rang out over the commotion and a dog barked in time with the rhythm.

Interested despite himself, Zacariah's head swiveled from side to side, as he tried to look at everything at once. Oh, it wasn't London by any means. By the Path, it wasn't even San Francisco for that matter. But in this tiny gathering of buildings, for the first time, he actually felt a part of the hustling confusion.

To his own surprise, he found it exhilarating.

"Afternoon, Becky," someone called out.

Zacariah turned to look at the speaker. A tall woman with weathered skin and tired eyes stood on a rise in the boardwalk. Her plain gray dress lay limply along her spare figure but the hands clutching an empty shopping basket against her narrow chest looked sun browned and strong.

"Afternoon, Doris," Rebecca answered, still keeping her horses at a walk. "How's Charlie feeling today?"

"Some better, thanks for asking."

"Glad to hear it. You tell him we expect to see him out at the house for supper soon."

"I'll do that." The woman smiled and the deep lines in her features fell into familiar patterns. As the Hale wagon rolled past her, she shouted, "Danny, I do believe you've grown since the last time I saw you!"

The boy stood straighter in the wagon bed and grabbed onto the back of the jump seat to steady himself. "Yes ma'am, I sure have."

The woman's curious gaze flickered over him. Zacariah chanced a half smile. She nodded politely and he turned around again to face front, pleased by the minor accomplishment.

"That's Doris Smalley," Rebecca told him as she guided her team of horses around a carriage headed right for them. "Her husband Charlie's been dying for twenty years."

"What?" He cocked his head to look at her. Twenty years? He'd like to know just who Charlie Smalley's Collector was. Hmmph! Gabriel punished *him* for being a few moments late?

Rebecca grinned and leaned toward him after a quick glance backward to make sure Danny wasn't listening. "Charlie Smalley is the laziest man God ever made. He's got more aches and pains and diseases than any big city hospital's yet to see."

"Ah . . ." He turned for another look at the tall woman before she disappeared into the cluster of people.

"Doc Jenkins's buggy has made the trip out to the Smalley ranch so many times, he swears his horse can find the place blindfolded in a fog." Rebecca shook her head. "I never have been able to figure what it is about dying that Charlie finds so blasted appealing."

"He wants to die?" In centuries, Zacariah had never once encountered a soul happy to see him. Even suicidal spirits generally had a change of heart once it was too late.

"Sure acts like he does," Rebecca said and nodded to the driver of a hay wagon. "But I guess not. Otherwise he would have gone out and shot himself long before this time."

Zacariah shifted his gaze away from her. He'd told Mordecai once that the mortals who actually ended their own lives were the brightest of a bad lot. He'd insisted that anyone anxious to leave such a miserable existence in favor of something better must be considered a superior being. He smiled to himself at the memory of Mordecai's outrage, then heard himself ask, "Wouldn't that be best?"

"What?"

"If he simply went out and ended his life." Zacariah shrugged. "If it's what he wants, perhaps he'd be happier."

She looked at him as though he was speaking in tongues.

"That is the stupidest thing I've ever heard!"

Affronted, he straightened up. A human? Questioning *him?* "You don't think it's stupid for a man to try to die for twenty years and not manage to complete the task?"

"That's not what I said."

"Then what did you say?"

She jerked on the reins as a horse and buggy darted out into the road in front of them. Shooting him a disgusted glance, she snapped, "I said, he doesn't *really* want to die. He just likes being sick."

"That makes no sense at all." But then what had he expected?

"What doesn't make sense is killing yourself," she grumbled.

He half-turned on the bench seat to look at her. Sunshine made her skin look warm and soft. Her eyes were squinted beneath the brim of her hat and her fingers worked the reins competently despite her agitation.

"If a man were ill, suffering," he said, trying to make

his point. "Wouldn't it be better—kinder—to simply give in? To go on to whatever reward awaits him?"

"Why hurry things along?"

"But why not?" This is what he couldn't understand about mortals. For all their professions of faith and their belief in the 'Promised Land,' none of them *wanted* to go!

"Because what if the damn fool kills himself, then the very next day some doctor decides that he could have cured him?" She glanced at him. "Then what?"

"All right, but what if that doesn't happen? Hasn't he simply saved himself from a miserable existence?"

"And what's he done to the folks he's left behind?" Shaking her head, she kept her gaze fixed on the busy street. "Don't they get a vote? Don't the people who love this man get a say in whether he goes or not?"

"Not usually."

"Exactly."

"What does that mean?" The woman talked in circles.

"I mean, when a body dies because it's his time, that's one thing. It hurts." She swallowed heavily, then went on. "But you can accept it. But if a body just gives up and quits . . . no. That I couldn't accept. Or forgive."

He sighed and leaned against the seat back. Two days he'd spent with this woman and he was obviously no closer to understanding humans than he had been when he'd arrived.

"Besides," Rebecca said and brought Zacariah's attention back to her. "There is a silver lining to Charlie's sicknesses."

"Silver lining?"

She flashed him a quick look and an even quicker smile.

Her moods shifted as easily as the swirling shadows of a Collector's appearance. And though he admired the flash of fire in her eyes when she was arguing a point, he preferred her smile.

"You mean to say that along with everything else, you've forgotten tired-out old sayings?"

The gleam in her green eyes told him she was laughing silently, but it was such an attractive shine, he found that he didn't mind overmuch.

"I must have," he admitted, intrigued. "What exactly is a 'silver lining'?"

"The old saying goes, 'Every dark cloud has a silver lining.' " She took another look at his still-confused features and explained. "It means that no matter what bad thing happens, there's usually some good in there somewhere. You just have to find it."

"Do you believe that?" Zacariah asked.

For an instant, a shadow flickered in her eyes, but then it was gone again. She steered the horses to an empty spot along the boardwalk and drew them to a stop. As she reached for the brake lever and thrust it forward, she said, "I have to."

"Hey Ma," Danny asked, poking his head between the two adults. "Can I go in and see Ellie and Jake?"

She brightened a bit as she looked at her son. "Sure, go ahead. We'll be right along."

The boy clambered over the side of the wagon and jumped to the boardwalk. His boots hammered against the wooden planks as he ran to the general store's front door. A bell jumped and clanged when he yanked the door open and went inside, leaving the wood panel to swing closed behind him.

Zacariah squinted into the afternoon sunlight and studied the small smile still curving Rebecca's mouth. He'd already noticed that the smile she gave her son was different from the one she gave others. It was warmer, somehow. Indulgent, proud perhaps. But definitely warmer.

She inhaled deeply, reached up and settled her dust brown hat more firmly on her head. The smile faded as the minutes flew past. Zacariah fixed her with a curious stare. What had she meant about *having* to believe in silver linings? And how did a person go about finding this lining? How would you recognize it even if you knew where to look?

"There's a silver lining to Charlie's diseases?" he prodded. The whole notion of looking for the good in something bad intrigued him.

Rebecca wrapped the reins around the brake handle, then turned on the seat. She tipped her hat brim back a bit to look at him. "I guess the silver lining is, that Charlie being the way he is makes Doris happy."

"Ahhh . . ." He nodded solemnly. Now *this* he recognized. And it was much more in keeping with what he expected of humans. "She wants him to die."

"No!" She laughed and gave him a playful slap on the arm.

"She'd rather he suffer?"

"He's not suffering." She cocked her head and stared at him for a long moment. "Aren't you paying attention? Doris doesn't want Charlie dead. She likes taking care of folks. And he's not dying, remember. He's not even sick. Why, the way Doris looks after that man, he'll live to be a hundred and fifty."

"She looked very tired," Zacariah muttered, recalling the heavy shadows beneath the thin woman's eyes.

"She's got a right. Does all of Charlie's work plus her own." Rebecca reached over the seat back and snatched up her shopping basket. "Then there's the kids. They've got four now and I'd be willing to bet they'll add another one or two before they quit."

"Then he is healthy enough to . . ."

She snorted a laugh. "Dead and in his grave, I believe Charlie would be healthy enough *to* . . ."

"Why?"

"Why what?"

Zacariah still didn't understand. "Why does this Doris work so hard to care for a man who gives her nothing in return?"

Rebecca shrugged. "She loves him."

"Why?"

She shot him a quizzical glance.

Zacariah shook his head. Gabriel was expecting miracles. A month was not enough time for him to understand humans. They made no sense at all.

Inhaling deeply, he said, "The man appears to be worthless. What could she possibly find to love about him?"

"Who knows?" She grinned and shrugged. "Nobody around here's been able to figure that one out either. But she does love him."

Love.

The most elusive of human emotions. Of course, love was not solely reserved for mortals. On the Eternal Path, love was a guiding force. A universal love that eased tired souls and mended wounded spirits. Love filled each moment of eternity and shone like the brightest star in the heavens.

And yet . . .

Human love was different. On the Eternal Path, love would never bring the misery that it sometimes did to mortals.

"Why is it, do you think," he asked suddenly, "that human beings tend to use love as a weapon?"

"A weapon?" She pushed her hat back further on her head and waited for him to go on.

"All right, maybe not a weapon. But certainly a game. To be won or lost. A challenge to be met. An obstacle to be overcome."

She turned her head slightly and looked out over the crowded street. "I don't know. Never really thought about it, I guess."

But then she hadn't had centuries to think these things through, had she?

"How many wars have been fought in the name of love?"

"Wars?"

He nodded and followed her gaze. All around him, the townspeople were going about their business. Women dragged reluctant children behind them. Cowboys leaned on hitching posts, rolling cigarettes and killing time. Shop owners industriously swept the boardwalk free of dust, even knowing that same dust would just cover the wood planks again.

"For love of country, of ideas." He snorted a choked laugh. "They've even been fought for love of God." Adding more to himself than to her, "All of that carnage in the name of love."

"When you put it like that, it doesn't seem to make much sense," she agreed. "But people being people, they'd probably fight each other even if there was no reason at all."

Exactly, he thought. Human beings made no sense. Hadn't he been saying the very same thing for decades?

"But," she added quietly. "Love is the reason wars end, too."

"What?"

"Sure. Compassion, pity, love. Wars end, wounds heal. Because of love."

Hmmm. He rubbed his jaw with one hand and cast a quick, sidelong look at the woman beside him as she reached over the seat back into the bed of the wagon. He'd thought all humans to be slow-witted. Uninteresting.

But then, he'd also thought using a hammer would be easy.

"Are you coming?" Rebecca asked, snatching up her basket and swinging around to climb over the wagon's side.

He looked at her and heard himself blurt out, "Your husband?"

She stopped short, one foot balanced on the wagon wheel, and looked at him. "Daniel?" she asked quietly. "What about him?"

Zacariah noted that her fingers were curled tightly around the basket's handle. Her knuckles gleamed whitely against her tanned flesh. But he had to know and the only way to find out was to ask.

"Did you love him like that?"

Her eyes widened in surprise. Perhaps he shouldn't have asked. But blast it, he was here to learn and he only had a month.

A long, silent moment passed while she watched him. He saw emotions flicker across her green eyes, but they moved so quickly, he couldn't identify them. The crowd on the street faded away. Noise disappeared into the strained silence that stretched between them like a taut cord.

Finally, just as Zacariah told himself she wasn't going to answer, she asked, "Like Doris does Charlie, you mean?"

"Yes," he said and was surprised to hear his own voice come out in a whisper. It felt as though there was a huge hand folded tightly around his chest. He could hardly draw a breath. And since he'd already become accustomed to breathing, the sudden lack of air was almost . . . frightening.

She shifted her gaze away from his momentarily and Zacariah studied her profile. She seemed to be looking beyond the dusty little street and the afternoon crowds at things only she could see. The longer she took to answer him, the more time Zacariah had to regret opening his mouth in the first place.

"Daniel was my best friend," she said and Zacariah's wandering attention shot back to her. A sad, distant smile flashed across her face. "I loved him," she said, nodding, and Zacariah wasn't sure if she was convincing him or herself. She swiveled her head to look at him again. "But no. I guess it wasn't like Doris and Charlie."

"No?" Now he really was confused. Didn't all husbands and wives feel the same kind of love?

"No." She tossed her basket to the dirt and climbed down from the wagon. Looking up at him, she added, "Not many find that kind of love. It's . . . special."

Zacariah scratched his head.

"C'mon, Zack," she interrupted briskly. "Let's get the shopping done. I've got to get back home and start supper."

At the mention of food, he put aside his other thoughts for the time being.

"Apple pie?" he asked hopefully.

Rebecca's gaze narrowed again. "I don't believe I've ever seen a man eat like you do." She shook her head and continued, "But, I like a man who appreciates my cooking. Especially if he helps peel and slice apples."

He jumped to the ground, then bent to pick up her basket. "I can do that." He could only hope that a knife would prove easier to use than a hammer.

Or a razor.

Rebecca threaded her arm through Zacariah's as they walked to the Parkers' store. People rushed past, the men giving her a perfunctory tip of the hat and the women practically ignoring her in their fascination for Zacariah.

She glanced up at him from the corner of her eye. His gaze shifting constantly over the afternoon crowds, it was as if he'd never seen a town before. Rebecca smiled to herself. If he had, he'd apparently forgotten all about it. Absently, she wondered what the townswomen would say if they knew that the handsome man on Rebecca Hale's arm couldn't even remember his own last name.

She stopped short and he stopped right beside her.

"What is it?"

"Your name," she told him. "You have to have a last name."

"I don't see why."

"People will wonder about a man with one name. They'll ask questions you won't be able to answer, then they'll think I'm crazy for hiring a man who doesn't even know who he is."

He shrugged and nodded. "Fine then. What name shall I give them?"

"I'm thinking," she said. "Hang on a minute." Her teeth pulled at her bottom lip as she silently asked herself why she was going to all the bother of protecting him from nosy people. She didn't have a ready answer. But maybe it was enough for now that the man worked for her and his name or the fact that he claimed to not remember a blasted thing was no one's business but his. And hers.

She turned her head to look at the street, mentally going down lists of long-lost relatives' last names. A wagon rolled past and the signboard caught her eye. *Coleman's Feed and Grain, Denver, Colorado.*

Smiling, she looked up at the man beside her. "Cole. Zacariah Cole."

He considered it for a full minute or two, then nodded slowly. "Cole it is, then."

Her arm tucked in the crook of his, they walked the few short steps to the mercantile.

The bell over the door danced and echoed out a welcome as they stepped into the general store. Instantly, warm, familiar scents surrounded Rebecca and she felt her insides settle down. Immediately, she looked for Bear, the Parkers' dog and the store's unofficial greeter. The soft click of nails on wood announced the shepherd's presence just before Rebecca felt a cold nose press against her hand.

"Hello, Bear," she said and dropped to one knee to ruffle the dog's thick gray-and-black fur. As she stood up again, Rebecca glanced over her shoulder at Zack, who was eyeing the dog with a wary eye. "Hold your hand out, let him get your scent."

"As long as he leaves the fingers," Zack muttered as he dutifully stepped forward and held out his right hand.

Bear moved closer to the man, sniffed his outstretched fingertips, then whined piteously. Zack jerked his hand back and stuffed it into his pocket, but it was too late. Backing up, the dog's hackles lifted and the deep-throated whine became an uncertain, rumbling growl.

"What's the matter with you?" Rebecca muttered.

The big dog dipped his head, shot one last look at Zacariah and slunk away, tail between his legs, to hide somewhere in the rear of the store.

"Now what do you suppose got into him?" she said, more to herself than anyone else.

Zacariah scowled at the retreating animal. "Guess he doesn't trust me any more than I do him."

"I've never seen him act like that before." The big dog had almost seemed scared. As soon as the thought entered her mind, though, Rebecca dismissed it. Why would he be afraid? Zack had done nothing threatening. She glanced at the man beside her, and answered his confused expression with a shrug of her own. "Maybe he's getting old and cranky."

Zacariah gave her a slow smile.

Pushing thoughts of Bear to the back of her mind, she looked around the organized jumble of merchandise that was the Parkers' store. She didn't see anyone, though, so she moved to stand beside the counter to wait. No doubt Tom and Helen were upstairs, riding herd on their children.

Zack wandered off and Rebecca half-turned to watch him. His head swung back and forth as his gaze moved over the towers of merchandise. He pulled a thick book down from a high shelf and thumbed through it gingerly, his fingers touching each page as though it was made of glass. When he'd finished, he returned the book and moved on.

Rebecca rested her elbow on the countertop behind her and followed him with her eyes. He squatted to inspect a stack of jeans, then slowly stood again and studied a row of paint cans. It was as if he was seeing everything for the first time. Shaking her head, she watched him dip one hand into a barrel, pull out a cracker and take a bite. His eyebrows lifted and a smile tugged at one corner of his mouth. Apparently, he approved.

When he lifted the lid on the pickle barrel, Rebecca had to choke down a laugh at the expression on his face. The overpowering scent of pickling spices shot into the room and she held her breath as he reached for a sour pickle.

One bite and his face screwed up. He jerked his head back and stared at the damned pickle as though the thing had deliberately poisoned him. Then he looked wildly around for somewhere to put it.

Rebecca laughed out loud, despite the niggling voice in the back of her mind, asking, *Could a man really forget so much?*

"Hello, Becky," a woman called out as she walked the length of the room behind a dark pine counter.

"Helen!" Rebecca turned away from Zack's still puckered features and walked toward the other woman. "Danny upstairs?"

The obviously pregnant woman laughed gently and nodded. "Oh, he raced through here like the Devil himself was after him." She waved one hand at the stairs in the far corner. "He went up to see Ellie and Jake."

Helen's gaze slid from Rebecca to the man stepping up behind her.

"Helen, this is Zacariah Cole. He's working on the ranch for awhile."

"Nice to meet you, Zack." Helen smiled and reached up to tuck a fallen lock of dark red hair back into the coronet of braids atop her head. Turning to Rebecca, she said, "Glad to see you're getting a little more help out there. Maybe you'll be able to come in and visit now and again."

"It has been awhile since we had the time to sit and chat, hasn't it?"

Helen laughed, a warm, liquid ripple of sound, and caressed her swollen belly with one hand. "Since before 'Junior' here took up roost."

Good heavens. Was it really *that* long? Her mind raced back over the past several months and Rebecca groaned silently as she admitted to neglecting her friendship with Helen. And she really had no excuse for it, either. If six children and another on the way didn't keep Helen too busy for her friends, what did that say about Rebecca?

"I promise, we'll do it soon," she said and realized, not for the first time, how much she missed whiling away an afternoon with a pot of tea and good gossip. Why, she couldn't even remember the last time she'd come to town strictly for pleasure.

Her thoughts were splintered in the next instant by the clattering noise created by three children on the stairs. Rebecca turned and watched her son barrel out of the stairwell, Jake Parker hot on his heels. His carrot-red hair stuck up at odd angles around his heavily freckled, elfin features and his pants had holes in both knees. At a year older than Danny's six, Jake was a good two inches taller and a whole lot thinner. Helen swore that the child ate like a grown man, but a body would never know it to look at the boy. But then again, Rebecca had never seen Jake Parker sitting still for longer than a minute. He probably ran off every bite of food he took into his mouth.

Ellie followed the boys, her steps a bit slower. As she stepped into a bright patch of sunlight, Rebecca smiled at the sight. Only twelve . . . almost thirteen, as Ellie would be happy to inform you, the girl was already a beauty. Auburn hair the color of her mother's hung loose about her shoulders, falling in graceful, natural waves around her heart-shaped face. Delicate brows arched over soft green eyes and her cream-colored skin was pale enough that the few freckles dotting her nose stood out like gold dust in a sparkling streambed.

Rebecca sighed. Even in a yellow dress that she'd obviously outgrown, young Ellie Parker was a beauty.

"She's very pretty," Zack offered quietly.

"Yes, she is," Helen agreed, thanking him with a smile. "More's the pity."

Flicking a quick glance at Helen, Rebecca said. "Your Tom's going to have his hands full in a few years."

"Hands full?" Zacariah asked.

"Keeping the boys away," Rebecca explained.

He frowned. "Why would he want to do that?"

Rebecca shook her head.

Helen spared him a short look, then leaned her elbows on the countertop and cocked her head to stare at her daughter. "My Tom's *already* got his hands full. Do you know that Jenkins boy? From out past Finger Mountain?"

"Sure," Rebecca nodded, immediately seeing an image of the lanky teenaged boy in her mind.

"He's been coming around an awful lot here, lately."

"Mama," Ellie sighed and walked closer to the adults discussing her as if she wasn't in the room. "Billy Jenkins just wanted me to help him with his arithmetic."

Helen's eyebrows lifted. "You're twelve," she said.

"Nearer thirteen."

"Fine. Thirteen. He's *sixteen*." Helen propped her chin in her hands and watched her daughter with a knowing smile.

"But he's terrible at arithmetic, Mama."

"Maybe," she sighed. "But I'll bet he knows lots of other things."

Rebecca laughed at the tired note in Helen's voice and silently sent a prayer of thanks to her late husband, for giving her a son rather than a daughter.

"Isn't that good?" Zacariah wondered aloud. "For the boy to know a lot of things, I mean."

Rebecca ignored the look Helen shot Zack. "I'll explain later," she said.

He nodded.

As Ellie started past them, Rebecca noted the faint, bluish shadows beneath the girl's eyes. "Are you feeling all right, honey?"

"Yes ma'am," she answered too quickly, with a covert look at her mother. "Just a little tired is all."

"Come here, Ellie," Helen ordered and reached across the counter as her daughter grumbled, but came closer. Gently, she laid one hand on the girl's forehead. "No fever," she said.

"Is she sick?" Rebecca asked.

Zacariah moved up closer to the girl and seemed to study her carefully.

"I feel good, Mama. Honest." Ellie stepped away from the counter and moved again toward the front door.

"Not really," Helen allowed. "She's just been so tired lately."

"Is she sleeping all right?"

"Seems to be."

"Mama," Ellie interrupted the two mothers. "I'm not *so* tired now. I just want to take a walk. All right?"

Helen frowned, but nodded. "I suppose. You go on outside for awhile. Maybe the sun'll do you some good." Ellie went through the front door quickly, as if afraid her mother would change her mind. Helen called out after her, "You come back if you start feeling poorly!"

The door slammed shut on her words and Rebecca watched her friend stare at the empty doorway, lines of worry etched between her brows.

"You're sure she's fine?" she asked.

Helen straightened up and gave her a determined smile. "I'm sure. Doc says I worry too much. That she's probably having a hard time with her . . ." Helen glanced at Zack, then back to Rebecca. "*You* know."

Ah. Instantly, realization dawned and at the same moment, Rebecca knew that Helen wanted to talk and felt she couldn't with a man present.

"Why don't you go down to the livery, Zack?" Rebecca asked. "See if the set of branding irons I ordered is ready."

"Livery?"

She looked into those brilliant blue eyes of his and again wondered about how much of his memory a man could lose. And if he were lying about the whole thing, why would he pretend to be so ignorant about everyday things?

Mostly, though, she wondered why it mattered to her whether he was a liar or not.

Chapter ❀ Six

Zacariah leaned back against the slat-board fence surrounding the livery and glanced into the darkened building, where the blacksmith's red-hot forge gave off a strange, glowing light. As he watched, the powerful-looking smith stepped up to the fire and worked the bellows until flames roared and heat shimmered in the semi-darkness. He set a long metal rod into the very heart of the flames and once more applied the huge leather bellows until his forge looked like the fires of Hell. Finally, the smith drew the bar out of the heat and began to deliver sharp hammer blows to its glowing iron tip. Sparks flew and the air rang with the crash of metal on metal.

A stabled horse pushed its velvety nose into Zacariah's palm and he smiled. Tearing his gaze away from the blacksmith, he turned to stroke the animal's wide forehead and neck.

"You don't care who I am, do you?" he whispered. "As long as I pay attention to you, you're content."

The big animal shook its head, as if denying the statement, and Zacariah laughed. Sobering, he realized that he was becoming quite fond of laughter.

"By the Path," a voice heard only in his mind demanded, *"who are you talking to?"*

"Mordecai." Zacariah grinned and looked over his

shoulder at his friend. "It's good to see you."

"You seem to be no worse for the few short days you've spent as a human," the other Collector said.

"Actually," he began, "it's not entirely as bad as I'd thought it would be. I even—" He broke off when something at the corner of his eye caught his attention. A swirl of mist appeared on the ground and spun itself upward, into a cloud of fragile, silvery threads.

"By the Path," Mordecai muttered. *"Can't I have a moment's peace?"*

The hesitant swirl continued in staggered bursts until it became a vague blur of vapor. After several long moments, Mordecai finally reached into the murky haze and gave a hard tug.

Instantly, another being popped free of the mist and stumbled into the back end of the horse and continued on right through it. The animal whinnied, snorted and side-stepped frantically, trying to escape.

"Fenwick," Mordecai sighed, *"how many times have I explained to you the proper way of stepping through the mist?"*

Zacariah smothered a smile and studied the new Collector covertly. Smaller than most of the others, Fenwick also labored under the burden of a most unprepossessing face. His features were unremarkable, save for the fact that even in the afterlife, he was cursed with an oversized Adam's apple that bobbed distressingly. His ears stuck out from the sides of his too-round head like the slats of a windmill around its center. And even his shimmering gray robe seemed somehow duller than it should. The garment hung from his narrow shoulders limply, and pooled around his feet in a vast excess of material.

As Mordecai talked, the novice Collector lifted the hem of his robe a good five inches.

"You're absolutely right, Mordecai." Fenwick dipped his head several times.

Zacariah winced as the new Collector's voice clattered loudly in his brain.

"You don't have to shout," Mordecai interrupted.

"Of course, of course," Fenwick answered, this time at a more manageable level. *"And I've been practicing the mist movement. I truly have. It was only that my robe twisted around my feet and I'm afraid that I tripped. I am sorry. It won't happen again."*

"Yes it will," Mordecai muttered, then turned to look at his friend helplessly.

Zacariah smiled widely. He'd never thought to see Mordecai's patience tested. Shifting position, he leaned one hand on the fence rail and winced, hissing in a breath.

"What is it?"

Reluctantly, he held out both hands, palms up to show the two Collectors evidence of his time spent as a human.

Fenwick clucked his tongue and shook his round head slowly.

Mordecai was less subtle.

"Actual blisters!" He glanced up from the raw, red flesh of Zacariah's hands. An excited, almost envious gleam lit his eyes. *"How did you merit those?"*

"I built a fence two days ago."

"With your bare hands?"

"I used tools," he said with a shrug and stuffed his hands into his pants pockets. Suddenly, he didn't want to talk about it anymore. Especially since he couldn't explain the mixed feelings he had about his hard-won blisters and calluses.

He was almost proud of his hands. Oh, they pained him, certainly. But the pain was somehow part of the pride. He had actually managed to build something. Something that would still be standing—hopefully—long after he returned to the Eternal Path.

Perhaps, he told himself absently, years from now, that corral fence would be a reminder to Rebecca and Danny. They would see his work and pause briefly to remember the stranger who had spent one long month with them before disappearing forever.

Scowling, he pushed the notion aside. What did it matter if they remembered him or not? Why did he care if they thought about him at all?

"Zacariah," Mordecai said, *"I came to see you for a reason."*

"What?" He looked from his friend to Fenwick and back again.

"I wanted to ask you again. Are you still determined to serve out the entire month of your punishment?"

"We've been through this before," he answered, idly stroking a nearby horse. "The Minions wouldn't release me even were I to ask."

Mordecai smiled and drifted closer. "I have reason to believe that they would."

"Who told you that?" His eyes narrowed slightly. It was discomfiting to know that he was the subject of conversation on the Path.

"Who, doesn't matter." Mordecai shook his long blond hair until it fell into graceful waves about his head. *"What matters is that I've been assured that if you were to beg and plead sufficiently, anything is possible."*

Zacariah's hands curled into fists at his sides. The humiliation they'd showered on him with this punishment wasn't enough. The Minions apparently wanted to see him crawl. His eyes narrowed thoughtfully. He hadn't begged for *anything* in over six hundred years of existence. He wouldn't start now.

Shoulders stiff, he lifted his chin defiantly. "I won't bow and scrape, Mordecai. I've already told you that."

"But Zacariah, this could all be ended with just a bit of compromise on your part."

"No. The Minions made their decision to send me here." He drew a deep breath as if to emphasize that human he was and human he would remain—for another three weeks. "I've made mine. I'll stay and serve out my time."

Disappointed, Mordecai shook his head. *"Your pride gets in your own way, my friend."*

"Pride? This is not about pride, Mordecai."

"Isn't it?"

Zacariah's lips thinned into a grim slash across his face.

"Oh, very well. I don't understand your unbendable nature, Zacariah. But I see that it's doing no good to argue the matter with you."

He gave him a half smile and tipped his head slightly.

"For now."

Mordecai never had been one to give up easily.

"For the present, Fenwick and I have to leave." The new Collector straightened up to his less than imposing full height and began to shift from foot to foot impatiently. Mordecai cautioned, *"Really, Fenwick, curb your eagerness. Collections are a serious matter."*

Fenwick complied. Barely.

"It was good to see you, Mordecai," Zacariah said and tried to ignore the small stab of imminent loneliness pricking him.

"I'll . . . we'll come back when we can," he said. Then in a whisper of warning, he added, *"In case I don't see you again before your month is out . . ."* He glanced over his shoulder to make sure that Fenwick was keeping his distance. *"Before you return to the Path, Zacariah—do not fail to make your Collection. The Minions are already planning what they will do if you don't bring that soul with you on your return."*

Zacariah nodded, accepting his friend's warning, even though he had no intention of missing another collection. He wasn't about to give the Minions an excuse to come up with an even more elaborate punishment. Who knows what might be next? A month as a tree slug, perhaps?

He shuddered and watched silently as the silvery mist twisted and spun, then faded away entirely.

He was alone. Again.

Inhaling sharply, Zacariah turned around and his surprised gaze locked with the blacksmith's.

"What the hell are you doin' mister?"

"Just waiting for Mrs. Hale's branding irons."

The man stepped through the open doorway and gave a quick look around. When he saw no one but Zacariah, he eyed him warily. "You always talk to horses, do ya?"

Zacariah rubbed one hand over his jaw and shrugged. "Sometimes, they make more sense than people," he said simply.

The smith wiped streaming sweat from his brow with one brawny forearm, then slowly nodded. A glimmer of a smile lifted one corner of his mouth. "You're right about that," he said. "Though when I looked out here and saw you talkin' to nobody, it gave me a queer feeling."

Zacariah grinned. "Must have. Sorry."

"No need, no need." The man laughed at his own wild imagination and turned back into his shop. "I'll have those irons for ya in a minute or two."

"I'm in no hurry," he told him and glanced at the horse giving him another nudge. "I'll just pass the time with my friend, here."

In the shadowed alleyway between the general store and the barbershop, three children hunkered down behind a stack of empty crates.

Jake dragged the match head against the bottom of his shoe and grinned when a tiny flame sputtered into life.

"If I tell Mama that you stole cigars from the store, she'll tan your hide good," Ellie warned.

Danny glanced at the girl, then at the still unlit cigar in his hand. His mother would do the same thing if she found out that he and Jake were smoking. But, he thought as he leaned in toward the lit match, she wouldn't find out.

Jake waited until Danny's cigar was glowing, then lit

one for himself. Only then did he answer his sister.

"I snitched one for you too, Ellie."

Her lips twisted as she thought about it, but then she shook her head. "No, ladies don't smoke cigars."

Danny thought she looked disappointed and told himself silently that ladies sure didn't seem to do much fun stuff. Ever since Ellie'd stopped wearing braids and started talking to Billy Jenkins, she didn't want to do anything anymore.

Used to be she could run faster and climb higher and throw further than most of the boys in town. Now, all she wanted to do was fix her hair and sit still. Seemed foolish to Danny.

"But you won't tell Mama, will you?"

"Don't see why I shouldn't," Ellie sniffed and waved one hand in front of her face. "Those things smell awful."

"You didn't used to think so." Jake grinned and lifted two orange-red eyebrows. "Besides, these here are ten-cent cigars. Real good ones."

Danny watched Jake carefully then imitated his friend's actions. He puffed on the cigar, holding the thick smoke in his mouth for a moment, then blowing it out in a stream in front of him. He coughed and frowned at himself for it. Jake didn't cough, so he wouldn't, either.

"I should tell Mama," Ellie said, more firmly this time.

"But you won't." Jake leaned against the store wall, and crossed his legs at the ankle. He smiled at his sister.

Danny took another puff and sat down beside Jake. "Why not?"

Jake shrugged. "If you tell Mama on me, I'll just tell her how you let Billy Jenkins give you a kiss last week."

"Jake Parker, I did not!" Ellie sat straight up and shook her long, loose hair back over her stiff shoulders.

"You did too, and I saw you."

Thick blue smoke settled into a foul-smelling cloud around the three of them. Danny swallowed heavily, glanced at his cigar, then rubbed his queasy stomach.

"Why'd you let him do that, Ellie?" Danny asked, more because he didn't want to take another puff of his cigar than because he was interested.

The girl's mouth twisted into a stubborn scowl, but after a long minute or two, her features relaxed into a half-smile. She tugged at her skirt hem, pulling it down carefully over her drawn-up ankles. "It was just a little kiss," she said softly.

"Yeah, and Billy looked like this," Jake teased and puckered his lips like a fish after a hook.

"Oh, he did not and shame on you for peeking."

Danny belched softly, licked his lips and set his cigar down on the dirt, hoping Jake wouldn't notice. His stomach churned uneasily and his head felt all fuzzy. "How come you let him?" he managed to ask through gritted teeth.

"'Cause she's set on marrying Billy," Jake answered for his sister and earned another scowl.

"You're gettin' married?" Danny asked, his upset stomach forgotten for the moment.

"Not right away." Ellie shrugged and rubbed the tip of her nose. "But in a year or two."

"If Mama doesn't chase him off with a broom first." Jake laughed and leaned his head back, taking another long draw on his cigar.

Ellie waved at the smoke again and scooted back a bit into a slash of sunlight. She coughed, sniffed and rubbed her nose. "You and that cigar are making my eyes sting and my nose run," she snapped.

Danny glanced at her. "Your nose ain't runnin'. It's bleedin'."

"Not again," Jake complained and stubbed his cigar out in the dirt. He pushed himself to his feet, then stomped on Danny's discarded cigar before going to his sister.

"Is it bad?" she asked.

"Nah. Just like last time is all." He glanced at Danny. "Come on, we got to take her home."

Danny jumped to his feet and swallowed back a sick feeling in his stomach. Then he hurried to the end of the alley where he waited for his friends.

Ellie stood up, wavered unsteadily on her feet for a moment, then took the hand her brother offered. Tilting her head back, she started walking, Jake leading the way.

"So who is this Zacariah Cole?" Helen asked and eased down onto the chair she kept behind the counter.

Rebecca avoided her friend's too-sharp gaze and stacked two pairs of men's jeans and three white cotton shirts next to the foodstuffs she'd already selected. "He just drifted in a couple of days ago," she said lightly and moved off to inspect a row of men's hats. Her gaze moved over them quickly and settled on a dust-colored, high-crowned hat with a curled brim. She picked it up and carried it to the counter, smiling to herself as she imagined Zack's deep blue eyes peering out from beneath the rim.

"That smile of yours makes a person wonder," Helen teased. "He *is* a handsome devil."

Rebecca frowned at her friend and plopped the hat down on top of her other supplies.

"I hadn't noticed."

Helen laughed delightedly. "Oh, I can see that." She laboriously pushed herself to her feet, keeping one hand on the mound of her stomach as if to steady herself. "You always buy new clothes and hats for the drifters who wander onto your place?"

"No, Helen," Rebecca smirked. "Just for the handsome ones."

"See?"

"What I *see*," she countered, "is my friend letting her imagination run wild." She set both hands on the counter, on either side of her purchases. "Now, are you going to add these up and give me my bill, or are they free?"

"All right." Helen laughed again and picked up a pencil and paper. As she checked the stack of supplies and wrote down the corresponding prices, she glanced at Rebecca.

"He seems nice enough."

"Yes, he does."

"I heard Danny telling Jake that he likes Zack fine."

"That's good."

"It does make things easier," Helen agreed and started thumbing through the pile of men's clothing.

"What makes what easier?" Rebecca lifted the lid on a glass jar filled with candy and pulled out one long red licorice whip. Sticking one end in her mouth, she waited.

"Well," Helen kept her gaze fixed on the paper in front of her. "It's good for a boy to approve of the man his mother's interested in."

The bite of licorice stuck halfway down Rebecca's throat and she choked, coughing and slapping herself on the chest until it finally went down. Eyes watering, throat raspy, she demanded, "Interested in? What gives you that idea?"

"For heaven's sake, Rebecca," Helen told her and lifted the jeans to count how many pairs of socks were on the counter. "Why are you so defensive? It's time you found a man."

"I had a man, thank you very much." She took another bite of licorice, despite the fact that it didn't taste very good anymore. Avoiding Helen's gaze, she dipped into her change purse and quickly counted through the few bills and coins there. Then, glancing at the clothes she'd picked up for Zack, she considered putting some of them back. But, their minor cost wouldn't make any difference in the long run. A couple of dollars more or less wasn't enough to keep the wolf from her door.

Helen clucked her tongue until Rebecca gave up trying to ignore her and looked up. "What?"

"Nothing."

"Good."

"It's only that . . ."

Rebecca sighed.

"Yes, you had a husband. But Daniel wasn't a . . ." She leaned closer and whispered, ". . . *lover.*"

"Helen!" Frowning, she argued, "I think you should remember here that I have a son? *Daniel's* son."

"Fine. You consummated your marriage. But Daniel was your friend. Not the love of your life."

"He was also my husband."

"Pooh!" Helen snorted and began to add up the column of figures. "Only because you both gave up looking and settled for each other."

"Thank you." Rebecca tossed the remaining licorice down onto her canned goods and turned away. When she swallowed that last bite, she muttered, "I like to think that neither of us 'settled.' I was happy with Daniel."

"Of course you were." Helen reached across the counter and laid one hand on Rebecca's forearm. "You'd known him most of your life. But happy with a friend is not the same as being in love."

"I'm not looking for love, Helen," she said. Silently, she added that if she *were,* she wouldn't be looking at Zack. Despite the things she felt whenever he looked at her. She knew nothing about him except that he was lying to her.

Why? she wondered again.

What was he hiding?

And more to the point, she asked herself, why did she care?

"When you're not looking," Helen went on, "is usually when you find it."

Rebecca shook her head. "I know you mean well, Helen. But nothing is going to happen between Zack and me. He's just passing through."

"Doesn't have to be."

"Yes, he does."

Whatever Helen might have said was lost as the front door flew open and slammed into the wall. The customer bell clanged furiously and Zacariah rushed inside, cradling an unconscious Ellie Parker in his arms.

The pair of branding irons lay in the dirt where he'd dropped them in his haste to catch Ellie when she fainted. Zacariah picked them up, then set them in the back of the wagon. Glancing over his shoulder at the general store, he found himself wondering if the girl was all right.

Ridiculous, he told himself and deliberately looked away. But he couldn't rid himself of the memory of Ellie's slight, fragile form lying limply in his arms. A pretty child. And so small.

The moment he'd caught her as she slumped to the ground, he'd searched her features for outward signs of the Path. There was nothing though, and he clearly recalled feeling a jolt of pleasure at the knowledge that she wasn't dying.

Pleasure.

What kind of reaction was *that,* for a Soul Collector to have?

He scowled and squinted into the sunlight. The fact that he'd seen nothing to indicate that Ellie was nearing the Path didn't mean a thing and he knew it.

When humans met their ends by way of an accident, there were no outward signs. It was only in the desperately ill that shadowy hints could be seen.

He pushed away from the wagon and thrust one hand through his hair. So, what did this mean? Was her illness a slight one? Or was she not close enough to the Path yet?

Shoving his hands into his pockets, he paced the boardwalk restlessly. He paused at the mouth of the alley when he heard a soft moan. Cocking his head, he concentrated on blocking out the sound around him and heard a gagging noise.

Walking into the narrow passage, he stepped over discarded trash and startled a scrawny cat scavenging for food. As he threaded his way through the obstacles to the end of the alley, the sounds of misery grew louder.

He walked around the edge of a tower of wooden crates, and stopped short. Danny knelt in the shadows of the boxes, his arms wrapped tightly around his middle. The boy moaned piteously, then his small body jerked as his already empty stomach protested again.

Zacariah stepped closer to the boy, knelt down beside him and held his head while the sickness gripped him. Had Ellie's faint upset the boy this much? he wondered. But almost as soon as that thought entered his mind, he noticed the crushed cigars lying only a couple of feet away.

He smiled to himself and shook his head. Humans. Even knowing that something would make them ill didn't keep them from it.

Danny finally quieted and leaned back against Zacariah's chest. He smoothed the boy's sweat-soaked hair back from his forehead and asked, "Feeling better, now?"

A short nod pressed into his chest.

"You smoked one of those, didn't you?"

Danny shuddered violently.

Unthinkingly, Zacariah rubbed the boy's back. "You going to do it again?"

"No sir," Danny's voice was tired, muffled. "You gonna tell Ma?"

Zacariah stood up slowly and pulled the boy to his feet. A small, pale face turned up to him and he couldn't stop himself from smiling gently. "I guess not," he said and wondered at the warmth shimmering inside him. When had the boy stopped being annoying?

Danny sighed in relief.

"It looks as though you've suffered enough."

The child grimaced and wiped his mouth on his sleeve. "Zack?"

"What?" he asked and didn't even bother to acknowledge that he'd grown accustomed to hearing his shortened name. If he did, he might have to admit that he'd actually come to like it.

"Is Ellie all right?"

"I don't know," he said gently and ruffled the boy's hair.

"She's sleeping," another voice spoke up and they both turned to look at Rebecca.

"Ma . . ."

She shook her head. "It's all right, Danny. We'll talk about the cigars another time."

The boy's chin dropped to his chest.

Rebecca looked up into Zacariah's eyes and his heartbeat staggered slightly. Understanding, gratitude and something he couldn't identify shone in her clear, green eyes as she smiled at him.

"I think," she said, her gaze never leaving his, "that Zack's right. You *have* suffered enough for now." Glancing briefly at her son, she added, "Go get in the wagon, Danny. We'll be along in a minute."

The boy scuttled away quickly, glad for the reprieve.

For a long, silent moment, the two of them stared at each other. Zacariah's gaze moved over her, pausing briefly at the rapid rise and fall of her breasts. His body tightened painfully and he widened his stance, hoping to ease the discomfort.

"Thank you," she said.

"For what?"

"For helping Danny. For bringing Ellie home. For . . ." she broke off and shrugged gently. "Just, thank you."

"You're welcome," he answered, his voice as hushed as hers.

She stared hard at him another moment or two before dragging her gaze away. When she spoke again, her voice shook. "The doc thinks Ellie's having 'female troubles.' "

"A bloody nose?"

She tucked a fallen strand of hair behind one ear and Zacariah's gaze followed the surprisingly graceful movement.

"I know. Ridiculous," she said. "I think Doc says 'female trouble' when he hasn't got the slightest idea what's wrong." Rebecca shrugged and turned toward the mouth of the alley. Zacariah fell into step beside her.

"I don't like how pale Ellie is," Rebecca went on. "But hell. Maybe the doc's right. Helen believes him."

As they walked, his hand brushed against hers and an arc of heat jolted him. She looked up at him sharply and he knew she'd felt it, too. Zacariah had to fight every screaming instinct inside him to keep from reaching for her.

What was happening to him?

And what was he supposed to do about it? By the Path, had the Minions *planned* this much torture for him? Or did he just get lucky?

Chapter ❁ Seven

Rebecca checked her figures once, then .again. Disgusted, she tossed her pencil down onto the table and leaned back in her seat. She glanced around the lamplit room idly, her gaze moving from one person to the next.

Scotty perched on the end of a bench, a bridle held between his knees. As he worked to repair the leather straps, he kept his head bent, seemingly oblivious to the others in the room.

Near the hearth, Buck was engrossed in carving a stallion, in full gallop. The older man repeatedly tipped his head up and down, looking over and then through, the half-glasses resting at the end of his nose. Apparently, he couldn't decide if he needed them or not.

Lastly, she glanced toward the corner where her son and Zack faced each other over a checkerboard. The boy said something she couldn't hear, but her breath caught in her throat when Zack's features split into a wide grin.

Taming her suddenly racing heart wasn't easy, but she determined to try. One thing that ought to do it, she told herself, was going over the ranch books one more time.

Mentally, she ticked off the horses she'd lost in the last few months. At least thirty animals so far, including two half-wild stallions that would have brought top dollar if she'd had time to break them properly. Plus, who knew how many foals had been born on the range only to be stolen along with their mothers. Rebecca sighed heavily. And those were only the losses they knew about. All of the range land hadn't been checked yet and they could come up even shorter.

"How's it look, Becky?"

She jumped, startled by Scotty's voice coming from directly beside her. She hadn't even noticed him moving.

"It's not good," she muttered.

"We found a few more on the craggy knoll," he told her off-handedly.

She shot him a quick, hard look. "Why didn't you say so earlier?"

"Thought we'd just wait and tally 'em up together when we finished the search," Buck offered from across the room.

"How many?"

"Five mares, one gelding," Scotty said.

"At least that's something," she muttered and quickly wrote them down in the ledger book. "What about Pine Creek?" Rebecca asked. "Have you been over there yet?"

"In a couple of days," Buck told her and stood up slowly, careful to keep the curls of shaved wood falling from his lap on the blanket he'd laid down in front of him.

Again, she tossed her pencil to the tabletop. Then lifting both arms, she stretched her cramped muscles.

"I win!" Danny shouted.

"Again."

Rebecca glanced at the pair quickly enough to see Zack's disgusted stare as he studied the checkerboard and tried to figure out what he'd done wrong.

"I'm for bed," Buck announced to no one in particular.

"Don't worry, Becky." Scotty laid one hand on her shoulder and lowered his voice. "We'll find a way out of this mess."

She shot him a quick look. Since when did he call her 'Becky'? Only Daniel had. And Buck. Warmth from his hand seeped into her and it felt cloying. Rebecca shifted slightly to move out from under his touch. Ridiculous to be so bothered by a simple gesture, but she couldn't help herself.

"Time for bed, Danny," she said and gave him a sharp look when he wanted to argue. As her son shuffled off to his room, Rebecca let her gaze slide over Zacariah before turning to Buck. Hoping to ease her own discomfort, she chuckled and said, "I suppose I could always go to town. Take a job at the saloon."

Buck snorted, then scowled at her.

Scotty gave her shoulder another pat and Rebecca stood up abruptly. She stepped into the center of the room, deliberately keeping a safe distance between herself and the cowhand. Grinning like an idiot, she went on with her joke, hoping that Scotty wouldn't notice her avoidance.

"I don't know," she said. "I might look good in feathers."

The blonde shook his head patiently. "It'll be all right, Becky. You'll see." Then he turned and quietly left the house.

Buck was right behind him, his new carving under his arm, blanket over his shoulder. "I dumped the shavings into the fire," he said, then wagged one finger at her. "And no more talk about feathers, Becky."

She shrugged, but nodded. It wasn't as though she'd actually considered working in the saloon.

"You comin'?" Buck called to Zacariah at the same time Danny yelled out from his room.

"Zack! Come here a minute, will ya?"

Zacariah shrugged and stood up. "I'll just go see what he wants first," he said and headed for the boy's room.

Thoughtfully, Rebecca watched him go. She knew exactly what her son wanted. "You might as well not wait for him, Buck. Looks like Danny wants Zack to check for monsters tonight.''

Buck shook his head. ''Monsters, feathers, the whole durn world is crazy.'' He marched across the floor, muttering to himself, then left the house, quietly closing the door behind him.

Taking a deep breath, Rebecca crossed her arms over her chest and wandered down the hall to Danny's room. For the first time, her son hadn't asked *her* to reassure him of his safety. A pinprick of hurt jabbed at her like a lost needle in a pile of bedding.

Obviously, Danny had come to care for Zack, even though the man made no secret of the fact that he would be leaving in just a few weeks. She hugged herself tightly and silently admitted that Danny wasn't alone. There was something about Zack that reached her, despite her suspicions. Despite her own natural wariness.

When she'd found him with Danny that afternoon, gently helping the boy through his well-deserved bout of sickness, a spiral of warmth had opened inside her. It was more than his handsome face. More even than those vivid blue eyes that seemed to mesmerize her whenever he looked at her.

There was a kindness behind his remote facade. A gentleness in his hands that blended with the quiet steel in his voice to create a singular sort of fire in her blood.

A fire of need that flickered with wild flames of desire.

Something she'd never felt before.

Rebecca stopped in the doorway and watched as Zacariah went down on his knees, lifted the blankets and peered under Danny's bed.

''Nothing there,'' he reported solemnly.

The boy nodded and snuggled down deeper under his quilt.

''You figure Ellie's all right now?'' he asked, his voice muffled by the covers.

"I think so," he answered and pushed himself to his feet.

"G'night, Zack," Danny whispered and as his gaze slipped past his mother, he added, "G'night, Ma."

Zacariah turned to look at her and her knees turned to jelly. She clamped one hand on the doorjamb and managed to say, "Good night, Danny. Sleep well."

Those eyes of his locked on her and Rebecca felt heat roar through her. When he turned away long enough to blow out the lamp beside Danny's bed, she took advantage of the moment to draw air into her starving lungs.

She moved into the hall and heard him fall into step behind her. In silence, they walked to the front door, where her hand tightened around the brass knob until the cold metal bit into her palm.

Chancing another look into his eyes, she immediately knew she shouldn't have. Lamplit shadows flickered in their depths, illuminating wants and needs much like her own.

She cleared her throat, nudging aside the rock that had lodged there. "Thank you for that."

"You don't have to keep thanking me for spending time with Danny," he said softly. "He's a nice boy."

"Yes." She drew one long, shaky breath. "He is."

"He's still upset over Ellie," Zacariah said and his voice was a caress that fell around her gently, like the softest of shawls drawn up close on a cold night.

"We all are."

This was the strangest conversation she'd ever had in her life. Beneath the quiet words, there were other words shimmering in silence. Words that neither of them could speak. Words that clamored to be heard.

In self-defense, she turned the knob and pulled the door open, hoping he would leave for the bunkhouse before she lost all of her common sense.

Zacariah turned and stared out at the night for several

long moments. Then he looked back at her and found her gaze waiting for him.

Rebecca held her breath. She saw his jaw tighten and something flash in his eyes. He leaned toward her, as if he couldn't help himself. She went up on her toes and tipped her head back. Before he could straighten up, she kissed him. A soft, hesitant brush of the lips that sent spears of heat lancing through her body.

Immediately, she pulled back and watched him touch his fingertips to his mouth as if caressing her kiss. Then gently, he reached out to touch her lips. His hand was warm, his touch almost hesitant. Her mouth trembled as his fingers explored and traced the contour of her lips. She shivered in response.

"You would look good in feathers," he said softly, then left her, a half-smile still curving his mouth.

Zacariah straightened up and stretched his aching muscles. He smothered a groan as he rolled his shoulders. Reaching for the shirt he'd tossed aside more than an hour before, he wiped the sweat from his forehead then squinted at the blazing sunshine overhead.

Resting the garden-hoe handle against one shoulder, he rubbed his palms together. Even through the thick, protective gloves, he felt the difference in his hands. In only four or five days, the soreness had disappeared and even his blisters were almost healed over. Idly, he wondered if he would carry the scars of his hard work back with him to the Path.

"Now will ya tell me some more stories about them Roman kings and their soldiers?"

"Not kings, Danny," Zacariah corrected him. "Emperors."

"Emperors." The boy jerked his head in an abrupt nod and sent his hair tumbling down into his eyes.

Hardly a week at the Hale ranch and he could barely remember a time when he hadn't cared for this child. Like a puppy that refuses to believe he's unwanted, the boy had worn away his defenses, insinuating himself into Zacariah's heart.

Danny cocked his head, closed one eye against the fierce sunlight and grinned at him. Instantly, a different kind of warmth blossomed in Zacariah's chest. And unlike the sun's impersonal heat, this genial burning went beyond his bones to settle in his own, long-forgotten soul.

His breath caught at the unexpected magic of the moment. Centuries of existence hadn't prepared him for the flash of wonderment to be found in a child's smile and trusting eyes.

A dark slash of regret that he would never see this boy grow up shot through him and left him stunned.

"Zack?" Danny prodded. "Zack? You goin' to tell me some more stories?"

He nodded stiffly. "I will if your mother doesn't have another chore for me to do."

"Ah, shoot." Danny kicked the toe of his shoe against the newly turned garden dirt. Jamming his fists into his pockets, he went on, "Ma's a bear for work, Zack. If you tell her you're finished with the vegetable garden, she's sure to think of somethin' else."

"Well then, whatever it is, I'll just have to do it quickly so we have time for another story or two."

"Ya mean it?" The boy looked up again, his disappointment gone as quickly as it had appeared.

"I mean it." Zacariah enjoyed telling his stories every bit as much as the boy did hearing them. Heaven knew, he had more than enough tales stored up in his memory to keep the child entertained for years.

Glancing at the freshly turned earth at his feet, he smiled to himself. Dark, rich, dirt lay broken, ready for planting. Because of him. He'd done it. A sense of accomplishment welled up in him, despite the fact that he knew any human could have done the same thing. He'd actually come to enjoy this feeling of satisfaction at a job's completion.

But he'd also learned that when one job was finished, another was waiting to be started. "I'd better get over to the barn and find your mother. See what she wants done next."

An invisible band tightened around his chest at the thought of Rebecca. Since that moment when she'd kissed him two nights before, she'd been on his mind almost constantly. The memory of that heart-stopping moment stayed with him, night and day. She haunted his dreams and tormented his waking hours.

He wanted to feel it again. That rush of life and heat that had surged through him the moment her lips met his. He wanted to hold her close and feel her warmth pressed to him.

"I know where she is," the boy said and splintered Zacariah's imaginings.

Danny started walking alongside him, futilely trying to match his much shorter stride to Zack's. "She's with Sky Dancer."

"Who is that?" Zacariah slowed his pace a bit to accommodate the boy.

"One of the mares. She's goin' to have a baby."

"Ah. When?"

"Ma says anytime now, but nobody knows for sure except the foal."

"True enough." Zacariah smiled. A heartbeat later, his smile dissolved into a sea of memories. How many times over the years had he arrived for a Collection just before or after a baby's birth? His presence at a birth had always brought sorrow down on those he visited. In the midst of their joy, he would arrive to make a collection, shattering peace and tainting happiness.

He shifted uneasily against the sudden discomfort.

Once, though, he'd spared a baby, too, he reminded himself. But a voice in the back of his mind laughed at him.

It wasn't by his benevolence that the Winters infant still lived.

It was only through his carelessness.

"Ma says Sky Dancer is goin' to stay right there in the barn till after she has her baby, 'cause she don't want some no-good rustlers sneakin' in and stealin' her."

"That sounds like your mother," Zacariah said, admiration coloring his voice. Despite suffering losses, she refused to admit defeat. Somehow, she managed to keep her ranch going with only Buck's and Scotty's help.

And she was raising a son to be proud of. Alone. Not an easy task for anyone.

"Your mother is a smart woman."

"She sure is." Danny scowled and bent to snatch up a fist-sized rock. Immediately, he half-turned and threw the stone, watching as it clattered against a watering trough then fell into the dirt.

An interesting reaction. "You don't like having a smart mother?"

The child looked around him furtively, then crooked one finger at the man.

Obligingly, Zacariah bent down until he was at eye level with the suddenly serious boy. "What is it?"

"Shhh." Danny tossed a quick look at the wide-open barn doors, then turned back again. "Ma's got ears like a hawk. She's all the time hearin' stuff I don't want her to."

Smothering a smile at the boy's solemn disgust, Zacariah nodded and whispered, "Sorry."

"That's okay," Danny whispered right back, then rubbed a dirty hand across his freckled nose. He left behind a clean mark on his dusty face. "See, Zack," he said and leaned in closer. "It's 'cause she's so smart that I ain't got a pa."

"What?"

"Well, it ain't her fault that my real pa got killed. But it is on account of her that I can't get me a new pa." The boy added earnestly, "Honest. In town awhile back, I heard Buck talkin' to the barber, Mr. Peterson?"

Zacariah nodded, intrigued.

"And he said that menfolks're scared of Ma 'cause she's smarter than they are."

Surely human males weren't that stupid.

"Y'know my friend Jake? At the general store?"

Zacariah nodded, remembering the freckle-faced red-head and his too-pale sister.

"Him and his pa go fishin' and huntin'. And they hide out from Jake's ma when she's lookin' to put 'em to work."

Danny's eyes glistened and his features twisted into a wistful expression.

Trying to help, Zacariah said, "I'm sure Buck or Scotty would take you fishing if you asked them."

"Ah." He kicked at the dirt again and watched as a pebble skittered across the open ground. "That ain't the same at all. I guess Buck'd be all right, except he's always busy."

"What about Scotty?" he asked, though just the thought of the blond, short-tempered cowboy was enough to make Zacariah forget all about the peace of the Path.

"He only wants to talk about Ma and a fella don't want to talk about his ma when he's fishin'."

"I see." Zacariah's jaw tightened at the reminder of Scotty's interest in Rebecca. "He isn't afraid of your mother like the other men?"

"Don't seem to be," Danny said. "But he wouldn't make a good pa anyway. He gets mad too much."

Even the boy had noticed.

"So, Zack," Danny asked after a long moment of staring at his own feet. "Are you scared of Ma, too?"

"Of course not." Zacariah laughed shortly. Whatever he felt for Rebecca, it certainly wasn't fear. "I like your mother very much," he said and knew it for an understatement.

"Ya do?" Danny gave him a gap-toothed grin that lit up his entire face.

"Sure, I do."

"And do you want to go fishin' sometime, too?" Danny asked breathlessly. "Just you and me?"

Zacariah stood up and smiled down at the boy. It felt *right* to make the child happy. Besides, how difficult could it be to actually catch a fish, if Danny and his friends could do it? "I'd like that. Just you and me."

"Oh, boy!" Taking off at a dead run, Danny sprinted across the last few feet of dirt separating them from the barn. "Hey Ma! Zack and me are goin' fishin'!"

"That's fine," Buck snapped. "I've been waitin' on you for nearly two hours and when you *do* show up, you haven't got the missing horses with you."

Scotty sighed and climbed down from the saddle. He half-heartedly tied the reins to a dried-out twig of a pine branch, then stepped around his horse to approach the small cook fire Buck had going. It had been a long day already and he was in no mood to listen to sermons.

"Hell boy, we've already lost more horses than we can afford! Why Rebecca don't just fire you is beyond me," Buck said in disgust.

It surely was. But Scotty knew why she kept him on when she couldn't really afford him. And the reason didn't have a damned thing to do with how good he was with horses.

She wanted him.

He could tell.

It was in her eyes every time she looked at him. Every time she smiled, he knew she was asking him to touch her. To kiss her. Of course, she hadn't said it out loud yet. But she would. When she was hungry enough.

And she would be soon. He licked suddenly dry lips and painted a mental image of the woman who'd haunted his every moment for the last several months. Briefly, he thought about how friendly she'd been to the new man at the Hale place. But even as he thought it, Scotty told himself that Rebecca would never be so foolish as to throw herself at Zacariah. Not when she could have *him*.

No, it wasn't Rebecca he had to worry about. It was Zack. Pretending to not know a damned thing. He didn't fool Scotty. Hell, it wasn't so bad that Rebecca'd been taken in. After all, she was only a woman. But Buck! Even if he was older than dirt, he should have been smart enough to see that Zacariah, whoever he was, was lying.

No man just up and forgets who he is and where he comes from.

"The way I figure it, there should be at least twenty horses runnin' in the box canyon behind Twin Peaks."

Scotty smiled and nodded.

"If you find more than that, it's to the good. But boy, we've got to get those horses rounded up before these damned thieves steal the damn rocks out of the damn dirt!"

"Wish I could catch those bastards."

"I know ya do boy. Me too." Buck tossed the remains of his coffee into the bushes. "I'm too damn old to be sleeping out under the stars," he went on. "But you ain't. So you can just stay out here tonight and find them horses first thing tomorrow. Then bring 'em in to the ranch."

"Anything you say, Buck." Scotty gave the older man a slow smile. "You're the boss."

"And don't you be forgettin' that, either." Buck scratched his whiskered jaw thoughtfully. "Sure hope the Army still needs horses. Becky's got to sell at least a few head just to have enough cash money for next winter."

"The Army always needs horses," Scotty said. He dropped to one knee, tested the coffeepot handle with the tips of his fingers, then picked up the pot and poured himself a cup of Buck's thick, black brew. Absently, he was aware of the old man yammering on, but he didn't bother to listen. It was the same old crap he'd been hearing for months now.

He flicked him a quick glance over the rim of his tin cup. Buck's face was red and what little hair he had left was standing up all over his head. Looking away again, Scotty told himself that the old man had about reached the end of his tether.

Buck's voice droned on, but Scotty paid no attention. It wasn't like he *had* to. Soon enough, him and Rebecca would be together and then the old fool would be taking his orders from Scotty. Or he could take himself off somewhere.

If everything went like it was supposed to, he'd only have to be patient a little while longer. He'd waited this long to take his rightful place in Rebecca's life. A few more weeks, give or take a week, didn't really matter that much.

A solitary lamp was lit, creating a small circle of light in a darkness that seemed to be drawing nearer. Shadows dipped and swayed on the stable walls in time with the lamp's flame.

The big animal thrashed on its straw bed, kicking out blindly at the pain.

"Shhh, Sky Dancer," Rebecca soothed and ran the flat of her hand down the horse's sweaty neck. "It's all right, girl, you're doing fine."

Sky Dancer's wide brown eyes rolled back in her head, and the swollen mound of her stomach writhed with the life she was laboring to deliver.

"Come on now, pretty Dancer." Rebecca's voice was faint and gently singsong. "A little more work and we'll see your baby."

The animal whinnied sharply and fresh tears spilled from Rebecca's eyes in sympathy. And worry. This was all taking too long. Sky Dancer had given birth before.

Twice. And each time, the labor had been short and hard, but the foals had come as they should.

This time, there was something wrong.

The animal knew it.

So did Rebecca.

They both needed help.

Her first thought was for Scotty. As much as he made her uncomfortable, there was no one better with horses. But Scotty had stayed out on the range. A few years ago, Buck would have been able to handle this problem, too. But he was older now and Rebecca had a deep-seeded feeling that a lot of strength was going to be needed.

That left Zacariah.

She'd tried to avoid spending time alone with him since the night she'd impulsively kissed him. Her attraction for the man and her growing feelings for him were enough to convince her that being alone with him wasn't safe.

But now she had no choice. She needed Zack's help. Fast.

Easing to one side, Rebecca gently lifted Sky Dancer's head from her lap and stood up. Her legs trembled as blood rushed to her feet. A tingling, prickly sensation raced along her flesh as her limbs came back to life after being cramped in one position too long.

Another pain crashed down on the midnight-black horse. All four feet lashed out, the edges of razor sharp hooves coming within a hair's breadth of slicing through the worn jeans covering Rebecca's legs. She jumped back, out of range.

"It's all right, Dancer. I know you're hurting." From the dozen or so stalls lining the shadowy barn came sympathetic whinnies from the other stabled horses. Rebecca backed carefully out of the stall, reluctant to leave the straining animal, yet desperate to get help. "I promise I'll be back. Zack will help us."

Sky Dancer screamed and the sound sent a cold chill shooting down Rebecca's spine. With the painful cry still echoing around her, she turned and raced for the door.

Zacariah woke up instantly when he heard someone approach the bunkhouse at a dead run. He jumped out of his narrow bed and snatched up his jeans from the floor. When the door opened, he was already tugging his pants on.

"Zack?"

Rebecca.

Barefoot, he moved across the room silently and glanced over his shoulder at Buck, sound asleep in a spill of moonlight. A deep, gravelly snore rumbled through the bunkhouse and Zack's eyebrows lifted.

He'd never get back to sleep.

With one hand, he pushed his hair back from his face, then slipped through the slightly open doorway. Cold air smacked against his bare chest. As he joined Rebecca on the top step, he winced at the icy feel of the boards beneath his feet.

In the pale light of a half moon, Rebecca's face looked ghostly and her green eyes shimmered with an emotion he'd seen often through the centuries.

Fear.

Discomfort instantly forgotten, he reached out and grabbed her upper arms. "What is it? What's wrong?"

"Sky Dancer," she whispered, and reached up to snatch one of his hands. Tugging him from the porch, she started for the barn, speaking in a rush as she went. "She's been trying to deliver her foal for hours. Something's wrong and the baby's not coming."

"Hours?" he asked and ignored the stab of pain when his bare foot slammed down on a rock in the yard.

She tugged on his hand harder. "I couldn't sleep. Got up a couple of hours ago and decided to check on her. She was down and in pain. Had to have been like that for awhile. I figured to stay with her until the foal was born." Rebecca threw him a wild glance over her shoulder. "But it's not coming."

Then they were at the barn and racing into the shadows where no moonlight penetrated. From Sky Dancer's stall came a soft, yellow light that seemed somehow to make the darkness surrounding it even blacker.

Thicker.

Rebecca dropped his hand and sprinted the last few feet to the stall. He heard her whispered words and then lost them when the laboring animal let loose with a high-pitched scream.

Zacariah forced himself to go on. He felt the straw and dirt beneath his feet and knew he was walking. Other horses poked their great heads over stall doors and watched him. The light at the end of the building grew brighter as he approached and Rebecca's whispered rush of words became more clear.

"It's all right, girl. Zack's here. He'll help your baby. Everything will be fine."

He inhaled sharply and stepped into the straw-littered enclosure. In the suddenly eerie light of the single lamp, he looked at the scene and knew he was in trouble.

Rebecca held the horse's head in her lap and ran her hands up and down the animal's neck, comforting it with her touch and the soothing sound of her voice. Sky Dancer's belly, swollen with her baby, tightened as the animal strained again to deliver the foal.

And nothing happened.

Zacariah rubbed one hand across his face and tried to do battle with the feeling of helplessness that was swamping him.

"Zack?"

His gaze shot to hers.

"You've got to pull the baby out. I think it must be turned wrong."

Something tightened around his chest, making it difficult to breathe. He wiped his sweaty palms on his thighs.

"Zack, she needs help."

"I know," he snapped, then shook his head, disgusted

with himself. Punishment was one thing. But what right did the Minions have to punish Rebecca and the mare? They needed his help and he was useless to them.

Or was this what his superiors had had in mind all along? To set him amongst humans who would expect his help only to have him let them down? He hadn't given the Minions nearly enough credit. They were far more diabolical than he'd thought.

What did he know about bringing life into the world? His entire existence had been built around easing humans out of this life and into the next.

He looked at the pain-wracked animal and tried to overcome the feeling of helplessness swamping him.

"I'll hold Dancer's head," she told him. "There's a bucket of water over in the corner." She jerked her head to show him where. "Wash your hands and arms."

He took a single step toward the bucket, then stopped. Staring into her eyes, he forced himself to say, "I don't know how to do this, Rebecca."

She swallowed heavily and nodded.

"What happens if I do it wrong? If I hurt her?"

Fresh tears welled up in her green eyes, but she blinked them back, allowing only one or two to trickle down her pale cheeks. "I can't answer that," she said softly. "But I do know that if she doesn't get help soon, she'll die. And her foal with her."

Admiration for her strength rose up in him. He'd never realized before, just how difficult life could be.

Zacariah nodded, already steeling himself for the trial about to start.

"All I ask is that you try," Rebecca said softly. "I'd do it myself, but I'm not strong enough to pull that foal free."

"I'll do my best," he said, hoping desperately that it would be enough.

"I know you will."

Zacariah drew courage from her quiet conviction and greedily held her words tightly within him.

When he'd washed thoroughly and taken up his position, Rebecca said, "Carefully, put your hand inside her and see if you can feel the foal."

His features tight, Zacariah did exactly that. He felt the horse's muscles clamp down on his arm and wrist as another labor pain rippled through the mare. He clenched his jaw against the pressure and waited for the animal to relax once more.

What seemed like hours passed before he was able to move again. Sweat rolled down his forehead and stung his eyes. Beads of perspiration tickled along his spine and he was surprised to realize that he was silently muttering prayer after frantic prayer.

Then everything changed.

He looked up at Rebecca. "I feel it!"

An uncertain smile flashed briefly across her features before she asked, "Can you feel its head?"

"No." He licked dry lips feverishly and shook his sweat-soaked hair back out of his eyes. Concentrating, he forced his fingers to explore the infant horse he'd only just discovered. "Legs. All I feel is legs."

"Dammit." Rebecca caught herself and lowered her voice instantly. "He's trying to come out backwards. Maybe we shouldn't try to turn it. This has gone on too long already."

"What do you want me to do?" he asked, ignoring the sharp pains lancing down his shoulders and arms.

She kept her hands smoothing over Sky Dancer's neck and jaw as she said, "You have to get a hold of the back legs. All I can tell you is to feel around as best you can. Try to separate the tangle of limbs gently, then draw the hind legs back toward you."

He saw the fear in her eyes again and knew that the same emotion was glittering in his own. Fear. He hadn't realized that it would have its own taste and smell. He'd never guessed that fear could pound and pulse in one's soul like a heartbeat. He hadn't realized, either, that even when you were afraid, you still had to act.

Nodding solemnly, Zacariah pushed everything from his mind but the mental image he had created of the foal and its position inside its mother. Slowly, gently, he moved his hand. Inch by tantalizing inch, he worked to free the infant from its nest.

Pain after pain crashed down on Sky Dancer and in turn, on Zacariah. His hand and arm ached from the pressure and the need to go slowly. But then he felt something different. Movement. It was as if the foal had suddenly understood what it was supposed to be doing.

It shifted lazily and stretched out its legs toward Zacariah. He grinned as his fingers smoothed over the tiny animal's flesh, assuring himself that these two legs were the ones he was supposed to be tugging on. Then, when the next pain erupted deep inside Sky Dancer, he began to pull.

Gently at first, to get the foal moving, then a bit harder as the baby hurried to be born. "It's coming!"

"Come on Sky Dancer," Rebecca urged. "Just a bit more."

In a rush of blood and water, the foal slipped free of its mother. Zacariah fell backward in the straw, the tiny, fragile horse stretched across his bare chest.

"Clean his face," Rebecca said on a half-laugh, half-cry.

Obediently, Zacariah wiped his hand across the horse's mouth and nose. When the foal shook its head and snorted indignantly, he laughed out loud.

Almost at the same moment, Sky Dancer lurched to her feet. A bit unsteady at first, the mare walked to her baby and began to sniff and examine it.

Zacariah leaned back against the stall wall and watched the mother and child for a moment or two. Amazing. After hours of pain and terror, Sky Dancer looked none the worse for it.

As for himself—covered in blood and muck, he looked as though he'd been through a war. He grinned and stared at his hands as if he'd never seen them before. For one brief instant of time, he'd actually *touched* a new life. He'd actually been the one to *save* it.

Joy pulsed through him and he felt as though he could get up and run for miles, just for the pleasure of it. He chuckled to himself. An amazing reaction for a man who hated to walk. Still shaking his head at the abrupt change in his own nature, he moved to the bucket to wash himself.

As the icy water sluiced over him, washing away all evidence of the heated battle he'd just won, Zacariah felt his muscles tremble. He needed to sit down. Finishing quickly, he carried the bucket of dirty water outside the stall and set it down.

Wet and exhausted, he stumbled back into the enclosure, then plopped down onto the floor and leaned back against the stall wall. He couldn't seem to tear his gaze away from the new mother and child.

"Are you all right?"

He looked up to find Rebecca had moved to sit beside him.

All right didn't begin to explain what he was feeling at the moment. But he also realized that he didn't have the words to describe it. "I feel wonderful," he finally said and noticed that he couldn't stop grinning.

She took one of his hands in both of hers and squeezed it gently. "So do I. Now."

He tried to pull his hand away, saying, "Rebecca, I'm still pretty dirty."

"With *life*," she answered and tightened her grip.

A quick look over her shoulder had her smiling again. Sky Dancer had already convinced her new baby to stand up and nurse.

As the foal balanced itself on trembling, stick-like legs and dipped its head beneath its mother's belly for its first meal, Rebecca turned back to Zacariah.

"Thank you."

He wanted to thank her, too. He wanted to tell her what it had meant to him—a Soul Collector—to have helped a new life begin. But he bit those words back and contented himself with, "You're welcome."

The lamp flame flickered and shadows danced.

One moment stretched into another as their gazes locked and held. All sound seemed to fade away. It was as if nothing existed outside the small circle of golden lamplight. Something strong and undeniable shivered in the air between them.

Slowly, Rebecca leaned toward him. Zacariah's heartbeat staggered, caught and then began to pound erratically. Her eyes closed just before her lips met his. As her breath fanned across his cheek, his eyelids fell and he wondered how the night could suddenly seem so bright through closed eyes.

Chapter ✿ Eight

She laid one hand on his bare chest and he felt the imprint of each of her fingertips burn into his flesh. Zacariah wasn't sure what to do next. That small, quick kiss they'd shared hadn't prepared him for this. And it was suddenly very important that he make no mistakes. Frantically, he tried to recall instances when he'd witnessed mortals kissing. Though those times were few and had always been interrupted at his arrival by an unexpected death, he hoped to at least remember *something*. Zacariah tilted his head to one side as she moved toward him again. But Rebecca did, too and their noses bumped. Before he could worry about it though, she cocked her head to one side and he moved opposite her. As their lips met, he told himself it was as if they'd been made for each other.

His body tightened quickly, uncomfortably. Pressure built in his groin and he gritted his teeth against the exquisite torture.

Bolder, driven by the need raging in him, Zacariah reached out, wrapped one arm around Rebecca and drew her across his lap. Her arms encircled his neck and he bent his head to press his mouth more firmly to hers.

Slowly, her lips parted beneath his and the tip of her tongue delicately, teasingly caressed his mouth. He jerked his head back and stared down at her, startled.

"Zack?"

He stared at her as if he'd never seen her before. Rebecca shifted uneasily, but didn't look away. What had she done wrong? Why had he stopped kissing her? Was it possible that she'd shocked him? Maybe she should have waited for *him* to deepen their kiss. But she didn't know the rules to this age-old game. She'd only been with one man in her life. Daniel.

Her hands fell from his neck and she finally shifted her gaze from his. Sitting up straight, she told herself it was useless to try for dignity while seated on a man's lap. Instead, she opted for honesty.

"I'm sorry. I shouldn't have done that."

"You're sorry? You didn't like it?"

"It's not that," she said and hazarded a quick glance at him. Confusion still reigned in his eyes, but now, she thought she spotted a glimmer of disappointment, too.

A bit embarrassed, Rebecca tried to push herself off his lap, but he held her in place. "Yes, I liked it," she said. "But apparently, you didn't."

"It's not that I didn't like it."

"You could have fooled me."

"Why would I do that?"

"What?"

"Never mind." Zacariah's arms tightened around her again, pulling her close. She braced her hands on his bare chest and beneath her palms, she felt his racing heart. His warmth soaked through her, easing away the discomfort she'd experienced only moments before.

"To kiss like that," he said, his gaze moving over her face like a touch, "*feels* different than it looks."

Her insides trembled under his steady regard. His breath puffed against her cheek as he bent his head closer to her.

"You surprised me," he whispered and lifted one hand to caress the line of her jaw with reverent fingers. "But even more, I find the touch of your tongue . . ."

She closed her eyes briefly and swallowed past a knot in her throat.

"Exciting," he finished and lowered his mouth to hers.

Her lips parted for him and her breath caught at his tongue's tender invasion. Hesitantly, as though she were the first woman he'd so kissed, he explored her secrets and brought her to a trembling height of passion that she'd never known before. She leaned into him, tilted her head back and met his caresses slowly, eagerly.

Her palms slid over his chest, tracing the hard, smooth planes of his body. Her slightest touch brought a reaction from him and she felt his muscles quiver beneath her hands.

She arched toward him and Zacariah wondered if she wanted him to touch her as she did him. Hesitantly, he lifted one hand to imitate her actions. Rebecca's breath caught as his palm cupped one of her breasts.

He broke their kiss and looked down to where his palm cradled her flesh. Staring in awed wonder, his thumb moved across her nipple and Rebecca gasped at the sparks skittering through her bloodstream.

She watched his features as he looked at her . . . really looked at her.

"May I touch you?" he asked quietly.

She ducked her head, suddenly, ridiculously shy. If she said yes, would he think she was a loose woman? But *could* she say no and spend the rest of the night wondering what it would have been like?

"Yes," she said, before she could lose her nerve.

With slow, careful fingers, he undid the buttons on her shirt and she held perfectly still, terrified that she might break the spell surrounding them with any sudden movement. When the buttons were freed and her shirt lay open, he glanced into her eyes briefly before slipping one hand beneath the fabric to touch her.

Even through her chemise, Rebecca felt the magic of

his flesh on hers. Her breath staggered. Her heart pounded. Mouth dry, she watched him admire her.

His fingers skimmed the crest of her nipple and she arched into him, jolted into movement by the heat of his touch. Delicately, as if she were made of the finest spun glass, he cradled her breast.

Rebecca had never felt more . . . *cherished*.

She'd never felt more wanted.

Nor had she ever experienced such want herself.

When he at last lifted his gaze to hers again, she saw the sheen of emotion glittering in his eyes just before he bent to claim another kiss.

Damp heat spiraled in her center. Her heartbeat pounded erratically. Rebecca slowly lifted one hand to cover Zacariah's, holding him to her breast, trying to silently tell him what she was feeling.

He groaned and shifted uncomfortably. Still perched on his lap, she felt the hardness of his body pressing against her. Another curl of desire licked at her insides and her whole body ached with the need gripping her.

When his tongue dipped into her mouth again, she met him, stroke for stroke. Their tongues danced and twisted together in a silent parody of what they both wanted.

Sky Dancer snorted, blew and whinnied loudly, as if reprimanding them for such behavior in front of her newborn.

The intrusion splintered the cocoon of desire and Zacariah pulled his head back.

He'd completely forgotten where they were. But, he'd become so engrossed in Rebecca and the startlingly new sensations rushing through him, he wouldn't have noticed a fire.

Everything in him ached.

He could still taste her.

As she moved off his lap and out of his reach, he noticed how empty his hand felt without her breast filling it.

Why had he ever thought the human practice of touching tongues to be disgusting? It was nothing of the sort. On the contrary, it was more exciting that he would have guessed.

And he wanted more.

Now.

Rebecca, though, moved away and knelt on the straw-littered floor beside him. As he looked at her, a throbbing pain that seemed to march in time with the beat of his heart thundered through him and it was all he could do to listen to her.

"I can't do this, Zack."

His head fell back against the stall wall and he looked at her steadily as he labored to breathe. In the lamplight, her face was flushed and her lips looked full and ripe. Something new flickered in her eyes, but he couldn't identify it.

"Yes you can, Rebecca," he said finally, when he could trust his voice to work. "Actually, you were doing very well."

She choked out a strangled laugh then reached up and pushed the stray wisps of hair out of her face. Cocking her head, she looked at him for a long minute before speaking.

"You're right," she said. "I suppose it's not that I *can't* do it. More like I won't."

"But why?" Surely she had felt the incredible explosions of delight that he had. And if she had, wasn't she now feeling the same sort of pleasure/pain that held him so tightly?

"Because I hardly know you."

He frowned. "You have known me for almost a week."

"That's not long enough for us to be doing . . ." She waved one hand mutely. "*This.* Especially here. In the *barn.*"

Zacariah shook his head. "I don't understand." He inched his back up higher against the wall. His body twitched at the movement and a new wave of need and want rippled through him. "What difference does it make where we are? And how long must you know me?"

Rebecca sighed and came down off her knees to sit on the floor. Keeping a few inches distance between them, she too leaned against the stall door. Her hands moved restlessly over her thighs and Zacariah wondered again if her body was as uncomfortable as his at the moment.

"It's not a matter of how long, I guess. But how well." Both hands lifted, then fell onto her lap again. "As for the other, I suppose it doesn't matter where we are. It's just that I've never . . ." She shrugged. "A *barn?*"

Unself-consciously, Zacariah rested one hand against his groin and pressed down hard, hoping to ease the discomfort of his swollen flesh jutting against the heavy denim.

Rebecca inhaled sharply and looked away.

"Lord, Zack, what are we doing?"

He had no idea what they were doing now. But a few minutes before, they'd been engaged in something completely wonderful.

"Rebecca . . ."

"Zack," she said at the same time, then held up one hand, silently asking him to let her speak first. He nodded. "As much as I want to lie back down in your arms, I won't do it. Not now, anyway."

"But why not?" Had he bungled everything? Could she tell that he'd never kissed a woman before? True, he didn't know anything about this business, but he was certain that he could learn quickly.

"Because it's not just me I have to think about anymore."

"Don't worry about me," he blurted. "I want to, too."

She snorted a laugh and glanced at his groin. "Yes, I noticed."

"Then . . ."

"It's Danny."

Danny? What did the boy have to do with what went on between them?

"I'm his mother first and a woman second."

"Yes." That he could understand. He'd seen her love and devotion to her son. But how the fact of her motherhood interfered with their kissing each other was beyond him.

"I can't just give in to what the woman in me wants without a thought as to how it will affect the mother in me. And my son."

"I still don't understand," he whispered and reached out one hand toward her.

Sky Dancer whinnied gently and both of them looked at the horse and foal. Rebecca took advantage of his distraction and stood up. Slowly, Zacariah did the same.

She shouldn't have kissed him again. But since that brief kiss two nights before, she'd thought of nothing else. And in that moment of celebration over the safe delivery of Sky Dancer's foal, Rebecca had felt more of a connection to Zacariah than to anyone she'd ever known. It was as if they had gone into battle together and come out the other side, victorious.

The proud happiness on his features had mirrored the delight splintering inside her. The awestruck wonder in his eyes as he held that new life in his arms had drawn her to him instinctively. She sighed. Who knew what might have happened between them if Sky Dancer hadn't objected.

Zacariah was a drifter. A man with no past. No name, except for the one she'd given him. And for all she knew, he had no future, either. He could be a fugitive. He could be married.

A surprisingly strong curl of pain settled in her chest at the thought. When had she begun to care about him? How had he come to be a part of her life in such a short time? She knew nothing about him. Only a week ago, he'd been a stranger.

''You're a dangerous man, Zack.''

Surprise widened his eyes. ''Dangerous?''

''Oh, yes.''

''I wouldn't hurt you,'' he said.

''You already have.''

''What? How?'' His gaze slipped over her as if looking for bruises.

She shrugged. ''Not physically. But dammit all, you've played hell with everything else.''

''What are you talking about?''

Pacing briskly in the confining stall, she started talking. ''You make me feel too much.''

''What?''

''You. Me.'' She lifted both hands as if in supplication, then let them fall to her sides. ''This. I'm trying to tell you that it's not safe for me to be around you.''

He took a step toward her, but she skipped backward.

''Why'd you come here, anyway?'' She glared at him briefly and demanded, ''Why are you so nice to Danny? And why are you there when I need you?''

''Rebecca . . .''

''Mostly though, *why* do I need you?''

He took another step closer and this time, she shook her head to stop him.

''Don't,'' she said. ''I'm having a hard enough time saying this. If you touch me again, my brain'll turn to mush and I'll never get it said.''

She shoved another fallen lock of hair out of her face. ''Zack, until you came along, I didn't know my body could feel like this.''

''Ah.'' He nodded slowly. ''You feel this . . . *pain,* too.''

She stopped suddenly and shot her gaze to his. ''Pain. Yes, I guess it is pain. But it's more than that, too. It's want. And need.'' She spun around and paced again in short, almost angry steps. ''I've never *needed* a man before. And I don't know if I like it much.''

"But you were married . . ."

"Yeah." She wrapped her arms around herself as if huddling against a deep cold. "Yeah, I was. To a man I'd known my whole life. My friend." She threw him a quick glance. "Don't get me wrong, Zack. I loved Daniel. But damn him, he never made me feel the way you do."

He straightened his shoulders and had the nerve to smile.

"I shouldn't have said that."

"Why not?" He took a step closer.

"Because it doesn't change anything." She backed up. "There's still Danny. I can't act like some silly girl, sweet on a cowboy for the first time."

One corner of his mouth lifted in a pleased smile and she wanted to kick him.

"Don't look so proud of yourself."

"Rebecca . . ." He moved in close.

"Look, just leave me alone for tonight, Zack. Please. I need to . . . think."

"If that's what you want."

She nodded, turned, then stopped. Coming back to face him again, she rose up on her toes and planted a brief, hard kiss on his mouth, then stepped back before he could react. Quickly, she spun about and started walking toward the barn door. She felt his gaze boring into her back with every step.

"Rebecca," he called softly just as she reached the double doors.

"What?" She looked over her shoulder at him, but he was only a silhouetted figure against the lamplight.

"Is there a silver lining in this?"

Yes, she told herself. The silver lining here was that she'd come to her senses before ripping her clothes off and making love with him on the stall floor beneath Sky Dancer's watchful eye.

But she could hardly tell him that. After a moment or

two's thought, she said, "Yes. At least we have that awkward first kiss out of the way."

She could almost hear his frown when he asked, "You thought it was awkward?"

Rebecca's head fell forward until her chin hit her chest. Then, even though she knew he couldn't see her in the dark, she raised her head to look at him. Whatever else there was between them, she wasn't going to lie to him.

"No, Zacariah. I didn't."

Dammit.

Hell, it hadn't even been their first kiss.

She left quickly then, disappearing into the slice of moonlight that speared through the partially opened barn doors. Zacariah stared after her for several long moments as he tried to control his rampaging emotions.

With her kiss, she had shown him something that he'd never dreamed existed. A burning without flame. She'd created fire with a touch. Madness with her sighs. She'd tortured him with such sweet pain that his body still ached.

The Eternal Path had nothing like this.

Forcing herself to walk, Rebecca moved through the dark house toward her room. She didn't need a light to find her way around the furnishings. Not one stick of furniture had been moved from its proper place in ten years.

She stopped short and laid one hand on a chair back. Lord, she was just like her house. A place for everything and everything in its place. She'd been Daniel's wife, then Danny's mother. Now, when given a chance to simply be *Rebecca* . . . she didn't know what to do with it.

She stepped into her bedroom, closed the door behind her, then walked to the wide bed where she lay every night, alone. Flopping down onto the mattress, she threw one arm across her eyes and tried to keep from imagining Zack lying next to her.

* * *

The solitary rider entered the narrow canyon just beyond Pine Creek. Soft moonlight lit the well-worn trail and he kept his gaze moving, shifting from side to side. The steady beat of his horse's hooves against the rocky ground sounded out loudly against the otherwise quiet night. He rode through mooncast shadows of the boulders lining either side of the old trail. His sharp gaze swept over mesquite bushes and the occassional straggly pine.

Keeping his ears attuned for the slightest sound, he listened for anything out of the ordinary. A boot sliding on rock. The hammer of a gun being cocked. But there was nothing beyond the sound of his own passage and the distant cry of a coyote.

As he rode deeper into the canyon, he began to relax. No stranger would have made it that deeply into the canyon without being stopped by the two men waiting for him up ahead.

Grimly, he turned his horse down the sharp incline that led to the mouth of the canyon. Now that he was closer, he heard the unmistakable sounds of a standing herd of horses. Softly, the animals called to each other and the muffled pounding of dozens of shod hooves against the dirt sounded almost like heartbeats.

He snorted at his own fancies. It wasn't hearts beating he heard. It was the sound of cash on the hoof.

A man stood up from the shadows and stepped onto the trail to meet him.

"What are you doin' here tonight?" he asked quietly. "We weren't expectin' you back again for another week or so."

"There's been a change in plans," the rider said and leaned both hands on the saddle pommel. He waited until the other man moved into a slice of moonlight before speaking again. "I want you and Joe to hurry things up some."

"Why?"

A lightning-like surge of anger filled him and was

beaten down just as quickly. As much as he hated to admit it, he still needed Hank and Joe. He couldn't afford to lose his temper and shoot anybody he'd be hard-pressed to replace this late in the game. Once that final sale was made to the Army, though, he was through explaining himself to *anybody*. "You don't have to worry about the whys of it. Just do what you're told and you'll get your money."

The man cradled a rifle in the crook of his left arm, and scratched his whiskered jaw thoughtfully. "All right, what do you want done?"

"Round up as many of the remaining horses as you can in the next few days. Leave the ones by Twin Peaks. I'll take care of them."

"Then what?"

"Then we sell them." The rider shrugged. "Just like the others."

"I know that," the man said slowly. "I meant, you want us to take them in, or wait for you?"

He scowled at the man. He had no intention of trusting these two thieves any further than he could see them. He wasn't about to tell them how to contact his Army buyer. No, he'd have to go along when it was time to sell, or he'd never see his share of the money.

"Wait here," he said. "I'll come back in a few days, then we'll go."

"You're the boss." The man shrugged, turned his back on him and disappeared into the shadows.

The boss.

He liked the sound of that.

The rider smiled as he pulled his horse's head around and headed back the way he'd come.

"You did a good job," Buck said and rested his forearms on the top slat of the corral fence.

"Thanks," Zacariah answered and took a spot beside

the older man to watch the mare and her foal wander around the paddock.

Across the yard, the front door of the house opened and closed. Buck's gaze shifted to the man beside him long enough to see Zacariah's gaze shift to follow Rebecca.

His bushy gray eyebrows arched high on his forehead and he deliberately looked away. There was something going on here, he told himself. And it didn't have a damn thing to do with staying up all night birthing a horse.

All morning long, Becky and Zack had been stepping carefully around each other, like they were walking barefoot through a rattlesnake pit. The two of them had been silent as the grave.

A half-smile hovered around Buck's mouth and he rubbed his face with one hand to hide it. All right, so he'd been wrong about the man. He would admit to being worried—letting a stranger come in and settle down among them. But for all his odd ways, Zacariah was, at least, a worker.

Buck slanted a quick look down at the bent nails holding the fence rails in place. He wasn't much for working with his hands, but give that boy a hoe and nobody could stop him. Seemed a good sort, too. Didn't know a damn thing, but at least he was willing to learn.

"Danny!" Rebecca's voice rose up in the still air and Zacariah's head swiveled around as if drawn to the sound.

Buck glanced in her direction and saw her, kneeling on the freshly turned earth in the garden. Her long, auburn braid shone like a rope of fire down her back and when she smiled at her son's approach, her whole face seemed to light up.

His family.

Oh, maybe not by blood. But Daniel, Becky and their son were the only family Buck had ever had. Now, with Daniel gone, it was up to him to look out for Becky and the boy.

"What's going on between you and the boss?" he

asked suddenly, watching Zacariah's eyes carefully.

"What?" The man's clear blue gaze shifted to Buck.

Those eyes of his sometimes made Buck feel like squirming. They were too . . . knowing. Too *familiar* for comfort.

Uneasily, he changed his question. "Just what are you doing here, son?"

"What do you mean?"

"I mean, why are you here? At the ranch? What is it you want?"

Zacariah's head fell back on his neck and he stared up at the startlingly blue sky as if looking for answers. After several long moments, he whispered, "A place to stay. To live."

"That's all?"

The man straightened up and stared into Buck's eyes again. He tried to look away, and couldn't.

"What more could I want?" Zacariah asked.

This wasn't working at all. What he needed was to get Zack away from the ranch and loosen him up some. Get him to talking so that maybe he'd spill a couple of the secrets he was obviously keeping.

The older man grinned suddenly. He had just the thing.

"Zack," he said suddenly, "I do believe it's time me and Scotty took you to town and introduced you around."

Zacariah frowned. "I've been into town a few times already."

"Not to where we'll take you." Buck grinned and winked. "We'll go tonight, after Scotty gets back."

Chapter ❁ Nine

It was mid-afternoon before Scotty showed up at the ranch, driving six horses ahead of him.

When Rebecca saw him, she left Danny to the bean planting and stepped out of the garden to meet him. She brushed her dirty hands against her thighs as she walked across the yard. Absently, she noted the thunderheads gathering atop the mountain peaks. Another storm coming and the roof still wasn't fixed.

Once Buck had slammed the gate shut and latched it securely, Scotty swung down from his saddle and tossed his reins over the closest fence rail.

"Six?" Buck nearly shouted as he stomped up to stand beside Rebecca. Staring into Scotty's smiling face, he asked again, "Six horses? That's all you found at Twin Peaks?"

"That's it, Buck." The cowboy shrugged and his easy smile slipped a bit. "Sorry boss, looks like our rustlers are at it again."

"Did you see any sign of them?"

"Nothin'," Scotty told her and pulled his hat off and wiped his forehead with the back of his sleeve. "These boys are good, whoever they are."

"Scotty, tomorrow I want you to go back out. Cast around. Find tracks. *Any* tracks."

"Now, Rebecca," he started.

"I want to know who's stealing my horses and where they're taking them. I don't care how long you've got to be out there, Scotty. But you find something before you come back. You understand?"

He snatched his hat off and slapped it against his thighs. "Why don't you send Zack? Let him earn his keep."

"He earned his keep last night," Buck broke in. "If it weren't for him, Sky Dancer and her foal would prob'ly be dead right now."

"What's this about Dancer?" Scotty asked, his gaze flitting from Buck to Rebecca and back again.

"She delivered late last night and Zack helped Rebecca with the birth."

"You and Zack, huh?" Scotty stared at her, waiting.

"Yeah," she said. "If he hadn't been here . . ." Her voice trailed off as memories filled her mind. Then other, even more vivid recollections leaped into life and she felt heat and color rush to her cheeks.

She heard Scotty's sharp intake of breath and spoke up before the cowboy could utter a word.

"Buck, why don't you go dig those old shingles out of the barn for me? We've got to get that roof fixed before a new storm hits." She glanced skyward. "There's enough daylight still to make a good start of it."

When Buck had left, Scotty reached out to smooth a stray lock of hair away from her eyes. Rebecca took a half-step back and he let his hand fall to his side.

"Why don't you let me help you?"

She shook her head and turned away from him. "The only help I need from you is your skills with horses. You can rest up tonight, but tomorrow, you get yourself a fresh horse from the barn and head back to Pine Creek canyon. Find out what's happening to my stock. *That's* what I'm paying you for."

She'd only taken a few steps toward Danny and the garden when his voice stopped her again.

"Why don't you just quit?"

"Quit?" she echoed.

"Hell, you can't make a go of this place with the few miserable head of horses you got left." He reached one hand out for her, but Rebecca stepped away from him. Her shoulders lifted and fell in an unconscious effort to shake him free.

"That's where you're wrong, Scotty," she said softly. She glanced around the yard of the ranch that would one day be her son's inheritance, then looked back into the cowboy's pale, gray eyes. "I'll make this place go if all I've got left is a three-legged burro."

"You're losing horses every damned day."

She stopped on her way to the blasted vegetable garden and looked back at him over her shoulder. Forcing a smile she didn't feel, she said, "But the silver lining is, I don't have to worry about having to feed them, do I?"

Clouds of heavy, foul-smelling smoke rushed at him, as if looking for someone new to annoy. He sniffed, then wrinkled his nose at the combined odors of unwashed bodies, liquor and the cloying, flowery scent that drifted in the wake of a woman who brushed past him. Another woman's shrill laugh cut through the overlying hum of male voices and an occassional angry shout was heard above the clatter.

Zacariah reached for the small glass on the table in front of him. He frowned as his hand slid past his drink completely. Odd, he didn't recall having the slightest bit of trouble picking up the first four drinks. Carefully, he moved again, this time mentally willing his fingers to curl around the glass.

Scotty snorted and shifted his gaze to sweep the crowded saloon.

Zacariah tossed his drink down his throat. The now-familiar fire rushed through him, bringing tears to his eyes and a growing sense of contentment. He couldn't imagine why he hadn't liked the taste of this fine liquor right away.

He poured himself another drink, wincing as some of the liquor splashed out of his glass to be wasted on the scarred tabletop.

The older man chuckled, then began to wheeze and finished by coughing until his cheeks flushed and his eyes filled with water.

"Jesus, Buck," Scotty snapped. "You gonna die right here in the saloon?"

"Die?" Zacariah attempted to straighten up in his chair, but felt himself tilting dangerously to one side. Was someone dying? Buck? When? He blinked and stared hard at the older man. Was there something he should be noticing? He focused his eyes harder, then blinked again and shook his head.

Why did Buck look . . . fuzzy?

And why did Scotty suddenly sound so faraway?

"I'll let ya know when I get ready to die, boy," Buck said and lifted his drink to drain the whiskey in one long gulp.

"Or I will." Zacariah nodded abruptly and *felt* his eyes roll in his head. Very strange.

Buck squinted at him for a long minute, then slammed his empty glass back down onto the tabletop.

"So, you're Becky's hero now, huh?"

He turned to look at Scotty and immediately wished he hadn't. The room started spinning.

"Shut up," Buck said.

"No. It's just us here," the younger man went on. "You wanted to bring him along. Well, now that he's here, he can damn well talk."

"About what?" Zacariah asked.

"About Becky. And you." Scotty leaned both elbows on the table and fixed him with a hard stare. "Just what in hell are you up to, anyway?"

"Up to?"

"With Becky, damn you," he nearly shouted, then

glanced around him, making sure no one else had heard.

"I'm not 'up to' anything."

"So nothin' happened between you two last night?"

"It's none of your business," Buck growled and the cowboy flicked him a quick, unconcerned glance.

"I've told you before, *Becky's* my business."

Zacariah laughed, and something behind his eyes popped. He reached up and rubbed his temple thoughtfully.

"This ain't funny."

"Yes, it is," Zacariah insisted. He wasn't drunk enough not to notice that it was jealousy driving Scotty. And as much as he might wish things were different, the cowboy had no reason to be jealous.

"I saw how she was lookin' at you today."

His insides tightened. "How was that?"

"Like she was a cat and you the cream."

A broad smile creased his features, then he frowned as he realized his lips were stuck to his teeth.

"You all right, Zack?" Buck asked and leaned toward him.

He nodded and ran his tongue over teeth that suddenly felt *soft*.

"Hell yes, he's all right," Scotty muttered and pushed away from the table. "Why wouldn't he be? He's got Becky all tied up in knots over him. Even *you*," he added, glaring at Buck, "think he's all right." His stare shifted, pinning Zacariah to his chair with icy shards of anger. "Well, he don't fool me any. And mister, I for one want you the hell out of here."

He spun around and stomped through the crowd, pushing men out of his way until he reached the bar. There, he propped one foot up on the brass rail and draped one arm over a woman's shoulders.

"How about another?" Buck asked and picked up the bottle again.

He heard liquor splash into a glass.

"So you want to tell me," Buck asked, and leaned in close to him, "just what is it that's goin' on between you and Becky?"

Zacariah stared at the older man and watched, horrified, as his friend slowly grew another head. He blinked furiously and was greatly relieved when the two Bucks joined together again.

"What is what?" he asked, despite the sudden thickness of his tongue.

"You and Becky have been acting real strange all day. Not talking. Avoiding each other. For the first time in a long time, I figure Scotty's right. Something's goin' on and I want to know what it is."

Becky. Zacariah smiled to himself and licked his numb lips. He slanted a quick look at Scotty and the woman again and saw that the cowboy's hand had slipped down to caress the woman's bottom. Hmmm. He would have to remember that.

"She seems to like you, boy," Buck was saying and Zack turned back to look at him. "And I'll admit that you've been good for Danny, too."

"Nice boy."

"Yeah, he is."

Zacariah reached for his drink and quickly downed it.

"But I'm a careful man, son."

"Of course you are." Zacariah finally managed to raise his head and looked Buck directly in his eyes. All four of them.

"And no matter what you say, I'm *sure* I know you from somewhere."

"Impossible." Zacariah waved one hand and laughed shortly.

"Why's that?" Buck demanded.

"Because you're human." Zacariah chuckled softly.

Buck's eyes bugged out and he jerked his head back in surprise. "Human? So're you."

"Oh, sure. *Now*." He told him and held out his glass toward the bottle.

Buck pushed the bottle at him and scowled. "Shit, I got you *too* drunk. Even *you* don't know what you're sayin'."

Zacariah laughed and grabbed the bottle neck. As he poured the whiskey with a shaky hand, he said, "I know, but you don't know. So nobody else knows, either."

"God damn it," Buck muttered and reached for his own glass.

Someone pitched a chair through a window and silence dropped over the crowd like an old, unwanted blanket. In seconds though, an angry, young voice shattered the silence.

"Let go of me!"

A cluster of people slowly drifted apart, leaving an angry young man standing alone.

A boy, really, he had sandy blond hair and bright red splotches of color staining his cheeks. Too thin, his limbs had the long, ungainly look of a work in progress. In a few years, he might be a powerfully built man. At the moment though, he was a furious boy, looking for trouble.

One of the perfumed, feather-bedecked women stepped up to him and laid an arm around his shoulders. He jerked back from her, swiped his forearm across his eyes and shouted at the bartender.

"All I want's a drink," he demanded. "And this fella won't let me pass." He jerked his head at a solemn-eyed man dressed almost entirely in black. The man shrugged massive shoulders.

Sighing, the bartender shook his head at the boy. "Go home, Billy. You're too young to be in here."

A trickle of mutters rose up from the interested crowd, but died again when the boy began to argue.

"Too young?" He laughed and stared wildly around the room. Even from a distance of fifteen feet, Zacariah saw the shadows of despair lurking in the boy's eyes.

"Too young for a drink, too young for . . ."

"Billy," the bartender said softly. "I know what's eatin' you and you can't cure it in here."

"Dammit, where, then?" Billy Jenkins rubbed his eyes with one hand and asked his question again. More softly this time. "Where? Tell me where and I'll go there."

"Go home, Billy," the perfumed woman in the bright green dress said gently as she took his hand and led him toward the door. "Go on home now. Get some sleep."

The boy threw another hostile glare at the crowd, then rushed across the room and through the doors.

Slowly, the voices around him started up again only to be drowned out by the bartender.

"Sorry folks," he said, with a slow, sad shake of his head. "Young Billy's sweet on Ellie Parker, y'know. And I hear she's not perking up like she should be."

Ellie.

The young girl from the store.

Zacariah stared blankly at the tabletop, remembering the girl's pale, still features. Overriding that memory came the pain in Billy Jenkins' eyes and voice. The boy's suffering was real, he knew. What he didn't understand was the depth of emotion.

"Poor kid," Buck muttered.

"Why is he so angry?" Zacariah wondered aloud. "He isn't a part of the girl's family. Why is *he* so upset?"

"Sometimes, Zack," Buck said, clearly disgusted, "I wonder about you more'n usual. That boy's in love. Young he may be, but love don't know anything about ages. And right now, young Billy thinks his world's ending."

Zacariah frowned and stared thoughtfully at the doorway through which the boy had run.

She reached up for him, rising on her toes to meet his lips. She felt his breath brush across her cheeks, heard him whisper her name. Her heartbeat pounded frantically in her chest and her fingers curled into his shoulders.

"Ma!"

The dream image splintered. She opened her eyes to darkness and found herself clutching a pillow to her chest tightly. Every nerve in her body was alive and humming and she felt as though her flesh was on fire. Rebecca drew one long, shaky breath into her lungs and released her hold on the feather pillow.

She pushed her hair back from her face, then eased into a sitting position. She yanked at the quilt and sheets twisted around her legs and tried to tell herself that the trembling in her limbs was caused by being trapped in the bed linens.

But if that was so, why were her hands shaking, too?

She scowled into the darkness.

"Ma! Come here, quick!"

Danny.

Rebecca threw the covers back and swung her legs over the side of the bed. Spears of shimmering moonlight filtered through the pale ivory fabric drawn across the partially opened windows as she hurried to Danny's room.

Sitting up straight in his bed, her son was turning his head from side to side, frantically inspecting the shadows shifting and twisting over the walls in his room.

Rebecca sighed quietly and went to him.

"Ma," he whispered and buried his head in her chest as she sat down on the mattress beside him.

"It's all right, honey," she said softly. "I'm here, it's all right, now."

"It was here, Ma. It was here." His voice broke and when he continued, his words were muffled against her body. "It had red eyes and it tried to get me, but I called you and it went away, under the bed."

Rebecca's eyes closed as she rested her chin on top of his head. She felt his small body tremble and his quick, shallow breaths tore at her. Within minutes though, his small, terrified fingers on her back loosened. Rebecca smoothed his hair off his forehead and she bent to press a kiss on his clammy skin.

"Better?" she asked.

"Uh-huh," he said and nodded jerkily.

"That's good," she whispered, then began quietly humming. Gently, Rebecca rocked her son, cradling his small, warm body close. When he fell asleep at last, her mind began to wander.

Naturally, it wandered directly to Zacariah.

There was something about the man that drew her to him, despite the fact that she hardly knew him. There was kindness in his eyes, along with a tired sort of wisdom that somehow made her ache for him. A strong man, with a hard voice and quiet strength, he made her feel more alive than she ever had before.

Passion stirred in her. Like a carefully banked fire, the coals of desire still burned in her blood, and apparently it took only the thought of him to fan them into a blazing inferno.

Her arms tightened around her son and when he shifted, snuggling in closer to her, she reached for his blankets and pulled them up over his bare legs. She couldn't give herself blindly to a man. Not with Danny to consider.

But the boy cared for Zack, too.

This was all his fault, she told herself. If Zacariah had never come to the Hale ranch, she'd be a perfectly happy woman. At least, all she would have had to deal with then were the rustlers stealing her horses.

And that would be far easier than trying to protect herself from a drifter trying to steal her heart.

Rebecca stared at the man sitting at the table and almost found herself feeling sorry for him. Thankfully though, her better judgement leaped into life to prevent it.

She'd awakened still angry with him for disrupting her perfectly pleasant life, only to find that he was doing a much better job of punishing himself than she could have.

Elbows braced on the table, he held his head in his hands.

"You look terrible."

"I'm not surprised," he croaked and winced at the sound of his own voice.

Sitting down opposite him, she slid a cup of coffee under his nose and grinned when he inhaled the steam like a dying man. A hangover was an ugly thing and he looked to have a dandy.

"Why'd you do it?" she asked quietly, her smile fading.

"Do what?"

"Go out and get drunk. Was it because of what didn't happen between us?"

He lifted his head, opened one eye and looked at her. "What makes you say that?"

She shrugged. "Just wondering."

He reached for the cup and lifted it carefully. Taking one long sip, he said, "I don't know why I did it." He took another swallow or two. "But I won't be doing it again, I know that much."

"Ah," she said. "The morning-after promises."

"What?"

"Nothing. I've just heard them before, is all."

"From who?"

"Daniel. My husband." She held her cup between both hands and stared down into the inky coffee. "Every Sunday morning, he promised to stay away from the saloon. But by the following Saturday night, the hangover was a memory and so were his promises."

"Rebecca . . ."

She shook her head. "Never mind. It was a long time ago."

"Were you that unhappy?" he asked.

"With Daniel?"

He nodded.

She thought about it for a long minute. Unhappy? With Daniel? "No. He was my best friend."

Zacariah rubbed his eyes with his fingertips, then looked at her. "But you didn't *love* him. Like you said your friend Doris loves her husband."

She shifted uncomfortably. "I trusted him."

"It's not the same thing."

Even though his eyes were red-streaked and blurry-looking, they seemed to see too much. Too clearly. He was right. Love and trust were certainly not the same thing.

She'd trusted Daniel but hadn't been in love with him. Was she now falling in love with a man she couldn't trust?

Rebecca straightened up on the seat. The conversation was taking an uncomfortable turn and it was time she set it back on track.

"Rebecca . . ."

"So," she interrupted smoothly, "you won't be wanting any breakfast this morning?"

"No," he groaned through clenched teeth.

"Well then, you may as well get started on your day," she said and stood up.

"Get started?"

"Sure. Scotty's horse is gone from the corral, so he probably rode out before dawn. Buck's busy in the barn," no doubt napping, she added silently. "So, you should get going, too."

He sat up on the bench and grimly looked her in the eye. "What do you want me to do?"

She'd thought carefully about that since she'd seen him and Buck drunkenly arrive home well into the morning hours. Zacariah, whether he'd meant to or not, had robbed her of sleep, tormented what few dreams she'd managed to have and teased her with a passion she couldn't claim.

Now, she would have her revenge.

"I have to go see the sheriff today and after that, I'll

be up on the roof, finishing up the shingling.''

He winced and she knew he was imagining the constant pounding of a hammer.

"But because you're feeling so poorly," she went on with a small smile, "I've decided to give you the day off."

"Thank heaven," he sighed into his coffee.

The front door flew open and crashed into the wall behind it.

Zacariah jumped, then moaned quietly.

"Danny, how many times have I told you not to slam the door?"

"I didn't slam it," the boy countered. "I opened it. Hard."

Shaking her head, she asked, "You ready to go?"

"Yep. I just come for Zack, is all." The boy raced across the room and slid to a stop directly in front of him. "I've got the poles and I dug for worms and I don't think it's gonna rain today, so let's get goin'."

"Hmmm?"

"Fishing," Danny said and glanced from Zack to his mother.

Zacariah blinked his eyes furiously, took a long drink of coffee and welcomed the heat. Hopefully, it would help burn off the murkiness still clouding his mind.

"Ma says you and me can have the whole day to catch us some fish."

His gaze shifted to Rebecca and he felt his eyeballs scrape against the inside of his head. She smiled at him.

"You said you wanted to go fishin', just you and me."

"So I did." He tore his gaze from her to look at the boy whose features were slowly slipping into a mask of disappointment.

"Don't you want to anymore?"

What he *wanted* to do was tear his head off and carry it gingerly back to bed where he could wait quietly for the Collectors to arrive and claim him.

Danny looked from his mother to him.

When the boy's eyes met his, he knew he was lost. Forcing a smile, he stood up and fought the urge to sink back down. Ruffling one hand through the child's hair, he said, "If you're ready, let's go."

"Oh, boy!"

Oh, Lord.

Chapter ❋ Ten

Sheriff Tall Cooper looked her up and down dismissively, then went back to tossing playing cards into an empty spittoon across the room. Big feet propped on the corner of his desk, a cigar burning in the ashtray and a pot of coffee within reach, he looked as though he'd picked his spot for the year and had no intention of moving.

Rebecca leaned both hands on the cluttered desktop. "Are you going to come out to the ranch or not?"

"Well now, Miz Hale," he said lazily, "don't see no reason to do that, if you're willin' to come all the way into town."

Disgusted, she threw her hands up. This sheriff would never lock up her rustlers—unless the thieves came to town themselves and demanded a jail cell. "What about investigating? Can't you get out there and look for tracks?"

He yawned, displaying a set of crooked teeth, then stretched like a fat old cat near a warm hearth. "You already got Scotty out lookin', don't ya?"

"Yes, but—"

"No sense in me crowdin' the boy, then."

"Sheriff—"

"Mustn't get yourself overset now, Miz Hale. Wouldn't want you to suffer a case of the vapors."

"*Vapors?*" Rather than fainting, Rebecca was within a hair's breadth of leaping across that messy desktop and throttling the sheriff. "I don't get the vapors."

"Good, good." He tossed the Queen of Hearts and sighed his disappointment when the card sailed past its target. "Now honey, until Scotty comes in and tells me that he's found something, we don't even know that them horses of yours was stolen."

Unbelievable.

Even for Tall Cooper.

Hands at her hips, she leaned toward him. "If they weren't stolen, Sheriff, just what do *you* think happened to them?"

He shrugged and blinked past a lock of greasy black hair hanging over one eye. "Oh, they prob'ly just wandered off and you're gettin' yourself all in a twist over nothin'." He paused before aiming his next card to tell her, "Hysterics ain't a pretty thing, Miz Hale."

She glared at him and he at least had the decency to look cowed. Briefly. But what he said next caught her completely off guard.

"Been hearing some odd things about the new man out at your place."

She tilted her head and looked at him from the corners of her eyes. As she would any other snake. "What do you mean, odd?"

He flipped another card toward the spittoon and almost crowed when it dropped in. Half-turning to face her, he said, "J.T. came in to see me the other day."

The blacksmith? "So?"

"*So . . .*" he gave her a satisfied smirk. "J.T. says he saw your man in his corral, talkin' to *nobody.*"

Rebecca laughed at him. "That's what you call odd? Hell, everybody in this town talks to themselves at one time or another. Especially when they come in here!"

It took a moment or two, but the insult finally sank in. He shook his head sadly. "No call to be nasty, Miz Hale.

Besides, didn't say he was talkin' to himself. Said he was talkin' to somebody else. Somebody who wasn't there.''

"Then how . . . ?"

"J.T. says this fella was asking questions of thin air, then noddin' his head and even laughin' at some of the answers he was gettin'. From nobody."

"Sounds like J.T.'s been visiting the saloon regularly again."

"Awww." Cooper shook his head slowly, as if disappointed in a wayward child. "There you go, bein' nasty again."

She sighed.

"J.T.'s been sober as a judge for nigh on to two years as well you know."

Rebecca turned away from the desk and marched across the room to look blindly out the window. Even if it was true, what did it mean? Nothing. Lots of people talked to themselves. Didn't mean they were crazy. She smiled inwardly. Hell, she was doing it herself, right now.

Glancing over her shoulder, she said as much.

"True, but I hear tell that your new man says he don't remember a damn thing about himself, either."

She spun around to face him head-on. Resting her bottom against the windowsill, she folded her arms over her chest and crossed her feet at the ankles. "What are you getting at, anyway?"

He shrugged. "I'm just sayin', that it seems almighty peculiar that you have a real strange new fella at your place around the same time you claim to be missing horses."

A sly smile crept up his face and Rebecca was forced to admit that Cooper was the only person she'd ever known who looked *worse* smiling. As for his idea . . . ridiculous.

"I was missing those horses before Zack showed up and you damn well know it." She uncrossed her legs and stomped right back to his desk, staring the worthless man down until he shifted his gaze from hers uncomfortably. Slapping one hand down onto the desk, she pointed her other index finger at him. "I've been in here every couple of weeks for the last few months, hoping to blast you out of that chair."

Sheriff Cooper huffed indignantly and dropped his feet to the floor. "You ain't once brought me proof that you've got rustlers, Miz Hale."

"And just what do you call proof? Do I have to bring the thieves in here myself, all hogtied like a Christmas present?"

"Just proof." He wagged his head sagely. "That's all I ask."

Straightening up, her hands balled into fists, she growled deep in her throat.

Cooper's eyebrows lifted high on his forehead and he clucked his tongue at her. "Now, now. There you go, gettin' all hysterical again."

Hopeless. This was hopeless.

"If I was you"—he leaned in toward her, obviously unaware of how badly she wanted to smack him—"I'd fire that drifter. Run him off your place. Even if he ain't a rustler, he's plenty damned odd, if you ask me."

"Well Sheriff," she shot back as she started for the door. "I don't recall asking you."

"Your funeral," he said with a tired shrug and aimed another card at his target.

She grabbed the tarnished brass doorknob and turned it. Before stepping outside, though, she looked at him over her shoulder and said one last thing.

"Come next election, *Sheriff,* it'll be *your* funeral. I will find *someone* to run against you," she promised. "Even if it's me."

The card went far afield, sailing into the corner behind a potbellied stove that hadn't been cleaned in years.

A guttural laugh started low in Cooper's chest and rumbled up along his throat until it spilled into the room with all the music of sand on glass.

"A female? *Sheriff?*"

Rebecca left before she could give in to her instinct to hit him with something heavy.

Sunlight washed down over them and touched the surface of the lake with diamonds. The water glittered and sparkled with every touch of the breeze.

Zacariah inhaled sharply, pulled the brim of his hat down low and squinted against the brightness. Two hours of sitting on the bank, staring at the water, had finally begun to calm the pounding in his head.

Of course, it might have stopped sooner, but for the little boy beside him.

"This is fun," Danny said and cocked his head to grin at him.

Zacariah nodded carefully, ran one finger around the inside of his collar and tossed a quick look at the sun overhead. Not a cloud in sight. The shadows from the trees along the bank were lying in cool dark patches, too far away to be any use as shade.

"Hot, ain't it?"

"Yes."

Danny immediately began to tug at the buttons on his shirt and Zacariah admitted silently that the boy had a good idea. When their shirts had been tossed aside, they settled into an easy silence that was soothing to the remnants of Zacariah's hangover.

"You want a sandwich?" Danny asked as he turned and began to rummage through the basket of food his mother had packed.

"No." For the first time, food didn't sound good at all.

"Okay." The boy forgot about eating, picked up his pole again and stared thoughtfully at the end of his line where it disappeared into the lake. Idly, he scratched at an old scar on his forearm, then glanced at Zacariah.

"How come you don't have any scars?"

"What?"

"Scars." Danny pointed to his own arm and said, "I got this one when I fell off the corral fence last summer. Scraped it open on a nail." He glanced up and grinned. "There was lots of blood and Ma looked real scared when she saw it."

He nodded.

"But Buck told her that all menfolks get scarred up. It's like a badge of honor, Buck says." Danny's narrow chest swelled with pride and he gave the mark on his skin a last pat before asking again, "So how come you don't have any?"

Zack glanced at his palms. The broken blisters and callouses had barely healed, so weren't really in the class of scars.

"Buck's got one right here," Danny said and reached around awkwardly to point to a spot on his own lower back. "Some no-account shot him a long time ago."

He certainly couldn't compete with an old bullet wound.

"And up here," the boy went on and pointed to the center of his chest, "there's a mark where a cow stomped him the night my pa died."

"That must have been painful."

Danny jerked him a nod. "Buck says he durn near flickered out that night."

That sounded like Buck.

"But he didn't," Danny said more quietly. "My pa did."

"How did your father die?"

"A stampede," the boy muttered. "Back when I was a kid."

Despite the sun's blazing heat, a shaft of ice settled in Zacariah's chest. He tore his gaze away from the boy beside him and focused instead on the glittering water. A stampede?

"Buck says he didn't suffer any and Ma sold all the cows right after." His small hand dropped to the ground and his fingers began to tug at the new grass. "She said she didn't know anything about cattle, but I think it was because she was mad at the cows."

Cattle.

Stampede.

Buck, injured in the same incident.

The old man thinking him familiar.

"Did you ever see a stampede, Zack?"

He nodded stiffly. "Once." In over six hundred years, he'd been at the scene of only *one* stampede.

"I never saw one, but Buck and Scotty told me about it."

Images flashed through his mind. Dust. Screams. Blood.

"Don't say nothin' to ma, all right? She didn't want me to know about it."

He nodded again, caught somewhere in between this calm, sunny day and the memories of a long night, four years ago. His mind raced back, through the countless faces and places that he'd seen and visited since that one night. He sifted through the remnants of memory until he'd found the one he needed to recall.

He could almost hear the newly liberated soul ask, *"My son? My wife? Will I see them again?"* Zacariah had stood silent as his Collection had whispered to Buck, *"Good-bye, you old coot."*

"Buck says Pa didn't want to leave us," Danny said softly. "But he had to."

Every muscle in Zacariah's body clenched painfully and he realized that the relatively minor pain he'd felt earlier wasn't even a shade on this new, soul-deep agony.

"You think my pa misses me?"

Zacariah glanced furtively at the child beside him. Tears welled up in his eyes and Danny's face became blurred, indistinct. He inhaled sharply, blinked away the blinding water and willed himself to control.

"I'm sure he does," Zacariah said and hoped the boy wouldn't notice the roughness in his voice.

"I don't remember him much," Danny whispered.

Those simple words were like a knife in his chest.

His mouth dry, his heart thundering, Zacariah realized that it was *he* who had collected Danny's father.

Rebecca's husband.

It was *he* who had ruined their family and made the last four years so difficult for them.

For her.

"Zack? You all right?"

Why hadn't he seen this sooner? Why hadn't he put it all together before this? But he knew why. His memories were crowded with faces. Faces of the dead. Faces of liberated souls. Too many deaths. Too many souls for him to remember each one individually. The faces blurred together in a long, unending chain, forged so tightly that no one link stood out from the rest.

Not even Buck's insistence that he knew him had been enough to dredge up the memory.

Zacariah rubbed one hand across his face. He pretended to be one of them, but he didn't even have the courtesy to remember those people whose souls he had touched.

By the Path, he'd taken this child's father.

Instantly, he remembered everything Danny had said to him during the last week or so. He recalled every wistful expression on his small face. Every question a fatherless boy had hurled at a friendly stranger. Every devilish grin. Every laugh.

Everything that Daniel Hale had missed.

True, he hadn't caused that stampede. It wasn't his fault that Daniel Hale had died. If not him, Zacariah admitted, there would have been another Collector there for Danny's father. It had been the man's time. Nothing could have changed that.

And yet, regret filled him, surprising him with its

strength. Even knowing that Daniel now existed in a world of beauty and peace wasn't enough to overcome this strange feeling of . . . *distress.*

His mind raced and his nerves tingled. He needed to move. He wanted to run. To feel the aches in his legs. To feel his chest burn for want of air. To feel his heart pound from exertion. To feel everything he had denied Daniel Hale.

"Zack?"

His breath caught. He turned to look into Danny's eyes and knew he wouldn't run away. He couldn't.

"Jake says Ellie's goin' to die," the boy whispered and water rushed into his eyes with the words. "Is she?"

His chest tightened another notch. Instinctively, he reached for the child.

Danny dropped his fishing pole into the water and moved into his embrace gratefully.

Cradling the small warm body against him, Zacariah whispered helplessly, "I don't know, Danny." He cursed silently, viciously, because it was the truth. He didn't know. And because even if he had known the answer, it wouldn't have been a comfort.

He threw a quick, furtive look at the sky and mentally bowed to his superiors. The punishment they'd devised for him had been a clever one. Despite himself, he was learning from these humans.

He wasn't sure quite when it had happened. And he would have been willing to wager heavily against it *ever* happening. But somehow, he'd actually learned to *care* for a child.

Danny pulled back in the circle of his arms to look up at him. "Kids can die too, can't they? Not just grown-ups?"

Zacariah swallowed heavily. Looking into eyes so like Rebecca's, he suddenly wanted to shout, "No! Children don't die! Children don't suffer!"

"Yes," he finally said and congratulated himself on

being able to squeeze the word past the unexpected knot in his throat. "Children can die, too."

"Does it hurt?"

Zacariah brushed the boy's hair back from his forehead with a gentle touch, then shook his head slowly. This, at least, he could give him.

"No, Danny. It doesn't hurt."

The child studied him for several long moments, then, apparently satisfied with what he saw, he nodded and leaned back against him. "I'm glad," he whispered and one of his tears burned its way down Zacariah's bare chest. "I don't want her to hurt any."

Tightening his arms around the child, he rested his chin on the boy's sweet-smelling hair. "Neither do I, Danny." And his words were a prayer. "Neither do I."

Zacariah climbed the ladder to the roof and carefully stepped onto the splintery wooden shingles. His boots slid on the weathered wood and he threw both arms out, searching for balance.

"Back so soon?" Rebecca called out.

He looked at her and every other thought in his head disappeared. Even dressed in dirty workclothes, she was lovely. Sunlight caressed her auburn hair, making it burn with a dark fire. Her nose was pink and perspiration dotted the front of her blue shirt.

She sat straddling the roof's peak, one long, jean-clad leg on either side, and she held a hammer poised over an obviously new shingle.

"Where's Danny?"

He jerked his head toward the barn and caught himself as his balance wobbled. "With Buck."

She nodded, then looked down and pounded the hammer onto the roof a few times. Zacariah winced slightly, thankful that the worst of his headache was gone.

"Why not just hit me in the head directly?" he asked and began to make his way to her.

Rebecca threw her head back and laughed. The sound rolled over him in musical waves and he drank it in, luxuriating in it.

"Oh," she finally said with a shake of her head, "it's been too long."

"Since what?"

"Since I laughed that hard."

A shadow of that laughter remained in her eyes and kept her lips in a gentle curve. She should laugh all the time. It made her eyes sparkle.

"How long has it been?" he heard himself ask as he eased himself down onto a spot directly opposite her.

Rebecca ran one hand over the hammer's head, then glanced up at him. "Since before Daniel died, I guess," she said, so wistfully that it tore at him. "We used to laugh a lot together."

"You miss him."

"Yes."

This is why he'd gone to the roof. To learn exactly what the loss of her husband had meant to her.

"But you didn't love him."

Her fingers tightened around the hammer. "I don't want to talk about Daniel anymore."

"I have to know."

"Why? What difference can it make to you?"

"I can't explain it," he said and knew that for the truth. He couldn't explain it even to himself.

He only knew that all afternoon, he'd thought about her and Danny and what his Collection four years before had done to them.

"How was your love different?" he asked.

Rebecca set the hammer down, wiped her palms on her thighs and stared at him. "What are you getting at, Zack?"

He had to ask.

He had to know.

"I'm trying to understand," he said, even knowing that

she would likely think him an imbecile. "You love Danny. You love Buck. You loved Daniel."

"Yes?"

"The same way?"

"Of course not."

He sighed and shook his head.

"Jesus, Zack," Rebecca said and tilted her head to stare at him. "You really expect me to believe that a man could *forget* things like that?"

"That doesn't matter. I just need to know."

"And if I answer your questions, will you answer mine?"

"What questions?"

"How about who are you, really? And why are you here? What do you want from me?"

He reached for her hand and covered it with one of his. "You wouldn't believe me if I told you."

She choked out a harsh laugh. "I don't believe the stories you've already told me."

Humph! He hoped the Minions had heard *that*.

"Rebecca, please," he said and the steel in his voice slashed at her. "Don't ask for things I can't give."

She inhaled sharply and squared her shoulders. "Fine. What do you want to know?"

"Daniel. You miss him."

"Sure I do," Rebecca said. "I miss having someone to laugh with. To talk to. To help me with Danny."

"And you would miss Buck?"

"Of course." She shook her head. "Zack, what are you—"

"Danny," he interrupted. "You would miss Danny most of all?"

She jerked her hand out from beneath his and turned her head to stare out over the ranch. "I don't want to even think about that," she whispered. "I don't know what I'd do without Danny."

Zacariah nodded, his features grim. Slowly, he turned

his gaze to look in the same direction, though he paid no attention to the varying shades of green splotched across the landscape. Instead, he saw again Rebecca's wistful smile at the memories of her husband and the almost frantic shine in her eyes at the thought of losing her son.

He rubbed his eyes with his fingertips, hoping to ease the still-throbbing pain in his head. But thinking such deep thoughts weren't helping his headache. These lessons he was supposed to be learning were too painful. Too hard.

Why did he need them?

He wasn't going to be a mortal forever.

"To better understand them," a voice in his mind whispered.

Zacariah wasn't sure if it was his own conscience talking to him or a stray Collector hoping to help him out. Either way, though, he knew it was true. He was there to learn all he could in order to be a better, more compassionate Collector.

Who better to understand pain than one who had experienced it?

In a sunburst of awareness, he suddenly understood Billy Jenkins's pain. He wasn't related to Ellie Parker, but the boy loved her. Rebecca hadn't loved Daniel as desperately, yet her pain at his absence was obvious. Billy's heartache would be even deeper. More wrenching.

Then how much deeper would Rebecca's pain at losing Danny be? He shuddered at the thought of such grief.

"Anything else?" she asked and her voice sounded tight.

He looked at her and realized that one day, Rebecca, too, would die. Her eyes would cease to shine. Her laughter would be stilled.

She would be gone.

Something inside him twisted viciously.

Daniel would probably be waiting to greet her on the Path when her time came.

Inside him, that unnamed feeling twisted again. Harder.

In a couple of weeks, he would be leaving her forever. He wouldn't know when she smiled. Or cried. He wouldn't be aware of her triumphs or her losses. He wouldn't even have the small comfort of knowing that he would one day see her on the Path.

They weren't family.

They shared no connection to ensure that they would meet again.

How he would miss her.

The realization slammed into him. He would *miss* Rebecca. His eyes widened and his already overtired brain raced to figure out exactly what that meant. He'd never missed anyone before. He'd never *had* anyone to miss. Did this mean an unending sort of torture for him? Centuries of feeling as though something was lacking in his existence?

Eternity stretched out before him and loneliness was his only companion.

"Zack?"

He forced himself to meet her gaze. Staring into green eyes that would haunt him forever, he steeled himself to ask the one question that was suddenly more important to him than his next breath.

"What about me, Rebecca? Will you miss me?"

Chapter ❁ Eleven

She dropped the hammer from suddenly nerveless fingers.

It hit the roof, slid across the shingles, dropped off the edge and plopped onto the dirt below.

Her gaze locked with his, she tried futilely to slow the racing beat of her heart. Sudden, gut-deep anger roared up inside her and battled with the rising tide of passion just looking into his eyes caused.

"Will you?" A muscle in his jaw ticked nervously as he repeated his question.

What did he have to be anxious about? It wasn't *his* world that seemed to be teetering wildly on a daily basis. She grabbed hold of the roof and curled her fingers into the aging wooden shingles. Why hadn't he asked his question when they were both on the ground? Where she could turn and stomp off? Why here? On the roof. Where the only way out was through him.

"Rebecca . . ."

"Yes!" If he asked that damned question again, she just might jump from the roof and take her chances. How bad could a broken leg or two be?

"Yes?"

"Yes, I'll miss you, dammit!"

Something flashed across his features but whether it

was pleasure or relief, she couldn't be sure. It disappeared as quickly as it had come.

Taking a deep breath, she squared her shoulders and waved one hand at him imperiously. "Would you mind backing up? I'd like to get down off this roof."

"Not yet."

"I answered your question," she shot back. "And you won't answer mine, so we're through talking, Zack."

"There's nothing I *can* tell you."

"Can't? Or won't?"

His jaw tightened and that muscle flinched again. His vivid blue eyes looked hard, unreadable. "There are things you can't understand."

"Sure." Rebecca nodded stiffly. "Now, you've had your say. Either get out of my way, or I'm going to jump off this damned roof."

He wanted to argue. She could see it in his face. But she also saw that he believed her threat. As he backed up to the ladder leaning against the house, she followed him. Zacariah went down first and as her foot touched the bottom rung, she felt his hands at her waist.

Immediately, she jumped clear of the ladder *and* his touch. At the moment, she didn't trust herself that close to him. Anger alone might not be enough to keep her from giving in to her desire to feel his arms around her again.

He took a single step toward her, but she lifted one hand, palm toward him and he stopped.

"Zack, you're leaving. I'm staying." She shrugged and shook her head. "I've admitted that I'll miss you. What else is there to say?"

Hands at his hips, he tilted his head back and stared at the sky for a long moment. When he looked at her again, he said, "I'll miss you, too."

She took a step back and tried to ignore the sudden rush of illogical hope fluttering inside her. If he would miss her, then he must care. But he was still leaving.

"Then don't go," she said.

"It's not that easy."

She laughed shortly. "Easy? You want *easy?* Nothing comes easy, Zack. That's one thing I've learned in the last four years. But this is only as hard as you would make it. You don't *have* to leave."

"Yes, I do."

Hope died a quick death and anger rushed back in to fill the empty spaces in her soul. Spinning on her heel, she started for the front door.

"Then why not leave now? Get it over with. Danny's off somewhere, you wouldn't even have to say good-bye to him. Is that *easy* enough for you?"

She heard him run up behind her and tried to sprint for the door. She didn't make it. His hand closed around her upper arm and yanked her around to face him.

His dark features were flushed. His eyes wild with something she couldn't identify.

"You think this is *easy?*"

"I don't know what to think anymore." She pulled her arm free and glared up at him. "You tell me lies about not having any memories. You talk to nobody. You kiss me like I'm the first woman you've ever touched—yet you can't wait to get away from me! What *should* I think?"

"I *can't* stay."

"So you said," she snapped. "Leave then. Now."

"I can't leave yet, either."

This time her laugh choked past a knot of helplessness in her throat. "Can't stay. Can't leave. You don't know *what* you want, do you?"

He spun away from her and shoved one hand through his hair. "No, I don't. Path help me, I don't. But it doesn't even matter what I want, anyway."

"What do you mean it doesn't matter? Of course, it matters."

He threw her one wry glance over his shoulder before staring blankly out at the surrounding mountains. "Maybe it should," he muttered thickly. "But it doesn't."

"That doesn't make sense, Zack." She paused. "Hell, none of this does." Inhaling deeply, she crossed her arms over her chest and demanded, "Why did you even come here?"

Slowly, he turned around to face her. His features tight, eyes grim, he looked like a man who'd been pushed too far and couldn't find his way back. "Do you think I *wanted* to come here? By the Path, I would have done almost *anything* to avoid it!"

He crossed the few feet of space separating them in two long strides and grabbed her upper arms tightly. "God's Blood, this wasn't my idea! None of it! I didn't want to be here. I didn't want to stay once I *did* arrive."

"Then why did you, damn it? Why did you stay?" She tried to pull herself free of his grasp, but his hold on her tightened. "Everything was fine. I was *happy.* Danny was happy. Then you show up and make me want things to be different! Damn you for ruining everything. Damn you for coming here."

His eyes glittered.

Rebecca stared up into those eyes and whispered her last curse. "And damn you for leaving me."

He flinched.

She drew her foot back and swung it forward, slamming the toe of her boot into Zacariah's shin. He yelped at the starburst of pain in his leg, then released her abruptly. Focusing on the pain, he savored it as another man might a bottle of wine. As long as he had the pain to concentrate on, he didn't have to think about anything else.

Silently, he watched her storm into the house and slam the door behind her.

"Did you talk to the sheriff?"

Rebecca snorted. "I sure did."

Buck grimaced and nudged Zacariah into passing him the pepper. "What'd he say this time?"

"About the same as always." She shook her head and reached for her coffee cup. "Told me not to 'worry my pretty head about it.' Said it was sheriff business."

"Sheriff my great aunt Sadie's—" Buck broke off with a quick look into Danny's interested gaze. "Hat."

Rebecca went on. "He also says that we don't have proof that the horses have been stolen."

"They ain't here," Buck shouted. "He don't think that's proof?"

"Nope." She took a sip of coffee, then set her cup back down on the table. Glancing at her still-full plate, she pushed it away. Since her confrontation with Zack, her appetite was gone. Why had she said all those things? What had she been thinking?

She shot him a covert glance, then looked away again quickly.

"Why is this man the sheriff?" Zacariah asked no one in particular.

His voice lanced her heart.

"Nobody else wanted the job," Buck snapped. "And Cooper's just useless at it. Hell, that man wouldn't come outside that office of his if the place was on fire."

"Of course," Rebecca interrupted, forcing herself to take part in the discussion. "There *is* a bright side to all this."

Danny laughed.

Buck groaned as his head fell forward until his chin rested on his chest. "I swear, woman, you'd find the bright side to being mauled by a bear."

She smiled at Buck, and avoided looking at Zack. "Since Cooper doesn't believe me about rustlers, we don't have to worry about him interfering."

Buck snorted. "*That's* a bright spot? He don't interfere in anything!"

Rebecca frowned at him. "It's *my* bright spot." Toying with the handle of her coffee cup, she asked, "When are you expecting Scotty back?"

"Who knows? You told him to find either horses or tracks of the rustlers." Buck shrugged. "He could be out there days yet. He took enough supplies."

Rebecca nodded. It wasn't the first time Scotty had been gone for days at a time. For that matter, there had been plenty of times that Buck had spent days living in a line cabin on the range. When just a few men had several hundred acres to ride herd on, it didn't make sense for them to come back to the home ranch every evening.

But there were risks to such a life, too. Death courted cowboys through all manner of catastrophes. Beyond the weather, stampedes, landslides, snakes, wolves, flashfloods—a person still had to worry about the human kind of misery. And not just thieves or killers, either. Even a careful man could get killed all too easily and that wasn't even taking into account sickness. If a cowboy got into trouble while on his own, it could be days or even weeks before he could expect help. Sometimes, that help came too late.

"All right," she said finally. "We'll give him a few more days."

The older man nodded grimly.

"Buck," she said softly, "I know how you feel about Pine Creek Canyon, but . . ."

He cut her off with a quick glance at Zacariah. "It's all right, Becky. If we don't hear from Scotty in a couple of days, me and Zack'll head out lookin' for him."

"Pine Creek?" Danny asked. "Is that where . . ."

"Yes, honey," Rebecca interrupted and reached over to pat her son's hand.

"Can I go with you?" he asked.

Buck looked at the boy, clenched his jaw and shook his head.

Zacariah studied them, these people who'd come to mean so much to him. How had it happened? And when? Before coming to this place, he never would have believed that he could come to *care* for humans.

And now that he could admit he *did* care—what did it mean for him as a Collector? Would these new ... *feelings,* hinder him? Or help?

Zacariah's thoughts drifted away as he came back to the conversation at the table.

"Tell ya what, though, Danny," the foreman said softly. "How 'bout you and me ride out this afternoon and check the fence line on the south border?"

The boy's face lit up. Eyes wide and excited, he turned to his mother. "Can I, Ma?" he asked. "Can I?"

Rebecca gave Buck a small smile of thanks, then grinned at her son. "I think you'd better. This ranch will be yours one day, and you should learn everything you can from Buck."

"I'll go get ready now," Danny said, jumping up from the bench.

Zacariah watched the boy race out of the room, then his gaze shifted to Rebecca. The pain in her expression tore at him, forcing him to look away, directly into Buck's accusing stare.

He knew why the man was suddenly so hostile. He even understood it. Obviously, Buck had noticed Rebecca's agitation and had laid the blame, rightly, on Zacariah.

"How much longer you plannin' on stayin'?" Buck asked.

"A couple more weeks."

The older man tossed one last look at Rebecca's strained features, nodded abruptly, then pushed away from the table. The foreman left to follow Danny and silence settled in behind him.

Zacariah glanced at her, staring thoughtfully into her coffee cup, and a small twist of pain settled in him. How had this woman come to be so important to him? And why did it bother him to know that once he was gone, he would be forgotten by the very woman who would haunt him through eternity?

After several long moments, Rebecca spoke, keeping

her gaze fixed on her untouched coffee cup. "A couple more weeks?"

"Yes," he answered, his voice as hushed as hers.

She nodded slowly, then dragged a deep breath into her lungs. As if she'd made an important decision, she stood up and finally looked at him.

"Well then," she said. "We'd best make good use of the time we have left."

"The whole outside of the barn needs fresh paint," she said. "But we can start here."

The tack room, holding all of the saddles, bridles, leather-working tools and everything else required to care for and train horses, stood at the back of the barn. Jutting off the main building like a wart at the end of a witch's nose, the six-by-six room had no windows and no trim. It was as good a place as any to start painting.

"Buck sanded down the old paint job a couple of weeks ago, getting it ready. But then—" She shook her head and shrugged. "Well, something else always came up."

"Like the rustlers."

"And other things."

"Rebecca," he said quietly, "about what I said earlier."

A flush of heat rushed up her neck and stained her cheeks. She felt it and immediately bent down and dipped her brush into the brick-red paint. Turning quickly, she laid the bristles against the wood wall, then dragged the brush up and down slowly, making long, even strokes.

"Since you probably 'forgot' how to paint, too, this is how you do it." Her voice cracked painfully and she winced.

"Rebecca."

He wasn't going to let it go. She knew it as well as she knew that her insides were trembling just standing this close to him.

But she hadn't really expected to be able to forget the

things they'd said to each other. In fact, she didn't really want to. That confrontation with Zack had forced her to really look at what she wanted. And the sad truth of it was, she wanted a man who would be leaving all too soon.

Unless she could convince him to stay.

She didn't believe for a minute that he *had* to leave. He'd probably just gotten used to drifting. In the couple of weeks she had left with him, Rebecca was sure she could convince him that a home. With her. Would be better than anything else he might find.

All she needed now was the courage to do it.

The brush stilled on the wall. Her chin dropped to her chest momentarily as she sucked in one steadying breath after another. He laid one hand on her shoulder and she jumped.

"We don't need to talk about this again."

"Rebecca, it wasn't my intention to hurt you."

Sighing, she set the paintbrush down on the rim of the can and straightened up to face him. Squinting past the afternoon sunlight, she stared into the eyes that so disconcerted her. "I know."

He smiled and lifted one hand to cup her cheek.

"I didn't expect to find anything like you," he said.

His too-long black hair fell across his forehead and she reached up to smooth it back, allowing her fingertips to trace lightly over his flesh.

"You were a surprise to me, too."

A brief, sad smile lifted one corner of his mouth. "I wish I knew what to say."

"The truth would be nice," she told him, knowing that she couldn't fight what she didn't know.

A shutter dropped over his eyes and she knew even before he spoke that she wouldn't be getting the answers she wanted.

"I've told you the truth."

She shook her head. "Not all of it."

"What do you mean?" he asked, acknowledging that

he couldn't give her what she claimed to want. The complete truth now would end whatever time they had left together. And he wanted that time with her.

She reached up and covered his hand with hers. Warmth speared through him. Holding his hand to her cheek, she said, "I want to know why you're here. If you didn't want to come, why did you? Where are you from? Where are you going when you leave? All the things you're hiding."

"Rebecca." He shook his head slowly, regretfully.

She ignored him and went on. "I want to know how it is a drifter can stumble up to my ranch and into my life." She gulped a breath and continued in a voice tight with strain. "I want to know why I care that you're leaving."

Something inside him shattered.

What had the Minions been thinking when they'd sentenced him to a month of human life? Why hadn't they considered how his time here would affect the people around him?

They'd condemned him for his lack of responsibility, but were they any better? In using human emotions and feelings to teach him a lesson, they were bringing pain to the very mortals they expected *him* to treat with respect.

When faced with his continuing silence, Rebecca stepped back from him and stuffed her hands into her jeans' pockets. She let her head fall back on her neck and stared up at the deep blue sky overhead until she realized that Zacariah's eyes were that very color.

Perfect, she told herself as she straightened up. Now that she'd noticed, she'd never again be able to look at the sky without thinking of him . . . and this moment.

Damn him anyway for making her want him. Despite her own doubts and suspicions about him, she was drawn to him. His patience with Danny. His quiet strength. His willingness to work, all spoke to her.

But even those things weren't all of it.

It was, simply, him.

His touch. The feel of his arms sliding around her, holding her close. His mouth on hers, gently teasing, tempting.

She'd never experienced such wild, all-consuming passion before. With Daniel, lovemaking had been quick, almost furtive. As if being friends had robbed them of the right to become lovers.

Ironic, to finally discover passion with a man determined to leave her as quickly as he could.

"Rebecca . . ."

She pulled one hand free of her jeans and rubbed her forehead.

"If I could tell you what you want to know," he said softly, "I would."

She nodded and moved to pick up the paintbrush again.

He stopped her with one hand on her arm.

"Let go, Zack. Please."

"I can't do that, either."

A shallow breath shot down her throat and she held it, afraid that she wouldn't be able to draw another.

He stepped up close to her and bent his head to hers.

The breath in her chest eased from her lungs on a sigh as his lips touched hers.

Her knees gave out and she swayed against him. His arms tightened around her middle and she felt him easing them to the ground. Spring grasses cushioned them and lent a sweet, clean scent to the air.

He lifted his head and she opened her eyes to look up at him. Silhouetted against the sky, she squinted into the brightness and focused on the brilliant blue eyes studying her so intently.

Slowly, she lifted one hand and smoothed her calloused fingertips across his cheekbones and along his jaw. Every touch was like lightning. Every caress set another fire raging in her blood.

He smiled and carefully brushed her hair back from her forehead. Then his fingers slid across her features until he'd reached her mouth. Gently, he rubbed the pad of his thumb across her lips.

When her tongue darted out to touch his flesh, Zacariah's heartbeat staggered. He trembled with the ferocity of the feelings building inside him.

With the sun on his back and Rebecca held close beneath him, he experienced a sense of completion that he'd never known before. Slowly, he bent his head to hers and claimed her lips in a tender kiss. Her hands slid up his arms to encircle his neck and Zacariah told himself to remember. Remember it all, so that centuries from now, he would be able to draw on the memory and experience it all again.

Using his new knowledge, he parted his lips, inviting her inside. When her tongue slipped into his warmth, he groaned and held her tighter. In a silent dance of passion, their tongues twisted and caressed, promising each other fulfillment and even more hunger.

His hands moved over her reverently, exploring the rich curves he'd known so briefly during their last encounter. She gasped and arched into him as his palm cupped her breast.

He responded by brushing his fingertips across her hardened nipple and felt his own body react immediately. A groan slipped from his throat as he gently freed her shirt buttons, one by one. And then all that lay between him and her smooth flesh was a fine, white cotton undergarment, held together with pale yellow ribbons.

Mouth dry, heartbeat drumming in his ears, Zacariah tore his gaze from the treasure before him long enough to look at her face.

She gave him a small, nervous smile as her fingers tugged at the silken ribbons. Keeping his gaze locked with hers, he moved his hand to cover hers, so that together, they disposed of the fragile material hiding her from him.

When the last ribbon was free, Rebecca pulled a deep breath into her lungs and exhaled on a sigh. She lifted his hand to her mouth and keeping her gaze on him, placed a single kiss in the palm.

"Touch me, Zack," she whispered. "Touch me before I shatter from the wanting."

She watched him admire her and felt a flush of heat race through her. He looked at her with wide-eyed wonder and made her feel . . . beautiful. Gingerly, he drew one finger down the center of her chest and she shivered at the tender caress.

Sunlight lay across her naked flesh and a soft breeze brushed over her. From somewhere in the distance, she heard birdsong and she inhaled the sweet, springtime scent surrounding them.

Somehow, lying with him outside, under the cloud-dotted sky, seemed right. As if the heavens looked down on them in blessing.

Slowly, Zacariah smoothed his palms over her bared breasts and she swallowed back a moan of pleasure. She glanced at him and her eyes filled with sudden tears at the expression on his face. Like a blind man whose sight has been miraculously restored, he looked at her as though she was the most precious treasure on Earth.

His fingertips moved over the hardened bud of her nipple and he gasped along with her when her skin tightened at his touch.

She'd never felt more cherished.

She'd never experienced such . . . wonder.

Again and again, he repeated his caress until Rebecca was straining beneath him. She felt every nerve in her body screaming for his attention. Waves of affection and desire rocked her and in the heart of her, damp heat gathered in anticipation.

She reached for him, smoothing her hand along the front of his shirt, slowly undoing the buttons that kept her from touching him as he did her. When his shirt hung open, Rebecca trailed her fingertips along his muscled chest and smiled to herself when he trembled.

His body tightened and he shifted uncomfortably. Incredible sensations swept through him. Light and fire and peace and excitement clamored together in his chest and urged his heartbeat into a ragged pounding that shook him to his toes.

Drawn by his own growing need to feel all of her, to explore every inch of her warm, human flesh, Zacariah dipped his head and took one of her nipples into his mouth. His tongue swirled around the hard nubbin and her soft sigh was his reward. Loving her, tasting her, he marvelled at the fact that by bringing her pleasure, his own pleasure was doubled.

Emboldened by his success, he shifted slightly and moved one hand down along the line of her sun-kissed body. He followed the curve of her waist to the rounded fullness of her hip. His palm slipped across her flat abdomen to smooth over the length of her leg.

Her warmth seeped into him. Like candlelight in a cave, the glowing light eased slowly into the shadows of cold still hiding inside him.

He couldn't breathe and he didn't care. The rush of his own blood thundered in his ears and his heart pounded so violently in his chest, he thought it might explode from his body and *still* he didn't care. All that mattered was in his arms. All that mattered was Rebecca. Her next touch. Her next kiss.

He lifted his head finally, gasping in air like a drowning man plucked from the water.

"Zack," she whispered huskily. "I want to feel you. *All* of you." Her gaze lowered briefly before she looked up steadily into his eyes. "Make love to me, Zack."

His mouth dry, his throbbing groin pressing against his jeans, demanding freedom, he felt one glorious moment of incredible delight. Then worry set in. Not enough worry to stop the need driving his body, but enough to make him start thinking.

He had no idea what to do. How could he make love

to this woman when he hadn't the slightest notion on how to go about it? Oh, he knew that his own hard, throbbing flesh was designed to fit inside Rebecca's.

His heart began pounding even harder at the thought. But there was still enough panic in him to admit that he had no idea just how he was supposed to go about inserting himself where he should be. And what if there was something that all human males knew and he didn't? Could he hurt her?

She looked far too small to accommodate the part of him that was hard and ready.

"Zack," she said in a rush, "I need you. More than I ever thought possible, I need you. Now."

"I need you, too, Rebecca. I have for a long time," he said and knew it for the simple truth. "But . . ."

"No buts," she interrupted with a shake of her head. "And no promises. I'm not an untried virgin, Zacariah. I'm a widow. A grown woman. And I know what I'm doing."

He only wished he did.

Chapter ❈ Twelve

She reached up to stroke his chest and his eyes slid shut at the magic in her touch. When her fingertips strayed down further, he held his breath, hoping she wouldn't stop. She tugged at his belt buckle, her fingers suddenly clumsy. Half-rising, she lifted herself until she could brush kisses over his chest and graze his own flattened nipple with the tip of her tongue.

Zacariah gasped and quickly moved to undo the damned belt. Brushing her questing fingers aside, he yanked at the buckle, mindless with want and need. His worries cast aside for the moment, he fumbled with the buttons on his jeans while she did the same with hers.

He couldn't stop looking at her. Sunlight spilled over her, making her skin glow and her hair shine like a night fire. Her clear green eyes were hazy with passion and as she slipped out of her clothes and lay down again on the new grass, he realized that he would never again know a moment like this one. Eternity stretched out behind and ahead of him, yet here, in this one, sunlit moment of time, with this one woman, he'd found something he hadn't realized he'd been searching for.

The fact that this was a stolen moment—a moment that would end all too soon—only made it more precious.

She slowly untied the rawhide string at the end of her

braid. Then, she separated the ropes of her hair until the rich, reddish-brown mass lay in undulating waves about her shoulders and across her breasts. She held one hand out to him and Zacariah hurriedly stripped and lay down beside her.

He wanted to hold her tightly to him, feel her flesh against his and commit the sensation to memory so that he would always have her close.

His hands smoothed over her, exploring every valley and curve. He dipped his head to taste her breasts again and lovingly gave first one, then the other, his attention.

Rebecca's breath came fast and shallow, her head tipped back on her neck and her eyes closed on a sigh. His right hand slipped along her rib cage, and over her hip. She shifted beneath him, arching into his touch and parting her thighs.

Zacariah lifted his head from her breast, placed one soft, brief kiss on her lips, then began to stroke her heated skin gently. Again, she lifted her hips and this time, he understood her silent plea.

His palm covered her center and her breath caught. She turned her face to one side and bit down hard on her bottom lip. Concerned, afraid that he'd done something wrong, Zacariah lifted his hand from her body only to return it at her quiet moan of disappointment.

Damp heat pressed against his hand and he caressed her gently, sparking another moan from the woman desperately trying to hide her face from his gaze.

"Rebecca?"

Her fingers clutched at him. Her thighs fell further apart, even as she tried to burrow her head into his side.

"Lord, Zack," she whispered brokenly, "help me."

His mouth went dry. His heartbeat staggered. His body tightened until he thought he would burst. Why didn't he *know* what to do? Why must he guess?

She shivered in the circle of his arm and whimpered quietly. Her heat pulled at him, seducing him, urging him to touch her deeper. Unsure of what else to do, he gave in to his own desires and slipped one finger into the damp, warmth of her and groaned at the tight feel of her body. Here, he told himself, with sure, sudden knowledge. Here is the spot that was meant to cradle his flesh. He smiled to himself as he pushed his finger deeper within her.

Her hips lifted as she pushed her body into his touch. Another finger joined the first in her depths and he sighed as she shifted to welcome him. Zacariah pulled in breath after shaky breath and realized that he wanted to be buried inside her. He needed to become a part of her. To feel her body holding him to her.

And at that thought, his doubts rushed to the surface again. What if he did something wrong? What if he wasn't any good at the one thing that now seemed more important than anything else? What if he failed her?

Rebecca's hand smoothed down his chest until her fingers curled around his aching hard body and he flinched at the jolt of pleasure. He groaned quietly as her hand began to move on him, caressing, rubbing the rigid length of him until he was surging into her hand, his hips rocking instinctively.

His heart raced, his blood boiled and deep within him, a new and horrifingly overpowering feeling built. Her hand squeezed gently and he pushed himself into her grasp, needing her touch. Needing . . . *something*. His mind was lost in a jumble of thoughts. Nothing mattered. Nothing beyond the touch of her hand and the mounting sense that something incredible was about to happen.

Inside him, tension built. Eyes closed, he tried desperately to ease the mounting sense of expectation. He knew something waited for him, just beyond his reach. He felt it growing within him. His hips pumped frantically as Rebecca's mouth moved over his throat and chest. He felt her lips, her tongue, blazing trails of heat and wonder across his skin. Her breath washed over him like a blessing. He felt the imprint of each of her fingers as she rubbed and stroked his hard body.

His breath staggered. He opened his eyes to stare into nothingness as a wildness crept over him.

And then she released him.

He wanted to scream. He wanted to beg her not to stop. To touch him again. To make those feelings return. He felt like a drowning man, raised to the surface of the water, high enough to see the light of day—only to be thrown back into the deep.

She looked up at him and whispered, "I need to feel you inside me, Zack. Deep inside me."

He wanted that, too. He just didn't want to ruin this incredible moment with her by making a stupid mistake. But how to tell her? He withdrew his hand from her center, and she sighed her regret. Caressing her smooth, warm skin, he finally said, "Rebecca, I don't know—"

"What?" She turned her face to leave a kiss on his chest.

One of his hands moved to cup her breast, his thumb and forefinger teasing her hardened nipple. He swallowed his own fear of looking like a fool and admitted, "I'm not sure what to do. How to make you . . ." He gritted his teeth and closed his eyes, disgusted with his own ineptitude.

A moment or two of silence stretched out between them before Rebecca said softly, "You're doing fine, Zack." Her fingertips dusted across the base of his abdomen and his hips jerked in response.

"We'll discover each other together, all right?"

Emotion roared up within him. As she urged him to cover her with his body, he wondered wildly what he had done over the centuries that had brought him to this woman. To this time.

He knelt between her parted thighs. She lifted her hips in silent welcome. He glanced down at their bodies and watched as he carefully entered her. Slowly, afraid of hurting her, he pushed himself forward, inch by glorious inch.

And then he was buried within her.

Tight.

Hot.

Wet.

Zacariah's eyes closed tightly, his hips jerked violently and his world exploded into bright shards of color and texture. His body rocked in convulsions as he emptied himself into her. On and on it went in wave after wave of profound pleasure that seemed to know no beginning and no end.

He heard himself shout her name as he fell through space helpless in the grip of something more powerful than he had ever imagined. He collapsed atop her as the tremors finally began to ease into ripples of satisfaction. Opening his eyes again, he saw her face, just a breath away from his own.

From somewhere, he managed to dredge up the energy to lift his head long enough to kiss her. Then his eyes slid shut and he collapsed again.

A soft smile drifted across Rebecca's face. Her hands smoothed up and down his back and she took a moment to enjoy the solid feel of him lying atop her.

If he thought he was finished, though, he was sorely mistaken. Was it possible? she wondered. She'd noticed the awestruck expression he wore whenever he touched her. Had he actually been a virgin? She smiled again. That would certainly explain why her body was still humming with need and unfulfilled want.

She lifted her legs, locked them around his middle and arched into him.

He groaned slightly and his eyes opened wide. "We're not finished?"

"We're just getting started," she whispered.

Zacariah grinned and came up on his elbows to look down at her. "You mean there's more?"

"So much more," she answered softly and raised her head long enough to kiss him briefly.

He moved one hand to cup her breast and her insides twisted and shimmered with promises of delight. She'd never felt anything close to what she felt when Zack touched her. Sparks of awareness sputtered through her blood, igniting her body from within.

She sighed, rocked her hips slightly and felt him grow and swell inside her. He completed her as if God had designed his body and hers to be a perfect match. His manhood stretched and filled her body until nothing remained but he and she, locked together.

He rose up on his knees and looked down at her and at the place of their joining. Dragging the tips of his fingers across her belly, he said softly, "Show me. Show me what you want."

Rebecca's breath caught at the beauty of the moment. She wasn't a shy virgin. She was a grown woman with needs that she'd never acknowledged before. And she wanted this man more than she'd ever wanted anything in her life.

Slowly, she pulled his hand from her breast and drew it down to the spot where their bodies met. He nodded silently as she placed his hand against her center and then he quickly proved that he didn't need any more instructions.

He leaned back and slid his fingertips across her damp, sensitive flesh. She gasped and her spine arched into a bow. He seemed to instinctively know the one spot to concentrate his energies on and as he teased that tender piece of skin, Rebecca twisted and writhed beneath him.

Bright, gaudy colors swirled behind her closed eyes as her hips moved against his hand and the hard length of him. She felt him reach up and take one of her nipples between his thumb and forefinger and suddenly, she had three sensations crashing down on her at once.

His hard body pushed higher and higher inside her as

his hips moved in a rhythm as old as time. His finger on the bead of skin at her center rubbed back and forth until she wasn't sure if she could stand the torture another moment. All she *was* sure of was that if he stopped, she might die.

Her body limp with sensation, yet tense with expectation, Rebecca's legs tightened around his waist, pulling him deeper within her. She opened her eyes to watch him. She wanted to see his face. Feel his breath. Read the pleasure in his eyes and try to find the love she hoped was there, waiting for her.

Tendrils of fire spiraled up from her core. She welcomed the spreading heat. Felt the building intensity and she knew that satisfaction was within her reach. Ragged breaths tore from her throat. Her short nails dug into his shoulders. Her head tipped back into the spring grass as the first tremor shook her.

She arched into him, lifting herself off the ground to press against his body as she rode the crest of the wave tearing through her. She cried out at the explosiveness of the release. Unshed tears gathered in her eyes and spilled over as moment after moment passed and still her body shivered and quaked with a pleasure more profound than she'd believed existed.

Staring up into his eyes, she felt her soul shatter and come together again. She held his body locked within hers and knew he had touched her so deeply that she would never again be alone.

He groaned and his features twisted into a mask of painful joy. Her fingers curled into his shoulders as he pushed against her, cried her name and poured all that he was into her warmth.

Seconds stretched into minutes and still they lay on the grass, side by side, oblivious to the world around them. Still stunned at the wild explosions of sensation that had gripped him, Zacariah might have lain there, unmoving, for hours, if a familiar voice hadn't echoed in his mind.

"Zacariah, you've actually mated with one of them? Oh, what will the Minions say about this?"

"God's Blood and chalice!" he shouted, sitting bolt upright.

"What is it?" Rebecca demanded. "What's wrong?"

"Oh, Zacariah, I believe you really have gone too far this time," Mordecai told him.

He scowled at the Collector hovering nearby and snatched up his pants. Tugging them on, he just managed to keep from shouting at his old friend. All he needed was for Rebecca to see him yelling at thin air.

"Zack?"

He glanced over his shoulder to see her push herself into a sitting position. Torn between relief and disappointment, he noted that she was hastily gathering up her clothes and throwing them on.

"What's going on, Zack?"

Glaring at Mordecai, who politely looked away from the spectacle in front of him, Zacariah said lamely, "I, uh . . . thought someone was watching us."

Mordecai chuckled.

"Watching us?" she repeated as she stood up and pulled her jeans on. "Who? From where?" She swiveled her head around, taking in the empty yard and surrounding meadow.

"I don't know," he said. "It was just a feeling."

She pushed her hair back from her face and looked up at him. "Fine time to be getting 'feelings.' "

"Yeah," he grumbled and shot another disgusted glance at the Collector.

Mordecai gave him a half-bow.

Rebecca drew a long, shuddering breath. To have such a deeply intimate moment shattered so abruptly was disconcerting to say the least. She cast another quick look around the lonely landscape surrounding the ranch. She'd had no sense of an intruder. But then, until a few moments ago, she'd felt nothing but Zacariah and the whispered rush of passion stealing through her bloodstream.

And dammit, she wanted it all again. What she'd said to him earlier was true. She was all grown-up, with no one but herself to answer to. If she wanted to lie in the sunshine with a man who made her feel more alive . . . more precious than she ever had before, it was no one's business but hers.

And his.

She glanced at Zacariah and noted his stiff posture and the hard, almost grim set of his features. His head dipped in a barely perceptible nod, as if he was listening to someone or something she couldn't hear.

She laughed inwardly.

Ridiculous.

"Zack?"

He half-turned to look at her and his features softened slightly.

"Are you all right?"

He nodded and lifted one hand to touch her face gently before dropping back to his side.

"Zacariah, we must talk."

Scowling to himself, Zacariah wished his old friend anywhere in the universe but there.

"I think I'll finish painting, Rebecca."

"Painting?" she asked. "Now?"

He reached up and rubbed the back of his neck. "Yeah," he said with a shrug. "Buck and Danny will be back soon. It had better look like I've done something in the time they've been gone."

"All right," she said and stepped closer to him. When she wrapped her arms around his neck, his own arms went around her, pulling her close.

For a moment or two, he savored the feel of her against him once more. She left a kiss on his neck, then stepped back. "If you're going to be painting, I might as well go in and start supper."

She gave him a tender smile, then turned for the house. Halfway there, she turned and looked at him over her shoulder. "Zack? You're not sorry, are you?"

Zacariah shoved both hands into his pockets and shook his head firmly. "Not a bit."

"Good. Me either."

He watched her walk away from him and didn't tear his gaze away until she'd stepped into the house and closed the door behind her. Only then did he turn around to look at the Collector, patiently waiting for his attention.

"What do you want, Mordecai?"

"You're not sorry?"

"No." He bent down, snatched up the paint brush Rebecca'd left on the rim of the can and dipped it into the paint. No matter what the Minions decided to do to him for this latest transgression, he couldn't be sorry. And that was saying quite a bit.

"Fascinating. Simply fascinating." Mordecai shook his head and drifted to Zacariah's side. *"You're serving out a punishment because of your mistakes . . . and while doing so, commit an even greater one. Yet you don't regret it."*

One corner of his mouth lifted in a wry smile. He could hardly blame Mordecai for being surprised. Not so long ago, he wouldn't have believed it of himself, either. But, one thing he'd learned during his time as a human was that things changed. Daily.

Apparently, he was changing, too.

"Still," the Collector muttered, more to himself than to his friend, *"I don't believe I've ever heard of an immortal actually mating with a human."*

"But for the next couple of weeks, I'm not an immortal, am I?"

Mordecai brightened considerably. "That's true! Perhaps the Minions will take that fact into consideration.

*Although, I'm sure they were expecting you to conduct
yourself with a bit more . . . circumspection.''*

Zacariah slapped paint onto the bare wood and glared
briefly at the being beside him. "They made me human
for a month. Did they expect me to continue acting as a
Collector even though, for all intents and purposes, I'm a
mortal?'

*"They don't make me privy to what they do and do not
expect, Zacariah." Mordecai tugged at the sleeves of his
robe, then smoothed the fall of fabric with the flat of one
hand. "They merely inform us when they are displeased,
as you should remember all too well.''*

He did remember. Everything.

*"There is still time for you to redeem yourself in their
eyes, Zacariah.''*

"How?" His gaze narrowed suspiciously.

*"Come back with me. Now. Plead for forgiveness.
Prostrate yourself.'' The Collector leaned in closer. "I'm
sure they will be the very souls, pardon the expression, of
mercy, Zacariah.''*

He shook his head. "They sentenced me to a month."

*"Yes, yes." Mordecai waved one hand dismissively.
"But only the Path is eternal.''*

The Path and perhaps, Zacariah acknowledged silently,
regret.

He stared at the brick-red paint as it soaked into the
thirsty wood and realized that he was much like that paint.
He was being drawn deeper into the lives of the humans
from whom he'd been sent to learn.

As he layered more of the thick liquid onto the wood,
he wondered if he, too, would become a part of them, just
as the paint was now a part of the wall it had covered.

"Zacariah, you have only to—''

"Beg," he finished abruptly and shook his head, dismissing both his own wild thoughts and Mordecai's suggestion. "I won't beg them for mercy and that's the end
of it."

"Because of your pride."

"No, not just because of that." Zacariah turned a steady look on his friend. "I was sentenced here to experience being human, and that's what I'm going to do." He pointed one finger at the Collector. "And as long as we're talking," he added, "there's something else about humans that I'd like to experience."

"By the Path," Mordecai asked, *"what's left?"*

"Privacy."

"Ahh . . ." He inclined his head toward the ranch house and smiled. *"Going to do it again, aren't you?"*

A sudden, inexplicable yet undeniable flash of anger shot through him. His fingers tightened on the paintbrush and he had to grit his teeth to keep from actually shouting at his oldest friend. When he'd controlled his emotions sufficiently, he said softly, "Don't sneak up on me unannounced again, Mordecai."

"I do not sneak." The Collector shook his head. *"If I herald my appearance with a booming voice coming out of nowhere, these mortals will think they're hearing ghosts."*

"Fine. Thunder will do. A loud clap of thunder should be enough to let me know you're coming."

"Unless it's raining."

Zacariah smiled tightly. "I'll take my chances."

"You even sound mortal." After a moment, he asked, *"Tell me, Zacariah. Have you given any thought to the Collection you must make when your month is finished?"*

"No." He hadn't forgotten about it, but he didn't want to think about it, either.

Who was it? Buck? Scotty? Danny? *Rebecca?*

Then another familiar face swam into his mind. Ellie Parker. The small, too-fragile girl with the pale face and gentle smile. Was it she?

"No, I haven't given it much thought." Glancing at his friend, he asked, "Do you know who it is?"

Mordecai shook his head slowly. "You know better

than that, Zacariah. No one knows until the time of Collection is upon them.''

Zacariah nodded, and glanced over his shoulder at the ranch house. Only late afternoon and Rebecca had already set a lighted lamp in the window. Somehow, that bright glow reached across the yard to burn inside him.

Ignored, Mordecai moved away from the man. Waving one hand, he drew a swirl of mist up from the ground and as it twisted around him, he said, "I'm leaving now, Zacariah. But for the sake of the Path, remember who you are and why you're here. You can't afford to make the Minions angry again.''

Chapter ❊ Thirteen

Scotty picketed his horse in a patch of new grass near enough to the creek that the animal could drink when it wanted. Once his horse was taken care of, he tossed his saddle and bags down beside the campfire, then stretched out on the ground.

Too early to make camp, really, but Scotty'd done enough riding for one day. He'd travelled all over the far reaches of the ranch holdings searching for strays. He'd only managed to round up one or two head, though, for all his work.

Glancing to his left, he checked quickly to make sure that both horses were still securely tied to the ancient pine that sheltered his campsite. Restive and clearly unhappy, his untamed captives pawed at the ground and took turns tugging at the ropes binding them.

Scowling to himself, he fed another branch into the greedy flames and reminded himself exactly why he was doing all this.

Rebecca.

At once, her image rose up in his mind and his features softened slightly. The fire crackled loudly as it snapped over the fresh wood. Water in his coffeepot began to boil and he dumped a handful of grounds into the water.

Yeah, he was willing to put up with a lot for that

woman. Even riding his tail into the ground on a fruitless mission. Frowning again, he used the tips of his fingers to push the coffeepot closer to the fire. An immediate stinging sensation began and he jerked his hand back from the flames.

Lying down with his head resting on the worn leather saddle, Scotty promised himself that this nonsense would end soon. Once Rebecca saw how few of her horses were remaining, she was bound to admit that the ranch was lost. Then she would turn to him for comfort. For advice. And eventually, for love.

And what about Zack? his mind wanted to know. *What if she's cozying up to that drifter while Scotty was out getting blisters on his butt?*

Sure, he was taking a risk, leaving the two of them alone. But it was a chance he had to take. If he could convince her that he'd done his damndest to save her ranch, then she would be grateful to him. And gratitude was a good start.

As for Zack, well, Scotty would deal with him when the time was right.

Two days later, Rebecca drove the wagon right down the center of Main Street and tried not to notice how many people were staring at them. As the Hale wagon rolled down the wide road, couples paused on the boardwalk and exchanged a private word or two. Shopkeepers stepped outside their stores and one or two people openly gawked.

Rebecca shifted uncomfortably on the bench seat and shot a quick glance at Zacariah, seated beside her. Apparently, he hadn't noticed anything amiss. With one foot braced on the jumpseat's edge, he had his hat brim pulled down low over his eyes and a blank expression on his face.

That shouldn't surprise her, though.

Despite what they'd shared together only two days ago, neither of them had mentioned the interlude. She wasn't entirely sure why Zack wasn't talking. For her own part, Rebecca didn't know what she *could* say. Or how to say it. As far as she knew, there was no polite way for a lady to ask a man to 'please make love with me again.'

Odd, she called it. This feeling of being closer to a man than she'd ever felt before—yet still so separate from him, she had no idea what he was thinking most of the time.

"Ma." Danny leaned over the back of the seat and placed both small hands on his mother's shoulders.

"Hmmm?"

"You think Ellie's feelin' better now?"

"I hope so." Surely the girl was on the mend. Helen would have sent word to her if there was anything seriously wrong.

"Me, too." The boy turned his head to look at Zacariah. "Do *you* think she's better now, Zack?"

Rebecca flicked a quick glance at him and was almost certain she saw him wince. Strangely enough, knowing that Zack shared her concern was somehow comforting.

It had been too long since she'd had someone with whom to share her burdens.

"I don't know, Danny," Zack said softly, forcing a strained smile for the child. "We'll just have to see."

Rebecca brought the team to a stop just outside the general store. She didn't say a word when Danny scrambled over the edge of the wagon, jumped to the boardwalk and ran through the open doorway. After throwing the brake lever, she wrapped the reins tight around it and turned on the seat.

Zacariah had already climbed down and was waiting to help her.

Rebecca stood up, stepped over the side to the wagon wheel and handed her shopping basket to him. He set it down, then reached up and placed both hands at her waist. In one easy motion, he swung her down to the boardwalk. Instead of releasing her right away though, his hold on her tightened.

"It feels good to touch you again," he said softly.

Rebecca's knees wobbled and an instant surge of damp warmth rushed through her body to settle low in her center. If he enjoyed touching her, why had he kept his distance the last couple of days? To be fair though, she could have gone to him. And hadn't.

Why? It was certainly too late to try to keep from feeling anything for him. But she knew the answer. Danny. How could she allow herself to care for a man—let her son become attached to a man—who kept insisting he was leaving?

She stared up into those incredible eyes of his and tried to imagine never seeing them again. Emptiness yawned open inside her and a wave of cold washed over her. She felt the insistent pressure of his fingers at her waist and for a moment wished that the two of them were alone somewhere.

Anywhere.

"Zack . . ." she whispered, then glanced past him at the storefront. Reality crashed down around her and she took a reluctant step back from him. This wasn't the time or the place to indulge in the emotions Zacariah wrought in her. Taking one of his hands, she smiled as he threaded his fingers through hers, locking them together. He squeezed her palm gently as if he understood exactly what she was thinking.

She shot him a quick look. "We'd better go inside."

He nodded grimly, then turned for the Parkers' store.

The shadowy interior of the mercantile blinded him temporarily, but as his eyes became accustomed to the gloom, he saw the two people standing near the counter.

Helen's breath choked and she took a half step toward them.

"Oh, Lordy," Rebecca whispered and released him to hurry to her friend's side. She held the other woman in a tight embrace as Helen's silent weeping tore at Zacariah in a way that not even the most violent sobs had ever done. The tall, blond man behind the two women wore an expression that seemed carved out of stone. But his dry eyes were tortured.

Hesitantly, unsure just what to do in such a situation, Zacariah took a single step forward. To his right, he heard the quick scuttle of nails on wood and frowned at the shepherd dog slinking away from him.

"Zack?"

He swiveled his head toward her.

Keeping one arm tight around her friend's shoulders, Rebecca said, "This is Helen's husband, Tom."

The man jerked him a stiff nod. "Helen's spoken of you," he said. "I thank you for carrying my girl home the other day."

Zacariah inclined his head, then looked a question at Rebecca, wondering how the girl was doing.

She lifted one shoulder helplessly.

Helen sniffed loudly, straightened up and lifted her chin. "If you give me your list, Becky, I'll fill your order."

"Oh Helen . . ."

"Please, it helps to be busy." The woman rubbed one hand across the mound of her belly and smiled half-heartedly. "The baby is active, I might as well be, too."

"I'll get their order, dear," Tom said quietly and stepped up behind his wife to guide her to a nearby rocking chair. "I want you to rest for a moment or two."

Once his wife was seated, Tom took Rebecca's list and nodded toward the stairs. "You can go up and see her if you'd like. I'm sure she'd enjoy it."

Acting purely on instinct, Zacariah walked to Rebecca's side and took her hand in his. Squeezing her fingers slightly, he smiled when she returned the pressure. Together, they started for the stairs, only to stop again when clattering bootsteps announced the fact that someone was coming down.

Billy Jenkins looked far older than sixteen.

Sympathy stabbed at Zacariah and the jab was so sharp it almost stole his breath.

The boy's eyes were sad and tired, as if he'd lain awake for too many nights. When he saw Rebecca and Zacariah, he dipped his head in greeting before turning to the Parkers.

"She seems better today, don't ya think?"

Helen looked at him and smiled weakly.

"She even yelled at me some because I didn't pass that arithmetic test at school yesterday." His features held a look of such desperate hope that all four adults were struck dumb by the boy's pain. "That's good, ain't it?" He took a step or two closer to Helen. "That she got mad at me. It's good, right?"

"Of course it is, Billy," Helen told him, her lips twisting.

"I knew it" He nodded at her and smiled while a sheen of water filled his eyes and trickled over to run down his face unchecked. "I knew she was better. She even said that she'd give me what for tomorrow if I don't do better."

"She will, too," Tom assured him.

"Yeah." Billy nodded, then reached up and pulled his hat brim lower on his forehead. He wiped the tears from his face with the back of his hand and started for the slash of sunshine spearing through the doorway. "I'll be back tomorrow," he said just before he disappeared into the light.

When the boy was gone, Helen's head fell forward onto her chest and her quiet sobs began anew. The list forgotten, Tom hurried around the edge of the counter to his wife's side, then pulled her into his arms. Her head on his shoulder, she wept for herself and for the father wounded too deeply to cry.

Rebecca walked into the small room ahead of Zack. By the time he reluctantly entered, she was seated on the mattress beside Ellie, the young girl's hand firmly clasped in hers.

"Mornin', Mr. Cole." Ellie's voice seemed as fragile as she looked.

"Good morning, Ellie." He swallowed to dislodge the knot in his throat. "How are you feeling?"

"Better," she said and nodded her head as if to underline her own words. "Mama says I can get out of bed soon and go back to school."

"You miss school?" Rebecca laughed gently and patted the child's hand. "You're going to have to have a talk with Danny for me."

"Oh, I will." Ellie stared off through the open window on her right where sounds of the town outside slipped through to keep her company. She lay quietly for a moment, watching the green-and-white checked curtains flutter in the soft wind creeping under the sash. When she spoke again, her voice came slowly, like a spring breeze dying of cold. "He'll like school once he starts. I do. I miss reading and doing my numbers and I miss my friends most."

Zacariah couldn't speak. And even if he'd been able to scratch out a sound, what could he say? Damn the Minions for putting him in such a position. Damn his own growing emotions for leaving him open to such raw pain and confusion.

When Ellie's thin voice faded away, thankfully Rebecca was there to fill in the silence.

"We saw Billy leaving when we came in."

The girl turned her head on the pillow and smiled at Rebecca. "He comes to see me every day," she whispered.

"Is he your beau?"

"Uh-huh." Ellie looked down and began to pluck at the crocheted, white lace coverlet spread over her.

"And what does your pa have to say about that?" Rebecca teased and Zacariah hoped that Ellie didn't hear the catch in her voice.

"Papa worries," the girl's small voice admitted. She shuddered slightly and took a deep breath that hardly moved the sheet and blanket draped over her narrow chest. She looked up again and made a visible effort to strengthen her tone before she continued. "But I love Billy and I'm gonna marry him as soon as I'm old enough."

Rebecca sucked in a gulp of air and his admiration for her swelled when she grinned and said, "Don't you forget to invite me to the wedding."

"I promise," Ellie told her just before a stream of dark red blood poured from her nose. "Oh no." She sighed. "Not again."

Rebecca stood up quickly and pulled the pillow from under Ellie's head. Shaking it from its cotton slip, she tossed the pillow to the floor and hurriedly folded the fabric into a pad that she pressed to Ellie's nose.

"It's all right, darlin'," she whispered in a soft, singing tone. "It'll stop in a minute." Rebecca's free hand stroked the child's auburn hair back from her forehead, while at the same time, she continued her hushed comforting.

Zacariah stood like a statue, unable to move. Blankly, he stared at the small form beneath the covers now stained horribly with a wild, red pattern. He saw Ellie's delicate hands lying limply along her sides and heard her soft whimpers of distress.

His insides churned. Sweat broke out on his back and rolled along his spine. His hands clenched into helpless fists and his jaw tightened until he thought it would shatter.

This was what they felt.

This was why humans chanted and prayed and lit candles to hold him and his kind at bay.

This hideous, all-encompassing rage and pity and sorrow was what pushed humans into challenging the Minions, the Collectors and even God Himself.

Pain splintered in his chest until it almost blinded him. He took a halting step back, out of the way. His gaze locked on the whimpering child and the woman comforting her despite her own shaking hands.

Zacariah steadied his gaze on the girl and stared through her, beyond her, looking for a sign of an encroaching path. It only took a moment. His jaw clenched tight, he reluctantly identified the flickering shimmer of golden cobblestones already beginning to form around her.

Regret, cold and sharp, pierced him.

Ellie would be his collection.

"Zack?"

He flinched away from his own thoughts and looked at Rebecca. Judging by her expression, it wasn't the first time she'd called him.

"What?"

She frowned slightly, but never stopped stroking the girl's clammy forehead. "Would you go downstairs and get Helen?"

Ellie cried softly.

He winced.

"I don't want to leave her," Rebecca finished.

"Sure." He jerked into action. "Of course." Clutching his hat brim in one tight fist as if it was a lifeline, he left the room.

A half hour later, Rebecca stepped into the hall and closed Ellie's bedroom door behind her. She pulled in a long, shuddering breath that hurt Zacariah just to watch.

She must have sensed his presence in the shadows, because she turned unerringly toward him and a heartbeat later was pressed against him, her arms locked around his neck.

He hadn't been able to leave. As much as he'd wanted to, he hadn't been able to leave without Rebecca. Instead, he'd hovered outside the bedroom door, listening to the murmuring voices and waiting.

His arms closed around her, holding her to him until he could absorb the tremors rippling through her body. He felt each breath she drew, and heard tears in her voice when she started to speak haltingly.

"Doc says it's a cancer of the blood."

Zacariah's eyes squeezed shut as if he could push away the memory of golden cobblestones shining around the little girl.

"He says she might last another year, with luck."

Two weeks, he told himself. At the most.

"A *year!*" She buried her face in the hollow of his throat to muffle her agonized whisper. "With *luck*. How could he even *say* that to Helen and Tom? How can he tell them that their little girl needs *luck* to see another spring?"

Helpless to change anything, yet desperate to try, he ran his hands up and down her back, comforting, soothing, much as she had done for Ellie.

"And a year of what?"

"Rebecca . . ."

"No!" Her fingers curled into his shirtfront and held on tight. "A year of lying in bed? Getting weaker? Sicker?" A sob broke her voice, but she fought it down to continue raging. "Does she get to lie there for a year of pain? And fear?"

She held him tighter, harder and he felt her desperation.

"Dammit, this isn't *right*. It isn't *fair*."

"No," he groaned and ducked his head to her shoulder. "It's not."

"If she has to die, why does it have to be in inches?" She drew her head back and punched his chest with a hard, work-worn fist. Biting at her bottom lip, she hit him again and again.

Zacariah stood perfectly still, his arms still locked around her waist and let her strike out at him. He knew she needed to fight against the coming darkness and by allowing it, he knew he was helping her fight.

She pummelled him helplessly until her fists fell weakly to her sides as if she hadn't the strength to hold them up any longer. Resting her forehead against his chest, she sighed. "Why does she have to suffer?"

Her tears came then in a slow, silent flood of grief and he held her close, pressed against the reassuring beat of his heart.

So many different kinds of love, he thought as he rested his chin on top of her head. And so many different kinds of pain. He wasn't sure he had the strength to be human.

She wrapped her arms around his middle, lifted her head from his chest and looked up at him through watery eyes. "How will they bear it?" she demanded in a hushed groan. "How will they survive losing Ellie?"

"I don't know," he said softly, with a sad shake of his head.

She swallowed heavily. "When Daniel died, it was awful."

He stiffened slightly, but she didn't seem to notice.

"I felt so . . . alone. So . . . abandoned." She let her head drop to his chest again. "But I still had Danny. And the ranch. The ranch that will go to my child someday. My child." Rebecca shook her head frantically. "No, Zack. I couldn't do it. I couldn't bear to lose Danny. It would kill me."

"You haven't lost him," he said and lifted one hand to stroke the side of her face.

"And I won't."

"You won't."

She stared into his eyes for a long minute. Then she went up on her toes and brushed her lips across his. "Hold me, Zack. Just hold me."

He leaned back against the wall, cradling her close and pretended, however briefly, that he would always be there to hold onto her.

*   *   *

Later that night, Rebecca tried to concentrate on the
ranch's books, but the numbers kept blurring and her mind
kept drifting.

"Becky?" Buck asked quietly and she looked up,
grateful for the respite.

"What is it?"

He shot one quick look at the hall that led to Danny's
room, where the boy and Zack were busy hanging new
shelves for Buck's carvings. The solid thump of a hammer
on wood seemed to convince him that he wouldn't be
interrupted.

Rubbing one hand over the back of his neck, he started
haltingly. "It's Zack. You sure you know what you're
doin'?"

She stiffened and lifted her chin as if ready for a fight.
"What do you mean?"

"Hell, Becky," he muttered and got to his feet. "You
know what I'm gettin' at. I can see the way you look at
him."

"How's that?"

"Like you're a dyin' flower and he's the first spring
rain."

She twirled the pencil in her fingers, staring at it
blankly. "What's between me and Zack," she said, "is
between me and Zack."

"Figured you'd say somethin' like that."

"Then why'd you bring it up?"

"I'm worried about you, Becky. We don't know
nothin' about the man."

"I know what I need to know." She shifted in her seat
at the lie. She didn't know nearly enough. And the fact
that he had secrets ate at her. But not enough to keep her
from feeling what she did for him.

"Just go careful," he said and scratched his whiskery
cheek.

The rigidity went out of her spine and her shoulders

slumped. She shouldn't be getting mad at Buck. He just wanted what was best for her. She knew that. It was only the fact that his doubts raised her own that she resented.

"I will," she promised and bent to the task in front of her, effectively telling him to let the subject drop.

"Me and Zack are goin' out after Scotty tomorrow mornin'," Buck said softly and waited for her reaction.

She looked up from the account ledger and nodded, thankful he'd switched topics. "It's time, I guess. He should have been back by now." Tiredly, she tossed her pencil down onto the tabletop and rubbed her dry, aching eyes with her fingertips.

Reluctantly, she said what she'd been thinking about on and off now for days. Since he was preparing to leave, she couldn't put it off any longer.

"Buck, I know how you feel about going to Pine Creek Canyon—"

The older man stiffened slightly, then straightened up, squaring his shoulders.

"I hate to ask you to go back there," she said softly. "But it's got to be checked. I'm sorry."

"Don't be." Buck's gaze flickered slightly. "I'm the foreman here. Past time I started actin' like it."

He shook his head and stared down at his hands. "It'll be fine, Becky. I should've faced that canyon down a long time ago."

Maybe. But then, so should she. Rebecca'd avoided going to the spot where her husband had died four years before every bit at much as Buck had. And it was worse for him, she knew. After all, he'd been with Daniel the night of the stampede. Beside him when he died.

His ghosts were, no doubt, far more intimidating than hers.

"There's something else, though," he said suddenly and his voice sounded as grim as he looked.

"What?"

Lamplight played on his features, casting weird shadows that made his familiar face look different. Harder.

"First off," Buck started slowly, "I think you ought to get used to the notion that ol' Scotty's gone into business for himself."

"What makes you say that?"

"You know yourself he's been actin' mighty peculiar these last couple of months. And now this." He shrugged. "Scotty should have been back here yesterday at the latest. He ain't."

No, but did that make him a thief? Rebecca shook her head and shied away from the thought. Sure, he'd been acting strangely. But thieving?

She hated to think it of him. Not simply because of the betrayal. But also because, if Scotty was indeed stealing her horses, what did that say about her judgement? And if she could be so wrong about a man she'd known for a couple of years, how could she be sure about Zack? And what she felt for him?

A shiver raced down her spine and made her tremble.

No. She wouldn't accuse a man on suspicions.

She nodded abruptly. "We'll deal with that trouble if we come to it. Anything else?"

From a distance, she heard the hammer stop, Zacariah curse and Danny's helpless giggles. Rebecca smiled to herself absently.

"Zack."

The smile disappeared and she glared at him. "Not again, Buck."

"It ain't about the other—you were right. That's your business. This is different."

Another chill crept along her flesh and she shivered. "Spit it out, Buck."

"Don't you think it's awful strange that Zack shows up out of nowhere—with no recollection of anything—right when we're losin' our stock to rustlers?"

"What?" She jumped to her feet and folded her arms across her chest. "Are you tring to say you think *Zack's* stealing from me?'' She took a couple of quick, jerky steps. "A minute ago, you were accusing Scotty.''

"I ain't *accusin'* anybody.'' He shoved his hat down onto his head and glared at her from under the brim. "I'm just tellin' my *boss* what I think. That's still my job, isn't it?''

"Of course it is,'' Rebecca countered, dismissing his sarcasm. "But dammit, Buck. You can't go around calling first one man, then another, a rustler.''

"I ain't sayin' so for sure,'' he argued. "I'm only sayin' it's possible.''

"No, it's not.'' She pushed past her foreman and started pacing. The hard clicks of her boot heels against the wood floors sounded out in the stillness like an old biddy clucking her tongue.

When she reached the opposite side of the room, she spun about and faced him. "We were losing horses for *months* before Zack arrived.''

"Yeah, but he could've been ramroding the operation from somewheres else and only come down here for the finish.''

"He wouldn't do that.''

"You can't be sure.''

"I'm as sure as I need to be,'' she snapped and ignored the tiny trickle of doubt beginning to worm its way through her body. "Besides, he and Scotty don't even get along. What makes you think they'd be partners?''

He snorted. "Money has a way of bringing folks together.''

"I don't believe it. Zack wouldn't do that. To me or to Danny.''

She saw the sympathetic gleam in his eyes and flinched inwardly.

"Becky, I've known you a long time,'' he said softly. "Since Daniel died, I've been hopin' that you'd find yourself a good man . . .''

"I think I have, Buck.''

He sucked in a deep breath while his shoulders slumped a bit in defeat. "And if he *is* a thief?"

She inhaled sharply and blew it out on a shaky sigh. "He isn't," she said firmly. "He can't be."

"I hope you're right, girl. For your sake."

She nodded and wrapped her arms around her own middle.

"We'll be leavin' at first light," Buck said gruffly and headed for the front door. "Should be back by tomorrow evenin'. Whether we find Scotty or not."

The door creaked slightly when he opened it.

"Be careful, Buck."

A long, thoughtful pause stretched out between. Then he inclined his head toward the hammering in the back room. "You too, Becky."

Alone, Rebecca turned to face the fireplace. Leaning both hands on the carved wood mantle, she stared down into the cheerful blaze as if expecting to find answers in the snap and hiss. A log split suddenly and she jumped, then watched as sparks skittered up the chimney.

Slumping down onto the stone hearth, she looked off into the shadows flitting about the room. Wearily, she thought of the monsters Danny was sure lived under his bed.

She couldn't help thinking that those monsters her son kept searching his room for were actually here.

In the dark.

Surrounding her.

Zacariah looked across the dark yard at Rebecca's house, his gaze locked on the soft yellow glow of lamplight shining from behind the main room's windows. With the moon hidden behind a bank of clouds, that hesitant halo of light was the only bright spot in the blackness around him.

Buck snored from behind him and Zacariah tossed a

quick glance at the sleeping man before moving for the door.

Rebecca.

His insides churned and his hands curled into tight, empty fists. He needed to see her. To hold her. To wrap his arms around her and feel the soft warmth of her pressed to him.

Mostly, though, he admitted silently, he wanted to pretend that he wasn't leaving in little more than two weeks.

Before he could think better of it, he slipped out the bunkhouse door and loped across the shadowed yard to the main house. Wearing only his jeans, he waited impatiently in the cold after knocking gently on the front door. Blowing on his hands for warmth, he wondered what he would do if Rebecca turned him away.

But then the door opened and she was there. Her hair fell in careless abandon about the shoulders of her white nightgown and he could see the dark flesh of her nipples beneath the thin fabric.

He drew a short, anxious breath before she flew into his arms, silenty answering the question of his welcome. Zacariah scooped her up in his arms and stepped inside, closing the door behind them.

Buck let go of the curtains and watched them fall into place. Jaw tight, eyes hard, he walked back to his narrow cot.

He'd seen enough.

More than enough.

Chapter ❀ Fourteen

Just before dawn, Zacariah kissed her one last time and left her bed. As he pulled his jeans on, he glanced at her, sitting straight up, a sheet pulled almost high enough to hide her breasts from his gaze.

He wanted to lie back down with her. Thread his fingers through her hair and revel in its softness. He wanted to bury himself so deeply inside her that nothing and no one would be able to separate them.

"Be careful," she whispered.

"I will."

"Zack?"

He paused in buttoning up his pants and looked at her in the hazy, lavender, early morning light.

She came up on her knees and settled back to sit on her heels. Still clutching the sheet much too loosely, she said softly, "I have to tell you something, *before* you go out with Buck."

"What is it, Rebecca?"

"I know you might not want to hear it, but I have to say it."

He waited, breath held.

"I love you."

He stared into her eyes, still dazed with sleep and the night's passion and read the truth for himself. Somewhere inside him, the last shadowy corners of emptiness and darkness were filled with light. A miraculous feeling swept through him and Zacariah knew that never again would he know anything like this.

In the next instant though, those fragile feelings splintered into thousands of pieces. He wasn't a part of her world. His time here was merely a punishment. Discipline.

A wry smile touched his features briefly. Ironic to know that the Minions had granted him a gift *and* an injury with the same sentence. The gift of love—and the agony of losing it.

"You don't have to say anything," she told him. "I don't need words." She inhaled sharply. "Or promises. I only told you how I feel because I've never felt this way before and I wanted you to know it."

"Thank you." He set one knee on the mattress, leaned in close and kissed her, long and thoroughly. He took his time, moving his mouth over hers and memorizing everything. Her scent. Her taste. The puff of her breath on his cheek.

When he finally pulled away, he walked across the room to the door. Quietly, he left her and just as quietly shut the door behind him.

The landmarks around him were familiar.

Too familiar.

Buck shuddered and ducked his head to avoid looking at the crooked pine tree that stood at the mouth of the box canyon. Faintly, he heard the musical sound of the creek, running high with mountain runoff. A breeze rifled through the trees and sounded like a sigh.

A chill of uneasiness crawled up his spine and he wished briefly that he was anywhere but here.

Four long years had passed since the night Daniel had died and still Buck was haunted by the memories. Sure, he'd seen men die over the years. Probably helped a few through those pearly gates himself.

But Daniel's death was different. He'd been like a son to Buck. The pain of losing him was as clear and sharp as the day he'd died.

Yet even that wasn't the whole reason he'd avoided the canyon since that terrible night. There was something else, too. Something that played at the edges of his mind, teasing him, taunting him with his own forgetfulness. He'd tried to remember. But nothing came.

He shot a glance at the man riding beside him. It had taken everything he had to keep his mouth shut when Zack had slipped back into the bunkhouse just before dawn. But he'd promised himself that if he found out Zack was playing Becky false, he'd tear the younger man's head off with his bare hands.

They approached the mouth of the canyon as quietly as they could. But even at a slow walk, the muffled thuds of their horses' hooves pounded like heartbeats.

Ahead, sheer rock walls jutted straight up, stretching reddish-brown, ragged fingertips of stone toward a sweeping expanse of deep blue sky. Sprinkled over the face of the canyon, in startling clumps of green, bushes clung to the rocks, thriving, despite their precarious hold on life.

Zacariah cast one quick look at the man beside him and immediately wished he hadn't.

"All right," Buck whispered and waved the pistol he'd drawn from his holster. "You stay ahead of me when we ride in. Where I can see ya."

Staring into the cold black muzzle of the pistol, he nodded silently. He couldn't blame Buck for feeling protective of Rebecca and Danny. In fact, it was an urge they shared. Though obviously the older man wasn't convinced of that.

From somewhere in the distance, a horse whinnied softly. The barely heard noise echoed off the canyon walls until it drifted to Zacariah and Buck like the call of a phantom beast.

"Reckon that settles that," the foreman muttered. "The

horses are in there. At least, some of them.'' His own mount sidestepped nervously as if sensing its rider's agitation. Buck shot Zacariah a hard look. "What I'm still figurin' out is if you knew that already.''

Surprise flickered through him.

"You think *I'm* stealing Rebecca's horses?''

"I think anything's possible.''

He didn't know whether to be angry or amused. Then he took the time to study the hard glint in Buck's eyes and reacted in kind. A slow, simmering anger began in the pit of his stomach.

True, he'd been at the Hale ranch only a couple of weeks. But he'd done *nothing* to warrant being accused of forcing Rebecca from her home. Whoever was behind these thefts was bent on ruining her. Stealing her ranch, her *life* from her.

"I'm not a thief, Buck,'' he said, battling the anger bubbling within. "But there's not a damn thing I can say to prove that to you.''

"Sorry to hear that, boy.''

If anything, the man's grip on the pistol tightened as his features became even sterner, more forbidding.

"Look,'' Zacariah said with a quick glance back at the canyon. "Why don't you let me ride in there first? If there's trouble, you'll hear it and be able to go for help.''

If there *were* thieves in among the rocks, he would rather face them alone. Should they start shooting, their weapons wouldn't hurt him. Buck, on the other hand, could be killed.

Since his month as a human wasn't yet finished, he knew that *he* wouldn't be Collecting Buck's soul that day. But there were *other* Collectors.

"Not a chance, son.'' The older man shook his head slowly. "I'm hopin' you're tellin' the truth. For Becky's sake, if nothin' else. But if you're lyin' and you are a no-account thief . . . why in hell would I let you ride on in there and warn your friends I'm comin'?''

He had a point.

"As to the other, I can't afford to ride off and get help, either." A frustrated scowl briefly crossed his leathery face. "Who knows how long that bunch'll be there?"

Buck waved him on and Zacariah gave in, spurring his horse forward. The other man followed just a pace or two behind.

The air seemed still. Heavy. The canyon walls felt suffocating. Buck's gaze bored into his back and he felt a stir of uneasiness creep into the raw emotion churning in his stomach.

As they rounded an oversized boulder, they saw him.

A lone man, his back to them, stood close to a slipshod corral where thirty or more horses wandered aimlessly in circles.

"Goddammit," Buck muttered thickly.

For the first time since becoming human, time seemed to slow down. Seconds crawled by. Zacariah stepped down from the horse and, never taking his gaze from the man, started for him. He didn't stop to think about Buck. He didn't consider the fact that there might be more men stationed in the rocks. Instead, he followed the demands of the towering anger that threatened to choke him.

Images of Rebecca rose up in his mind as he crossed the rocky expanse of ground separating him from his goal. He remembered all the times he'd seen her bone weary. And worried. And desperate, in the face of overpowering losses, to save her ranch for her son.

His hands clenched as he ran, his boot heels sliding on rock. At last, the man whirled around, his movements still slow, dreamlike, surprise etched into his features. Zacariah kept moving, thinking only of getting his hands on the man who'd come so close to costing Rebecca her home.

The man's surprise faded quickly as he clumsily drew his pistol, took aim, then fired directly at Zacariah's chest.

Flame exploded from the barrel of the pistol. Sound

deafened him. He staggered as the bullet crashed into his chest. Still moving slowly, as if suspended from reality, Zacariah glanced down and gaped at a scarlet stain blossoming in the center of his plain white shirt.

He looked up again and saw the man pull back the hammer of his gun to fire again. Rage erupted in Zacariah. Hot, pulsing, mind-numbing rage.

As his own pain receded, he charged across the last few steps separating him from the thief. It didn't matter if the man fired once more or a hundred times. Fury tightened its grip on him.

Nothing could defeat him. He couldn't be killed and he wouldn't be stopped.

Another shot rang out from behind him and dirt to the right of him flew up with the impact of a bullet fired from somewhere above.

His gaze didn't shift.

The man stared at him, eyes wide and terrified. He fired again but the shot went wild, arcing off into the canyon. Before he could fire it a third time, Zacariah's fist slammed into his face.

The man's head snapped back. New pain shot up Zacariah's arm but a rush of satisfaction blunted it. Centuries of existence hadn't prepared him for the elation that filled him as he met and vanquished an enemy for the first time. Instantly, he recalled the howls of victory he'd heard rising from bands of Celtic warriors. The thunderous shouts of knights on Crusade. The earsplitting shrieks of bagpipes playing joyful tunes when militiamen turned back the King's army during the American Revolution. The bloodcurdling call of Confederate troops when charging a Union line. The war whoops of Indians sweeping down on the settlers encroaching on their lands.

He felt it all. Felt the tremendous swell of energy, gratification . . . and, for the very first time, understood it.

The thief lay on the ground, blood streaming from his split lip. A wild, frantic look shone in his eyes as his boot heels dug into the sandy dirt in a frenzied attempt to push himself backward, away from the man hovering over him.

His blood pounding in his ears, his breath ragged, Zacariah ignored the man's attempts at escape. He bent down, curled his fingers into the thief's shirt and yanked him to his feet. He swayed unsteadily.

"I shot you, mister," he managed to say, just before one last furious blow took him under the chin. Then his knees gave out and he slumped to the dirt, eyes closed. Zacariah stood over him, dragging one deep breath after another into his heaving lungs, trying to ready himself for the next step in this battle. He knew the fight wasn't finished.

Something whizzed past his ear and thudded into a corral post. Zacariah ducked and spun around in time to see Buck lean to one side in his saddle, take careful aim at the canyon's rim, then fire his own weapon. The solid "thump" of a bullet making contact with flesh followed. A man on the edge of the rocky wall teetered unsteadily for a long moment, then fell lifelessly to the ground below.

In a velvety gray mist, a robed figure drifted to the fallen man's side. Zacariah squinted against the sweat nearly blinding him. The Collector paused in his duties long enough to glance at Zacariah and nod. Then, the Being reached out and gently guided the dead man's soul from his body.

The canyon and the others around him fell away as Zacariah concentrated on the liberated soul. Surprise gave way to pleasure as the former thief took the Collector's hand. He looked back at his own broken body, lying in the dirt, and a look of puzzlement flashed across his features briefly. Then he turned eagerly toward the golden Path.

As the two figures disappeared into the Eternal mists, Zacariah sighed. Even after all that had happened in this canyon, he found himself hoping that the thief wouldn't end his journey on the Dark Road.

Before he could take a single step, he heard the now all-too-familiar "click" of a gun being cocked.

Close by.

Slowly, he looked to his left and his gaze locked with a pair of furious, pale gray eyes.

Scotty.

Buck's outraged voice shouted to be heard above the restive movements of the caged horses. "You goddamned traitor!"

Scotty smiled softly, kept his gaze and his gun locked on Zacariah and yelled back, "Shut up, you old fool. You don't know a damn thing!"

"I know a lyin', thievin' son of a bitch when I see one."

The blonde's smile faltered and something cold flashed in his eyes. "I told you to shut up, otherwise I shoot your friend here straight off."

Buck obediently fell silent.

"It's time to deal with this drifting trash," Scotty said.

Zacariah watched the man carefully, taking note of the white-knuckled grip he had on his pistol and the hard, implacable shine in those too-pale eyes.

"How can you do this to Becky?" Buck shouted a moment later. "How can you watch her lose everything?"

"I'm not doing this *to* Becky, you old bastard. I'm doing this *for* her."

The soft, muffled hoofbeats of Buck's horse sounded out as the older man came steadily closer. "*For* her? You're doin' her a favor by stealin' her home out from under her?"

"You stay where you are, Buck, or so help me, I'll shoot this drifter right now."

Buck drew his horse to a stop just ten feet away.

"Your friend already tried shooting me," Zacariah told him, hoping to distract him.

Scotty glanced at the bloodstained shirt and shook his head. "A bad load in that bullet," he said. "Not enough to do real damage." He shrugged. "My loads, I do myself. When *I* shoot ya, you'll be dead."

Hatred glimmered in his eyes and warred with a jealousy that had been simmering for two weeks.

"All of this is your fault," Scotty said in a conversational tone that belied the gun still aimed at Zacariah's chest. "If you hadn't wandered in and started making cow eyes at Becky, none of this would've happened."

"You'd still be stealing her horses, you no-good lyin' son of a bitch!"

"Yeah, but you wouldn't have known about it," Scotty slid one fast look from the corner of his eye at the furious older man. " 'Cause you never would have come to this canyon, would ya, Buck?"

The man sucked in a gulp of air as though mortally wounded. "You bastard."

Scotty chuckled and lifted the barrel of his gun an inch or so, aiming for Zacariah's heart, and said, "With you afraid of ghosts and Becky leaving the range to me, everything was going fine." His features tightened. "Pretty soon, all of her damned horses would've been gone."

Ghosts. Realization blossomed in Zacariah's mind. The stampede. This canyon was the place he'd visited four years before. The place where Daniel Hale had died. The place where Buck had seen a Collector and lived to tell about it.

It almost seemed fitting to be back where his connection with the Hale ranch had begun.

"Why the hell do you hate her so much, boy?" Buck asked with real puzzlement.

"Hate her?" Scotty spared the other man a quick look. "I *love* her."

"Love?" Buck snorted. "You're tryin' to ruin a woman ya claim to love?"

He sounded surprised, but Zacariah wasn't. He'd existed too long for that. He'd seen viciousness and villainy done in the name of love for eons.

What was one more?

Scotty's lips thinned along with his patience. "Once her herd was gone, she'd have had to give up on this goddamned ranch. She'd have nobody but you and Danny, then. And you're old, fixin' to die." He moved a step closer to Zacariah, wildness growing in his eyes. "She would have turned to *me*. Me! Then she'd have seen that I love her. And we would've left this blasted place behind and made a new start somewheres else! Just her and me."

"What about Danny?" Zacariah asked.

"He's just a kid. He'll do what I tell him."

"What about me?" Buck prodded.

"Hell, you're almost dead already." Scotty snorted a laugh that scratched across the other men's ears with the sound of madness. "I'd have been doin' you a favor, hurrying you along."

"You son of a bitch." Buck's voice was tired. Weary with disappointment.

Scotty laughed again, more to himself than anyone else and Zacariah took the split-second advantage offered him. He lunged for the gun, his fingers curling around the barrel and jerking it skyward. A chamber exploded and a bullet went flying harmlessly into the empty canyon.

Scotty growled, low and furious as he swung on the man whom he saw to be the cause of all his problems. Zacariah ducked, stepped in closer and threw a punch of his own, landing a blow squarely on the other man's jaw. Scotty staggered, released his grip on the gun and went for Zacariah, determined to crush him in his bare hands.

Together they hit the dirt, Scotty's knee smashing into Zacariah's ribs. Some of the corralled horses rose up onto their hind legs, then shifted, running from the fight to the farthest corner of their pen.

Zacariah bent one leg then straightened it abruptly, flipping Scotty backwards over his head. By the time he landed in the dirt, Zacariah was already rushing him. Scotty dodged the charging man, rolled to one side and leaped to his feet.

"Damn you, drifter. I'll kill you for this. You ruined it all. You ruined *everything*." He raced at him, diving for Zacariah's legs. Again, they hit the dirt and a rock stabbed in Zacariah's back. He winced with the lancing pain then forgot it as Scotty's fingers began to tighten around his throat.

The edges of his vision darkened. Splinters of light, like jagged stars, drifted in and out of the blackness, but he shook them off, refusing to give ground to the man straddling his chest. If he surrendered, Scotty would then turn on Buck. And after, perhaps Danny. Even Rebecca wouldn't be safe from this man's *love*.

New strength born of desperation rose up in him. Zacariah reached up and set both hands under Scotty's jaw. Shoving hard, he forced the man's head back, hoping to loosen the fingers choking off his air. But it wasn't working. If anything, the choke hold on his throat tightened, bringing the blackness in closer and splintered shards of light to a brightness that was at once beautiful and terrifying.

A solid, heavy "thump" sounded out.

Above him, Scotty sat up straighter, eyes wide. His grip slackened and Zacariah gasped in a gulp of dusty air, relishing the sweetness of it.

Scotty blinked, stared down at him blankly, then slowly tipped to one side where he sprawled in the dirt, eyes closed, arms wide.

Zacariah sat up, running one hand across his bruised throat. He stared at the fallen man for a long minute, then cautiously turned his gaze on Buck.

The older man stood over him, his rifle butt still high after smacking into the back of Scotty's head. Buck's boots crunched on the dirt and rocks underfoot as he stared down at the unconscious man. "Hoped I was wrong about him." He flashed a quick look at Zacariah. "Really did. But there was somethin' not right about him for a long while now."

On their left, the first man Zacariah had fought stirred. Calmly, Buck walked to his side and slammed his rifle butt into the man's forehead, effectively silencing him again. Then the older man turned around, raised his rifle barrel until it was trained on Zacariah and said, "Now that all the hoo-rah is over, I want to know one thing. Who in the hell are you?"

Dread spiraled out of control in his chest. One battle finished, another just begun. He pushed himself to his feet, staggering only slightly. Slowly, he lifted his gaze to Buck's.

The older man inhaled sharply, suddenly. His face paled just before a fresh rush of color stained his cheeks. "It's from *here* I know you. I saw you that night. Four years ago."

Zacariah muttered a curse.

"I'm right, ain't I?" Buck demanded. "It *was* you here, the night of the stampede?"

"I was here," he said, knowing it was pointless to deny it now. The man had been trying to remember for weeks.

"You're different now, though."

"I'm human. Like you."

Buck snorted. "You may be human, but you ain't a damn sight like me!" He waved one hand at the spot where the thief's bullet had collided with Zacariah's chest. "If he'd shot me, I'd be dead. You ain't even winded."

Not very observant, Zacariah noticed. He was more than winded. He was exhausted. Every bone and muscle in his body ached with the abuse he'd heaped on it in the last several minutes.

"You mind if I sit down?" he asked and without waiting for permission, dropped to the ground. He drew one leg up and rested his forearm on his knee as he watched the other man gather his newly recalled memories.

Buck lowered his rifle barrel until it lay along his side, pointed at the dirt. Gesturing to it, he said, "Guess a gun won't do me any good. I already saw that bullets don't stop ya if you don't want to be stopped. So, what happens now?"

Zacariah shrugged. Lifting one hand, he cautiously touched his swollen, bleeding lips. "We take these men to the sheriff and go back to the ranch."

"That's all you got to say?"

"What more can I say?"

"Plenty," the man snapped. "For starters, you can tell me how it is a ghost man is here. Alive."

"I'm not a ghost."

"You ain't a man, either," Buck told him angrily. "If you *were* a man, you'd be a dead one."

Zacariah looked down at his shirtfront. The damning stain of dried-blood covered flesh that had already closed over the bullet wound.

"Just who—or *what* are you, mister?"

He lifted his head and stared at the man across from him. There was no choice. Buck had seen and *remembered* too much. The only thing that would satisfy him now would be the complete truth. Zacariah tossed a glance heavenward and wondered what the punishment for confiding in a mortal would be. He shrugged again. No doubt, he'd find out soon enough.

"I'll tell you," Zacariah finally said. "But you must understand—you can say nothing of this to anyone."

"What about Rebecca?"

"*Especially* Rebecca." Just the thought of her knowing him for what he was sent cold chills racing down Zacariah's back. By the Path, he didn't want to spend his last couple of weeks as a mortal watching Rebecca's eyes cloud with fear every time she looked at him.

Buck nodded despite the fingers of dread and denial squeezing his heart. He would have promised anything to get the answers he needed. Whether he kept that promise or not depended. On a lot of things.

Zacariah started talking and as crazy as his story sounded, Buck knew it to be all too real. The proof lay in his own memory. Images of Zacariah, bent over Daniel, rose up in his mind. Memories of other gray figures drifting with the wind and settling on the broken bodies of the men caught up in the stampede.

He looked into Zacariah's cool blue gaze and felt a chill of recognition that stirred every buried fear of the unknown he'd ever had into life again.

Death.

No matter that he called himself by the name Collector.

Death was his business.

Zacariah lifted one dark brow and shifted his gaze away from the older man's dumbfounded expression. All things considered, Buck was taking the truth fairly well. No shouting, no keening and despite his feelings, he hadn't run, either.

"One month, huh?"

"That's right."

"And you're down to about two weeks?"

Zacariah sighed. Afraid or not, Buck obviously wanted him gone. Soon. "Yes. About that."

The older man nodded thoughtfully, narrowed his eyes and scratched his whiskery chin. "And when you leave, you ain't comin' back?"

"No." A bitter smile crossed his face briefly. Whatever the Minions did to him next would no doubt be far more creative than sending him back here.

"Good." Buck jerked him a nod. "Least ways then, things'll go back to normal around here."

Zacariah stiffened.

"What?" the old cowboy demanded. "I saw you flinch. What is it you ain't sayin'?"

Wearily, he stood up again and shoved one hand through his hair. He looked around for the hat he'd lost while fighting and spotted it a few feet away. Slowly, he walked over to get it. Anything to avoid that question.

"You ain't said it all, Zack and I want to hear it. Now."

He snatched up the hat, dusted it against his thighs, then settled it firmly on his head. Pulling the brim down low on his forehead, he shot a hard look at the other man. He wanted the truth . . . he could have it. All of it. "When I leave, a soul will be leaving with me."

"A soul." Several heartbeats of silence passed. Buck stepped closer, cocked his head and peered deeply into Zacariah's eyes. "You mean, somebody's gonna die when you leave."

"Yes."

"Who?" Fear streaked Buck's voice and seemed to shimmer in the air around him. "Who is it? Who are you taking? Rebecca? Danny?"

His insides twisted at the thought. Rebecca? His breath tore at him. Danny? Each beat of his heart stabbed at him.

He gritted his teeth and turned to stare at the wild, penned horses. The lingering silence prodded Buck into action.

The older man dropped his rifle, closed the distance between them and grabbed a handful of Zacariah's shirt. Shaking him viciously, he shouted, "Who? Goddamn you!"

"I don't know!" He shoved free of the man's grip and glared at him. "I don't know," he repeated and heard the pain in his own voice.

Air staggered into Buck's lungs with ragged gasps. A dull, throbbing ache settled around his heart and he absently rubbed his chest. When he realized what he was doing, a whisper of relief fluttered through him.

It was him.

It had to be.

No doubt his old heart was getting ready to quit. Hell, he was an old man. He'd lived a long, hard, full life and it was past time for him to die.

Not that he was anxious to go, by any means. But if there was a choice between him and those he loved, he'd go and gladly. He snorted a short laugh. Somehow, he'd always imagined fighting death tooth and nail when it came his turn. But knowing that his going would keep Rebecca and Danny safe, he found that he was almost looking forward to it.

At least he wouldn't have to put up with another Colorado winter!

"Zack," he said softly, "I believe I've got this figured out."

"Really?" A wry grin lifted one corner of his mouth.

"I think I'm the one goin' with ya."

"What makes you think so?"

"I'm older than dirt, for one. Ask Scotty." He glanced at the unconscious man. "When he wakes up."

"That doesn't mean anything."

"I know, we can't be sure." But Buck knew he was right. "Rebecca and Danny are safe from you while you're here? I mean, you can't kill 'em accidental-like, can ya?"

The Collector scowled. "I haven't yet."

"True, true." Fella seemed a little testy all of a sudden. But then, why shouldn't he be? Certainly couldn't have many friends, what with being Death and all.

"Well son, I reckon you and me better get these two thieves to the sheriff." He shook his head. "Guess that old fool will listen to Rebecca from now on when she talks about rustlers."

"You'll say nothing?"

"Hell, who'd believe me?"

Zacariah nodded grimly.

"One thing, though, Zack," Buck said, his features suddenly serious. "Maybe it'd be best if you kept a distance between you and Becky now."

"No."

"Boy, this'll only get harder. When you leave, she'll—"

"I can't stay away from her."

"Can't?"

"All right," Zacariah admitted. "Won't."

"Now see here—"

"No," he interrupted, "*you* see." Blue eyes blazing with eternal fire, he turned on Buck. "You know who I am. You know I'll be gone in two weeks."

The older man stood his ground, though everything in him was telling him to run. "Yeah?"

With an obvious effort, Zacariah swallowed back the rage shaking through him and said more quietly, "I'll never see her again." Staring hard into Buck's eyes, he vowed, "And damn it, I won't leave her before I *have* to."

"You tryin' to tell me that you *love* her?" Fear forgotten, Buck asked, "Is that possible?"

Zacariah inhaled sharply and turned away.

Stunned, Buck stared at him. *Somebody* in Heaven had messed things up good and proper.

And he wasn't quite sure how to fix it.

Chapter ❁ Fifteen

Rebecca heard their horses and jumped off the settee. Hurrying to the door, she threw it open and stepped into the night. All day long, her thoughts had jumbled together. Her conversation with Buck had repeated itself over and over in her mind, dredging up suspicion, striking down hope.

She relived every moment of the night before. In memory, she felt each of Zacariah's caresses and experienced again that sense of belonging that she found in his arms. Her brain tortured her with "what if's." What if Zacariah really was a thief? What if he was working with Scotty? What if he had no feelings for her at all, but had been merely using a foolish widow for his own ends?

By nightfall, her nerves were a wreck. She'd sent Danny to bed early, despite his protests, so that she could have a little peace before the men returned.

She shivered as she stepped off the porch into the dirt. Wrapping her arms around her, she admitted that she couldn't bear the thought that Zacariah might have betrayed her.

Two riders entered the yard and Rebecca held her breath.

Indistinct, moonlit shadows shifted over them, making Buck and Zacariah look like phantoms. When the horses came to a stop a few feet from her, Buck climbed down and for the first time actually looked his age. Zack dismounted too and gave her a slow smile.

Her gaze swept over him hungrily and she gasped. Dried blood stained the front of his shirt, covering the center of his chest like an obscene flower.

"I'm all right," he said.

"He ain't hurt, Becky." Buck's voice cut through the wild imaginings in her brain.

Thankfully, she set that worry aside, promising herself to to find out more about the bloodstain later. For now, she needed answers.

"It was Scotty," Buck said simply.

Not Zack. She started breathing again.

"Did he say why?"

"He wasn't makin' much sense." Buck shot an odd look at Zacariah before continuing. "Zack and me took Scotty and his pals into town. Two to the sheriff. One to the undertaker."

Rebecca nodded stiffly. She'd known when they'd set out after the thieves that there might be gunplay. That someone might die. She was only grateful that it hadn't been Buck or Zack.

"Cooper kept us in town forever," Buck complained. "Had more questions than a fussy schoolteacher."

She nodded absently and let her gaze slide to Zack. Her foreman kept talking and she knew she should be listening. But she'd already heard the important part. Buck and Zack had taken the thieves into town. That could only mean Buck was convinced that Zack wasn't a part of the rustling.

She hadn't been wrong about him.

He was just what he appeared to be.

A drifter. A man without a past. And maybe—a man with a future that began on the Hale ranch.

"Zack," Buck said, loud enough to let her know it wasn't the first time he'd said it. "Why don't you go put the horses up? I want a word or two with Becky."

Zacariah stiffened slightly, his jaw tight.

The older man ducked his head, to avoid Zack's stare.

Rebecca watched the two of them curiously. A thin curl of worry began to stream through her. Was there something no one was saying? Was Buck still suspicious of Zack after all?

"Rebecca . . ."

She looked at Zacariah, then back to her foreman when the older man interrupted sharply.

"Becky, it'll only take a minute." Not even glancing at the other man, he said, "Go on now, Zack. And give the horses a few extra oats. They had a long ride today."

Zacariah looked as though he wanted to argue, but finally, grimly, he snatched Buck's reins and drew both horses away, toward the barn.

She watched him go, head up and shoulders squared, like a man walking to his own execution. That uneasy feeling kicked up again as she swiveled her head to look at the man who'd been like a father to her.

"What is it?" she asked. "Why the secrecy?"

He shot a careful look over his shoulder and didn't speak until the other man was inside the barn. Then he looked at Rebecca and started talking in a rushed whisper.

"I know you don't want to hear anything from me about what's between you and Zack . . ."

"Damn it, Buck!" She pulled a shaky breath into her lungs and let her chin drop to her chest. "You scared me. I thought maybe you'd found out something bad about Zack."

"Not exactly," he hedged.

Her eyes narrowed and she cocked her head to look at him. She'd never known Buck to mince words. Whatever he had to say, he said it and damn the consequences.

"What's that supposed to mean?"

"Becky, he ain't a thief, if that's what you're thinkin'."

"Then what's the problem?"

"Maybe nothin'."

"Buck . . ."

"All I want to say is, hold onto your heart, Becky."

"What?" The sliver of moon slipped behind a cloud and even the vague, silvery light was lost. Buck was no more than a blacker shadow against the night.

"Don't love him, Becky," he whispered frantically. "The man will be leavin' in a couple of weeks."

"Maybe not," she argued with a quick look at the barn. "Things are different, now. Better. We . . ."

"No, Becky. He's leavin'. Believe me." Buck reached out in the darkness and dropped both hands onto her shoulders.

Moonlight again peeked out from behind a drifting cloud and lay across Buck's features. Concern flashed in his eyes and Rebecca took a half-step back, moving out from under his touch. Determined to prove him wrong, she said, "He won't leave me. Not now. I know he won't." She glanced at the barn again, then shot her gaze to Buck's. "He loves me."

"Has he said so?"

"No, but I can tell."

He nodded slowly and drew in a long, deep breath. "Maybe he does, honey. But like I said, he *is* leaving. And Becky, you've *got* to let him go."

"Why?"

"I can't say. Just remember what I told ya, and keep a hold of your heart."

"It's too late," she whispered, moving away from him. "It was too late a long time ago." Rebecca turned her back on him and everything he'd tried to say and headed directly to the barn. And Zack.

He looked up when she entered and tried to read the expression on her face. Had Buck broken his word and told her everything? Had she believed him?

She hurried down the wide middle aisle toward the stall where he was unsaddling one of the horses. As she stepped into the circle of lamplight, he studied her features quickly and felt himself relax. Whatever it was the foreman had said to her, he had kept Zack's secret.

Their gazes met. Blue eyes locked with green. Silence stretched out between them and then, like a too-taut cord, suddenly snapped.

"I'm sorry about Scotty," he said.

"Are you sure you're not hurt?" she asked at the same time.

He smiled. "I'm sure."

Rebecca shook her head. "I'd better check. All that blood had to come from somewhere."

Zacariah cursed silently. He should have gone to the store while they were in town and gotten another shirt. How was he going to explain having a bullet wound that had healed completely over in a matter of hours?

"It's just a scratch," he offered lamely, hoping to discourage her.

It didn't work. She reached for his arm and determinedly pulled him out of the stall to her side.

"Scratches don't bleed like *that*."

Brushing his protests aside, she deftly undid the buttons of his shirt. Speaking more to herself than to him, she said, "I've tended more wounds than I care to think about Zack. Bullets, knives, broken legs, bumps on the head. When you live far enough from town, you'd better be good at taking care of your own hurts. A doctor isn't always handy. Especially come winter."

While she talked, he thought frantically, hoping for a decent lie to tell. But nothing came.

She finished with the row of buttons and pulled the fabric aside. Frowning, she stared at his sun-bronzed chest, looking for a wound.

Nothing.

Rebecca glanced up at him curiously, then tugged at him, turning him more toward the light.

"I told you," he said. "I'm fine." He tried to step away, but she held her ground.

"I don't see a thing here," she muttered.

"See? Just a scratch."

"Not even a scratch."

Staring hard at his chest, Rebecca frowned. There had to be *something*. That blood hadn't just appeared on his shirt. Then she saw it. So faint, it was no surprise she'd missed it the first time, there was a tiny mark in the middle of his chest. Rebecca slowly drew one finger across his skin to stop on that tiny imperfection.

He flinched.

"What is this?" she whispered and bent for a closer look. A small, pale red circle lay dead center of his breastbone. Though faint, the edges were clearly visible. But even as she stared at it, the mark grew paler until she almost believed she'd imagined seeing it in the first place.

"Zack . . ."

Quickly, he pulled her into the circle of his arms.

"I'm fine, Rebecca."

She nodded, still trying to figure out what she'd seen. Where that blood had come from. Then she remembered. Buck had said one of the men had been killed. No doubt, Zack had had to lift the dead man onto a horse. He'd probably stained his shirt in the effort.

"We found some of your horses in the canyon too," he said, smoothing his hands up and down her back.

Her head snapped up. She hadn't dared hope for this. Somehow, she'd assumed that the rustlers would have sold off all her stock by now. "How many?"

"About thirty," Zack said.

Thirty. Ripples of anger spread through her. How many head had Scotty sold off? Dozens? A hundred? Or were there pockets of animals hidden all over the ranch, waiting their turn to be driven off? And what about the money he'd gotten from selling her stock?

Deliberately, she tried to calm down. There would be plenty of time to question Scotty. For now, the bright side was, the thieving would stop and she had at least a *few* horses left.

Inhaling sharply, she said as much to Zack.

He grinned and winced. "The silver lining?"

Her lips twitched.

"Buck also said those horses we found were from the South pasture. He seemed very pleased about it."

"The *South* pasture?" A swell of pleasure washed over her. "You're sure he said South?"

"I'm sure. Does it mean something special?"

She reached up, wrapped her arms around his neck and gave him a long, hard kiss. When she pulled back again, she grinned at him.

"The South pasture mares are my best breeding stock," she told him. "Even with a few of them, we could make a go of it."

"That's good. Isn't it?"

"No. It's perfect." She reached up, plucked his hat off and sent it sailing into the surrounding shadows. "Everything's perfect. You're safe. Buck's safe. The rustling's over." She sighed in satisfaction. "I feel like celebrating."

He lifted one hand to frame her face and she turned into it, relishing the heat that flowed into her from his flesh.

"I love you," she said and held her breath, waiting.

His gaze moved over her face like a caress. His fingers slipped beneath her jaw to tip her chin up. Slowly, reverently, he bent his head and left a tender kiss on her lips. He pulled back to only a whisper away from her and said softly, "I love you, Rebecca. God help us both, I love you."

Her pent-up breath escaped on a sigh and she banished all of Buck's foolish warnings. Zacariah loved her. Now she knew he wouldn't leave. He couldn't. Any more than she would be able to let him go.

She leaned against him and gave herself up to an embrace that seared her soul and branded her heart. No other man had ever made her feel so loved. So cherished. No one had looked at her the way Zacariah did. And no one had given her this sense of completion that filled her each time they made love.

She needed him like she did air and water and sun. Each time with him only fed the flames consuming her, making them burn brighter, hotter.

Rebecca pulled back, then reached up to touch his bruised lips tenderly. "Hurts, I'll bet."

He nodded.

"I've got some witch hazel at the house."

He eyed her warily and she laughed.

"It'll help. Trust me."

A distant, low rumble of thunder rolled into the barn.

"Rain," she said.

"Sounds like it," he agreed, though doubt niggled at the back of his mind.

"We'd better get back to the house."

"All right," he said. "You go ahead. I'll finish with the horses and follow after."

"I'll even rustle up some food and have it ready."

Another clap of thunder rattled the plank walls. It was closer.

He pulled her into his arms for a brief, hard hug, then released her again.

"I'll see you in a few minutes?" she asked as she headed for the door.

He nodded as yet another crash of thunder blasted directly overhead.

She'd hardly left the barn before the voice came.

"Zacariah, what were you thinking?"

"Hello, Mordecai."

"Hello? That's all you can say? Hello?"

Zacariah moved into the barn and immediately went straight to the horse he'd abandoned in favor of Rebecca. "What do you want me to say?" he ground out.

"Zacariah," he began, then broke off quickly.

A smaller, grayer mist began to form in the corner and as Zacariah turned to watch, he saw Fenwick stagger from its center and smile shamefacedly at Mordecai.

"You're late," the Collector said.

"Yes sir," Fenwick bobbed his bald head. *"I know, sir, but there was a difficulty and . . ."*

"Never mind." Mordecai sighed heavily and turned back to his friend. *"I'm concerned for you, Zacariah. You seem to have become far too involved with these people."*

A bit late for *that* warning, he told himself with a wry smile.

"The Minions are not happy," Mordecai went on. *"They cannot believe you actually told that Buck person who you really are. And as to the . . . mating . . . well!"*

"Buck already knew about me." Zacariah smoothed the brush over the horse's back methodically. "He remembered me from four years ago."

"Sulphur and brimstone!"

"He hasn't told anyone."

"He will. He's human—they're entirely too talkative."

Zacariah lifted one brow and Fenwick chuckled.

"You are prepared to make your Collection . . . aren't you?"

He shifted uneasily as thoughts of Ellie Parker filled his mind. "I think I know who it is. The girl I told you about."

"Good."

"There's nothing good about it!" He whirled around to face his friend, his voice a strained, whispered shout. "She's just a child!"

Mordecai stiffened. "It's not for you to say. And the Minions will brook no more mistakes from you."

No. They wouldn't. Rage drained from him like water from a washtub. There was nothing he could do to save Ellie, anyway. The disease was killing her. He couldn't cure disease. That last infant had been different. The child was supposed to have simply . . . died. For no apparent reason. In that case, his late arrival had changed everything.

But he didn't have the slightest notion how to save Ellie. Still, should he try? He glanced at his oldest friend. "What could they do to me?"

Mordecai gasped, horrified. "Don't even ask, Zacariah. I'll pretend I didn't hear and so will Fenwick. Won't you, Fenwick?"

He nodded furiously, sending his hood flying off his head.

"We'll see you in about ten days. With your Collection."

"Ten days," *he echoed after a long moment.* "With my Collection."

"What's in ten days? Who are you talking to? And what do you collect?"

Rebecca.

Dread filled him as he slowly turned away from the disappearing mists to meet her confused gaze.

"Of all the stupid, insulting stories," she snapped and started pacing the length of the barn furiously.

Soul Collector?

She'd never heard such nonsense!

"It's not a story," he insisted from his position near the front door. "I didn't make this up!"

"Oh, of course not!" She stopped dead and whirled around to face him. Splotches of lamplight left small circles of yellow light dotting the interior of the barn. Zacariah stood in the shadows. Naturally. She couldn't see his eyes. Read his expression. And she didn't trust herself to get any closer to him.

Betrayal slashed at her, cold and deep. That he would invent such a ridiculous story only made the betrayal harder to bear. He didn't even respect her enough to give her a *good* lie.

But, if this laughable story was better than the truth—what could the truth *be?* Marching back down the center aisle, she stopped with a good five feet in between them.

"What's the truth, Zack? The *real* truth?"

"I already told you," he said and she saw his jaw tighten.

"Not that fairy tale! What are you really?" She took a half-step closer and glared at him. "A gambler? No. An outlaw?" She shook her head. Those weren't right, either. "We know you're not a horse thief. At least, you're not *my* horse thief."

He inhaled sharply, stuffed his hands into his pockets and glared right back at her. "I'm not a thief."

She gasped as a sudden, horrifying thought occurred to her. "You're married!" Lifting one hand to cover her mouth, she went right on talking. "Where is she? Do I know her? Oh, Lord, not this. Somebody tell me I didn't go to bed with a married man!"

"Rebecca, it's not that simple."

"Simple? You think having a wife is *simple?*" She took a staggering step back. "Oh God, you have *two* wives!"

"Rebecca . . ."

"*More* than two?"

"I'm not married at all! I told you, I'm a Soul Collector."

Shaking her head viciously, she stumbled toward the door. She tried to brush past him, but he caught her arm firmly with one hand and spun her around to face him.

"Rebecca, I told you the truth." He lifted one hand to touch her and she turned her head aside. "Why would I lie?"

She snorted a choked laugh. "Why?" Shaking her head, she pushed her hair back from her face and glared at him. "To get away from me, of course!"

"I don't *want* to leave."

"Sure. You don't want to. You *have* to."

"That's right."

"In ten days."

"Yes."

"Because all the other little Soul Collectors are waiting for you."

He sighed. "Yes."

She jerked away from him and stepped back. For all his lies, she wanted to rush back into his arms and let him hold her. Tell her this was all a mistake. A joke.

But she couldn't.

And he wouldn't.

Ten days. He probably wouldn't have even said goodbye if she hadn't caught him talking to his invisible friend.

Lord. Invisible friends. Soul Collectors.

She snapped him a look and asked, "Were you even going to tell me that you were leaving? And if you were, when? The morning you left? Perhaps the night before, after making love to me again? Or maybe you were just going to disappear from my life as mysteriously as you came into it."

"Do you think I want this?" he demanded and took a step toward her. Sparks of anger lit up his cool, blue gaze. "After what we've shared together, do you *really* believe I want to leave you?"

"I don't know what to believe." Her head hurt. It felt as though a dozen blacksmiths were pounding on tiny anvils behind her eyes. "I watch you talking to a man who isn't there. You tell me some outrageous story. And still all I can think about is being in your arms."

He reached for her but she jumped back, holding one hand out, palm up, to stop him.

"No." She shook her head solemnly. "Why ten days, Zack? Why not five? Fifteen?"

"I told you."

"Right." She laughed and nodded. "Some people in Heaven are expecting you."

"Rebecca . . ."

"Don't treat me like a fool! Why don't you just admit that you were looking to spend a few nights with a widow who happened to be handy and let it go at that?"

"It was more than that and you know it."

"How do I know?"

"If I were going to lie," he snapped, "wouldn't I have told a better one?"

"Maybe. And maybe you're just a terrible liar." She threw her hands up and shook her head in wonder. "Then again, perhaps you're better than I think. A *Soul Collector.* Not many men would have thought of it, Zack. It's something you can't prove, after all." She paused thoughtfully. "You can't, can you?"

"No." He scowled, then brightened a bit. "There's the bullet wound."

"What?"

"Where I was shot. Earlier."

"Shot?"

He ripped his shirt open and buttons flew around the barn, skittering into the shadows. "See?" he said and rubbed his chest. "Nothing there. You said it yourself. That blood just didn't appear. I was shot, but my body healed itself over."

She nodded and smirked at him. "In a few hours."

"Dammit Rebecca," he shouted suddenly. "Can't you trust me?"

It was as though he'd slapped her. Trust? He talked about trust while telling lies bigger than any she'd ever heard before? Instead of answering his ridiculous question, she asked another of her own.

"If you're Death, why haven't you killed any of us?"

"It's not your time." He sighed tiredly and shoved one hand through his hair.

"And when *is* it my time?"

"I don't know."

"Oh, yes." She nodded sagely. "Only the *Onions* know that."

"Minions."

"Onions, Minions, *carrots!* I don't care!"

She was shrieking. She heard her voice rise and felt her insides go with it. She should have known. She sholdn't have cared. Dammit, why had she fallen in love with a man so desperate to leave her that he would make up lies a crazy woman wouldn't believe?

"Rebecca, if you could just trust me," he said softly.

"How can I?" She crossed her arms over her chest again and squeezed. "Why should I believe you? You let me care for you. Fall in love with you. And even worse than what you did to me—you lied to my son."

"I never lied to Danny."

"Not in so many words, maybe," she shot back. "But with your silence, you let him believe that you cared."

"I do."

"Damn you, you *don't!*" She spun in a tight circle as if looking for one stable spot in her tilting world. Finally, though, she stood stock-still to face him again. "If you don't want me, just say so. Don't insult me with tall tales that even Danny wouldn't put up with."

"I *do* want you," he groaned and took another step toward her.

"Just not enough to stay."

"I can't."

"Or won't."

He reached out and grabbed her arms. Pulling her to him, he ignored her futile attempts at escape and held on to her until she'd settled down a bit. Finally, she lifted her eyes to meet his.

Everything he'd ever dared dream about lay in her eyes.

In shattered splendor.

"Rebecca." He drew a long, shaky breath. "If there was a way for me to stay, I would do it. In an instant. With no hesitation at all. The Minions will not allow it."

"Tell them," she demanded as if she believed him. "Tell them you want to stay."

He shook his head slowly. "It wouldn't do any good. I was only sent here to experience life in the first place as a punishment."

"Life? A punishment?" Confusion and fatigue warred in her eyes.

Zacariah prayed silently that she was beginning to believe him.

"Punishment for what?"

"It doesn't matter now."

"Of course it matters," she said. "If one month was a punishment for some small misdeed—do something unforgivable!"

"I already have," he told her and lifted one hand to cup her cheek. "I've fallen in love with a mortal."

Tears welled up in her eyes, but she blinked them back. "I wish I believed that, Zack. I wish I believed it all."

Regret and sorrow swelled in his chest until they threatened to block off his air completely. He saw the pain he'd caused in her eyes and felt its twin echo inside him.

"Believe this then, instead," he whispered. "I have never known love before coming to this house." He stared into her eyes, willing her to read the truth in his. "I have wandered alone for centuries and the only warmth I've found is here. With you. I would give up my soul for the chance to be with you."

She bit her lip and one tear spilled over the corner of her eye to roll down her cheek.

"If nothing else," he said, "believe that I love you."

He kissed her. A tender, gentle brush of his lips across hers. After a long moment, he lifted his head and smiled at her sadly.

She slapped him.

Hard.

Chapter ❀ Sixteen

Her fingers stung and she shook her hand as she took a step back from him.

"By the Path, Rebecca . . ."

"Don't you think you can sweet-talk me or kiss me into forgetting about all this, Zacariah."

"I wasn't trying to—"

She cut him off again and he threw his hands in the air before letting them fall to his sides in disgust.

"Don't even tell me what you were *trying* to do. I'm not in the mood for any more fairy stories tonight." Spinning around, she marched through the open doorway, headed for the main house. She hadn't gotten far at all when she heard him.

"I'm not lying to you, Rebecca. About *anything.*"

She hunched her shoulders as if defending against a blow, and kept walking.

Three days and she'd hardly spoken to him.

Zacariah propped one foot on the lowest rung of the corral fence and stared blankly at Sky Dancer and her colt. His remaining two weeks were fast disappearing and it looked as though Rebecca had every intention of ignoring him for what time he had left.

Grumbling to himself, he admitted that she had a right

to be angry. Even furious. But the fact that she didn't believe he loved her was particularly galling. Stubbornness. An annoying human characteristic.

"You all right, boy?"

He snapped his head around to look at Buck. He hadn't even heard the older man walk up.

"Yes. Fine." His gaze shifted back to the animals strolling peacefully around the enclosure.

Buck snorted. "Forget I asked. It was a stupid question anyhow. I can see you ain't fine."

He slanted a look at the man who now stood beside him at the fence.

"I know you don't think so, Zack. But it's better she's mad at ya. Better for Becky and prob'ly better for you."

"You're right. I don't think so."

Buck whistled for Sky Dancer and the big horse trotted to him, her baby stumbling along behind. As his work-worn hands gently stroked the horse's nose and broad forehead, he went on talking. "If she's mad at ya, she won't be hurt so much when we leave."

Zacariah shifted uneasily. Buck's conviction that *he* was the coming collection was a bit unnerving.

"So instead," he answered stiffly, "she believes that I'm a liar and never cared for her."

Buck shook his head. "You got to admit, this Soul Collector stuff is pretty damned hard to believe."

Two dark brows lifted.

"I mean, if I didn't remember you floatin' around four years ago . . ."

Zacariah's lips quirked as the man droned on. He would miss Buck. In fact, there was much about this life that he would miss. Odd, considering how appalled he'd been when first sentenced to a month as a mortal.

But he'd learned quite a bit since then. He'd made friends. He scowled and focused on the far distance. For the rest of eternity, he would see Danny's eager, gap-toothed smile. He would hear Buck's snort of laughter and wheezing cough. He would smell the sharp, clean scent of pine in every breeze that never touched him.

And he would remember Rebecca.

Her smile: Her tears. The teasing glint in her eyes when she sparred with Buck. Her loving patience with Danny. The touch of her hand. The warmth of her breath on his face. Her lips on his. Her breasts pressed against him and her arms wrapped tightly around his neck.

Even her anger was memorable. Fury shaking through her. Fire dancing in her eyes. Her sharp tongue wielding words as a fencer did swords. All of these things and more would haunt him throughout eternity.

"Hey, Zack!"

He started and glanced over his shoulder at Danny, across the yard from him.

"Are ya ready?"

"Yes, I'm coming." He steeled himself for yet another confrontation with Rebecca and straightened up. When Buck didn't move, he asked, "You're not coming to town with us?"

"Nope." He glanced at him from the corner of his eye. "Like I said, I think Becky bein' mad is good. But that don't mean I want to be around her if I don't have to be."

Smart man.

He sensed the difference in the townspeople's attitude toward him the moment they rode in. Smiles, nods and tipped hats followed their progress down the main street.

"It seems word has gotten around about you helping Buck to catch my rustlers," Rebecca said.

Surprised, he answered, "I didn't do that much."

Her eyebrows arched high on her forehead. "A *Soul Collector? Humble?*"

His jaw clenched until his teeth ached. Zacariah shot a swift look at the woman beside him on the wagon's bench seat. As he watched, Danny came up from the rear of the wagon and leaned forward, wrapping his short arms around his mother's neck.

Morning sunlight shimmered around them in a warm, golden light. Danny whispered something in Rebecca's ear that brought a soft smile to her face.

Regret stabbed at him as he committed their faces to memory. Centuries from now, he wanted to be able to close his eyes and remember this one moment. This one heartbeat of time when two people he cared for were happy. And alive.

She turned to him and frowned, concern overriding anger, however briefly. "Zack? You all right?"

He forced a smile and nodded.

"Do I get to go see Scotty in jail?" Danny asked suddenly.

"No, you don't."

"Aw Ma," the boy whined and squeezed his mother's neck in a pleading hug. "I never knew a jailbird before."

"Jailbird? Where'd you hear that?"

"From Buck."

She sighed. "I should have known."

"So can't I see him? Please?"

"No." Rebecca turned another look on Zacariah. "Would you mind taking my bloodthirsty child over to visit Ellie while I talk to Scotty?"

Ellie or Scotty. Zacariah didn't know which of them he wanted to see less. But for the first time in days, she was talking to him. Asking for his help. Besides, he knew she'd purposely waited several days before going to see Scotty, hoping a few days in jail would make him ready to talk. If she had to take Danny with her, she wouldn't accomplish anything.

"Sure," he said and swallowed back his reluctance to see Ellie. Facing the girl and having to pretend she wasn't dying was harder than anything he'd ever been called on to do before.

"Thanks." She smiled at him and he realized how much he'd missed her smiles.

"Will Ellie be all better, do ya think?" Danny asked.

Rebecca's smile faltered slightly, then faded completely. She reached up and patted her son's forearm, whispering, "I don't think so, honey."

"When *will* she get better?"

She sucked in a gulp of air and Zacariah opened his mouth, hoping to think of something comforting to say. Anything to help her answer her son. But Rebecca spoke up before he could.

"Ellie may not get better, sweetie."

Danny pulled his head back and looked from his mother to Zack and back again. "You mean, it's like what Zack said?"

"What did he tell you?" she asked, with a wary glance at the man beside her.

"That sometimes children die," Danny answered, his voice husky. "But that it doesn't hurt."

Her jaw tightened. Zacariah watched her blink back a sheen of moisature in her eyes. She sent him a long, thoughtful glance. "Yes, honey. It's like Zack said."

The boy leaned into his mother for a long moment, then whispered, "I'm glad it won't hurt."

"Me, too." Rebecca patted his arm again, then slowly, hesitantly, stretched out her hand to touch Zacariah. His fingers curled around hers and squeezed gently. When Danny moved to wrap one arm around his neck while keeping a firm hold on his mother with the other, a warm curl of acceptance flowered inside him. For the first time since becoming human, he felt like part of a family.

Satisfaction was small consolation for losing so much of her stock, but at least it would have been something.

Rebecca stood in front of the sheriff's desk and stared down at him in disgust. The lazy bastard didn't even have the decency to look shamefaced.

"I'm real pleased that Buck and that hired man of yours found your rustlers, Becky," he said and picked at his teeth with a dirty thumbnail. "Must be a real comfort to you, having menfolk around."

She crossed her arms over her chest and listened to the rapid tapping of her foot against the floor. "No more comforting than having a smart, hardworking sheriff to depend on."

He beamed at her, obviously unfamiliar with sarcasm.

Rebecca's eyes rolled heavenward as she told herself not to lose her temper. As useless as the man was, he could still prevent her from talking to Scotty.

"Can I see him now?" she asked, as politely as she could manage.

"Sure, sure you can." The big man scratched his swollen stomach absently. "Gonna be moving him to Denver in a couple of days. Hold the trial there, seein' as how we only got us a circuit judge and he ain't due in for another few months."

"Fine." She didn't care where the trial was. She'd be there to testify if they needed her, even if they held the trial in New York City. All she cared about at the moment were the answers to a few questions.

Then something the sheriff had said struck her and she had to ask, "Move him? Are you taking him to Denver personally?"

"Lordy, no." The sheriff waved one hand at her, like a parent at a particularly stupid child. "I'm a busy man, doncha know." He pulled his thumb away from his teeth, frowned at someting clinging to the nail, then shrugged and flicked it into the air.

Rebecca shuddered.

"Marshal from Denver's comin' down to collect them two horse thieves."

Relieved, she nodded. A marshal from *anywhere* had to be more competent than their town sheriff.

"Yes sir," he went on. "Those boys'll get a proper trial followed by a first-class hangin'."

Hanging.

Rebecca inhaled sharply and fought down a rising tide of nausea. She didn't want to think about Scotty hanging. No matter what he'd done to her, he didn't deserve that. He hadn't killed anyone. Luckily.

But a voice inside her whispered that Scotty had known the penalty for horse stealing long before he'd taken that first animal and sold it. Besides, if she was to believe Zack's story, it was only because he wasn't human that Scotty hadn't succeeded in killing him.

No. She wouldn't even *think* about that. Deliberately, she shook off every thought but the one uppermost on her mind.

"Can I see him alone?"

"Sure. He can't do nothin' from behind bars."

As Rebecca walked toward the door separating the sheriff's office from the cells, she heard him say, "Y'know, most everybody in town's talkin' about that new man of yours. Seems they don't care much if he talks to himself as long as he does the right thing when it's needed."

She glanced at him.

He shook his head. "Folks just ain't particular at all, I reckon."

That would certainly explain his being sheriff.

Turning her back on Cooper, she twisted the wrought-iron ring on the unpainted door and pushed the heavy panel open. Inside were two cells, opposite each other and separated by a walkway. Each of the two men had a cell to himself. Gunmetal bars formed the cages around the prisoners. Sunlight slanted through a narrow window at the end of the room and lay in golden, bar-like streaks on the dirty floor.

She looked to her right, saw a man she didn't recognize,

then turned immediately to her left. In the shadowy cell, a man lay on a cot, his back to her.

"Scotty?"

He tensed and slowly rolled over until he was looking at her.

Several days' worth of whiskers darkened his cheeks and his blond hair looked dirty. He'd been sleeping in his clothes and judging from the sheriff's own appearance, the man wasn't too concerned with giving his prisoners water to wash in.

But the pale gray eyes staring back at her looked the same.

He stood up, crossed the small cell and grabbed an iron bar in each fist as if he was going to try to shake the walls down. "It's good to see you, Becky."

"I wish I could say the same."

His fingers tightened around the cold steel. "I knew you wouldn't understand."

"Understand?" She took a step closer to the bars, saw him make a move to reach for her, and stopped. Keeping a safe distance between them, Rebecca said, "What I understand is that you were stealing from me. From my son."

"It's not like that," he argued and rested his forehead on the bars in front of him. "I wasn't *stealing*. I was getting a start for us."

"There is no us," she told him. "There never was."

The man in the cell behind her snorted a choked laugh and Rebecca stiffened.

Scotty smiled sadly. "There would have been. If not for that damned drifter."

"Zack?"

"I saw the way you looked at him. The way he looked at you." His grip tightened until his knuckles shone white. "He had no right. That's why I had to hurry up. I had to get the last of the horses sold so's you and me could get married."

Rebecca's insides twisted and something cold settled in the pit of her stomach. She'd noticed the odd looks Scotty'd been giving her over the last several months, but she'd never guessed that his mind had slipped so far from reality.

He lifted his chin proudly. "I did right by us," he whispered. "I got top dollar for those horses. The Army took all I could give them."

That cold knot in her belly hardened. *He* made top dollar? While she worried about keeping her son's legacy intact, this . . . *thief* was counting his money? Rebecca choked her anger back down a tight throat. She couldn't afford to give her fury free rein until she found out exactly what he'd done with the money.

"Where is it, Scotty?" she asked quietly. "Where'd you put the money?"

He glanced covertly at the man in the other cell, then looked back at her. Crooking a finger at her to come closer, he lowered his voice to just above a breath. "It's stashed someplace safe," he said with a smile that glanced off his icy eyes.

Rebecca drew a shallow breath and held it.

"Under my cot at the bunkhouse," he continued, "there's a loose floorboard. Money's all wrapped up in oilcloth. Safe."

She sighed and took one step back from him. What little light shone in his eyes, died.

"That's all you wanted?" he asked, stunned. "*That's* why you came to see me? The money? You don't give a damn about me, do you?"

Goose bumps raced along her flesh and made her want to run into the sunshine and wrap its warmth around her until the last of the cold seeped out of her. She took another step backwards, keeping her eyes fixed on the man who'd worked for her for years.

"You're gonna take that money and share it with *him,*

aren't you?'' he shouted. ''*My* money and you're going to give it to *him!*''

She staggered when she bumped into the jailhouse door. Her anger was enough to deal with a thief. Lord knew, she'd come to the jail ready to horsewhip Scotty herself. But the madness in his eyes and raging from his throat frightened her. Reaching around behind her, she fumbled for the iron ring and clumsily folded her fingers around it. Giving it a hard yank, she fell forward, dragging the door open.

Scotty's hand shot out and grabbed her braid. He tugged her toward him and Rebecca yelped, surprised by the sudden pain. Pulling her face close to the bars, he angled his own head near hers.

''I *loved* you!'' he snarled and gave her braid a vicious tug. ''I loved you and planned for *us* and you want to betray me? To throw everything I worked for away on a damned *drifter?*''

Tears stung her eyes even as fear tightened its grip on her heart. Somewhere along the line, Scotty had slipped over the edge into complete madness and she hadn't even noticed. *None* of them had noticed. She reached back and clawed at his hand desperately, hoping to make him release her. But his fingers only tightened in her hair.

''Don't you *understand?*'' he bellowed, giving her a hard shake. ''I was going to *rescue* you!''

''Here now,'' The sheriff's loud, booming voice sliced through Scotty's wild ravings and for the first time in her life, Rebecca was happy to see Tall Cooper.

Striding through the open door, the sheriff swung the iron skillet in his hand, smacking it against the steel bars just an inch or two from Rebecca's head. Scotty grunted and released her, hurling curses at the man who'd smashed a pan into his forehead.

She didn't waste time. After a quick thanks, she was out the door, Scotty's shouts still ringing in her ears.

*   *   *

"Is Billy still here?"

Zacariah leaned forward, dismayed to find that Ellie's voice seemed so much weaker than it had the last time he'd seen her. What little color that had remained in her cheeks was gone now, leaving her pale skin almost transluscent. Her hair lay spread out beneath her on the pillow like a bed of fire and even her cool green eyes seemed to be focusing on a world far away from the one she still lived in.

Snatches of conversations, an occasional shout of laughter and the unceasing roll of wagon wheels slipped into the room. A breeze fluttered the curtains at her window and Ellie shivered.

"You're cold," he said softly. "I'll close the window."

"No." She gave him a tired smile. "Leave it open, please. I like to hear everybody."

He nodded, wishing that he had something to do. Something to say. How had he ever thought mortals to be stupid creatures? None of the townspeople seemed to have trouble knowing what to do and say. It was only *he*, the Soul Collector, who stood dumbly by while others did the comforting.

When he and Danny first arrived at the store, he'd noticed people coming and going. There seemed to be a veritable flood of humanity, carrying hot food and warm compassion to the Parkers.

Even the boy had somehow known what to do to help his friend. Jake Parker, obviously frightened by his sister's illness, had stood stonily silent until Danny had drawn him outside to play. Once free of the store, and the aura of mourning clouding it, Jake had become a child again. For awhile, at least.

"Is Billy still here?"

He shook himself and looked down at the girl watching him through faded eyes. "You already asked me that once, didn't you? Yes, Ellie. He's here. Downstairs."

In fact, the solemn-eyed boy had planted himself on the

stairs and looked to have no intention of leaving anytime soon.

She closed her eyes briefly, then looked at him again. "I told him he should go home, but he doesn't."

"He loves you." Zacariah'd seen the boy's haunted features too often to not know what lay behind his pain.

"Yes, but he has to stop."

"Why?"

She moved, winced slightly and said, "Can I ask you something, Zack?"

"Of course."

"No one will talk to me about this," Ellie told him. "But I know I'm not going to get better."

A giant hand clamped down around his mid-section and squeezed. He fought for breath.

"I'm dying, aren't I, Zack?"

God help him. He looked into her eyes and knew he couldn't lie to her. She may have been a child in years, but she had earned the right to the truth. Carefully, he covered her fragile hand with one of his. "Yes, Ellie," he said past the lump in his throat. "You are."

Her eyes closed again and in the moment before she opened them, he called himself all kinds of a selfish fool. What did he know about human children? What did he know about life and death and suffering?

Everything he'd ever learned had been through watching, observing. Standing safely apart from the blood and the grief, untouched by anything stronger than a sigh of discontent.

But then those eyes of hers opened slowly and he saw that he *had* managed to give her something, after all.

Peace.

"Thank you," she said, "for not lying to me."

He nodded and cringed when she winced again. This suffering day after day wasn't right. Why must she wait for the end? Immediately, memories rushed into his mind. All the times when Mordecai had tried to tell him how important it was that a collection be made on time. Zacariah groaned inwardly as he recalled the many times when he'd arrived late, never thinking how much suffering his cavalier attitude had caused. He swallowed his own shame. Mordecai was right.

Every moment *did* count.

She turned her head slightly and stared at the spear of sunlight slashing through the room. Tiny particles of dust swirled in the brilliant light and sparkled like the sighs of diamonds.

"Mama and Papa are so sad," she said and he had to lean even closer to hear her. "They come in here and they try to laugh and joke with me and I can see that they're crying inside."

He ignored the stinging in his eyes and concentrated on her soft voice.

"I have to talk about it with somebody, though."

"I'm right here, Ellie," he said and almost wished for some of the distance he used to feel for the dying. "You go ahead."

She inhaled and the motion was so slight, the quilt-covering her small form hardly moved. "Do you think it hurts?" she asked. "The dying part, I mean?"

Something shifted inside him. At last, there was something he could do for her. Something no one else *could* do.

Zacariah slipped out of his chair and went down on one knee beside the bed. Leaning his forearms on the quilt-covered mattress, he took one of her hands in his and cradled it gently.

"It doesn't hurt, Ellie," he whispered and saw in her eyes that she desperately wanted to believe him. "It's over in less than a moment. Less time than a single heartbeat."

Her eyes widened and her teeth pulled at her bottom lip.

"You close your eyes and a beautiful silvery cloud swirls up around you."

"A cloud?"

"Yes." He smiled gently as he described a Collection. "A warm cloud, with all the colors of the rainbow and all the light of a thousand suns trapped inside it."

She sighed heavily. "Then what?"

"Then, you'll see someone."

"God?"

"No." He shook his head and smiled. "Not God. Not then." Although some of the Collectors he knew . . . including, at one time, himself, would be particularly pleased to be mistaken for the Supreme Being. "This *person*," he said for want of a better name, "is someone chosen specifically to come for you when it's your time to move on."

"Just for me?"

"That's right." He nodded and folded his fingers more firmly around hers. "And this person will be kind and gentle and will guide you to the Eternal Path."

She blinked, fascinated. "What's that?"

"A long, shining, golden road that stretches out past forever."

"Golden?"

"Yes," he told her tightly. "And it's more beautiful than anything you've ever imagined."

A long moment passed before she asked, "Where will the road take me, Zack?"

"To your new home."

"Heaven?"

"Some call it that."

"Will I be . . . *alone*?"

"No, Ellie." He bent over her, his voice hushed, his words spilling from him rapidly in his haste to reassure her. "Not for a minute. Your special guide will be with you until you're met by people who have gone on before you."

"Like who?"

Zacariah saw the gleam of interest in her eyes and hoped that her curiosity had overcome her fear. "It could be anyone," he said gently. "Do you have grandparents?"

"One in Illinois," she said. "But the others died when I was little."

He brushed her silken hair back from her forehead, then lightly drew one finger along the line of her cheek. Smiling, he said, "There's the answer to your question."

"What do you mean?"

"You wondered who would be there to meet you. Now you know." He bent down, left a quick kiss on her forehead and straightened up again. "Your grandparents will be waiting for you, Ellie."

"Are you sure?"

The knot in his throat tightened and the steel band around his chest closed another notch.

"I'm sure," he promised her solemnly. "Even now, they're probably getting ready for your arrival."

"Getting ready?" she asked. "Like for a party?"

"Exactly like that."

She thought about everything he'd said for several minutes. Zacariah felt the passage of time more keenly than he ever had before. Had it been enough? Had his words convinced her that there was nothing to fear in facing the coming journey?

Finally, she spoke again in a voice clouded by fatigue. "I'll get to see everybody again someday, won't I?"

"Yes, Ellie." Zack's dry throat thickened. "You'll be waiting for them when they arrive."

She nodded, then looked up at him, her gaze serious and old beyond her years. "Thank you for telling me," she said. "You make it sound really nice."

"It will be," he promised, "the most beautiful, joyous moment of your life."

"It almost seems like you *know* it's true."

He inhaled sharply and exhaled on a rush. His lips twisted as he nodded. "Maybe I *do* know, Ellie."

"If it's so nice, why are you crying?"

Startled, he lifted one hand to his own face, then drew it back to stare at the solitary tear glistening against his flesh. He gulped in air like a drowning man taking in water.

"I'm not . . . sure," he said.

Chapter ❀ Seventeen

"I think I know why." Rebecca stepped into the room and looked at Zack as he spun around in surprise to face her. Water filmed his cool, blue eyes, but couldn't dim the stunned expression shining there.

She'd heard only the last part of his conversation with Ellie. But that had been enough. Whether Rebecca believed his story about being a Soul Collector or not . . . he obviously did. And more importantly, Ellie believed. He'd been able to put the girl's fears to rest with his quiet words and gentle conviction.

If that were crazy, she much preferred it to Scotty's selfish, all-consuming madness.

"You know why Zack was crying?"

She smiled at the little girl. "I think so." She walked to the foot of the bed and curled her fingers around the curliqued, black iron frame. "I think it's because as nice as that other place is, Zack knows that we'll all miss you very much."

Ellie nodded solemnly and glanced at the man still kneeling by her bed. "I'll miss everybody, too."

He tore his gaze from Rebecca's and smiled at the girl. "No, you won't, Ellie. You'll be much too busy to give us a thought."

Even as he spoke, the child's eyes drifted closed and in moments, she was asleep.

Rebecca stole from the room quietly and Zacariah followed her. She was waiting for him in the hall.

"I didn't know you were there," he said.

"I know."

"You heard . . . *everything?*"

"No. Just the last part."

"And you believe me?"

"I didn't say that."

"But what you said to Ellie." He stared at her, confused.

"I saw what you were trying to do for her. I know she must be scared." Her voice broke and she drew one long, shaky breath before trying to continue. "Besides, I guess I wanted it to be true. For Ellie's sake."

He took a step closer and Rebecca allowed it. The last three days had been the longest of her life. She'd missed him. Talking to him. Laughing with him. Being held in his arms.

She looked up into his eyes and then let her gaze drift across his features. From the slash in his cheek where his dimple lay in hiding, to the night-black hair that fell across his forehead, to the eyes locked on her face.

She believed him. She had to. Her knees shook and she leaned against the wall behind her. A Soul Collector.

A silent laugh tore through her. Did believing him make *her* crazy?

She'd done a lot of thinking in the last few days. Enough to realize that his story would explain the mystery surrounding him. How a man came to be wandering around with no horse. No clothes. No knowledge of the simplest everyday things.

This bizarre explanation of his almost made the rest of it make sense.

Besides, believing that he was a Soul Collector and would *have* to leave her was better than the alternatives.

"Rebecca?"

"Zack," she whispered, "it's true, isn't it?"

He stepped closer, laid his hands on her shoulders and held her steady. "Yes, it is."

She slumped, but he caught her up and pulled her to him. His arms closed around her, and for a moment Rebecca did nothing but listen to the beat of his heart. A heart that he claimed wasn't real. Arms that weren't real.

Her eyes squeezed shut. She'd fallen in love with a man who said he didn't even exist. That he was nothing more than a temporary human, serving out a disciplinary sentence. A man who would leave her life forever in less than two weeks.

Unless she found some way to make him stay.

"Under his bed?" Buck's outraged voice boomed out into the room. "You mean to tell me the son of a bitch hid his loot right here under my own damn nose?"

"You couldn't have known," Rebecca soothed him as she watched Zack and her foreman tilt Scotty's cot over onto its side.

When the floor was exposed, she dropped to her knees and began to run her fingers over the planks. Even as she did, though, she told herself that perhaps Scotty had lied. Maybe he only *thought* he'd hidden the money here. "We don't even know if he was telling the truth or not," she grunted as she pulled at another plank. "He's crazy as a bedbug."

"Crazy like a fox, you mean," Buck countered and moved closer, slapping his palms onto his knees. "He fooled us for a helluva long time."

She scowled at the still-grating thought.

Then one of the narrow pine boards lifted under her searching fingers and her breath caught. Carefully, she pulled it out of the way and set it aside. Staring down into the blackness, she reached forward when Zack's voice stopped her.

"Maybe you should let me feel around for it. There might be snakes down there."

She jerked her hand back and glared at the gaping hole in the floor. Call her a coward, but the thought of sweeping her hand around in darkness and maybe snatching up a snake was enough to make her skin crawl.

Scooting to one side, she made room for him. Leaning down, Zack plunged his left arm through the hole in the floor and began to hunt blindly for Scotty's hidden treasure.

Seconds felt like minutes. Buck inched in closer. Rebecca strained to see into the darkness.

Finally, Zack crowed, "I found something."

Slowly, he straightened up, pulling an oilskin-wrapped package from the dark hole. Rebecca sat back on her heels and stared for a long moment before holding out one hand for it.

"It's heavy," he said.

She tested the weight of the package in her palm and heard the soft clink of coins.

"Well?" Buck prodded. "What're you waitin' on? Open 'er up. Let's see if Scotty was a better deal-maker than he was a workin' cowboy."

Rebecca nodded and carefully pulled at the tightly wrapped oilskin. When it had been unfolded, she stared down at the worn, leather pouch lying in her lap. She glanced briefly at Zack, then tugged at the drawstring holding the neck of the bag closed.

When the pouch was open, she held her breath and tipped the leather bag into her palm. A stream of gold coins poured into her waiting hand and over it to clink and roll on the floor. Hundreds, she told herself. There had to be hundreds of dollars here.

She wiggled her fingers and the golden coins shimmered in the late afternoon sun.

Buck whistled, low and long. "However crazy he is, he looks to have gotten top dollar for your horses."

Rebecca nodded absently. "He bragged about that."

"He would."

"With this much money," she said, ignoring Buck for the moment, "we can buy some new breeding stock. Make repairs to the ranch buildings." A harsh laugh scraped from her throat. "Hell, we can get *new* shingles for the roof."

"Rebecca," Zack asked, "are you all right?"

She looked up at him and smiled despite her watery eyes. "Yeah. I think so." Sniffing, she poured the coins back into the pouch and took the others that Buck had picked up and was offering her. "You know, Scotty stole more from me than the horses."

"What do you mean?"

Her gaze locked with Zack's. "He stole my trust. He made it harder for me to believe . . ." Her voice faded off. "But with this," she went on in a stronger tone, "at least I know I won't lose the ranch. I'll be able to hold onto it for Danny."

"Silver lining?" Zack asked quietly.

Buck snorted and straightened up.

But Rebecca gave Zack a half-smile. "I guess so."

She pulled the drawstring tight, securing the coins inside, then pushed herself to her feet. "Now, it's time I started supper or we're all going to go hungry."

She left without another word.

When the door closed behind her, Buck said, "You told her, didn't ya?"

Zacariah shot the other man a quick, hard look. "How'd you know?"

He shrugged. "Just a feelin'. She seems a bit sadder. And you said I shouldn't say nothin'. I told you it'd be best to keep your distance."

"I couldn't do that." He stared at the door where she'd disappeared and knew that he would do *anything* to have these last, dwindling days with her.

"Well, hell." Buck scratched his jaw thoughtfully. "Did ya tell her about me goin' with ya?"

Zacariah's gaze slanted toward the older man. "No.

Like I said before, Buck. We don't know—"

"Yeah, yeah. But you'll see I'm right." He lifted both hands and let them fall again. "I'm the only one who makes sense."

Collections didn't always make sense, Zacariah had come to realize. And if anyone should know that it was Buck. Hadn't he railed against Daniel Hale's dying too young? But then, maybe the man needed to believe that *he* was the imminent collection. And since Zacariah couldn't prove or disprove it, he wouldn't argue the matter.

Rebecca walked across the yard to stare out at the moon-washed meadow. Behind her, in the house, Zacariah was telling Danny one of his very involved bedtime stories. All she'd heard before coming outside was something about a gladiator doing battle with a chained lion.

Propping her forearms on the top rung of the corral fence, she admitted that Zack did seem to have an unlimited supply of stories at his command. She frowned at the thought. Despite preferring to believe his outlandish story, it was difficult to accept that he wasn't a man like any other.

Centuries. She shivered and rubbed her arms. Why was this happening to her? Why had she finally found the man she'd dreamed of as a child only to lose him to either a madness she couldn't cure—or a reality that was too bizarre to believe in?

She sighed and stared at the trees lining the ranch yard. Her gaze drifted across the open meadow that stretched as far as the eye could see to the foot of the distant mountains.

Emptiness.

She shivered again. Until Zack had arrived, she hadn't really noticed how much had been missing in her life. Then today, staring into the eyes of madness, hearing

Scotty accuse her of loving Zack, everything had suddenly slipped into focus.

She *did* love him. Despite everything. She breathed in the night air, savoring the magic and wonder of being alive. Too much of this existence was left to chance.

Daniel had died, unexpectedly. Violently.

Scotty had given in to the wildness inside him.

Ellie Parker lay at death's door . . . her life cut short before it had even begun.

Rebecca blinked back a sudden sheen of tears and told herself that she wouldn't risk losing her chance at happiness. Zack was here. And though he insisted on his ridiculous story—a story it shamed her to admit that she was beginning to believe in—she knew he'd been happy at the Hale ranch. She knew he cared for her. Loved her.

And maybe that was enough.

"Deep thoughts, Becky?"

She turned to look at the older man and smiled. "You making a habit of sneaking up on me in the dark?"

He shrugged and gave her a half smile. "Things've been mighty busy around here lately. We don't get much chance to talk anymore."

"You're right." She nodded and turned back to the view she'd been studying before he'd joined her.

"I got to say," he started, and leaned one hand on the fence next to her, "you're takin' Zack's news a lot easier than I thought you would." He tipped his hat brim up with one finger. "Oh, you was mad, I grant ya. But ya didn't lose your head over it."

"What?"

He met her surprised gaze and held it. "He told he that he talked to you. That you knew about . . . *him.*"

"Well, yeah," she said, a cold chill spreading through her. Buck knew about this? For how long? Why hadn't he said anything? Why was she so calm? "He didn't say that you knew."

"Guess he don't want it talked about much." Buck

admitted. "Reckon I can understand that. Can't be too easy, y'know . . . Him bein' Death, I mean."

"You *believe* him?" she asked, stunned. It was one thing for *her* to consider the outlandish. But Buck took nothing but the existence of *God* on faith. "Why?"

"I remember him." He shrugged, then narrowed his gaze as if staring at a mental image that he didn't quite like. "Gives me the shivers just to think on it, too."

"*Remember* him? You *remember* seeing Zack as a Soul Collector?" A cold breeze picked up from out of nowhere and fluttered past her.

"Saw him clear as I see you now." His leathery brow furrowed as he cocked his head to look at her carefully. "Didn't he tell you?"

Frustration, anger and a double serving of helplessness bubbled in her stomach. Her hands tightened on the corral fence rung.

"Do I *sound* like he told me any of this?"

"No, ma'am," Buck took a step back and looked around the empty yard as if searching for anybody who might distract her. "You don't at that."

"Don't you take another step, Buck," Rebecca snapped and jabbed one finger at him. "Just *when* did you see Zack?"

"Becky . . ."

"Don't 'Becky' me, just tell me the truth."

He sighed heavily and rubbed one hand across his face. "Dad blast it, I shouldn't have said nothin' at all, but he said he told you and I wanted to make sure you and me had a chance at a nice good-bye."

"Good-bye?" Rebecca knew she was repeating everything the man was saying, but somehow, she couldn't stop herself. She felt as though she was trapped in some strange nightmare and all she had to do was wake up and everything would be as it should be again. But how to wake up? "If you remembered seeing Zack before, why didn't you say anything to me?"

"Well, I . . ."

"And what do you mean, say good-bye?" She pushed away from the fence, turned on her foreman and glared him into submission. "Just what in the hell is going on around here, Buck?"

"Damn me and my damn foot in my damn mouth anyway," he muttered.

"Talk."

He sighed.

"What do ya want to know?"

"Everything." She jerked her head at him. "Start with this memory of yours. Where did you see him? When?"

"Four years ago."

She gasped, staggered and clutched at her throat. Three little words. How could three little words have the power to strip breath right out of her?

"Daniel?"

"Yeah."

She swallowed heavily, steeled herself and commanded, "Tell me."

As he talked, his words drew mental images for her. Zack, appearing out of nowhere. Dressed in a glowing gray robe and floating across the carnage left in the wake of the stampede.

Cold. She felt cold down to her bones. Wrapping her arms around herself, she felt as though she might never be warm again. Zack had taken Daniel.

It was the man she loved who had taken her husband's life.

Her knees shook. She swayed unsteadily and absently felt Buck's firm grip on her shoulder. If only she could draw air into her lungs, everything would be all right. But there was a rock lodged in her chest where her heart used to be and nothing could move it.

"Becky?" Buck whispered. "Becky, say something, girl. Are you all right?"

Slowly, slowly, she looked up into his worried gaze and shook her head. "No, I don't believe I am," she managed to say despite the growing nausea choking her. "But don't stop. I want to hear the rest of it."

"That's all there is, Becky."

"No." She jerked out from under his comforting touch and jabbed one finger at his chest. "You can't quit now. There's more and I know it. You said you wanted to give us a chance to say good-bye. What's that supposed to mean?"

"Ah, dammit . . ."

"Tell me, Buck!"

"When Zack leaves . . . I'm goin' with him."

"What?" She took another step or two back, shaking her head in denial. Instantly though, she retraced her steps and stopped when she was practically nose to nose with him. "Why are you going?"

"Reckon it's my time."

"Did Zack say that?"

"Not exactly."

"Tell me what he said. *Exactly*."

He inhaled, shoved his hands into his pockets and shrugged. "No reason not to. Ya know everything else."

Her nerves frayed and tattered, she said only, "*Buck* . . ."

"All right, what he said was, that when he left, he had to make a Collection, like he calls it."

"He didn't say who?"

"No, but I figured . . ."

"But he didn't *say?*"

"No. Hell, Becky. I'm the only one who makes sense."

"Sense?" She snorted a laugh at him. "You think Daniel or *Ellie* makes sense?"

" 'Course not."

"Then what the hell does *sense* have to do with who he's going to kill when he leaves?"

Buck shook his head firmly. "It's me, Becky. I got a feeling."

"Well, I don't," she snapped and shot a look at the

house as the front door opened and lamplight poured into the night. She watched Zacariah step into the yard and close the door behind him. "But I'm *going* to get some answers," she muttered just before she started running at Zack.

He heard her before he saw her. His eyes adjusted to the darkness just in time to see her enraged expression as she crashed into him at a full run. Zacariah dropped onto the dirt and Rebecca straddled his stomach before he could move. Her fists rained blows on his chest and face, smacking him good a couple of times before he managed to capture her hands in his.

"Stop it!" he ordered and wheezed as she raised up, then dropped down onto his stomach again. Her jean-clad knees jabbed into his ribs and he had to fight to draw air back into his body.

"Damn you!" she shouted. "When do the lies stop?"

"What lies?" he shouted right back. "I haven't lied to you. I told you that."

"Every time you keep a secret that I should know about, you're lying." She yanked one hand free and swung at him. He turned his head with the glancing blow to his chin and saw Buck slink toward the bunkhouse.

Buck!

God's Blood.

"It was you," she ground out and her voice was low and savage.

"What?" He tightened his grip on her wrists in his own defense.

"You took Daniel."

He went utterly still and looked up into wounded, angry green eyes. Her hair was wild, like an ancient warrior. Her mouth was twisted into a grimace of pain and he could feel the tension straining in her body.

Rocks stabbed at his back. His ribs ached. With her trying desperately to crush his stomach, every breath was a challenge. And it wasn't going to get any better.

"Well?" she demanded. "Are you going to deny it?"

"No," he said. "It was me."

A low, guttural scream of pure fury poured from her throat as she took another swing at him. Quickly, Zacariah rolled to one side, pinning her beneath him.

She bucked and twisted in a panic of movements. "Get off me!"

"No," he told her and held both of her hands down on either side of her head. "Not until you listen to me."

"No more." She turned her face from him. "I don't want to hear it."

"You will, though."

She glared at him briefly. "Damn you to hell."

"Very likely," he muttered and gratefully felt some of the fury seep from her body.

"What's *that* supposed to mean?"

"It's my problem."

"Trying to make me feel sorry for you?" She sneered at him. "Trying to make me believe that you're going to Hell for collecting Daniel? A little late, isn't it?"

"Not for collecting Daniel." He sighed and tightened his hold on her when she tried to escape. "That was my duty. My—*job*."

She snorted derisively. "Not much of a job. Killing people."

"I didn't kill him," he shot back. "The stampede did."

"Get off me."

"No." Though the moonlight wasn't strong enough to read her expression clearly, there was enough light to see that she was still furious. But the fire had swept through her, leaving only the cold, hard ashes of anger behind. "I want to tell you about Daniel."

"What is there to tell? You took my husband from me."

"Yes."

She coughed, sniffed and turned her head to one side again.

Hesitantly, he released one of her hands. Holding her chin with the tips of his fingers, he turned her back to look at him. "I didn't kill him."

"He's just as dead."

"Because of the stampede."

"But it was you—"

"Who collected his soul." He paused and took a long breath into his lungs. "Yes."

She shivered.

"That's who I am, Rebecca."

"It's an ugly thing to be."

"It can be."

"Did he"—she inhaled sharply—"suffer?"

"Not at my hands."

Her body slumped, relaxing as more of her anger fell away. He knew it was safe to get up now. To release her. But he couldn't let her go. Not yet.

Silent minutes crawled by as she adjusted to her new knowledge. A nightbird screeched in the distance. A cool, steady wind rustled the branches of the surrounding trees.

"Is he all right?" she asked grudgingly, as if it irritated her to be indebted to him for anything. Even this.

"Yes."

"Was it like what you told Ellie?"

Her voice was soft now, with an undercurrent of old pain and worry.

He nodded and watched her chest rise and fall with her slow, deep breathing.

"Who met him?" she asked.

"His parents."

She nodded and smiled slightly. Then, shoving at him, she grumbled, "Now, get off me."

Reluctantly, he moved away and rose as she stood on still-shaky legs.

"What about the other?"

"What are you talking about?" he asked. "And just how much did Buck tell you?"

She staggered, pushed her hair out of her eyes and glared at him defiantly.

"Why exactly did you come here, Zack?"

"I've told you already," he said and shifted his gaze to the dark, shadowy landscape surrounding the ranch.

"Tell me again."

He sighed. "As punishment."

"Yes," she countered and took a half step closer. "But why *here?* Why *this* ranch? Why Danny and me?"

Long, silent moments passed and the tension stretching between them grew tauter. Then slowly, knowing it was useless to prolong the agony, Zacariah turned to look at her.

Rebecca braced herself. Her knees locked in an effort to stay upright, her fists clenched at her sides, she forced herself to meet his gaze and immediately wished she hadn't.

In the vague moonlight, she stared up into the blue eyes she knew so well and recognized something she'd never seen there before.

Fear.

Chapter ❀ *Eighteen*

What could a Collector of Souls possibly have to fear?

In a heartbeat of awareness, the answer rushed into her mind. Her mouth opened and closed a few times before she was able to make her voice work. When she finally succeeded, it sounded more like a croak.

"Buck said that when you leave, he's going with you."

"Buck shouldn't have said anything."

"Is it true?"

He didn't speak. His gaze shifted away from her again and even in the dim light, she saw his jaw muscle flinch.

"Tell me, damn it!"

His head snapped around. His eyes locked with hers. "Fine. *Someone* will be leaving with me. I don't know if it's Buck."

"Who, then?" The words scratched her throat as they wobbled into the air.

"I don't know," he said through gritted teeth.

Fear galloped wildly in her blood, feeding on itself until the terror crashed over her, sweeping her away into a nightmare world from which she might never wake up.

"You *have* to know," she demanded. "I have no one else to ask! And dammit, you have to tell me. Who? Buck? Me? *Danny?*"

He stalked away stiffly and shoved both hands through

his hair, squeezing his skull between his palms until his knuckles whitened. "Dammit, I don't know! I told Buck the same thing. *He* decided that he was my Collection. I won't know for sure until the very moment of Collection arrives."

"Collection," she muttered thickly. "Too kind a word to describe stealing someone away forever."

She marched to his side and concentrated on the slap of her boot heels against the ground. The feel of the dirt and rocks beneath her feet. The cold wind as it brushed past her.

When she was close enough, she snatched at his shirt and yanked him around to face her. "I *have* to know who you're here for."

Zacariah reached out and grabbed her shoulders. Giving her a slight shake, he shouted in a strained whisper, "Don't you think I'd tell you if I knew? By the Path, I've already turned my back on everything I've ever known because I *love* you."

She pulled away, refusing to hear those last three words. She couldn't allow herself to be distracted. "You have to find out. You have to ask someone. *Anyone.*"

"I've tried, Rebecca." He tossed an angry glance at the impassive, black sky overhead. "I won't know until it's time."

She took one step backward and then another. True. All true. She felt it. She knew it. Deep in her bones. She staggered as her boot heel came down on a rock and winced as pain twisted around her ankle. Pain. Too much pain.

Well damn it, she'd had enough.

More than enough.

Tilting her head back, she lifted one fist and shook it furiously as she shouted to the heavens, "Damn you! Damn you all! You can't play with people like this!"

"Rebecca . . ."

"No!" She stumbled, kept her gaze locked on the night

sky and its benignly twinkling stars and shouted again. "You can't have my son!"

"This won't help, Rebecca," he said and stalked toward her.

She threw him a hostile look and shouted at him, too. "Tell me who to talk to, then! God? Those precious Minions of yours? The Angel of Death?"

His chin dropped to his chest.

"Dammit, *who?* What kind of place is this Path, anyway? Who the hell is in charge there?" She inhaled deeply and screamed out a warning to the heavens. "All of you! Do you hear me?" Her voice broke. "You can't have my son! You can't have Danny!"

On her son's name, she dropped to the dirt, bent at the waist and gave herself over to the terrified sobs shaking her.

In seconds, Zacariah was there. Beside her. He pulled her into the circle of his arms and she fought against the comfort he offered her. "Damn you too," she snarled, tears choking her words. "Damn you for making me love you and then destroying everything I hold dear!"

"Rebecca," he soothed, easily overpowering her struggles to draw her tightly against him. "God knows I'm sorry. If I could change it, I would."

She moved so suddenly, it caught him off guard. Sitting up straight, she grabbed two fistsful of his shirt and looked up at him through watery eyes. "Take me."

"What?"

"Take me, Zack." If he took her when the time came, Danny would be alone. No mother. No father. But he would have Buck. He would have the ranch. Most importantly, though, he would be *alive.* "Take me. Leave my son alone."

"Rebecca . . ." His agonized whisper couldn't stop her from making the plea again.

"Please, Zack. Let Danny live. Take me instead."

His hands smoothed her hair back from her face, then

cupped her cheeks tenderly. Pulling her head down to his chest, he cradled her close and whispered, "I could never take you, Rebecca."

She trembled and slumped against him.

"I want you to live," he went on and kissed the top of her head. "God help me, I want you both to live."

"Where *is* she?"

Buck tightened the cinch strap on his saddle, then flipped the stirrup down into place. "She's wherever she needs to be."

Zacariah glared at the other man's back. "She's been gone all night."

Gone since the moment she'd pushed him away from her and left him kneeling in the dirt. She'd raced through the house and in only a few minutes had come back outside and marched directly to the barn. Grimly, Zacariah remembered running after her, demanding that she stop and talk to him.

His hands fisted at his sides as he also recalled how she'd brushed past him as if he didn't exist. Then she'd saddled up one of the horses and ridden out of the yard as if the demons of hell were after her. He scowled to himself as he realized that was probably *just* what she had felt like.

"It ain't the first time Becky's taken off by her lonesome. And she's a big girl. Knows how to handle herself."

Rubbing his aching eyes, Zacariah turned and looked through the barn's open doorway at the house beyond. But he wasn't seeing the house. Instead, he saw her expression as she discovered the complete truth about him. He saw the anguish. The fear. The helpless fury. He saw it clearly.

As he had all night.

Where was she? And how could Buck—a man who

claimed to love her like a daughter—be so damned complacent?

"What's the matter, son?" The older man stepped up beside him. "Never been worried before?"

"As a matter of fact," Zacariah snapped. "No." He shot the other man a quick, disgusted glance. Buck almost seemed to be *enjoying* this.

"Sometimes she needs to go off alone. To think. To work things out in her own mind." Buck pulled his hat off and smoothed what was left of his hair. "This time, I reckon she's got more to think on than usual."

True. But that fact didn't make his uneasiness disappear.

A Soul Collector. *Worried.* He frowned thoughtfully. No doubt, somewhere on the Eternal Path, there were legions of Collectors laughing at him.

The front door of the house flew open and Danny charged outside. His jacket in one hand and a blanket roll in the other, he ran for the barn.

"You ready, boy?"

"Yes sir, Buck." The boy skidded to a stop in front of the men. "Don't you want to go with us, Zack?"

He ruffled the child's hair and took just a moment to enjoy Danny's gap-toothed grin. Ridiculous, he knew, but Zacariah felt a sharp pang of regret when he realized that he wouldn't be around to see the boy's new tooth come in.

"I'd like to, Danny. But I think I'll wait for your mother to come back."

"Okay, but Buck's gonna take me and Jake out fishin' an' we're gonna stay till we catch the biggest fish in the world. Even if it takes for-*ever*." He looked at the other man. "Right, Buck?"

"Forever, boy." Buck nodded at Zacariah and winked. "Or at least a couple of days." To the boy, he added, "Go tie your bedroll down, son."

After Danny hurried to do as he was told, the man said,

"When Becky gets back, tell her I took the boys to Shadow Falls. She knows where it is."

Zacariah nodded, only half listening. His entire body was actually straining to hear the sound of approaching hoofbeats, signaling Rebecca's return.

"I want to get Jake out of that store for a while. It ain't healthy for a boy to have so much sorrow heaped on him."

"It's good of you to take them."

"Nah, it ain't." Buck rubbed the end of his nose with the back of his hand, then settled his hat on his head again. "But it's about all I *can* do."

A half hour later, Zacariah stood alone in the yard, looking out toward the distant mountains. "Where are you, Rebecca?" he asked aloud of no one.

Silence answered him and he heartily wished she'd come back to the ranch and take another swing at him.

At least then, he'd know she was safe.

Rebecca packed up her gear, then poured a last cup of coffee. She leaned back against the fallen trunk of a lightning-struck tree and stared into the dying embers of her cook fire. She hurt all over.

Lying sleepless on the rocky ground all night made for a miserable morning. She glanced at the saddled horse cropping grass nearby and told herself she should get going. Get back to the ranch.

But she didn't move.

"Dammit, Comanche," she said aloud and the big chesnut lifted his head and looked at her. "What the hell kind of afterlife does Zack come from? What kind of beings are in charge of Eternity anyway? What were they thinking, to send me the man who took my husband?"

The horse snorted, dipped its head and went back to breakfast.

"Well," she said in response, "I think that about says it all."

Deliberately, she took one last sip of the scalding coffee, then tossed it onto the remains of the fire. Snatching up the battered tin coffeepot, she emptied that, too, onto the embers and listend to the angry hiss as heat drowned. Smoke curled up into her face and she waved it aside angrily.

Daniel.

For at least the twelfth time, she tried to draw up a mental image of him, but the picture had blurred and faded with time. Four long years.

Zacariah.

His image leaped instantly into her brain and her knees shook as she conjured up his fathomless blue eyes. Knowing that it was Zack who'd collected Daniel wasn't easy to bear. But at least, if she could believe the Collector, the passage to Eternity was a gentle one.

Her fingers curled tightly around the coffeepot's handle. She remembered all too well, the terrible injuries Daniel had suffered in that stampede. Had he lived, he never would have been the same man and that would have been a living, agonizing death for a man like him.

"You would have hated that, Daniel," she whispered. "And you would have eventually turned that hate on me. And Danny. *Anyone* who was whole and healthy."

Frowning, she walked to her horse and packed the pot and matching tin cup. Running her hand along the animal's neck, she smiled when the big horse turned into her touch like a dog begging to be petted.

The past was over, she admitted finally. Nothing could change it. And the passage of four years had muted the pain of loss.

It was the *now* she had to think about.

Danny.

Zack.

She slipped the reins free of the tree trunk, then swung easily into the saddle. Somehow, she had to find a way to protect Danny. To save him.

Zack would be at the ranch for another week at least. Surely she could come up with *something*. Some way to convince these . . . *Minions* to leave her son alone.

Rebecca threaded the reins through her fingers and tugged at the animal, turning him around toward home. Not until she was already moving did she realize how far she'd come in just a day or so.

Twenty-four hours ago, she hadn't believed Zack's stories about Collectors and Minions and whatnot.

Now, she was ready to bargain with the Devil himself.

An hour later, he was waiting for her when she rode into the yard.

Relief rolled through him. She looked fine. Tired, but fine. His insides churned. Right behind the relief, anger surged in.

"Where were you?" he shouted when she brought her horse to a stop right in front of him.

"Thinking."

"And you couldn't do that here?"

"Nope." She looked past him at the house. The barn. "Where's Danny?"

"With Buck," he snapped. "Buck's taking Danny and Jake Parker fishing at . . . Shadow Falls for a couple of days."

"Good. Both boys could use some time away."

He stared at her and cursed under his breath. He didn't want to talk about Danny. He wanted to shake her for making him worry all night long. Making him entertain terrifying visions of what might have happened to her. And then for acting as if there was nothing wrong. But, did it really matter where she'd been? Or even that she'd been gone at all? No, he decided quickly. All that mattered was that she was back. Safe.

Before he could say another word though, Zack heard a far-off shout.

"It's Buck," he muttered and Rebecca turned to look.

"Something's wrong," she whispered.

The older man had his horse in a high gallop. Bent low over the animal's neck, he raced for the ranch. As he entered the yard, he yanked back hard on the reins and brought the big black to a rearing stop.

"What is it?" Rebecca nearly shouted. "Is it Danny?"

"Danny's fine," the man said as he swung down and staggered a bit. "He's in town." Pulling his hat off, the foreman twisted the brim with his fingers as if needing something to do. "Seems little Ellie's failin' fast. Doc thinks she won't last out the mornin'."

"No," Zacariah muttered. It couldn't be. She still had more than a week. He wasn't leaving yet. It wasn't time. The month wasn't over.

He felt their eyes on him and deliberately avoided their gazes. What did this mean? How could Ellie be dying already? She was his collection. Wasn't she?

A deep cold settled over him.

If not Ellie . . . then who?

The boy raced through the general store, his small boots clattering against the plank floor. He rushed out the front door, a panicky look on his face. Tears streaked through the dirt on his cheeks, leaving strange white trails to mark their passage.

Rebecca's heart broke and she braced herself for the hard impact of his sturdy little body against her knees. She wanted to hold him. Pick him up and run from this place. To find someplace safe, where children were always happy and healthy. To where dreams never died and innocence wasn't crushed.

Danny glanced at her, then hurled himself at Zacariah. Rebecca blinked as an unexpected pain lanced through her.

Stunned, she looked at her son as the man beside her picked him up and cradled him close to his heart. Danny's tears came fast and furious. He buried his face trustingly in the curve of Zacariah's neck and his voice sounded muffled and thick.

"Remember, Zack?" the boy said, between hiccuping gulps of air. "You remember, you said it won't hurt her? You promised?"

Rebecca sucked a breath into straining lungs. Tears stung her eyes and she crossed her empty arms over her chest. She surrendered her own need to hold her son to his more important need.

"I remember, Danny." Zacariah ran one hand up and down the boy's heaving back, soothing, comforting. "I promise. It won't hurt."

"I'm scared, Zack." Danny's whisper tugged at her.

"I know, boy," he muttered. "I am, too."

Rebecca's throat tightened until she was sure she'd never draw an easy breath again. Almost blinded by the unshed tears gathering in her eyes, she reached out and laid one hand on Danny's shoulder. She felt the tremors rippling through her son's small body. Zacariah's hand covered hers. Comfort, strength flowed from his hand to hers and between them, to Danny.

Together, they walked into the store. Bear lay at the foot of the stairs, a low whine issuing from his throat. He raised his head briefly when they approached, then laid his jaw down on his forepaws again. Even the dog sensed that something more terrible than his fear of Zacariah was at work in the store.

The scent of hot candle wax hung in the still air.

How many times over the centuries had he heard these same whispered petitions? How many languages had been used in fruitless attempts to hold him at bay? How many candles had been lit against the coming darkness?

He'd once thought them foolish creatures. Now, he understood all too well. He ached to join in the prayers. He focused his will and hopes on the dying child, even knowing it was pointless.

Helpless against the forces of Eternity, Zacariah was one of them at last. He was finally, completely, human.

His gaze shot quickly around the room, moving from face to face, person to person. Billy Jenkins stood at the foot of the bed. His fingers twisted and strangled the bedpost as if trying to do battle with the enemy stealing Ellie from him.

The girl's brothers and sisters gathered close. An occasional choked sob shot from a tight throat and staggered the flow of prayers rising up around the small bed.

Jake Parker sat on his father's lap, staring at his sister with the shocked, bruised eyes of a child who'd seen too much suffering. Tom Parker's lips were a tight, grim slash of pain.

Helen sat beside her daughter, one hand comforting the child she still cradled in her womb, the other stroking Ellie's fragile fingers.

Standing beside him, Rebecca drew one long, shuddering breath after another. Her pain was masked but for the tight grip her fingers had on his upper arm.

For Rebecca. For all the others—he wished that there was *something* he could do.

Then again, maybe there was.

His gaze flicked to the far corner of the room, where a silvery gray mist began to form.

Rebecca blinked, stared and blinked again.

She wasn't imagining it. Shadows shifted, swirled and lifted toward the ceiling. Mocking the morning sunlight spearing through gaps in the curtains, a shimmering cloud of fog was rising in Ellie's bedroom.

"Zack . . ." she whispered, her fingers tightening on his arm. She shot a quick glance at the others in the room and realized that no one else saw it. Rebecca swallowed past a knot of fear and stared as the mist began to take shape.

Fear shut off her air.

A robed figure stepped from the heart of the cloud and

drifted soundlessly toward the bed. It took a position beside Tom Parker and his wife. No one noticed. Her gaze locked on the robed intruder, she tried to speak. To warn them all. To demand that *someone* look and see what she did.

She couldn't make a sound.

Instead, she threw a quick look up at Zacariah and didn't know whether to be relieved or terrified. His jaw tight, a muscle beneath his cheek twitched. She wasn't alone. He saw the Being, too.

In an instant, she recalled everything he'd told her. Every wild, crazy word came back to her and Rebecca felt her world rock. Any last, lingering doubts she'd had fell away.

Gutting candles spit accompaniment to whispered prayers. Then Ellie inhaled sharply and shuddered her last breath into the room.

Someone cried.

Helen groaned as if stabbed to the heart.

The robed figure leaned toward the girl and stretched out one hand.

Rebecca gasped.

Ellie's soul lifted from her body. She took the Being's hand and rose, smiling, from the bed. Her spirit shone so brightly, it hurt Rebecca's eyes to look directly at her. Yet, she couldn't look away.

Joy rippled from the child like waves on a windy sea. laughter spilled from her and she sparkled, like a star suddenly dropped into the room. The girl glanced at a brilliant light glowing from the mist behind her, then turned to look at Zacariah.

"It's just like you promised."

The robed Being clasped Ellie's small hand in his, then he, too, turned and nodded a greeting to Zacariah. Glancing at the child, he said, "We must go now."

Ellie took a step, then stopped. Looking at her parents,

she said, "Wait." She pulled away from the Collector and moved to her mother's side.

Helen's silent sobs stopped suddenly when Ellie brushed a kiss across her cheek. The bereaved mother paled and lifted one hand to her face.

Rebecca's heartbeat staggered.

"Ellie?" Helen whispered, a look of wonder on her features.

"It doesn't hurt, Mama," the little girl assured her.

Tom Parker's jaw dropped.

"Did ya hear her, Ma?" Danny's excited voice shattered the stunned quiet.

Billie Jenkins groaned and leaned into the bedpost for support.

"Don't be sad, Billy," the girl said softly.

The young man laughed shortly and squeezed his eyes tightly shut as if afraid to believe and terrified not to.

"Why did you allow this?" the Collector asked, looking directly at Zacariah. "Weren't you in enough trouble already?"

He stiffened and Rebecca instinctively moved closer to him.

Ellie waved to him, then stepped into the mist with the Collector. "I love you," she called back, just before shimmering folds of silver and gray shifted softly, swirled up and were gone.

Rebecca looked up at the man holding her son. She'd been granted something miraculous. They all had.

A single tear traced a course down Zacariah's face and the other Collector's words echoed in her mind. Zack had broken yet another rule to give Tom and Helen peace.

Chapter ❀ Nineteen

A nearly full moon shone down on the ranch yard, illuminating the night with a pale, ivory light. Zacariah tilted his head back on his neck. Clear and beautiful, millions of stars glittered against the blackness. A cool wind rustled through the limbs of the surrounding pines and somewhere in the distance, an animal howled.

With Buck in town, determined to get "seriously drunk," and Rebecca in the house trying to get Danny to sleep, the too-long day was at last ending. Every muscle in his body ached for rest, but he couldn't be still. His mind refused to allow it.

All day, he'd gone through the rituals of human mourning. Despite knowing that Ellie was safe and happy, he'd felt compelled to join the others in their tears. He finally understood that mortals cried not for the departed soul, but for those left behind. For the aching loneliness.

Danny's tears marked him still. Though reassured of Ellie's safety, there was no solace for a child who sees one of his own die and suddenly realizes that death isn't reserved solely for adults.

Tom and Helen Parker's pain had been blunted a bit with his gift to them. But Rebecca had haunted him throughout the day. He'd seen her watching him. Studying him. Had he done the right thing in allowing her to observe the Collector? To know and understand exactly who and what *he* was? Or was she too appalled now to even be near him?

How could he spend his last week of life with Rebecca looking at him in fear?

"Zack?"

He spun around to face her as she approached.

Moonlight lay gently on her and Zacariah committed another image of her to memory. Pale moon glow drifted over her unbound hair and eased the strained look pinched about her eyes. Firelight and moonlight, he thought. For eternity, he would see her in firelight and moonlight.

Her stockinged feet scuffed against the ground as she came nearer, then stopped just a few inches from him.

"Is Danny sleeping?" he asked.

"Yes." She tipped her head back momentarily, breathed the night air deeply, then sighed it out again. "Finally."

Straightening up, she looked at him directly. "It was wonderful, what you did for Tom and Helen."

"It wasn't much."

"It was enough."

He lifted one hand toward her, then let it drop again.

"What happens now?" she asked.

"Nothing's changed, Rebecca. In less than a week, I'll be gone."

"Are you sure they won't call you back early? After what you did for the Parkers, I mean?"

"I'm sure." There was another Collection due. Soon. Whatever the Minions decided to do with him once he returned, Zacariah knew he wouldn't be leaving until he'd made that Collection.

She dipped her head, lifted it again and met his gaze squarely. "Will I remember you? When you're gone?"

He froze. He hadn't thought of that. *Would* she be permitted to remember him? Or would the Minions remove all memory of his visit? "I don't know, Rebecca," he said softly. "I hope so."

She *would* remember. No matter what. She would see to it.

All day long, she'd waged a silent battle with herself. The decisions she'd come to the night before while away from the ranch had danced in and out of her mind, competing with the scene she'd witnessed that morning. Her brain had warned her repeatedly to stay away from a man with the power of life and death. His gift to Tom and Helen—though generous beyond anything she could think of—had also pointed out just how wide the chasm was that lay between her and Zacariah.

He wasn't even *real*. The man she loved didn't really exist.

She knew it. Believed it. But, as her heart had continued to remind her, it didn't matter.

A stranger had arrived at her ranch and in less than a month, had become the father Danny craved and the lover she'd waited for. Hoped for.

She couldn't turn away. Not when their time together was fast running out.

"I want to thank you," she said.

"*Thank* me," he repeated. "For *what?*"

"For what you did today. For all of us. But especially for Danny."

"Don't." He shook his head and turned from her.

She grabbed his arm and tugged him back around to face her. "You *helped* Danny. When I couldn't, you did."

"Rebecca . . ."

"No." She cut him off and started talking in a rush. "When Danny needed comforting, you gave it to him. Heaven help me, at first, all I could think of was, 'thank God it's not my son.' " Her chin dropped to her chest. "What kind of woman does that make me?" she muttered.

"Human."

She glanced up at him and saw a tired smile lifting one corner of his mouth. "Maybe," she acknowledged. "But I should have been feeling compassion for Helen. My *friend*. Today she suffered a loss no mother should have to bear."

He stepped up close and pulled her into his embrace. Rebecca went willingly, eagerly, longing to feel his solid strength and the reassuring beat of his heart beneath her ear.

His voice rumbled through his chest when he spoke quietly.

"Maybe I'm more human than I thought, too."

"What?"

"I was wondering a few minutes ago if you would simply turn from me in disgust. Or fear."

Her arms tightened around his waist. "I've been doing a lot of thinking since last night."

"Yes?"

She felt him stiffen, as if awaiting a blow.

"Thinking about Daniel. And Danny. And you and me."

"I'm sorry, Rebecca." He pulled back from her a bit, only far enough to look down at her and see her eyes. "My coming here has brought you too much pain. And I should regret it. But apparently," he added with a wry smile, "I'm too human for that. I can't bring myself to regret being with you. Loving you."

"I'm glad. Because I can't either. In spite of everything." She inhaled sharply and went on. "Daniel died a long time ago. What happened then is past. Done. And in a strange way, I'm almost grateful that it was you who collected him."

He frowned slightly and she reached up with one hand to touch his cheek.

"At least, I *know* he was all right with you." Her hand dropped to her side again and she lowered her gaze briefly before looking at him once more. "This is hard, Zack.

God knows, I don't know what Helen Parker's feeling right now and I hope to Heaven that I never understand it completely. But I do know that *life* is what's important. Not the inevitable dying. We *all* die sooner or later. It's how we live that matters."

She caressed his cheek again and his jaw clenched. She felt his muscles tighten beneath her hand just before he turned his face into her palm and kissed her calloused flesh. She closed her eyes and savored the tingle of warmth and pleasure that shot up her arm and lit up her insides like a Fourth of July fireworks show.

She'd made her decision. No matter what, she wanted her last few remaining days with him. Somehow, some way, she would manage to save her son, even if it meant her own death. And if Eternity waited at the end of the week, then she wanted to face it as a well-loved woman.

He reached to cover her hand with his, holding her touch to his flesh like a healing balm. He looked into her soft green eyes and saw all the Eternity he ever wanted to see shimmering back at him. His fingers moved over the back of her hand, still cupped to his cheek, and he savored the feel of her warmth. Each fingertip seemed to brand itself into his skin and he knew that throughout the centuries awaiting him, he would always be able to feel her phantom touch.

Reaching for her, he pulled her into his arms and lowered his head to claim a kiss. The kiss he'd hungered for all through the last, lonely, twenty-four hours. The kiss he'd feared he would never taste again.

Then his mouth came down on hers and Rebecca leaned into him, wrapping her arms tightly around his neck. She pulled him closer, reveling in the warm strength of him. In the hard, muscled body pressed to hers. In the wild fluttering of her heart.

Her lips parted for him and she welcomed him inside. A soft moan crept from her throat as his tongue caressed her frantically. Knees weak, she slumped in his arms and he scooped her up, holding her close. When he broke their kiss, he gasped for air and Rebecca laid her head down on his chest, stunned at the raw sensation unfolding inside her.

Without a word, he strode to the front door, then marched through the house, straight back to her bedroom. He closed the door, set her on her feet and in seconds, their clothing was off and tossed in heaps on the floor.

They came together in a frenzy of need and desire. His hands were everywhere, stroking, caressing, exploring. She touched him and felt him tremble. Her fingertips roamed his broad, muscled back, then circled around to smooth across his chest and stomach.

He walked them to the bed and together, they fell atop her brightly flowered quilt. She tipped her head back into the mattress and gave herself up to the feelings he aroused in her.

His thumb and forefingers tweaked at her breasts and ready nipples, then made way for his lips and tongue. He took the small rigid buds into his mouth, one after the other, and lavished attention on them until Rebecca's soft cries were the only sounds he heard.

She arched into him, demanding, needing more. Her fingers threaded through his hair, holding his head to her breast as if afraid he would leave her.

He redoubled his attentions and at the same time, allowed his hands to roam across her flesh. Down her rib cage, across her abodmen to the triangle of dark brown curls that guarded her secrets. He touched her and she jumped in his arms. Zacariah smiled against her breast and slipped his hand lower, to cup the heart of her. To feel her heat, to surround himself with her.

One finger dipped inside her and Rebecca strained upward to meet him. His tongue flicked against her nipple as another finger joined the first. As he slipped in and out of her body, his thumb moved across the sensitive piece of flesh she'd shown him the first time they were together.

She planted her feet on the mattress and rocked her hips in open invitation. He pushed her thighs further apart and moved his hand to caress all of her.

Rebecca sighed heavily and gave herself up to a touch that seared her soul and branded her heart. No one had ever made her feel so loved. So cherished. No one had looked at her the way Zacariah did. And no one had given her this sense of completion that filled her each time they made love.

She needed him like she did air and water and sun. Each time with him only fed the flames consuming her, making them burn brighter, hotter.

He lifted his head from her breast and before she could moan in disappointment, he trailed kisses along the length of her body. Tender, soft, gentle. Small darts of heat shooting into her soul. His lips forged a path of desire along her rib cage, down her stomach, across her abdomen.

He pulled his hand away from her center and she wanted to cry out at its absence. Instead, she held her breath and curled her fingers into the quilt beneath her as she felt him move to kneel between her legs. Looking at him, Rebecca saw the shadows of desire darkening his deep blue eyes.

Her gaze slipped lower to the hard, ready length of him, poised just outside her passge. He touched his body's tip to her sensitive flesh and she gasped with the need clawing at her.

"Hurry, Zack," she whispered huskily. "Be inside me. Become a part of me."

"Not yet, Rebecca," he whispered and gave her a slow smile.

He bent his head to kiss the inside of her knee and she shivered. In response, he planted another kiss a bit higher up her thigh.

"Zack . . ."

"I want to see all of you, Rebecca," he said softly and gently parted her legs further, opening her body to his gaze. "I want to kiss all of you. Taste all of you."

"Oh, God," she moaned and tensed as she realized what he meant to do. She should stop him. She'd never experienced this before and wasn't quite sure she should now, either.

His lips moved higher and his tongue darted against her thigh. She jumped. His hands stroked her legs, caressing, soothing, calming her and at the same time, stoking the fire inside her into an inferno.

Rebecca's hips lifted off the mattress and twisted, from anticipation or embarrassment, she wasn't sure anymore.

The pad of his thumb moved across the small nub of sensation he'd uncovered and Rebecca stopped thinking. She stopped caring whether he was looking at her or not. She didn't worry about anything but that he might stop.

Instinctively, her hips came higher off the bed, lifting for him, as she silently offered her body to him to do what he would.

She closed her eyes and waited.

She felt his breath first. Warm puffs of air brushing against her most intimate flesh. Then he kissed her and a world of passion she'd never dreamed existed opened before her.

As he'd done to her breasts, Zacariah used his tongue to torture her. Again and again, he licked at her, driving her to the point of madness and beyond. His strong hands cupped her behind and held her still and helpless. Her feet dangled above the mattress and her only grip on a steadily dissolving world was the fistsful of quilt clutched in her fingers. His lips moved on her, his tongue dipping into her heat and retreating, only to return for more. His breath dusted her body while his mouth brought her to a wild, heart-stopping release unlike anything she'd ever known before.

Pleasure washed over her, through her. She reached for him and held his head to her as her hips rocked with wave after wave of sensation.

While ripples of satisfaction still trembled through her,

he set her down onto the mattress and pushed his body into hers.

Completion, warm and heady, filled her as fully as his body did. Rebecca's arms and legs wrapped around him, holding him to her as he pushed her higher up the mountain she'd only just climbed. Together, they reached the topmost peak and together, they fell back to Earth, safely held in each other's arms.

The stunned hush of her breath brushed his cheek. Her heartbeat pounded frantically, in perfect tandem with his. Zacariah raised his head and dropped a gentle kiss on her brow. Then, exhausted, yet feeling more alive than he ever had, he rolled to one side and drew Rebecca close.

She draped one arm across his heaving chest and a moment or two later, her even breathing told him she was asleep. He held her tightly, and silently prayed that eternity would never come.

They buried Ellie two days later.

In the shade of an ancient oak tree, a circle of mourners surrounded the small casket.

The minister's voice became like the breeze sloughing over them. Soft, gentle, it hummed a comforting tune that had been sung for generations to people too wounded to hear.

When the service was ended, the people moved away, leaving freshly scarred ground to mark their grief.

Zacariah walked with his family. Buck, Rebecca and Danny. The small band held tightly together, as if to ward off anyone or anything that might threaten their solidarity.

Days and nights passed too quickly.

All too soon, the shortest week of her life had flown by.

Rebecca glanced at the man asleep in her bed, then turned to stare out her bedroom window at the night as her mind wandered.

With some of the money they'd recovered from Scotty's hiding place, Zack and Buck had visited neighboring ranches all week, buying breeding stock. Buck insisted on planning for the future, despite his belief that he wouldn't be around long enough to enjoy it.

While the men were busy elsewhere, Rebecca and Danny did the countless small chores around the house and barn that demanded attention. The nights, though, found all four of them gathered in the house, fire burning, lamps lit against the ever-encroaching darkness.

It wasn't right.

Rebecca should have been able to relax now. The rustling was over. They had money for stock and supplies. The ranch would prosper. It was all she had ever worked for.

Instead, though, she was tormented by the passage of time and the knowledge that Zacariah would soon be leaving her.

Forever.

And when he left, another piece of her world would be going with him. Daily, she asked herself, *who?* Buck was still convinced that he would be the one to make that long journey with Zacariah. He was content and unafraid.

But Rebecca couldn't share his conviction. There was too much at risk.

Still, knowing there was no danger to her son until Zack's month was up, Rebecca allowed Danny to spend whatever time he could with the man he wanted for a father. The two of them went fishing and played checkers by the fire. At bedtime, she and Zack tucked Danny in together and in the small circle of love they'd found, the boy's "monsters" were banished for good.

Then, when the house was silent, Zack came to her. Despite the threat hanging over them, Rebecca was determined to grab onto however much happiness she could find in this last week with him.

"Rebecca?"

She turned at the sound of his voice and smiled as he came close. Bare-chested, he'd pulled on his jeans, but hadn't bothered to button them. He pulled her to him and closed his arms around her.

"I didn't hear you get up," she said.

"Too much to think about?"

She nodded and listened to the steady beat of his heart. How many more beats? How many more hours? Minutes?

His hands stroked up and down her spine and she fought back tears.

"Do you leave at sunrise?" she whispered.

"I don't know." His arms tightened around her. "Won't know until the time of Collection."

She shivered.

"Come back to bed, Rebecca." He glanced out the window. "It'll be dawn in a few hours. You need to sleep."

"No," she said softly and pulled her head back to look up at him. "I need you."

Pain and desire flickered in his eyes just before he bent his head to hers and slanted a kiss across her mouth. She clung to him, encircling his neck with her hands, threading her fingers through his hair and pulling his mouth down more firmly on hers.

He carried her to the bed and lost himself in her. Kisses given and received. Hushed whispers and broken cries. Pleasure torn from the heart of desperation shone around them all too briefly. And later, as she lay against his side, he whispered to the lightening darkness, "I will love you forever."

Chapter ❊ Twenty

Dawn peeked between the folds of the curtain and fell across the bed, probing at Zacariah's eyelids. He ignored the light, refusing to acknowledge it. As if in response, the morning sun grew brighter, more demanding. Reluctantly, unable to fight the inevitable any longer, he opened his eyes and faced the truth.

His last day as a mortal had arrived.

Regret pounded at him. He tightened his hold on Rebecca, drawing her warm, nude body close. Her breath brushed across his chest and she instinctively cuddled into him, drawing one leg up over his.

He felt whole. Complete. Centuries of knowledge and experience hadn't prepared him for the realities of a deep, human love.

The Eternal Path and everything he had ever known meant less than nothing to him. His existence before coming to the Hale ranch seemed misty, indistinct. As if he'd never *really* existed at all, until finding this small family.

The only world that interested him was the one he held close in his heart. This woman. And the boy sleeping peacefully in his room. That these people were now threatened with rules set in stone by beings who'd forgotten what it was to live was horrifying. How could he make the Minions understand something even *he* wouldn't have believed a month ago?

"Zack . . ." she whispered in her sleep.

She snuggled closer, instinctively wrapping herself around him. For the first time in centuries, someone was counting on him. Not some nameless Collector. *Him.*

A cold, hard band of resolve tightened around his heart. He *had* to find a way to save them. No matter the cost, he must protect Rebecca and Danny.

She wasn't sure what had awakened her. But she stretched out one hand on the mattress and found Zacariah gone. Instantly, her eyes flew open in time to see him walking toward her bedroom door.

Dawn. He always left her bed at dawn. But *this* morning was their last. Quickly, she scrambled out of bed and raced past him to block the door.

"Rebecca." He kept his voice down, knowing that Danny was still sleeping.

"Don't go. Not yet." Her arms locked around his waist and she held on tight.

After a moment's hesitation, he returned her embrace, completing a small circle of warmth. Love.

"I have to go," he said softly. "Danny will wake up soon. It's morning."

"The last morning, you mean."

He sighed. "Yes."

The single word rumbled through his chest to quake in hers. Too soon, she wanted to tell him. The time had gone by too quickly. She wasn't ready to say good-bye. She needed more time. A lot more time. At least fifty years.

Her eyes squeezed shut and she told herself to remember everything. The gentle strength of his arms around her. The beat of his heart. The puff of his breath against the top of her head. The feel of his cold, metal belt buckle biting into her bare belly.

She needed to remember it all. Her memories would have to last her a lifetime.

"I'd better get to the bunkhouse."

"And pretend that this day is no different from any other?"

His hold on her tightened fiercely. "What else can I do? Do you want me to leave? To wait for the Minions somewhere else?"

"No," she said quickly. She wanted him there. On the ranch. She needed to know exactly where he was, today of all days. It was *she* who would leave.

She couldn't risk spending this last day with him.

"Zack, I'm going to take Danny to town." She drew one long, deep breath. "We'll be gone all day."

"Ah, Rebecca . . ."

"We can't stay. I have to keep Danny away from here. Away from . . ."

He flinched.

She paused, swallowed heavily and went on. "As much as I want every last moment with you, I have to leave."

"I understand." He kissed the top of her head and she considered it his blessing.

"Oh, Zack," she whispered and leaned back to look at him. "Why is this happening to us?"

His jaw clenched and something flickered briefly in his eyes.

Rebecca reached up and brushed his hair back from his forehead. "I love you more than I ever thought it possible to love anyone. But I *have* to keep Danny safe."

He gave her a slow, sad smile. "Of course you do." His fingertips trailed across her cheek and gently stroked the line of her jaw. "Go to town," he said. "Do what you can."

She bowed her head briefly, forehead resting on his chest.

"And," he added, "when this day is over, try to remember that I love you."

Raising up on her toes, she reached for a kiss. He bent his head and gently touched his lips to hers before releasing her. Then he took a single, difficult, step back.

Her soft green eyes sparkled with a sheen of unshed tears. Zacariah summoned what was left of his waning strength and left her while he still could.

Alone in the hall, he leaned against the closed door. Had he done the right thing? Should he have told her that her plans were useless?

It didn't matter if she and Danny were in town or in Europe. If a Collection was to be made . . . *nothing* could stop it.

"Buck?" She opened the bunkhouse door and stuck her head inside.

"Come on in, Becky."

Rebecca walked in and crossed the room to Buck's cot, where he was rifling through what looked to be everything he'd ever owned. Carving knives were laid out next to his saddle, his guns, razor and shaving mug made another pile and dozens of other, smaller items lay scattered over the blankets.

"What are you doing?" she asked.

"Settin' out all my worldly belongin's." He snorted a wry laugh and shrugged. "Ain't much to show for some sixty-odd years, is it?"

Oh Lord, he was making out a will of sorts.

She looked at the man beside her and felt a tug at her heart. "There's much more to your life than these *things*," she said.

He didn't speak, didn't lift his gaze from the cluttered remnants of the years.

Just in case he *was* Zacariah's collection, Rebecca knew she couldn't let him go without knowing how important he was to her. "Buck, you were Daniel's friend. You've been a grandfather to Danny."

He coughed and reached into his back pocket for a balled-up, red-and-white bandana.

"And to me, you've been father, friend, teacher . . ."

His faded blue eyes lifted to hers.

"Without you, I never would have been able to hold onto this ranch after Daniel died."

"Ah now . . ." He rubbed his eyes and nose with the kerchief, then stuffed it back into his pocket. "That's enough of that, girl. I want you to give most of this stuff to Danny when he's old enough, ya hear?"

"Buck."

"The shaving gear and the knives and all will come in handy when he's of an age," Buck said, effectively cutting off her protest. "But I want you to have the carvings." He shrugged again. "Some of 'em are pretty good, if I do say so. The rest you can hide in a closet or throw away."

Tears blinded her and clogged her throat.

He sniffed, then straightened up. "Now, no cryin' nonsense, girl. I'm an old man and I'm ready to go." He chucked her chin gently with his fingertips. "I had a good long run and that's the plain, honest truth."

"Buck, I don't want you to go." Rebecca bit back a groan. How could she stand this? Zacariah? Buck? Danny? The only way to avoid a never-ending pain was for *her* to be Zack's collection.

"Ain't up to you or me," he said gruffly. "You and Danny are my family, Becky. And I wanted you to know that, uh . . . well, hell."

"We love you, too, Buck. We always have."

He ducked his head. "I love you two something fierce. So you be sure and take care of each other when I'm gone, ya hear?"

"I hear." She nodded and blinked back the tears that hadn't left her all morning.

"Good then, that's settled." He snatched up his hat off the bed, then headed for the door. "Zack told me about you and Danny goin' to town for the day. It's a good idea. Don't want him around to see nothin', ya know." He yanked the door open. "I'll just go hitch up the wagon."

"Buck?"

"Yeah?" He glanced at her over his shoulder.

What could she say? Good-bye? Be careful? Nothing seemed to fit. Finally, she settled for, "Thank you."

He looked at her for a long, thoughtful moment, then stepped into the sunshine, closing the door behind him.

Rebecca dropped down onto the cot beside his belongings. Elbows on her knees, she buried her face in her hands and tried to stop shivering.

"Don't see why you can't come." Danny pouted.

"There's too much to do around here," Zack told him and picked him up. He gave him a quick hug, then solemnly lifted the boy into the wagon. Forcing a smile, he said, "Remember? You told me your mother was a bear for work."

"Yeah." After a moment, Danny brightened. "I'll bring ya some candy, all right, Zack?"

He inhaled sharply. Staring up into the child's clear, green eyes, he felt his heartbeat stagger. How he would miss this child and the daily adventure of his childhood. And how quiet the Path would seem without his laughter.

"Zack? Licorice is my favorite. Do you like it?"

"That'd be nice, Danny. Thanks." He didn't want to think about how hurt the boy would be when he returned home to find Zack gone. But there was no way to prepare him for that pain without terrifying him.

Rebecca came out of the house and walked to the back of the wagon. She lifted one hand and waved to Buck, across the yard. The older man then turned and disappeared around the side of the barn.

Zacariah moved to her side. "Rebecca."

She shuddered, then lifted her gaze to his.

He curled his hands into fists to keep from touching her one last time. If he did, he knew he'd never be able to let her go. All he could allow himself now was a final good-bye.

"I will miss you for Eternity," he said quietly. "But I will love you even longer."

She bit down hard on her bottom lip then reached up to brush the pad of her thumb across his mouth. "I will love you for the rest of my life, Zack. No matter *where* you are."

Without another word, she turned her back on him and stiffly walked around the wagon. Once she was seated, she clucked her tongue at the horses and drove the wagon out of the yard.

She didn't look back.

"Where's Zack?"

Rebecca bent down to stroke Bear's head, deliberately keeping from looking at Helen while she answered the question. "He's at the ranch, working."

Straightening up, she looked at Helen and forced a smile. "How are you?"

"Better." The woman's eyes filled with tears, but she blinked them back with a determined smile. Rubbing her swollen belly, she went on. "Not wonderful. But better. I miss Ellie every day, but this little fella here"—she glanced down at her abdomen—"keeps my mind busy most of the time." Helen walked along behind the length of the counter. "Besides," she added unnecessarily, "you were there. You heard her." She nodded to herself. "Ellie's all right. She's not sick anymore."

"I heard her," Rebecca agreed quietly. No matter what else happened, she would always be grateful to Zack for easing Helen's mind about her child.

"So," the woman said with a sniff. "Enough about me. What can I get for you?"

Buck glanced over his shoulder at the slightest noise. This waiting-to-die business wasn't as easy as it sounded. He'd tried mucking out the stalls, but he hadn't been able to stay indoors for long. If this was to be his last day, then dammit, he wanted to end it outside, under the sun and the sky. With the wind and the wide open spaces he'd always loved.

But with Zack in the barn now, Buck couldn't keep an eye on him. He wasn't sure exactly what he was waiting for, either. Lightning bolts, maybe? Still, he'd feel a lot easier in his mind if he knew just what Zack was up to.

"I'll need some flour and sugar to start with," Rebecca started, then half turned to look at the stairs behind her when she heard Danny's running footsteps. "I need coffee too," she added as an afterthought. She grinned at her son when he jumped the last three steps and ran across the store.

"I have to get it out of the back," Helen said and moved off.

"Ma," Danny blurted excitedly, "me 'n Jake are goin' to the blacksmith's, all right?"

"You're a pretty horse, Sky Dancer," Zack mumbled. "I think I'll miss you, too."

The big animal snorted and turned its head to stare at him.

He chuckled gently and stroked the brush over the horse's back and sides. It felt good to be busy. Keeping busy made thinking harder. And thinking wouldn't do any good, now. He was out of time.

All he could do was wait.

"Where is Jake?" Rebecca asked, looking past her son.

"Oh, he's comin'. He's just slow, is all."

She ruffled Danny's hair and told herself absently it was time for a visit to the barber. "Go ahead," she said. "I'll come for you in a while. Then we'll go to the hotel for something to eat."

"Thanks, Ma!" He grinned at her and she noticed the

beginnings of a new tooth coming in to replace the one he'd lost.

The boy ran back to the foot of the stairs and shouted, "Come on, Jake!"

The low rumble of a freight wagon rolling down the street drifted into the store through the open front door.

"Rebecca?" A soft, familiar voice echoed in her mind.

Terror skittered through her. She spun about to meet Zacariah's eyes. He stood in the shadows, just a few feet from her. It wasn't possible. She'd left him at the ranch. How had he gotten to the store?

Her voice strangled, she forced herself to mutter, "Who are you here for?"

Oblivious, Danny raced past her and Zacariah's gaze followed him.

She inhaled sharply and screamed, "*Danny!*"

Zacariah ran. He didn't think. He didn't consider what he was doing. He simply ran after the boy he loved like a son. In his Collector's mind, he saw exactly what was about to happen.

Danny would run out the door, across the boardwalk and jump into the street. He wouldn't even see the wagon that would crush him beneath its wheels.

Zack shot through the front door, just a breath behind the boy. He stretched out one hand, curled his fingers around the child's collar and yanked, throwing him back onto the boardwalk and safety. Zacariah saw the boy land, stunned, but unhurt, just before he fell beneath the wagon himself.

Someone screamed and the sound went on and on, drawing icy fingers of fear along Rebecca's spine. She tried to move, but her feet wouldn't cooperate. Her heart lodged firmly in her throat, she stood stock still, whimpering quietly.

Helen, her hands beneath her swollen belly, hurried to the boardwalk. A heartbeat later, she cried out, "Oh, God! Danny!"

The world shifted, splintered and began to sag down around Rebecca. Swaying slightly, she saw blackness at the edges of her vision and watched as the remaining light slowly narrowed.

Then she heard something else. Something that jolted her into moving again. Something that tore at her soul and filled her eyes with tears that blinded her as she half stumbled, half ran to the doorway.

"Ma?"

Danny.

Crying.

Alive.

Rebecca fell over the threshold and hit her knees to gather her son into her arms. She rocked him as the tears fell, listening to his frightened voice muttering things she couldn't understand. She thanked God and the Minions and Zacariah for the gift of her son and knew she'd never let him go.

Until other voices intruded. Other voices whispering in hushed awe.

"Did you see that?"

"Hell, never saw nothin' like that before."

"A hero, that's what he is."

"Durned if the fella didn't just jump in front of that wagon instead of the boy."

"I didn't see him," someone else shouted to be heard. "I didn't see him till he was under my rig! It wasn't my fault!"

"Rebecca . . ." Helen pulled Danny away from her, tucking the boy's face into her apron. She jerked her head toward the street, silently telling her to look.

Tearing her gaze from her son, Rebecca slowly turned around to stare at the crowd gathered in the street. Foreboding splintered inside her, allowing shards of emotion to slash at her soul. Holding her breath, she shifted her gaze to the man on the ground at their feet.

Zacariah.

Still and quiet, he lay in the dirt, his eyes closed, his body bent.

Somehow, she got to her feet and ran to him. Pushing and shoving her way through the people hovering over him, she dropped to her knees beside the man who'd given himself in place of her son.

One hand smoothed over his face, brushing his hair back from his forehead. No response. Those clear, brilliant blue eyes remained closed. She clutched one of his hands and pressed it to her chest. His fingers still felt warm, but there was no life in them.

Gone.

In less than a heartbeat, he'd saved her son and then left her.

She squeezed his hand and let the tears come. Alone. The years loomed ahead of her, dark and lonely. She would raise her son, missing Zacariah every day. She would sleep alone, always reaching for him. She would grow old without him.

Aching emptiness shook her and she tipped her head back to stare at the sky. Somewhere, he could hear her. She knew that now. She couldn't let him leave this way. She had to tell him. Ignoring the interested whispers fluttering about her, Rebecca shouted, "Zack! When it's my time, I want *you* to come for me!"

"Rebecca," someone said and touched her shoulder.

"No!" She shook them off and yelled again, as loud as she could. Loud enough to reach the Eternal Path and beyond. Loud enough to shake the walls of Heaven and tell them all what they'd done by taking Zacariah from her.

"You come back for me, Zack! I love you!" Her voice broke. "I'll always love you."

Mordecai clucked his tongue sympathetically as he looked back at Rebecca. "You should have told her that there was no need to screech so. That we can hear a whisper from the heart as well as a shout."

Zacariah looked at the woman for whom he'd risked everything. Her shouts followed him along the Path and comforted him. Whatever happened to him now, knowing Danny and Rebecca were safe would make the price he would pay more than worth it.

"The Minions are waiting for you, Zacariah," Mordecai told him. "And they're not a bit happy with you, I must say."

Fenwick nodded uneasily.

Well, Zacariah had expected to bear the Minions' wrath.

"What on the Path were you thinking?" his old friend asked. "How could you have thrown that child to safety like that? It was his time, Zacariah."

"I couldn't let him die," he said simply and knew that Mordecai wouldn't understand. He glanced at Fenwick, though, and saw that the Collector-in-training was looking at him sympathetically. Strange, that it would be Fenwick to understand.

Outside the Great Hall, Mordecai stopped. He looked at the filigreed, golden gates, then turned his gaze on Zacariah. "You're to go on inside. Alone."

"I know," he said softly and patted his friend's shoulder.

"Was it worth it, Zacariah?" Mordecai asked.

"Saving Danny?" He turned and faced the Gates as if ready for battle. "Yes. It was worth anything."

In the Minions' chamber, the five ancient spirits were waiting for him. They sat behind a scrolled table of shining silver and gold. Their robes dazzled in the light of Eternity and the cowled hoods hid their features—and their expressions—from him. Zacariah drifted forward to stand before them.

"You failed to make your Collection as specified," one of them said.

Another one spoke up. "You understand that we cannot have Collectors blatantly disobeying the rules."

"*Of course.*" He did understand. But that didn't change a thing.

"*Why, Zacariah? Why did you deliberately bring down censure on yourself?*"

He looked at them, each in turn. He heard confusion in their voices and knew that only a month or so ago, he would have felt the same way.

"*It was the boy's time,*" a voice intoned. "*These things are scheduled and not to be disrupted.*"

"*He was too young.*" Zacariah's voice was loud. Firm.

"*Too young? A soul has no age. You know that.*"

"*His soul, yes.*" Zacariah countered. "*But he's only a boy. And there's so much for him to do and see and feel in his time on Earth.*"

"*That's not for you to decide.*"

"*Besides,*" another one of them broke in before he could argue, "*a month ago, you didn't even like humans.*"

"*That's true,*" he said quickly. "*But wasn't that one of the reasons you sent me? That I could learn to respect them? To learn from them?*"

"*Yes . . . but rebellion wasn't one of the things you needed lessons in.*"

He nodded in acknowledgement, then said, "*I've learned much more than that.*"

"*Such as?*"

"*There are too many things to list.*" He paused, fighting the sadness of missing Rebecca already. It had only been minutes since he'd last seen her. How would he survive the coming centuries? The Minions shifted impatiently and he realized they were still waiting for an answer.

"*Love,*" he said at last. "*Mostly, I learned about love. The love of a woman.*"

"*Yes, we had noticed that. Surely you knew that mating with the female was well beyond a Collector's boundaries.*"

"I'm not talking about the physical act of love," he said and drifted closer. *"I'm talking about caring. Worrying for someone's safety. Shared laughter and quiet talks in the dark."*

Two of the Minions stared at each other in confusion.

"And the love of a child. A family. How it feels to know that there is one place in the world where you belong."

"You belong here."

Zacariah ignored that. *"I know what I did for Danny was against the rules. But I don't believe it was wrong. I want him to grow up. I want him to experience everything I did in the last month. I want him to taste his first beer. I want him to know what it feels like to scrape his face with the cold steel of a razor every morning. To fall in love. And yes, to know the magic of becoming a part of the woman he loves. To have children and watch them grow."* His voice faded away as he looked at the five beings judging him and knew that they weren't convinced.

He had to reach them somehow. Otherwise, they might very well reschedule the child's death and send another Collector after Danny. And Rebecca would never survive the pain of losing her son.

"I know that my pride has long been a source of irritation to all of you."

One of them sat up straighter.

"I've never once begged pardon of you." Slowly, he went down on his knees. *"Now, I offer you my pride. I'm begging you for the life of this child."*

"Zacariah . . ."

"Please," he interrupted. *"I'll do anything. Go anywhere."*

"There is no need for this, Zacariah."

"But there is. I love him. I love his mother. To protect the, I would dare anything. Risk anything." He stood up again and met each of their gazes, one at a time. *"Send me to the Dark Road."*

"This is highly irregular . . ."

"Do what you want with me," he went on, hurrying now. *"Send me to Hell. Sentence me to oblivion. Just don't take the boy. Let him live."*

"This is very moving, Zacariah. And it is good to know that you have at last learned that pride is not everything."

"But we do not understand," another voice spoke up. *"You do this for love, you say. Yet where is love more glorious than on the Eternal Path?"*

His head snapped up. *"The love I hold for Rebecca and her son is every bit as wondrous as the love to be found here."*

Someone muttered, *"Finally."*

Zacariah frowned in confusion, but went on, not daring to risk being still just yet.

"In my month on Earth, I discovered I was wrong. About many things. For centuries, I told myself that humans went through their lives never realizing that they were only one step away from death. The truth is, we exist never realizing that we are a step away from life."

"Because of this . . . revelation," one of them prodded, *"you saved the boy?"*

Zacariah smiled sadly. *"No. I saved Danny for several reasons. I love him. I didn't want him to die. I didn't want his mother to suffer his loss."*

"Have you finished now with your defense?"

"I would only beg you for mercy," he said. *"Not for myself. But for Rebecca Hale and her son. As for me, I await my punishment."*

In the next instant, a swirling mist rose up, enveloping Zacariah. Just beyond the grayness, he heard the low mutterings of conversation and knew the Minions were making their decision. He couldn't understand what they were saying. All he could do was hope that what he'd said had been enough to save Rebecca's son.

"Your punishment," a voice declared, *"has been decided."*

*   *   *

Her fingertips felt cool against his forehead.

Sunlight streamed through an open window and a soft breeze fluttered the white lace curtains. Zacariah frowned and turned his face away from the light. He tried to move and an agonizing pain burst into life in his left leg. He groaned and half sat up.

"Zack?"

His gaze shot to her. She looked tired, worried.

"Rebecca? What happened?" His mind was in turmoil. Only a moment ago, he had been on the Path, kneeling before his superiors. What was happening? He glanced down at himself and saw the rag-wrapped splint on his leg. From another room came the scent of a roast cooking.

His stomach growled.

"Where am I?"

"In the Parkers' storeroom," she said quickly. "We brought you in here for the doc to look at."

Somewhere far-off, a baby cried.

"What was that?"

Rebecca grinned. "You mean *who*. That is Tom and Helen's new baby girl. Your accident startled her into labor and little Mary Ellen arrived about an hour later."

"A baby." He dropped his head back onto the pillow. How long had he been unconscious? How long had he been breathing?

"Zack," she whispered, lifting one hand to touch his cheek. "Are you back to stay?"

"I don't know," he said and concentrated on the feel of her hand against his cheek. A touch he'd never thought to experience again.

A moment later, a whisper of sound entered his mind.

"The child, Danny, has been granted another sixty or seventy years of life."

Zacariah sighed. He'd done it. Danny was safe. But before he could tell Rebecca, the voice went on.

"There is a price for this change in plans, Zacariah."

"Yes." No matter the cost, it was worth it.

"It has been decided that for your failure to make your assigned collection, and for the countless *errors in judgment made during your recent punishment, you have been sentenced to a lifetime spent guiding Danny Hale and helping him to become a worthy adult."*

"Zack?" Rebecca demanded, glancing over her shoulder as if expecting to see the mist rise in a corner of the room. "What is it? What do you hear? Are they coming for you again?"

"No," he said quickly, snatching her hand and holding it tight.

"Your powers as a Collector have been stripped from you, Zacariah."

"I understand."

"What? What do you understand?" Rebecca's voice rose.

"Ask the female to be quiet for another moment or two please. Then she may speak to her heart's content, as we will not be here to listen to it."

Grinning, Zack said, "They want you to be quiet for a minute, Rebecca."

"I will not," she said firmly, sending a glare toward the ceiling. "Just you try to take him again. Or my son. I'll fight you every way I can."

Zacariah laughed.

"This is what you prefer to the peace on the Path?"

"Oh, yes." He smiled at her furious expression.

"It is decided." Someone sighed. "Soon, yours and everyone else's memories concerning the Eternal Path will fade. You will be simply Zacariah Cole, a man with no past."

"Just a future."

"An ordinary man."

"A grateful man."

"So be it." That voice drifted into nothingness and a moment later, he heard Mordecai for the last time. "I shall miss you, Zacariah."

"Good-bye, Mordecai."

"You realize Fenwick is taking your place?" He sighed. *"Be well, my friend."*

The voices faded and in a still-stunned whisper, Zack told Rebecca everything that had been said. Tears filled her eyes and she leaned in over him to brush a careful kiss across his mouth.

"You're staying?"

"I'm staying."

"Then there's one more thing, Zacariah Cole."

He grinned and reached for her, drawing her down to lay across his chest, her face just a kiss away from his. "What's that, Rebecca Hale?"

"As soon as that leg of yours heals, you're going to be a *married* grateful man."

A swirl of emotions raced through him but Zack ignored them all in favor of doing what seemed the most natural thing in the world.

He kissed her.

And as their lips met, promises were made and dreams were forged.

The storeroom door burst open, slamming back against the wall. Rebecca jumped, startled and moved out of the way just in time for Danny to hurl himself at Zack's chest.

"You're all right, Zack? Really?"

"Really."

"You saved me," Danny whispered reverently.

"That's what fathers do," Zacariah told him with a smile at Rebecca.

A slow grin eased up Danny's features. He shifted a quick look at his mother and she nodded. Turning back to the man in the bed, he said, "You're gonna be my pa?"

"If you want me."

Danny sucked in a breath. His eyes widened and he blinked a few times as if waking up from a long dream. Then he leaned down and hugged Zacariah tightly.

The former Collector held him close and accepted the boy's love with a full and grateful heart.

After a long moment, Danny straightened up and asked, "Can we go home now . . . Pa?"

Home. For the first time in centuries, he had a home. And a life.

Tears stung Zack's eyes and he groped blindly for Rebecca's hand. He had spent centuries on the outskirts of Heaven. An eternity walking along the edge of Eden. Yet it wasn't until he had found this woman and her son that he was finally able to claim a pocketful of Paradise for his very own.

Smiling at the boy, he said gently, "Good idea, *son*. Let's go home."

Kathleen Kane

"[HAS] REMARKABLE TALENT FOR UNUSUAL,
POIGNANT PLOTS
AND CAPTIVATING CHARACTERS."
—*Publishers Weekly*

DREAMWEAVER

As a Dreamweaver—a spirit who must deliver dreams (and sometimes nightmares) to sleeping humans—Meara refuses to upset the slumbering innocents. In order to hide from her punishment, she is whisked down to earth…and onto the Nevada ranch of Connor James. Soon they both discover an attraction as intense as the Western sun—but can a man of the earth, and a woman from beyond ever make their two worlds meet? 0-312-96808-6___$5.99 U.S.___$7.99 Can.

THE SOUL COLLECTOR

A spirit whose job it was to usher souls into the afterlife, Zach had angered the powers that be. Sent to Earth to live as a human for month, Zach never expected the beautiful Rebecca to ignite in him such earthly emotions. 0-312-97332-2___$5.99 U.S.___$7.99 Can.

THIS TIME FOR KEEPS

After eight disastrous lives, Tracy Hill is determined to get it right. But Heaven's "Resettlement Committee" has other plans—to send her to a 19th century cattle ranch, where a rugged cowboy makes her wonder if the 9th time is <u>finally</u> the charm. 0-312-96509-5___$5.99 U.S.___$7.99 Can.

STILL CLOSE TO HEAVEN

No man stood a ghost of a chance in Rachel Morgan's heart, for the man she loved was an angel who she hadn't seen in fifteen years. Jackson Tate has one more chance at heaven—if he finds a good husband for Rachel…and makes her forget a love that he himself still holds dear. 0-312-96268-1___$5.99 U.S.___$7.99 Can.

To save her town—and her heart—she'd have to...

WISH UPON A COWBOY
K A T H L E E N   K A N E

A wonderful new novel from the acclaimed author of
The Soul Collector and *Simply Magic*

Jonas Mackenzie isn't sure what to make of the beautiful stranger who showed up at his Wyoming ranch with marriage on her mind...Hannah Lowell isn't thrilled at the idea of marrying a man she doesn't know—until she gets a good look at the cowboy who will be her destiny...But how is she going to convince a man who doesn't believe in magic, that he's got the power to save a town from a terrible fate? And that it all boils down to the most powerful magic of all: their love.

"True to her talent, Kane keeps the conflicts lively to the end and fills the plot with many surprises."
—*Publishers Weekly*

**COMING SOON FROM
ST. MARTIN'S PAPERBACKS**